Eatheria

Michelle Lovrine

OAK MUSE PUBLISHING
Eatheria
Michelle Lovrine

Cover Art: Tais Teng

Published in the United States by Oak Muse Publishing
ISBN 978-0-9914886-0-5

Printed by CreateSpace, a DBA of On-Demand Publishing, LLC

DEDICATION

This book is dedicated to Jason, who made sure the dogs didn't eat
the couch while I was writing. Sometimes.

PROLOGUE

The eyes give her away, they always do. That's why I'm fascinated by human eyes. They're hazel, that mutable color that camouflages with the greens and browns around her. She thinks she is further concealed by those downward gazes.

But I see the flash in those eyes, the fire that forges the true gold color of her eyes. She'll see me in a wolf form later, on the desired timelines. Fierce, but loyal.

But those eyes also gaze far away, into my world, though that isn't as far as the humans normally think. Eyes of a dreamer, that one. They all have those dream eyes, the Eatheria sensors.

We puzzle, try to figure out what causes it, why some can see the ethereal realm. No answers are forthcoming. They tend to reproduce less, yet the ability keeps on persisting, sometimes where you would expect it least.

Take the girl. The one I've been charged with. Shouldn't have a trace of the ability, the royal ones hardly ever do. But she does, so I watch.

It hasn't been a normal life for her. It never is for them. Those dream eyes make her seem weak to the others, so she stays quiet, which exacerbates the problem. Everywhere she goes, she stares at the floor, hoping they won't see that spark: at balls, with her sisters, during the etiquette lessons meant to drill those habits out of her. A royal lady knows her place in the human world, and that is a place where every acquaintance is an opponent to stare down.

She does it at that rotten religious school they all attend from the age of three on, never looking at her teacher, never looking at her classmates. They get them early. Tell them that spark is to be feared. So she keeps her head down as people wonder why she won't stand up.

But the risk in the human world is great, to be sure. I've seen my charges burned, tortured and maimed before they can even realize their potential. Before they even know what they are.

But those who survive have the crucible of challenge with which to mold themselves. Then, hopefully, the dreamer eyes will stop being just dreamer eyes. They'll use those eyes to truly see and those dreams to guide...

CHAPTER 1

"Ah, a self referral, I understand." Dr. Iland looked over his parchment at Kiadora, who was sitting on a wooden table. "Fainting spells, you told my assistant?" Kiadora nodded.

"When do they usually happen?" Kiadora glanced nervously into the doctor's eyes. Should she be honest?

"Um, when…when I go into the woods." The sentence came out in a rush. She hoped she wouldn't have to repeat it.

"The woods," the doctor repeated for her. "I see. Any other symptoms with it?"

"Dizziness. I get very dizzy, and then I fall over." The doctor nodded, jotting down notes on his parchment that he had placed on the counter. The shadow of his hand danced madly across the paper as he scribbled, suspended in the torchlight from the four kerosene lamps that hung from the ceiling. Kiadora gazed down at the floor as he wrote. Maybe she shouldn't have come. Now her shame would be on record.

"Are there any other symptoms with the fainting? Hives, rashes, sweating, anything?"

"Heat." The doctor regarded her for a moment, expecting her to go on. "Just, like I'm warm all over," she elaborated. "Even on cold days." The doctor nodded and returned his is note-taking.

"Is that all?"

"Yes."

"This certainly is a strange case. Usually when people complain about natural adversities, it's a simple allergic reaction. But I've never known anyone to faint from it. Then again, you could be different. It could be a new type of reaction that's uncommon. How has your diet been? Eating normally?"

"Yes, I've had no other changes."

"No other changes," the doctor repeated. "How long has this been going on?"

"It started recently. The fainting, I mean. I've always felt the heat." Kiadora hesitated. "There's…there's something else." The doctor turned away from his notes, rotating on his stool. Kiadora looked up at a portrait of a wild-looking man with a large amount of dreadlocks. His face had been painted yellow. She looked down at the well-groomed doctor before her in his slick, black coat over his black pants. This man had slicked back his dark hair with oil, as if to match. He waited patiently has she tried to collect her experiences into the best way to tell them without earning herself a psychiatric recommendation.

"When I get near plants, I feel an electrical charge, sort of, like when you rub your hand over a carpet for a while in the middle of winter." The doctor's brow creased. She knew she should have left this part out.

"I don't quite understand." He had leaned toward her and put his hand on his chin. He was staring to the side, evidently deep in thought, as he seemed to shuffling through a mental library. "I don't believe I've heard of anything like this. I'll need to spend some time looking into the subject. In the meantime, before you leave, are there any other symptoms of this, or is it just merely something you feel? In other words, are you able to show me?"

"It's mainly only in the feeling I get, as far as I know. But I can show you. Do you have a plant?" The doctor stood up and walked to the door, holding it open for Kiadora to pass. She jumped off the table, her dress fluttering around her.

They went out the main door, down the steps to the walkway and went around the building. They passed under the trees that surrounded the small, two room practice. And just as always, it started. She felt an electrical charge, starting directly from under her skin closest to the nearest tree. Soon a warmth spread through her as though she had just stepped into the boiler room at their family's large estate. She felt light-headed, but the sparse number of trees allowed her to stay conscious.

The doctor led her between his general practice and a dentistry next door. All the buildings on this block were medical related since they were in the Health District, two blocks of housing mostly consisting of general doctor practices, save a few specially buildings devoted to certain ailments. Kiadora had been spooked by an old woman on a porch who started babbling at her loudly. The woman was wheeled inside by a man who was decorated with several amulets. A home for the incurable possessed.

The back of this practice had a small porch, where the man had several elder trees and flowers planted. Kiadora gasped.

"Are you growing wild plants yourself?"

"Yes. Naturally it is my wish you do not tell anyone. I have no need to be thrown in prison." He motioned for her to come over to the edge of the wildlife, squatting next to some ground up turf. It was a dark, rich brown, and Kiadora had never seen anything like it.

"But…why? The risk can't be worth it. There is plenty of wild land, if that is what you want." She felt freighted for him, and was afraid for herself to go near the tamed and controlled plant life. She looked up at the walls that enclosed the area, looking for windows, as if The Priest of the Church might be staring at them himself.

"There is nothing to fear," the doctor reassured. "See? No windows. And no one has reason to come back here. This area was intended to be used for repairs in the underground heating ducts, but the lines have been rerouted since they expanded to the east of here. I was very lucky to come across such a land, no one owns just raw dirt in an urban area like this. I wanted to enjoy a bit of nature for myself, without drawing curious eyes. So I merely replanted a few trees and flowers."

"It's still beautiful," she said. With the lack of windows about, she decided to come over to the patch of wild. Kiadora wondered if the fact that it was tamed and replanted would affect its power. As she walked toward it, her answer was given in the return of the tingling sensation. She looked at Dr. Iland, who was staring at her intently. She could see beads of sweat on his face, and she thought he must be burning under his black garments.

"Please kneel down, by the flower bed." She did as she was instructed, the scent of tilled earth more powerful that she had ever encountered. It looked even richer when she was closer. The tingling increased to a faint buzzing beneath her skin from within her veins.

"Do you feel anything?" the doctor asked, eyeing her skin closely.

"Yes. The tingling I mentioned, it feels almost like a faint buzzing when it gets this tingly."

"A buzzing?"

"God this is so hard to explain." She looked around hoping something would cue her on how to describe what she felt. "It's like…it's like…that." She pointed to a light green plant that had spiky leaves. "Like that is cursing through my veins, just under my skin, pulsating."

She kept looking at the plant, and as she looked closer, it did not look that painful. She reached out to touch the plant, and it was furry rather than prickly. She glanced at the doctor, who was regarding her with a kind patience, though his mouth was set in a firm line of concentration as he tried to understand. She knew she wasn't making this easy. "Ok, no, it's not that. But do you know the prickly plant, the ones that grow on the ground? Surely you must have stepped on one barefoot as a kid. Everyone does."

"Ah, yes," he said. "Hell's Paws, we used to call them. So is there a pain?"

"It is not really a pain, but it is a mild version of stepping on one of those, all over." He nodded. The look on his face said he was on the verge of understanding.

"Could you hold out your hand to the plant, I would like to see if there is any skin irritation. If it gets too intense, pull away." He indicated a catacomb-shaped purple flower. She nodded and held her hand over the flowers.

"Now it's a warmth, like I'm in heated water or outside in the sun." They were in the shade of the building next to them. The doctor bent down to look at her skin, just hovering above the plant. He peered in between the gap between her and the plants. And then it started. She felt dizzy, sleepy, slow. The world spun, and the last thing she saw as she toppled into the grass was the black coat of the doctor over her.

She awoke in Dr. Iland's office, on the wooden table again. She jumped as the first thing she saw was the harsh man with the painted face and the wild bird feathers in his hair. Just the portrait. She sat up and looked over at the doctor, at his desk, scribbling away once more.

"Oh, no," she gasped. "How long have I been out? I hoped that would not happen!" He turned around in his chair to face her.

"You've only been out a few minuets or so. Maybe ten at the most. I carried you in after you fainted." She looked down at her lap, ashamed that she had such weakness. Here was a man willing to risk his freedom to enjoy such pleasures, and for her it was too much.

"You don't need to feel ashamed," he said, wheeling over to her on his stool. She looked up at him. His eyes were filled with compassion. "It is unlike anything I have seen, but we can fix this. You're merely sick, and you'll feel better soon. There is no shame in catching a cold, is there?"

"If you're stupid enough to go out unprepared for the weather, yes."

"True, but oftentimes someone close is sick, and it cannot be helped. We're going to get you back in working order."

"Did you see anything?" she asked. She had wondered if she ever broke out into a rash of any kind when she fainted, hoping it was an allergy that attacked her nervous system.

"Actually, not really. Your skin appeared to be flushed slightly, so I took your temperature from under your arm and found your body temperature had risen slightly above normal, three degrees above the average. Tell you what, you head home, come back tomorrow in the morning. I'll look into it and see what I can find. Are you able to come back tomorrow?" She nodded, and jumped down from the table.

True to her word, Kiadora found herself walking down the streets of the Health District once again the following day. She walked in an aimless fashion, almost as if drunk from being low on sleep. Kiadora had stayed up all night worrying over what today's appointment would bring. At one moment in the night, she feared him finding something worse, a life altering illness that could only be controlled by forced confinement. She had a short-lived dream of herself in old age, muttering to herself on the porch of the house of the possessed. Her legs were withered from sitting idly at a table or strapped to a bed her whole life. Dry and crimped gray hair flowed down around her.

Later, she became more frightened he would not find anything at all. She would go through years of testing, observation, being watched over like a pet rat to see which way she would turn in her maze. Wall after wall would come up to meet her as she never found her way.

But she had to know.

She walked up the steps to Dr. Iland's office and knocked gently on his door. He swung the door open with a rush of cooler air, now mingling with the warmer day.

"My lady," he said brightly. "Come in." He stood to the side the let her in, and she walked through the main waiting area to a room he had at the back. No one was in. It was early, and she had come before his normal hours. She walked to the back room and stood by the table as he sat at his counter again.

"Please, have a seat," he said, indicating a chair next to the counter. She sat at the edge of the chair tensely, as if it would spring shackles and hold her there. "I have done research on this case long into the night. It is most interesting. Unfortunately, the closest I can find to it is what I thought initially. It appears to be some sort of aversion to plant life. An allergy, if you will. In rare cases, those allergic to certain plants will have an elevated temperature. Although I have never seen fainting before, I think it is best if we try some allergy pills."

"Pills? That's all?" She looked at the floor for a moment. Kiadora had considered asking him if she belonged in the house of the possessed, but if he did not bring it up, why should she?

"Is something on your mind?" he said, giving her that intense stare again.

She would always wonder.

"I don't…I don't belong in the house of the possessed, do I? I worried about it all night long. And what if these pills don't work?

Will I be placed there then?" The doctor sighed and looked down at his papers. Kiadora wiped her sweaty palms on her dress as Dr. Iland let the silence linger.

"The house of the possessed is there for people who are a danger to others," Dr. Iland finally said. He was still staring at his papers. "In fact, I do not even believe they are possessed." Kiadora was shocked to hear such things. Next to this, the spectacle out back was only a weed in the sidewalk.

"Then what causes such madness?"

"I am not sure, but I believe it is an aberration in the mind. I am not allowed to study such things, of course."

"How did you discover such an idea?"

"We have reached such a point the community where we view everything else as a bodily ailment, but we take the extreme occurrences and liken it to something beyond us. Why do we not view those large occurrences as something merely non-mystical?" Kiadora only stared at him, wondering if it was a direct challenge for her to figure out the nature of the universe. But still the seed was planted.

"Yes, why not?" she agreed. "But why do you say all of this to me? How do you know I will not run to tell the authorities?"

"You assumed this was a physical rather than spiritual ailment first. You cannot be terribly religious, am I right?"

"No, but I should be."

"But you are not. Most of the people that come to me are not. Many still go to the Church to cure them for things as large as what you are experiencing. Others come to me." Kiadora had never considered it before, but she was beginning to understand where her loyalties lay. But that wasn't the issue at hand.

"So, these pills? How often do I need to take them, and for how long?" The doctor reached down to a drawer next him, and brought up a dark brown, glass bottle. She could see the small pills inside, only a slightly lighter brown, struggling to shine through the darkness of the bottle.

"We'll keep you on for two weeks and see how you react."

"React? Is there anything that could happen?"

"Some have reported nausea and other minor ailments, but that is why this is a trial run." Kiadora looked at the dingy bottle again. It was worth a try.

Back at home, in her room alone, Kiadora looked at the bottle in her hand. On a piece of parchment, the doctor's neat scrawl read, "Take two daily. One in the morning, one in the evening." The beginning and the end, the end all and be all, Kiadora hoped. It was evening, she might as well start now. She poured one little pill out of its dingy prison of a container, the white now shining brightly. As instructed, she put the pill on her tongue and took a drink of water. She did not know what to expect, if there would be an effect right away. She had never taken a pill before.

She gulped down the water. The pill was so small, she merely felt like she had just taken a drink of water. Kiadora decided she would let it work through the night, take another in the morning. She'd test it then. She wondered how long it would take to work.

The next morning, after taking her pill early in the morning, she went outside. The warm mid-spring sun shined over her family's expansive estate. A small portion of the land was not tamed; the ground was not level, so it could not be turned into fruit fields. Anyone with land was expected to use it, not enjoy it. The produce profits made a nice side income to her father's political work governing the schools. Farm hands came cheap, after all.

A wave of fresh spring air hit her nostrils. Today would be the day of her freedom. She walked over to a small plant, behind a shed so no one would see. She knelt down by it and put her hand over it.

Oh, no. The prickling. Her heart turned to stone. No, all of this was supposed to be over. She put her hand closer, and the pickling grew worse, just as it usually felt before the warmth overtook her.

Maybe it would take a few days to work. She got up to go back inside, and her stomach did a flip as she stood up, cramping badly. Hopefully that would go away, too. Or maybe it was just from anxiety.

Later that day, Kiadora's stomach was still feeling upset. She refused lunch, and retreated to her quarters. Her younger sister, Ashila, gave her an overly concerned look. Her mother and oldest sister, Dehlia, merely looked at her from the side, as if she was a whining puppy. If her being sick meant skipping a meal with her sisters, that would be fine by her.

She lay down on her bed, her stomach doing turns and cramping badly. She remembered what the doctor had said about some people having problems with nausea. She had to give it a few days, she had to try.

Later in the middle of the week, she was not doing any better. Her stomach felt as if the lining was disintegrating. She had only been able to choke down marginal amounts of food in her quarters, telling her family that she had a stomach flu. Further, the prickling feeling she had when she was outdoors remained. Somewhere around the middle of the week, she began to vomit. Her only salvation, and her body was repelling it. Later that afternoon found her in the doctor's office once again, the cloudy container half empty between them on the doctor's desk.

"I've been vomiting, having an upset stomach and what's worse is that I still feel the same way around the woods. I swear, worse in fact. Usually I can stay conscious if I stick to the path through it, but today I barely made it through," Kiadora was saying. She was hunched over slightly in the chair, both arms folded in front of her stomach. She was paler than usual today, the ashen tones of her skin matching the dull, light brown of her hair.

"I see," the doctor said. "We will have to take you off of these immediately. I have another type of allergy pill you can try. Different people react differently to various treatments. We'll find the one that fits." He brought up another bottle from under his desk. This one was an even darker brown, with pills of a darker color inside. "These carry the same instructions," he explained. "Try them for a few days, and if you do not react well, we'll find something else."

It was the middle of the next week, and Kiadora felt similar. There was no cramping, but she was vomiting once a day at least. Her family was just about to send her to their family practitioner, when she stopped taking the pills. She didn't know why she didn't want them to know what she was feeling and that she was seeking to treat it. Her family always knew she had something different going on, but they could never place their finger on it. Perhaps it was because she felt dirty, ashamed, weak, so she tried to keep everything hidden.

Her father, being a noble lord, was always very concerned about his family's image. If instability was known, he would be overthrown, fast. There were always threats, but a crazy person in the family tended towards suspicions that the whole family might be about to erupt into madness themselves. These things did run in lines, everyone knew. It would be just the thing to unite an uprising.

Now that she could not even be treated for it effectively made it worse. She was now an official political burden. And if she stayed sick, she would only draw attention. She looked at the pills, these a slight brown to match the bottle. It was as if they had been white, but the drab nature of the their home had leaked onto them.

She wondered about going back to the doctor. Would he wonder, contact her family if she did not return? If the treatment was not helping, how much could she go through before she really messed herself up and became a liability anyway? She wondered what these things were doing internally to make her feel so terrible. If she was on them for a week and felt this way, what would she be like in several years?

She picked up the bottle and went outside to bury it, increased sensations or no. When the doctor's follow-up letter came, she did not respond.

CHAPTER 2

"I'm glad you could join us for dinner tonight. It's good you're better," Ashila beamed at Kiadora. Ashila had a round face that would have the radiance of the sun, if it was not for the pasty translucence of her skin. Kiadora always thought of the full moon. Ashila was perpetually doomed to only cause a gentle glow, when Kiadora could tell she wanted to illuminate the whole world.

Next to Ashila, Dehlia made a disdainful noise that she was well practiced in. "I liked it better when she was dying in her room," Dehlia shot. Kiadora felt her heart rate rise, but said nothing. It was not worth it, it was never worth it. And yet...

"I hope you get the virus I had and are too weak to survive it!" Kiadora shot back.

"I would get over that sickness in twice the time you did, you little slug. You're too weak to throw off anything I couldn't. It's your mental illness that weakens you." Kiadora stared at her, silent. She fought tears. That was why it was never worth it, it always came back to that.

"I don't have a mental illness," Kiadora muttered at her plate. The truth was, she didn't even know herself sometimes.

"Besides, you better watch how you treat me, or I'll tell Father about those little lapses you have in the forest." Kiadora never knew what she looked like when she fainted. Sometimes she didn't pass out completely, she just hovered in another realm, somewhere between sleep and consciousness. Dehlia had found her a few times.

"I'm not letting you hold that over me; maybe I'll tell them myself!"

Ashila just sat watching the exchange, her brow furrowed.

"Kiadora's right, you shouldn't hold this above her head, Dehlia. She can't help the way she is. You should really seek help about this," Ashila said, looking at Kiadora. "They haven't been able to help Relan, but they may be able to do something for you." Relan was their cousin who babbled in a strange language and pointed at the sky constantly, as if he had been raised among a wild tribe. This was on good days.

"Curse it, I'm not Relan," Kiadora bust out. "I never tried to wonder out of the house wearing nothing but a jar of lard on my head." Dehlia laughed, as she always did when that incident was mentioned.

"It was sad," Ashila snapped. "And made Glarish rather hard to learn while I stayed there. The family should put him in a home, but instead they keep him a closely guarded secret."

"Why don't you say something, if you're so concerned?" asked Dehlia. "Get the brat put away."

"Me? No, I'm not getting involved with family politics."

"Your pity is enough?" Kiadora asked. Since Kiadora was in such a biting mood today, she had another question she was meaning to ask. "And what's the point of learning a dead language? You can't use it."

Ashila looked at her, her expression one of profound hurt. She looked at both her sisters for a moment, now also fighting back tears herself. "It would be foolish to get involved in these things. The family, I mean," Ashila said loudly, waving her fork. "Besides, there's nobility to learning heritage, you know. Something called culture."

Kiadora looked over from where she was poking at her meat with her own fork. Well, the girl could get mad. Ashila looked down at her plate, as if suddenly aware she had been fighting.

"I'm sorry, I should not have raised my voice. Let's not talk about such matters. Has anyone heard of the wedding between Prince Marsh and Lady Lina?"

Later after dinner, Kiadora sat in her room sewing. She hated sewing, but she needed something to get her mind off the infuriating dinner conversation. It felt good to take her dinner in her quarters alone the previous week. Her primary thought was that she hated having Dehlia hold her own life over her head, simply because Dehlia had walked in on her having a few trances.

Then she thought, so what if her parents knew? What would they do? She was so petrified that they would find out that she let Dehlia walk all over her. Sometimes Kiadora felt no better than Ashila for her own meekness. Kiadora was mostly terrified that her father and mother would throw her into a home for the possessed, but they, like her father's brother and sister-in-law, would not want to risk such news getting out into the community. But would she be held captive in the estate? Though when she thought about it, she already felt like a captive of her sister's cruelty and her own fear.

'I should talk to them,' she thought. Really, what was the worst that could happen? But why did they need to know? Maybe they were happy not knowing? Why drag them into it? Perhaps so she could get Dehlia off her case. No, that was not the only reason. She sat focusing on her sewing for a few minuets, holding the thought at the back of her mind, waiting for her mind to provide her with the answer she already knew somewhere deep down.

Then it hit. She wanted someone to accept her, to not act as if she was ill, needed pity or was a funny, misshapen hound to be laughed at. But why would she have any reason to get that from her mother and father?

There was a knock at the door. Lisera, one of the family's home servants, was standing at the door. She looked solemn, her expression as dark as her long raven hair.

"Our lord and lady would like to speak with you," she said. Kiadora frowned at her and stepped into the hallway.

"What about?"

"They would not say, they just looked upset." Dehlia, getting the upper hand again. Whereas Kiadora was spacing out during their royal etiquette lessons, Dehlia took them to heart. Lesson one: always take the upper hand. Kiadora tried not to look panicked, even when she was considering running from the estate.

"Good luck," said Lisera, with a demure smile on her face. She vanished down a perpendicular hallway. The walk to her parents' room was usually a long one, but today, it felt like the walk was as long as the one to town. When she reached their door, she stood hovering outside of it for a moment. They had to know, and she tried to figure out what she would do once and if they did. She thought about the acceptance she had desired from them, and now realized how foolish it was.

Maybe it wasn't even about that. She knocked.

"Come in," called a stern voice from behind the door. Kiadora breathed deeply and took a step in. Her father was sitting as his desk as usual, behind a stack of scrolls. He was scribbling on one as she walked in and came over to his desk. She stood in front of it, as her father doggedly finished his scribbling.

He finally finished and set his pen down. "Dehlia tells me something disturbing," Lord Belac said, finally looking up at her. She sometimes felt as if he was trying to see past her.

"And what would that be?"

"You've been having visions in the forest…or lapses, I forgot how she described it, but it isn't normal."

"I don't see what she means," said Kiadora. "I'm fine, Dehlia's always telling stories." Kiadora's flushed complexion said otherwise.

"This is serious, Kiadora. I won't have you lying to me," Lord Belac said in a grave tone with that deep rumble he always got in his voice when he was slightly angry. Kiadora always saw him as such a bull of a man. She was glad he did not have horns, or she would be impaled on them right now.

"Well, so what? It doesn't hurt anyone!"

"It does, and you know that. What is it that happens to you, tell me exactly." Kiadora looked at his eyes. She would tell, he would see to that. She had hoped she wouldn't need to explain it again to anyone, it always seemed so stupid. And her father was no-nonsense man.

"It's...it's a tingling, and a warmth, when I get near plants, and water. And fire. You know that place, right before sleep? Sometimes I...get trapped there. Like I'm conscious, but not. Sometimes I just faint, but not usually. Past that, I cannot describe it. It's like I have some sort of affinity with nature."

She instantly regretted that last sentence. Her father nodded. She could see the muscles in his jaw wavering as he clenched them tight. His eyes unconsciously drifted over to the family tree hanging on the wall, and she could tell he was going over in his mind what the other nobles would say. And how that would rebound.

"How long has this been going on?" he asked quietly, now.

"A few weeks," she lied.

"Well, it's not long term. Perhaps...perhaps it is just a phase. This can't stick around for too long. No, not in my family. We're fighters, right Kiadora?" he beamed at her, with all the artificial light of a kerosene lamp. She felt indignant at this, as if what she was down to the core would fade away with age and wisdom. As if this were that time Ashila was convinced she was going to grow up to be a street performer. Knowledge of the world has shown her sister, and it would completely erase the slate for Kiadora as well.

"No!" Kiadora yelled at her father. His gray eyes widened, shocked that she would talk to him like this. Already she could see the hint of red anger in his face. "It's not something that will just go away, it's part of who I am."

"For several weeks only?"

"It's always been like this. I never told anyone. I never fainted."

"Are you telling me this will get worse?"

"I don't know..." Kiadora was cut off by her mother, who had just walked in the door that connected her father's studies to their chamber. She took a look at Kiadora and quickly turned back into the other room again. Kiadora stared at the door hitting the frame, making the exclamation that Kiadora could tell her mother just barely choked back.

"Is she *afraid* of me?" Kiadora demanded of her father.

"You know how your mother is," Lord Belac said. "That's why I think it's best we keep this quiet and just wait for it to work itself out." He was sitting back and staring at his desk now. Kiadora glared at him, held back a rude remark and rushed to the door her mother had disappeared behind.

Her mother was sitting on a sofa, paging through a book. Kiadora could tell she was going too fast to get any actual reading done. Her mother kept looking at the book, a book on famous paintings, as Kiadora walked toward her. Kiadora sat down in front of her mother on a large over-stuffed chair. Her mother's eyes darted up to her, her frail form quivering slightly.

"Are you going to pretend I'm not here until I go away?" Kiadora asked. Her mother put the book down and looked at her, large eyes bugging out at Kiadora as if she were looking at a circus animal. Her mother's own light, ash brown hair was pulled back from her face, making her look like a skull. Kiadora tried not to wither under the gaze of the fearful dead.

"Kiadora..." her mother said nervously. "Do you know what you are?" Her eyes darted to the door, as if she was a frightened doe about to bolt from a hunter.

"Human?"

"Not necessarily."

"What? Mother!" Kiadora had now jumped to her feet. Her mother flinched and sat back slightly. "Why are you so afraid?"

"Because I don't know what you are!" the second woman shouted back. She was now on her feet as well, although distinctly keeping a distance. "I think you may be a Shiekita, but I don't know." The uncertainty failed to lessen the blow. The word hung like a heavy, poisonous gas between them. Shiekita, the religious name for the demon possessed. Of course.

"So I'm a monster now?" Kiadora felt close to weeping. Just as her mother opened her mouth to say something, her father burst in from the adjoining room. She could tell he had just heard everything they said, as they had been shouting.

"Enough of this!" Lord Belac yelled back. "It is nothing! She is not a demon, Melanone. It is a phase, this will pass. No one in this family has been accused of being a Shiekita, and it will not start here. Tomorrow we will go to Church like normal and act civil. We're a pious family, and nothing will touch us." He strode out of the room, the word of the house lingering in the air. Lady Melanone looked at her daughter.

"You better go to bed," Lady Melanone whispered, and she turned to go into the bathing quarters behind her.

CHAPTER 3

"You know, if you pull that bonnet down more, you might be able to cover up some of that insanity," Dehlia sneered at Kiadora from the side. They were both standing in front of the mirror, getting ready for the weekly Church service. Kiadora simply turned red, which turned Dehlia's sneer into a genuine grin. Kiadora hated how Dehlia could get a noticeable rise out of her, despite how hard she tried to stay calm.

"Stop it," Ashila said. "Don't aggravate her before service. We are to fully focus on God, and Kiadora doesn't need to be angry. She needs all the focus she can get right now with her..ailment and all." Kiadora glanced at Ashila, turning even redder at the mention of a mental deficit. Kiadora decided today she would just turn and walk away, as she sometimes did. This time she was finished getting ready and didn't have to discern her reflection in a silver bowl in the kitchen.

At the gates, the family poured into the carriage to be taken to Church. The ride there was the usual early morning silence of the still groggy, with an added tension that simmered in the air like previously exploded fireworks.

When she got to the Church, she stepped down from the carriage to see Tahn, a scruffy boy from the village that she always hung around.

They smiled at each other as she was ushered into the Church and to the seating for the nobles. Kiadora walked in, and she sat down at the front.

An engraving on the altar table near her read, "That they may all be one in salvation," which shone at her in gold lettering. A quote from the Holy Text. Kiadora silently scoffed at it, as she did every other service. She looked back at the lesser section, to where Tahn sat.

They caught each other's eye again, and both smiled and waved. He had his boyish grin, despite being 18, and she knew he was happy to be at Church. She also knew, as he made it painfully obvious, that he harbored feelings towards her, but their social status kept them apart. A relationship with Tahn would have made last night seem like an enjoyable family banquet. They even had to keep their friendship on low profile.

"That doesn't stop any of the other royals," Tahn had said on the subject. "I don't know if anyone told you this, but there's this five-year-old boy in town that has a striking resemblance to Prince Hershick."

"I don't doubt that, but do you want be to be like him? He's a chauvinist and an all-around jackass."

"Yes, but you get my point..."

"It's out of the question," she had said, in a tone the reminded her of her father a little too much for her own liking.

Things had been slightly awkward after that, but their friendship remained intact. When they had avoided each other for two weeks, Kiadora decided it was silly to argue. Then they saw each other at the market and both had acted natural. They had pretended the whole thing had never happened. Kiadora could tell he never got over his feelings for her, as she sometimes caught him looking her over in uncomfortable ways. He never knew of her affliction, of course.

Kiadora snapped out of her thoughts; she daydreamed too much. Noticing The Priest was not yet up from his quarters, Kiadora judged they had arrived early. She looked over to the left and a motion Dehlia was making caught her eye. She was pulling her bonnet down around her face repeatedly, only to be hit lightly by Ashila. Kiadora reddened again and looked down at the pew. To not have the think about her sister, she grabbed a copy of the Holy Text and opened to the table of contents.

The text was divided into sections ranging from Holy Days to sins to what type of foods to eat. One section caught her eye, a subsection under the sins. "Those to be Considered Unholy," it read. Just for kicks, Kiadora opened up to the section to see if her sister, or any of these people, could be counted among them. As she scanned down, she saw the usual. Liars…cheats…those who have sex with the same sex… those who mate out of wedlock…There went Hershick, who sat somewhere around the high royal seats.

Now *there* was something that caught her eyes. It resonated from the conversation last night. "The most Cursed Shiekita." She turned to the corresponding page to read the text following the same heading as the contents page.

"The most vile of Creatures, they are known to bend the Creation of God in a direct Rebellion to His Supremacy. They have a special affinity for Natural Elements, some favoring one over others. They are most often female and best dealt with via Termination."

Kiadora suddenly went white, losing holding of the book in her hand as it dropped down to her lap. She stared numbly forward. So this was what her mother thought she was, and it sounded oddly true. She looked at her sisters sitting next to her, whispering together. Her father stared straight ahead, and her mother was turned around, lost in conversation with a family behind them. Would all these people turn on her further if they accepted what she was- might- be? A thousand questions raced through her mind, the most prevalent was, 'what exactly is involved in Termination?'

Suddenly feeling as if the book itself was going to erupt into flames if she held it, she closed it and put it back in the pew. Should she even be in the house of God, if she was so vile and such a rebel? She considered bolting out of the Church, but as soon as she became convinced she had to, it was too late. A rotund man at the front stood up and greeted the audience. There would be no escape now without everyone seeing her run out; their attention was now focused toward the front of the Church. He spread his arms out, his white robe spreading outward in the process.

"Welcome to the house of the Lord!" He smiled benevolently, like a father looking at his children. "I am pleased you could come to worship today." Kiadora pictured that benevolence turn to rage as he found out what she was. A Shiekita. She glanced around, seeing the attentive faces in the Church, picturing them turning to shock, some mingled with rage.

"Let us raise our voices to the heavens, so that we may be delivered from our earthly shackles," The Priest proclaimed. Kiadora joined in with a chant that they usually began the service with. It was an inane

31

thing that merely droned, "We praise the name of God, Lord of Air and Sky. Save us." Kiadora had only started mouthing the words long ago when her physical reaction to the other natural elements started. The Priest stood up at the front, passing incense around the altar at which he stood. He was sanctifying the altar with the powers of Air.

Kiadora could feel her face grow redder and redder as this portion of the service continued. She felt as if her presence was soiling their grasp for God.

"I'm...I'm going for some water," she whispered to her mother, who looked at her and nodded. Kiadora would tell her it was a fever later, she knew her face still burned red. As the chanting of a thousand rapt voices rumbled through the Church, she made her way down the side of the isle.

They wanted the area sanctified so she would help.

A few people glanced at her and seemed to be in an internal struggle of their own: obey God and keep chanting or kneel before a noble. Many glances were replaced by a few fledging, reverent stares at the floor.

As she slowly crept out of the large, oak doors of the chapel, she felt the immediate coolness of the lobby, an area unchecked by masses of people. She walked across the lobby, out of an even larger set of doors and through the courtyard of the Church. In the middle of the courtyard stood an ancient well. Kiadora knew that it was used as a wishing well by people who were considered subversive to the Church. Tahn had told her.

Remembering Tahn's jibe to the element, she walked over to it and gazed down the well. Cool air rushed up towards her. She put her head on the side of the well, enjoying the coolness wafting up from within. Kiadora stared down, looking into the blackness. Even though it was dark, Kiadora thought she could see something moving below. She felt a shiver go up her back, but the shiver had a warm quality to it. It was something akin to what she tried to show the doctor. If felt like someone was pouring warm water down her back. Her thirst completely forgotten, she backed away from the well. As she turned she looked up at the heavy doors.

She realized she couldn't go back in now. They would be doing group prayer, and she would cause a disruption. More of a disruption than her existence already caused, she thought bitterly. Besides, she would ruin their perfect area. Only the adherents to the element of Air could be in the Church. The other elements, those of sin, seemed to call to her. Would God miss her or indeed want her there?

She walked over to the steps of the Church and sat down. The lines in the Holy Book kept running through her mind. "Most vile of Creatures," it had said, not even human. Like her mother had said, too. It used similar language for other beasts, such as the serpent that once rose out of the earth, bringing the fires of Hell along with it. She had learned about it during the youngest years. It had seemed so factual and impartial then, like learning about weather patterns.

Could she be on that level, at that stage? Would she fall to a level of corruption that would cause her to burn entire towns all in the name of chaos? What that her fate?

"No, I would never do that," she said out loud. There was the local museum, which showed pictures of charred skeletons. It was a terrible time: people were consumed by red-hot fire, which resembled earth.

"That is why, to this day, Earth is only a temptress. We must look deeper, further and beyond for happiness. Surely, it is not in this world," the guide had said. Kiadora had looked back at the drawings of a red snake bursting from the top of a mountain, surrounded by drops of red.

"And Skira, King of the Shiekita, still hunts for us," the guide had continued. "He is soul hungry, and conniving. You must always focus on what is beyond and above, for from there will come goodness."

So that was it, Kiadora thought. She was a creature of Earth, doomed to instill fear and destruction wherever she went. Or was all this simply Skira trying to tempt her? She would talk to Tahn, he knew about these things. She would wait for him until he came out after service with the rest.

After what seemed like an eternity, the doors swung open, spewing forth a red sea of people. Red dye had just been made popular by a cheaper method of squeezing a newly usable berry. Previously, goone berries were thought to be poisonous, so people dared not use them for dye. Kiadora had asked Dehlia why it mattered, if it was not being digested.

"Because, some poisons seep through the skin and kill slowly, stupid, and no one wants to take the chance," Dehlia had said. Until recently, when a boy accidentally ate half a bush of the berries and had not died. Word spread quickly, and the best doctors in the area came to examine the boy. After two years of observation, they informed the council, who sheepishly changed the listing of the berry to nonpoisonous.

As a result, goone berry pies and cakes and teas sprung up. Girls had found a temporary hair dye, and children's watercolors now included at new, brighter shade of red. The berry was also cheap to grow and took excellent to wool as a dye. Awed by the new color added to the spectrum of clothes to wear, women everywhere could not be found without an item of red clothing. And so it was with the sea of people who flowed down the stairs. Streams of scarlet flowed down the steps of the Church. Kiadora was instantly reminded of Skira and his seas of red flowing from the mountaintop.

CHAPTER 4

Kiadora searched the crowd for Tahn. He would be first since he sat in the back with the lower classes. They could not be seen conversing in public, so when she finally spotted him, she walked past him and muttered, "Behind Burg's, noon hour." He gave a slight nod. Kiadora walked over to her sisters, who were now walking daintily down the stairs.

"Where did you run off to? You're always running off, but in Church? What in the Otherworld?" Ashila said.

"I wanted water, and then I didn't want to disturb the service coming back in, I felt like I had a fever," Kiadora said in a rush.

"Let's go shopping," said Dehlia. Kiadora made a face of disgust. "Not you," she said scathingly to Kiadora.

"Fine," said Kiadora, and they went their separate ways, Ashila giving Dehlia a sharp glare. It was always customary for the family to go around to the shops after Church. Kiadora hadn't gone with her sisters for a while, even though as a royal she was not supposed to be wandering the streets alone for security reasons. Usually the streets

were safe. It was crowded enough where an assault on a lord's daughter would be noticed. She meandered around the shops, frantically
checking the clocks on metal poles that lined the walks.

At noon, she headed over behind Burg's, one of the many bakeries
of the town. Tahn was there, hands in the pockets of his tunic, as he
dug his toe into the grout between the cobblestones of the alley. As he
heard Kiadora walk toward him, he looked up and grinned.

"What's going on?" They usually met like this, but Tahn's grin fell
as he saw the stricken look on Kiadora's face. She refused to make eye
contact, her eyes darting every which way instead, like a child who just
realized she had been caught for having a dead frog.

"I need to ask you something," she said as she approached him,
finally bringing her eyes up to meet his. She was now blushing. She
took a deep breath. "Do you know anything about Shiekita?"

"Sure, what do you need to know about them?" Kiadora knew he
had immensely questioned his primary teacher about them, as he did
about almost everything mentioned in the Holy Book, while Kiadora
had been in another class daydreaming.

Kiadora's eyes started to shift again, and she frowned as she tried to
think of the right question to pose. She had gone over it for the past
hour, only to blank when she stared Tahn in the face. She decided to
go the indirect way.

"Is it possible for a human to be a Shiekita... because I saw a woman manipulate fire."

Tahn's brow furrowed. "Who?"

"I...I don't know. Just a woman on the street. I didn't get a good
look at her. Her bonnet was obscuring her face." She could sense

Tahn becoming alarmed. "But I don't know," she emphasized.

"What did she do?"

"Well, she wove her hand. And I'm sure the candle that was burning next to her went out. This was last night."

"It had to be a coincidence. Maybe a wind blew it out. Shiekita are terrible, terrible creatures, Kiadora. They've been known to start hurricanes and the like. They're fundamentally workers for the Dark One, Skira.

"It is written that they were created in an inverted process from us. Where we were created from the purity of the sea and take our life from the air, they were created from the hard stones of the earth and take their life from the flame. That is why we are made mostly of water and spill liquid when we bleed. They only know to follow the Dark One, where we are given the blessing to follow God."

Her heart leapt. She bled. "So they cannot be born as humans? They are not a direct threat outside natural disasters?"

"No chance they could be born as humans. But they aren't to be taken lightly. They're tricksters by nature and take human hosts. That is why we have never seen one, but they are there, causing havoc."

"Do you mean the fire a year ago at Mac's blacksmith shop?"

"No. He just left the kiln on, he admitted. He had to run out because he got word his wife was having birthing troubles. When he came back the shop was ablaze. Well, the community pitched in to rebuild it. As long as we are strong as a community, we can rebuild. But it is believed that they turned to a larger form of new trickery because of this fact. The mind is harder to rebuild than a shop."

"What do you mean?"

"They can take over a person's mind, Kiadora. See, subjugate a person from their mind, and that person cannot be trusted, even by themselves. They are reduced to the level of an animal, something wild, to be locked up. It's not as simple as a Shiekita binding to a soul anymore. You know the town crier's daughter, shrieks and shrieks all day long?"

"So they cause madness…"

"Yes, but not only the obvious kind. Sometimes, they merely bend a person's view on facts, so you will not follow God's will."

Kiadora could feel her face shift from the look of intense curiosity to fear.

"Why?" he asked. "What's been going on?"

"It, uh, well…."

"What," Tahn urged, "This is very serious!"

"Well, I don't know how to explain it, exactly."

"Do you think one's following you?"

"How would I know?" Kiadora shrieked. Tahn took a breath. Kiadora could tell he realized that it would not help if he panicked as well.

"It's unique to the individual," he breathed. Kiadora shrunk back slightly, he seemed to be intently staring her down, as if he would see the thing lurking there. "What has been happening?" he pressed, finally breaking his gaze and leaning against the wall. There was no going back, she had to know.

"It's just, I think I'm going insane. I know my sisters have always teased me about being odd, and insane, but now I think it is actually happening."

"What's wrong?" he asked, looking over at her. He looked fatigued, as if the only thing that was keeping him upright was the side of the shop.

"Do you know the woods?"

"Yes, of course…"

"When I go there, I get a…a feeling. Like, oh, it's so hard to explain. Like, tingling and warmth. All over, but usually in my chest," she said pressing her chest, as if trying to protect it from ever having that feeling again. Every time she told it, she realized she was able to get more of the details out, like she was purging Skira himself.

"Tingling and warmth," said Tahn. He had stood up straight again, revived by his desperate attempt to understand.

"Yes. The longer I stay in the woods, the more it consumes me. At some point, when I do not think I can take it anymore, I become drowsy, but I do not fall asleep. It's somewhere between sleep and awake. I don't know the exact term for it."

"A trance," said Tahn. "Sometimes The Priests enter it, for higher enlightenment. They speak with God there. But theirs is Air-based. They breathe incenses and practice breathing to connect to God. But yours seems to be collated with Earth. That's not a good sign. Do you see anything in these trances?"

"No, I can feel myself usually hovering in darkness, usually. Sometimes, I can feel green." This was the part that she felt was even too weird for her to describe to the doctor.

"Feel green. Is that like smelling yellow?"

"No, it's just, with the warmth comes shades of green. Like the warmth is coming from the color. I guess I see something."

"Anything else?"

"Today, I saw something move at the bottom of the well in front of the Church. Just vague figures, I could not tell how they looked specifically. It's never been like this, Tahn. I could always feel something. But never these trances or that feeling."

Tahn looked sad now, as if he knew for sure what it was and what would happen. He stared at the ground for a moment, deep in thought. He seemed to be debating something.

"What should I do?" she asked. He still looked at the ground for a little while longer, his frown getting deeper. Finally, he looked up at her, his expression grim.

"I'll take you to the Church. They'll know what to do."

"No! What will they do? I won't go!"

"They will not kill you. They can cure you. Get rid of the Shiekita." Kiadora looked toward the street, where a steady flow of people went past on their errands. "Kiadora, this is a matter of your soul. You need to be purged. If you keep at this, you will fall to the ways of Earth, then you will go insane for good." Kiadora merely regarded him for a moment. She had the sudden urge to hug him and never let go. If this is what he thought was best...

"All right, I will go."

CHAPTER 5

Kiadora shook as they made their way back up the steps of the large cathedral. On the warm day, Kiadora could feel the coolness radiating off the lifeless stone. She began to shiver worse than before, and her steps halted.

"It's fine, come on," Tahn urged. He now supported her arm at the elbow, as if she was a frail elderly woman. "They'll help you."

Kiadora gazed up at the oppressively large stone building. She had not noticed it much before. She had always just come here, not given the edifice a second glance. Now it loomed, dark and cold, as if to say that this had always been her torture chamber. She just hadn't realized it.

"What if I don't need help?"

Tahn looked pointedly at her. But there was a hint of worry underneath the hard stare. It shone from the pit of his eye.

"It's happening. You're turning away from God. This is how it starts." She regarded him for a while. Eventually, she broke under that worry and concern. What if he was right? Could she afford it if he was?

She marched forward. The coolness increased as Tahn swung a door open. There was a hollow thud as the doors hit the outside wall. She continued to march. Tahn was still holding her arm.

They walked through the lobby of the Church, into the chapel itself. At the end of the middle isle stood an altar boy, cleaning up from the service. As they walked down the isle, father supporting nervous bride, the altar boy turned with his arms full of extinguished candles.

"Telan, we need to see The Priest." Telan looked at Kiadora, who was now leaning against Tahn, barely able to support herself.

"Right away," said Telan, and he dashed out of a side door.

"This isn't good, this isn't good," Kiadora muttered. "He'll see me as a monster. I'm weak, I'm worthless. Other people can withstand these things. Other people are not affected."

"No one knows for sure why they prey on whom they do," Tahn said. He sighed slightly. "But actually, they usually affect women who stand apart."

"Stand apart?"

"People like you, who have few close. They are independent. It's not that you are weak. It's that you are alone."

The side doors Telan had just disappeared behind now swung open. The Priest, whom she had only seen from afar at parties put on by her family and whom she had watched speak every service, now strode straight at her. He immediately bowed.

"Your Grace," he said. She should have been the one bowing. For all the bowing and averted eyes, she still felt as royal as the local barkeep.

"You may rise," she squeaked out, still shaking as much as ever.

"What do you want to see me for?"

"Your Holiness," Tahn said, bowing and straightening up again. The Priest looked taken aback by a commoner speaking for a royal, even more so when she did not stop him. Tahn looked at the old Priest solemnly.

"It's a Shiekita."

The Priest made a small gasp. His large, green eyes widened, making his face look even more wrinkled than it was. "You poor girl," he said to Kiadora. "But we can help, we can fix this." Somehow this did not reassure Kiadora, as if he were another doctor prescribing a pill with horrible side effects. She did not feel sick. Not once in the woods did she feel in danger, just…right. It was all the fuss that made her frustrated and frightened with the whole thing.

"I have to contact your father first." This comment whisked her away from her thoughts.

"No!"

"My dear, I have to tell the lord what I am doing with his daughter. To not would mean my head."

"But wouldn't that just reunite you with God, and take you from this foul world?" It had not been an honest question. The Priest looked her up and down, unfazed.

"And I told my father." Kiadora was standing on her own now, not leaning on Tahn. "He said it was a phase."

"His Highness probably knew very well what it was, but did not want to accept the truth. These things are hard to bear. I'll send him word at once and tell him what it is. We need to take action at once. I think it's best if you stay here. Telan," The Priest called to the next room. The altar boy bustled in again. "Take our lady to the chambers."

The chambers? But nothing else for it now. She started forward, feeling jolted when Tahn did not follow. She looked back to him despairingly.

"It's fine," Tahn repeated. "They will take care of you. You'll be better soon." She stared at the floor, torn between fear and indignation. It was as if she was being admitted to a sick house, and few people ever came back from those. All she could do was follow the altar boy and try not to make a mad dash out of the place.

He led her into the side chamber, where she saw clergy flow in and out all her life. She had sometimes wondered what it looked like in there. Upon walking through that mysterious door, the similarity to the main sanctuary was slightly disappointing. The walls and floor were also flagstone, with a few wooden furnishings: a chair, a small desk, and an altar to kneel at. Light incense burned from the altar, where the Holy Text was laid out next to a centerpiece of feathers arranged like a morbid flower bouquet. Bright orange feathers mingled with cool blue and some iridescent teal ones stuck out of the back. A picture of the Church's mascot, a large Blue Jay, hung from the wall.

They walked through another door on the other side of the room and down a flight of stairs. The lower level was uncommonly warm. Still, only more stone. Doors became more frequent as they passed down a hallway, and they stopped at one on the right.

"It's not much," said Telan as he fumbled with some keys. "But I hope it's to my lady's liking." He swung open the door to reveal a room furnished mostly like a standard bedroom: a modest bed, a single brown and dingy rug on the stone floor, no vanity mirror. A single nightstand stood by the bed with a stone bowl on top.

"All we have on stock are robes, if my lady would like to change."

"That will be alright," replied Kiadora, stepping into the room before Telan. She noticed on the table there was a rack supporting the Holy Text. She realized, as her heart raced, that she would rather be back on the agonizing pills than read the damn thing.

'What is wrong with me? Is this the demon?' She felt afraid to be alone, but still she wanted to reflect on what Tahn had told her. She had barely had time to think about it.

"Well, if there is anything else, my lady has only to ask," Telan said as he made a slight bow and ducked out. The door shut with a miniature thud she heard every service.

Termination, what could that be? Why had she not paid more attention in Church school? Because she had been daydreaming. Usually about playing outdoors. Everyone had thought she was a freak because she loved Earth so much, and now she had picked up a Shiekita.

But it had always been this way. Could she have picked it up as a child? Maybe it had been with her all her life, and now it had started to manifest itself in extreme ways? That didn't feel right, though. Shouldn't she feel…a presence? But there was nothing except the dull, stone cellar. Only her. *It's because you are alone*, Tahn had said…

She gazed around the room and looked at the Holy Text again. What was that intense hatred towards it earlier? But her hate had felt subversive, good and more pure than anything she had been told out of that book. Maybe that really was how the Shiekita attacked, by feelings such as those. Hate. Aversion.

She knew she should go pick up the Holy Text and read; pray for wisdom and read until she had the answers. But she could not bring herself to do it. Last time, it had given her nothing but what sounded like a death threat. And before that, it gave her stories from men of ancient times, fighting off monsters from the forest with nothing but prayer and nerves. Creatures she had never seen before, in all her wandering.

She had never been big on Church, but the more she reflected, when she was in a situation she could not control and therefore could only fear, she realized how little it spoke to her.

After a few minutes of staring blindly at the wall, unable to process her realized apathy and lack of inspiration, she wondered if her sisters knew or cared where she was. Would her father be irate? Hopefully, they figured she took a longer stroll in town than usual. Tahn's family would hopefully assume the same as well. Her heart ached at the idea of getting him in trouble.

Curse it to the Otherworld! Why was she thinking of such mundane things? She was up for a ritual, and she didn't even know what it consisted of. It could be an execution, for all she knew.

But she could not outrun the Church, that she knew. If it was a Shiekita possession, it would be made known to all eventually. It was getting worse. And she didn't want to disappoint Tahn, who really believed there was something wrong with her. Tahn wouldn't put her in danger. For the first time since she could remember, she needed to trust the Church.

Lord Belac sat perusing papers detailing yet another dispute over new textbooks. He looked up at the wall to give his mind a break from the morning of reading and then went back. As he was just beginning to refocus, there was a knock at the door.

"Come in," he called, in his usually deep, gruff voice. A court scribe came in, looking uneasy.

"I have a message from the Church." Tithe matters again.

"Yes?"

"It…It's about your daughter." It was all Belac could do to not slide off his chair. The Church was sometimes in charge of reporting deaths.

"It's not as bad as you think," the messenger plowed on. "The message concerns Kiadora. It seems she has been brought to the Church by a peasant boy. She's not injured, not in a physical sense." The messenger glanced at the door, as Belac rose to his feat. "The report is that she has a Shiekita. The Priest would like the permission to examine her. She is being kept in a chamber safely, my lord."

A Shiekita. Of course, why did he not see? But…

"No one in my family had ever been possessed."

There were families where it ran in the lines. Generation after generation worried over the things. He assumed his line was stronger than that. What if the dishonor of this got out?

"The Priest says he will most likely perform the Termination ritual."

"Of course," said Lord Belac. If it could cure things. "Tell them they have my blessings…and tell Kiadora to be brave."

Across town, another knock echoed across the walls. Kiadora looked up from her reverie. The altar boy was back. He stood just outside the door.

"The Priest got an acceptance from your father to examine you." He thought about giving the full message, to be brave, but he decided against it. No need to upset the poor girl more than she already was. The lord had such a way with people. Fortunately, she seemed to have calmed down.

Kiadora nodded as she rose, hoping what she was doing mostly for Tahn's sake would not be too painful. She gave a deep breath, to calm her fears.

She followed Telan up the stairs, and they entered one of the many side chambers of the main Church. Kiadora had heard there was a maze of them back here, but was never permitted to see them. The Priest was waiting for her.

The room looked like her chamber, and the rest of the Church, with minor changes. There was scant decor, though no rug. In the middle of the room was a single, stone dais high enough to remind Kiadora of a buffet counter. A small table set to the right of the dais held several small instruments she could not see completely from where she stood.

There was no window, and the only light came from lit torches attached to the wall, rather than from the free-swinging candelabras she usually saw. It was strange, because the swinging candelabras were used to represent the enlightenment one could receive from the element of Air. Kiadora had picked up that much in her years of Church attendance; the lighting of the candelabras was part of each service.

49

"I'm glad we could commence," said The Priest. "It is a terrible thing, if such a possession is taking place. Has Tahn explained any of this to you?" As The Priest advanced, she noticed several objects hanging from his neck: a blue triangle pointing up, a golden outline of a Blue Jay, a cone of incense in a glass bottle.

"He explained a little. He mentioned it causes madness."

"Yes, if left for too long. Initially, it starts as a feeling of discontentment, then moves into small actions: disobedience, refusal to participate in many social activities. Next, there is a refusal to believe in God's will, and feeling lost to him, feeling isolated from him. Later, delusions start, usually Earthly in nature. Victims see things that are not there, hear things that are not there. After a while, the victim will lose their mind." Kiadora was not surprised, it was her life's story. Almost.

"So no physical symptoms or manifestations?"

"That is not the way the Shiekita typically work. They are subtle creatures, careful not to let slip their true appearance. They prefer to leave doubt over their existence, but it has not worked. They sometimes poorly trick us. They try to switch up the order of the stages of their possession, erasing some symptoms and creating others, or lengthening stages to appear as if it was just a part of the victim's personality. That is how they sometimes fly under our vision for a while."

"Oh." So that was why she was like this for so long. Possibly. "I suppose we should get this over with?"

"Yes, it is best. Telan? Go get the plant." Kiadora wondered what "the plant" could be, a type of poison? Telan disappeared out the door. Kiadora glanced around the room, and for the first time, got a closer look at the items on the table. A single wood wand and a box. Mostly, she wondered what was in the box. Whatever it was, there was nothing she could do about it now.

Telan walked back in with a pot covered in a slicked burlap bag. Despite the burlap, and the wax that appeared to be covering it, she still felt a tingle. It was the same tingle she got when she was afraid her arm was falling asleep. She moved it slightly without a problem.

"Kiadora," said The Priest, "please sit on the edge of the dais for me." Kiadora moved forward up the steps and sat down as instructed. She sat facing The Priest, as Telan moved to the side and picked up the box. The Priest reached over and picked up the stick. He walked to about three feet away from her and stood facing the east side of the wall. He began chanting in a strange language, with a breathy voice, unlike the voice he had in service.

His chanting gained momentum and speed, became strong in sound. He began to circle the room, waving the wand around in sweeping motions, as in service. Kiadora knew he was sanctifying the area in the name of the element of Air. It was a form of protection. But Telan never followed him with a box before.

Telan followed The Priest around the room, chanting as well, and on their second rotation he threw down a trail of bird feathers in his wake. Kiadora almost blanched. How morbid. Had the birds been killed? As they passed, she examined the feathers. In the flickering torchlight, she could glimpse fresh blood on the end of the feathers. She turned to look at The Priest and Telan and saw shadows cast from the falling feathers on the wall, wavering and vaguely menacing.

They came back to the original spot, and the area was now encased in a circle of feathers. The Priest waved the wand in each direction. He was calling the Four Winds, asking for their protection. Kiadora didn't know how the winds could possibly give them protection after they murdered the Air's creatures. The Priest walked over to her, while Telan stayed at the outer edge of the circle.

"The area is now sanctified, we can progress. While in the circle, the Shiekita can do us no harm."

"But it's still here. Wouldn't sanctification prevent it being here?"

"That requires more extreme measures, but it is pacified for the time being." Kiadora felt no different, especially with the plant present. She was also shocked at her bluntness. But she had to know. That was how she felt lately. She'd follow that need to the pits of the Otherworld, if she had to.

"We are now going to test you to confirm our suspicions. Telan," he said, turning back to the boy. "Bring forward the plant." Telan walked forward with the pot and held it in front of her. As Telan took off the bag, she expected to feel a large surge, but the tingling stayed the same.

She examined the plant. It appeared to be a small sprout of an apple tree. Her family's estate had apple trees, and she recognized the oblong shape of the leaf and the slightly jagged edges. They always aggravated her the most. The Priest brought the plant forward, after taking it from Telan's hand.

"This may be painful for you, but I am going to request that you touch it." She looked over to Telan, who had a scroll out now on a slab of wood. A fountain pen was pointed at the ready.

For the first time, she was truly afraid. She had avoided touching them all these years because of how she felt just several feet from them. After a moment's hesitation, she reached out and grabbed it with her left hand.

The pinpricks grew worse until they turned into an intense warmth. The warmth traveled up her arm and into her chest. It started to reverberate down her torso and through her legs. It reached the other hand, and at last, filled her head. It was nothing like the searing pain she imagined it would be, but rather pleasant, like basking in the sun.

Unlike usual, she did not feel drowsy, or fall into a trance. She grinned at this feeling, or knowledge rather, as her strength began to grow. She wished she could have gone through this experience alone, not as part of a cold ritual.

Just as she had this desire, the torches went out in unison. She could hear Telan yelp. The Priest suddenly yanked the sapling away, and the warmth died with it. She started to feel cold. The subtle pinprick returned.

Telan, from a few feet away, started to chant a prayer under his breath. "The Lord keep me from all the filth of this world….The Lord keep me from all the filth in this world…" she could hear. The Priest was rummaging around in his robe for something. She heard his steps go to her right side, and the room sprang into light as he lit a torch. He was stranding on the outside of his bird-brained circle. The single torch played past the back of his head, masking his face. Kiadora cringed. Some of the feathers were now attached to his metal sigils and in his hair.

The Priest looked over, clearly noticing the scowl on Kiadora's face.

Kiadora knew that in his world, the Shiekita had possession. It was angry at him for turning on the light. Telan was still watching all of this and then started his frantic writing.

"I think we can confirm this is a Shiekita. We will need to start the Termination process."

Kiadora gripped the edge of the dais. She had hoped they were wrong, that this wand-waving fool could not possibly detect a Shiekita that, as far as she was concerned, did not exist.

"It will happen in three stages. One to capture it, one to make it know God's love and another to release it." The Priest reached inside the box. He pulled out a gold talisman. The symbol of a bird flying on a triangle pointed upward. "This has been consecrated, and will fully nullify the Shiekita, like when we are in the circle and it cannot harm us. It can still wreak havoc, but it cannot cause true harm."

"Like fires?" asked Kiadora.

"Exactly, although this has not been seen in a while. We still cannot discount what it is capable of." He gave her the talisman by hanging it around her neck. The cold metal pressed against her bare flesh, but other than that, she felt no different. She examined the gold, flickering in the light. So this was supposed to save her soul?

She looked up and could see the last of the feathers being swept away by Telan.

CHAPTER 6

Back in her chamber, Kiadora sat thinking about what had happened with the plant and the torch. So, she could control things. But it seemed to happen only with the plant. Nevertheless, she looked at the small candle on the table next to the bed. She stared at it, while the flames leapt as usual. She started to think about how she wanted them to go out. Nothing.

'Come on, go out.' The flames remained resilient as ever. "Damn." Apparently, the plant was everything. She reached over and turned to the candle with the snuffer.

They were back in the chamber again, the circle of feathers around the dais already. Kiadora was perched on the dais same as before. She almost wished part of the ritual would be to bring the plant back again. She'd show these fools.

"Today, we will capture the Shiekita," said The Priest. "This is basically the same way you would capture a bee in a box. It will be trapped in a small part of your soul. We will lock it in with element of

Air, which will act as a sort of binding."

The Priest walked over to the table that contained a few large censers and picked up a censer, opening the lid. He reached inside his robes and picked out some matches. He bent down, struck one on the floor, and stood up slowly to light the incense that was apparently waiting inside the censer.

He blew inside the small, golden container and smoke began to issue out in large quantities. He did the same with three other censers. As he walked toward Kiadora, she could smell the smoke. The usually sweet smoke of service now had an edge to it. It smelled spicy. He began to circle the area, just inside the feathers. He walked with one censer in each hand. Telan had picked up the other two and was following, copious amount of smoke still pouring out of the censers.

They began to chant once again as they circled her. With each circle, both men came closer to her, making a spiral pattern. The smoke trailed after them, now turning the air into a bluish haze. The spiced smell started to make Kiadora dizzy.

As her head was swimming, she could see The Priest sit down in front of her. The censers had been placed at four points on the circle of feathers, each evenly spaced. The smoke had become so heavy that she could only see The Priest's outline. She had to struggle to keep her consciousness. She saw Telan's outline over her. Why were they not affected? She squinted through the haze and saw The Priest reach down and pick something up. She heard the rustling of some paper.

"In thy Holy Name, give us the clarity to understand," she heard The Priest say through the haze, and he began to read, "And on the third day, he was found on top of the mountain. He prayed and prayed for deliverance from Earth's temptations. Upon the mountain, he hoped he would have escaped from the lure of Earth and would be closest to the sky and his Father Air..."

Kiadora's lungs started to burn now, and she stopped listening to the reading. The mention of Air made her think of her own smoldering desire for it. Soon, her eyes began to water from the smoke, and she blinked several times to get the tears away. But the tears kept coming. Her eyes stung, and she pressed her fingers to them try to alleviate the pain. It helped only slightly, and when she took her hand away, her eyes only started to water more.

She blinked the tears away for a moment and looked up to see Telan peering at her calmly through the smoke. His eyes seemed to be clear, and he showed no sign of having breathing problems. Kiadora became aware of her own rasping breath. These fools were going to kill her. Was this how they got rid of the Shiekita? They choked her to death?

She could see The Priest leaning forward through the haze. As he came forward, the smoke swirled violently around the man and cleared slightly from Kiadora. She blinked at him, gasping, and realized it must have looked like she had been crying. The Priest looked pleased, as if this was exactly the way everything should have been going. His mouth was still moving as he peered at her, and she struggled past the burning in her eyes and lungs to hear what he was saying.

"Thus he was exiled back to the mountain from which he came to reach further for God. He was to leave everything, his family, his house. And so he went back to the mountain. He lay on the stones for two more days, and then something miraculous happened. He heard God speak and tell him that the only way to find goodness was to leave this world he knew; that not until he moved on would he find his answers or true happiness."

They were going to kill her. She jumped up, and as she did so, her head swam worse than ever. The entire world tilted to the right, and she was forced sideways with the pull of it. She staggered to the left and was caught by Telan, whose arms reached out of the smoke to her. She saw only the outline of his head as he dragged her back to the dais. She wanted to just drift into unconsciousness, but she didn't dare when they were trying to expel her from this world. Although she knew whatever she tried, she would not be able to fight back.

Despite her weakness, Telan and The Priest had come over and were both holding her down from both sides. Telan was pinning her left arm with his and had his elbow pressed on her chest. The Priest was restraining her right arm.

"Good, we moved it to pain," said The Priest to Telan. "Start the Wisdom." The two men began to chant, this time in yet another tongue. It came out in a harsh rasp, more guttural moans than words, as far as Kiadora could tell. Was this the language of the Shiekita?

After a time, the smoke was finally too thick for Kiadora to stand it. She had spent time around incense her whole life, but there was something else about this variety Kiadora couldn't identify. It was like trying to see the rain droplets inside a gray cloud. The chanting stopped, and she was overcome with darkness. The last thing she felt was Telan releasing his grip.

Kiadora sat up in bed, her head pounding. Her throat felt like someone had shoved a splintered piece of wood down it, and her nose was
slightly stuffy. She noticed a pitcher and a cup sitting on the bedside
table and poured herself some water. The soothing water helped with
her dry throat.

She sniffed as she looked into the cup and noticed her reflection.
Her face had an ashen look to it, as if it had been trying to blend into
the smoke. Was this the face of a woman who had a demon bound to
her? Besides the side effects of the smoke, she still felt no different
than normal.

What was tomorrow? Oh, yes. To make her know God's love.
Could it be possible it would be worse than today?

Day two found Kiadora on the dais yet again. Today, the Holy Book
was on the table. Light incense burned around the inside of the circle
of bird feathers. Not enough to affect her as badly as yesterday, and it
had the usual sweet aroma. The throbbing in her head has stopped,
but the dizziness had not. Still, she was coherent enough to sit up on
her own without the world tilting, as if she had been bucked from a
horse.

The Priest walked over to her from where he was drawing a sigil in
the air with his wand in a circular motion.

"What was the incense yesterday?" Kiadora asked.

"Sandalwood, one the the holiest varieties and the most potent. I
take it the Shiekita did not take well to it?"

"Something like that," Kiadora said.

"Today, as you know, is the day when we reform the Shiekita. Right now, we have it captured in the Heart Chakra. It cannot see us, it only hears us. Do you feel as if there is a scratching when you breathe?" Kiadora nodded. "That is the demon attempting the break free from where it is captured. Right here," The Priest said, as he put a finger on her chest, right where the breastbone was. Kiadora looked down, for the first time afraid of what may be in her.

"But now we will begin to purge it," The Priest continued. "It is important to know that there will be no paralysis." Kiadora's eyes went wide and her body went rigid. She felt Telan come up from behind and force her down. She started to struggle, but this time she was aware of how strong Telan was. As he brought his arm down on her, she had a glimpse under his sleeve briefly and she saw that he was quite muscular. He would surely stop any effort of hers to run. The door was locked, anyway. But she still felt the overpowering urge to struggle.

"Is it the Shiekita again?" Telan shouted at The Priest, as he placed a knee on her upper thigh to restrain her. It dug into her leg, and the more she struggled, the more her muscles were compressed and in pain.

"No," said The Priest, standing over her. "That is not possible. This time it is only fear. I had phrased it wrong, I would have been freighted as well," he said, now addressing Kiadora. "This may hurt, but we are doing what is best for you. We promise you will walk out healed." She still struggled, Telan holding her down tight. "Surely, when you were a child you received at cut?" The Priest continued, starting into her eyes, adjusting his gaze as she tried to look away. "Do you remember a nurse putting on a liquid that stung?" Kiadora stopped struggling, remembering back to the genthea liquid. It had stung, and she had cried. She nodded, now looking at him unblinkingly. He smiled down kindly.

"You remember it was used to rid impurities, so that you would not become ill? This is much the same. It will hurt for a while, but you will be protected from becoming more ill." Kiadora thought of her lungs that still burned slightly, and as she did, she began to cough.

"That is your body trying to rid itself of the Shiekita. It's a sort of natural defense, once the body can identify that it is cursed." As much as she hated pain, she knew she could not escape. And she knew the Church would not harm a noble lord's daughter, once she thought of it. Still, she knew of doctors that would cut off both of a person's legs to save them from an illness.

"It will be alright, we will not cause you lasting damage," said Telan, still reacting to her frightened expression. She looked up into his eyes. The earnestness of them made her relax. They were the eyes of someone who sincerely wanted to help and meant the truth.

"Alright," she said at last. "What must we do?" The Priest set down a rope he had carried over. She would struggle no more. He looked pleased with her and even smiled as she looked over at him.

"We need you to kneel on the floor," The Priest instructed.

She did as she was told, stepping down from the dais and pressing her knees uncomfortably to the hard floor. She saw Telan move to the back side of the dais. She could hear something sloshing. He made a hoisting movement and she saw him walk toward her with a pail. He came around and put it down in front of her. She looked inside.

It looked like water, ordinary water. In the flickering torchlight, the liquid was clear and her pale reflection shined back up at her, as if it was her from another world.

"We will expose the Shiekita to that which it revels in most: Water, Earth and Fire," The Priest explained. "It will know the corruption of its ways and be driven from your body."

"Where does it go?" Kiadora asked.

"We believe back to the Otherworld, reformed." Kiadora wondered what he meant by the word "reformed," but was then distracted by The Priest and Telan moving next to her and grabbing her on each side once more. The Priest grabbed the back of her neck and plunged her head into the pail.

The shock of the water forced the air out of her. It was cold, as if she had been transferred to the top of the Aethia Mountains. As she cried, only bubbles erupted. Her voiced sounded muffled to her. She had closed her eyes, but now opened them to see the blurred bottom of the bucket. Her shock made her draw in a breath and inhale water. She started coughing slightly, but was terrified to inhale again.

She had heard in the Before Times, the time before the Church and the God-sanctioned noble lords took over and before Aethand was even a country, people had gone into the lakes and the rivers of their own free will, merely for leisure. Was this what it was like?

She had stopped breathing, and her lungs started to feel like they were on fire once more. She started to thrash around, but the two men held her firmly.

When she thought she could no longer stand it, she was brought up again, coughing. Water poured out of her mouth, and she was once again able to draw air. It was the sweetest breath she had ever taken of the life-sustaining stuff. She knew the lesson here.

Again, they forced her down. This time, she was ready with her breath held. She felt the chill of the water seep through her as she tried to hold her breath. Again she was brought up, allowed but a few short gasps, and was forced down once more. After a time, the coldness was replaced by a gentle numbness, the same she felt during winter walks.

Each time she went down, though, she was held just a little bit longer than the last time. At first, holding her breath was no trouble for her. As time went on, she started to reach the point where she could no longer hold her breath comfortably. Each time, her lungs burned slightly worse. As she was brought up, each gasp of air was more precious than the last. As she went under, she felt like her lungs were twisting in on themselves, and she would have traded her entire family's coffers for a breath of air.

And still the length of time she was kept drowning was lengthened. The lack of air started to become dizzying. Just as she was about to lose consciousness, she was hoisted away from the bucket and placed on the top step of the dais. She slumped against it. She realized she was shivering, and her whole head was numb. She felt like she no longer had ears.

Kiadora sat gasping large amounts of air, her head still swimming, as The Priest and Telan looked down at her. As she gasped for breath, the dizziness started to recede, and the stars that had begun to dance in front of her vision seemed less numerous. A small amount of feeling began to return.

The two men then reached down and grabbed her arms once more.

The Priest put his hand on the back of her neck again.

"No," she gasped, for all the good it did. She was plunged into the bucket once more. The coldness was as sharp as ever. The areas where feeling had begun to return were where she felt the bitter cold sharpest. Her ears felt burned as she held her breath.

And so it continued for what must have been hours. She was allowed to sit for bursts of air and relief, only to be returned to the icy depth of the bucket. After a while, she seemed to have distanced herself from her body. It was as if she was no longer there. Her world only consisted of stifling cold, and desperate, mad gasps for air.

Finally, she was forced to sit on the steps of the dais once more. Her head throbbed, and each breath she inhaled seemed to never be enough. Water dripped down her long hair, the part that was soaked dripping over what was dry. Despite being out of the water, she still shivered.

Slowly, she began to come back to herself. The pounding in her head receded with each breath, and a blanket was draped around her shoulders. The Priest stood over her, gazing down as usual.

"The Air is your salvation at the moment, is it not?" he said in a somber tone. She looked up to meet his green eyes. "Every breath slowly gives you back life. Remember the lesson."

The next day she was in the chamber once more, this time warm and dry. Kiadora still had a headache, akin to what her sister had described as a hangover after she had been into the wine cellars a few years back. Kiadora was tired today, as she endured an entire night of frantic dreams of being drowned in the lake by their estate.

Today, there was a crate in the middle of the room: long, rectangular, large enough to fit a person inside. Her steps slowed slightly as she walked into the chamber, and she had to be urged in by Telan behind her. The Priest was already waiting for her as usual, next to what must have been 15 buckets. As she drew closer, she could see that they were full of dirt.

"This time, we are going to learn about Earth's vices." Kiadora gulped. This could go either horribly wrong or she would go into one of her trances and feel nothing. "As you will find out," The Priest went on, "Earth is stifling, crude and most dangerous. I need you to step into the box. Kiadora looked into the empty box and back at the buckets of dirt. She knew exactly what they were going to do.

"You are going to burry me. How will I breathe?" she pleaded. Telan reached into a pocket in his robe and drew out a straw.

"Through this. Don't worry, our most important job is to make sure nothing plugs it." He gave her an earnest, comforting smile. Still...

"And if you fail?"

"You will only be in a few inches of dirt. You can be recovered immediately," said The Priest. "We will monitor you through this." He brought up a strange brown box with a window on it that had a needle inside. On the end of a cord leading out of it was a small narrow mouthpiece. "We put this in your mouth, and as you breathe, it will monitor the changes of pressure in your mouth. The needle moves from side to side as you're breathing."

"I told you," Telan said. "Though uncomfortable, it will be safe." She looked at the monitor for a moment, then stepped into the box and reclined back. Telan handed her the straw and the mouth piece to the monitor as The Priest set up the barriers again with his waving and chanting.

Kiadora had always wondered what it would be like to be in the earth, completely surrounded by it, a part of it. She thought she may have come close to it during her trances, but she was not sure.

The Priest had finally finished making circles around them and drawing sigils in the air. He was now standing over the crate.

"Put the straw in your mouth, as well as the mouthpiece. Make sure the straw is pointing up as straight as possible." She put both in her mouth and used her lips to point the straw as directed. "Keep your mouth shut tight." She pressed her lips around the two tubes. "We will proceed." The Priest brought up a bucket and poured it around her feet. Telan brought up a bucket and was pouring it around her body, first next to her ribs. She expected to feel the typical pinpricks, but she felt nothing. It was just musty, dry dirt separated from the outdoors.

The dirt piled in, and she began to feel its weight press down. She closed her eyes as it was poured around her head. She had begun to shake slightly, as she pulled air through the tiny straw. She was beginning to understand how uncomfortable this would be. A whole life of taking large breaths of air, and now she was given a tube. The air flowed in slowly, forcing her to take long breaths.

The dirt had now covering her body. She looked down to see the last of her green dress disappear under the dull brown of the dirt. She quickly closed her eyes and angled the straw higher as Telan stood over her with a bucket. Her lungs were already burning slightly as she struggled to take in air through the constrained tube. The dirt poured around her face with a rumbling finality. She tried to shift slightly, but the dirt was holding her in place. Kiadora could feel the added weight of still more dirt pouring in around her.

She continued to draw air out of the straw, but as the dirt was added, it was harder to breathe in. Her chest was restricted by the surrounding dirt. Still, she drew air, faster, more desperately. How heavy would the pressure be once they stopped?

After a time, she felt them stop, right when the pressure on her lungs was at its capacity. She could still draw breath, but every intake was a challenge. She felt the straw with her tongue. It was a strong straw, and she felt a tiny bit relieved that the chance of it collapsing was small. If it was not accidentally plugged with dirt. But still she could feel the edges of panic as the little bit of air she drew never seemed to be enough. She wanted to scream and burst from her coffin, but she knew if she did, they would only force her back in once more. She willed herself to stay composed, as much as was possible when she was buried alive.

After a time, the ebb of panic receded and she was overcome by a strange weightless sensation. It was akin to her trances, but lacking the warmth and feeling of complete well-being. Here, she felt like she was only floating aimlessly, adrift in a void, a sea of blackness. Kiadora felt suspended, vaguely peaceful, but then suddenly felt like she was falling. She jerked as she felt like she hit a hard surface, as much as her constraints would let her. Suddenly she remembered the constraints. Her head started to pound again. The lack of air was making her delirious.

She could not stand being confined like this much longer. Once more, her lungs started to feel like they were completely burning, smoldering under this prison. At that moment she wished she could be Skira springing forth to freedom, wreaking havoc on those two near. She could not stay locked up like this.

She started to wiggle her foot and push up. They said the dirt would not be that deep. A last she felt a small shred of freedom as her foot broke from the dirt. She moved her toes, relishing the freedom, hoping they wouldn't notice this much. If only she could have the same freedom of breath as they did. As she moved her foot, it broke completely free and hit something hard. No, they could not do this. She really was trapped. She hit it again, but it would not buckle. After a while she felt dirt flow around her foot once more. She imagined the top of the crate slamming shut and being encased again.

While she was ensnared like this, there was nothing she could do but wait for freedom, if it ever came. How she hoped it would come. What if it didn't? No, she had to be strong for…for, God? No, he had let her be infected by a Shiekita. He had gotten her into this mess. Then for whom? For…Tahn. She could be brave for him, her dearest friend. She remembered the worried expression he showed when she told him what she felt. He was always so wise, and he had a faith she could only dream of. And so she waited, enduring the pain in her lungs, hoping the pain in her head would not reach too high of an intensity.

Her worst fear was losing consciousness, then she would not be able to control her breathing completely. Her mouth may slack, she may drown in her prison. Her greatest task was to keep her mouth controlled and direct the air flow. She wondered if she could lose focus, take a nap. She had done it while in the trance. Her mind kept racing. What would she do if they forgot about her? How long could a person go without water? A day, wasn't it? Three?

No, she would wait and have faith like Tahn. Still, what would happen when the dehydration kicked in?

'No…here…100…99…98…97…96…'

After some time of counting, she started to drift off for the first time, and her mouth did start to sag as her breathing grew steadier. She lost her grip on the straw, and the flow of air stopped. Her mind erupted in fear. 'Clamp down, clamp down.' She grabbed the straw once more and continued breathing. Her mouth had opened slightly and piles of dirt had fallen in. She swallowed the granules, being careful to keep them from both tubes. Sleep would not be possible, and the burning in her lungs had increased. Her headache had intensified itself to migraine proportions. All she could do was lie there, and in spite of her anger, pray they would unearth her soon.

After what felt like days, she felt a hand hit her leg as they started to dig her up. As the dirt along her face was brushed aside by a hand, she spit out the straw and mouthpiece. Kiadora let in a gasp of air. It was like being given sunlight after having spent a lifetime trying to sew by a match. She gasped for air, and as she had after the water, felt like she could never have enough. Kiadora had taken for granted the ease with which she breathed normally.

She hadn't even noticed she was free of the dirt. She brought up her legs, which had started to feel cramped from the pressure and from staying still for so long. She swung them around to the top of the crate and jumped out. Then she saw stars and she felt the world spin again. She fell backwards slightly and had to steady herself on the edge of the crate. Telan was standing next to her and took her arm to help her sit down on the steps once more. She rested her forehead on her hand as she tried to steady the world. Slowly, the stars cleared and everything returned to focus.

"The necessity of Air, again? Is that my lesson?" she said, looking up at The Priest.

"How did you feel while buried?" he asked serenely.

"Like I was trapped. I was panicking, afraid you wouldn't let me out. Like you would forget about me. My lungs burned, and my muscles started to ache."

"You felt forsaken and alone. That is all Earth has to offer. Do you know the story of the desert dwellers?"

Kiadora shook her head.

"All they have is Earth. They are alone and forsaken out there. They hardly even have Air because it is clouded with dust particles from Earth. Remember that loneliness. Tomorrow, we will release the demon. And cover the last element."

That night Kiadora lay in her bed under the covers, gazing up at the stone ceiling. A similar panic had returned to her as in the crate. She wondered if she would keep the power of the element. All she could think of were its negatives. The solitude, the entrapment, the lack of freedom. She knew very well nature was beautiful and vibrant. Would that be all she was allowed the feel from now on, the pain? She rolled over in her bed toward the wall. Tears came to her eyes as she wondered what they were doing to her.

The next day she walked into the chamber, her eyes downcast like they usually were around her sisters. She had to fight the urge to cry.

On this day, she saw a plate with a pile of heated coals in it on the table. Next to that was a pail and something that looked like a smooth brander for steer. She halted once again, and Telan had to force her in today by grabbing both shoulders firmly and steering her while shutting the door with his foot. She looked at The Priest, who was there to greet her as usual.

"This is going to hurt a lot today," said Kiadora in a panicked shriek. "You're going to burn me. You said I would not be permanantly harmed."

"Paralyzed," Telan corrected. "You will be able to live normally after this."

"No," she screamed, as she spun around. They might as well have robbed her of her four limbs already. As she spun around, she wrestled free of Telan's grip on her shoulders and ran for the door. She grabbed the heavy handle and started to pull frantically, shaking the door only slightly. As the light booms resounded around the room, she felt something hit the side of her head. She fell sideways and saw Telan standing above her holding the brander before everything went dark.

When she came to she was strapped to the dais, ropes holding her hands and feet down. She pulled her arms and feet up, even though she knew there was no use. The ropes were tied tightly.

"I'm sorry we had to do it this way," Telan said. "You will thank us." That sincerity, that honest belief in his eyes. He really trusted in what he was doing. Still, she struggled harder than ever, knowing that even if she did break free, she would have the locked door, as well as two men to catch her. She sighed and was still.

"Get it over with so I can get out of here."

She had already sworn to herself that she would find a way to still feel the sensation when she got near Earth. She didn't quite know why it was necessary to preserve that feeling, or even if it was truly gone, but she felt it was important. It was a part of her that would be a shame to lose. It didn't hurt anyone… only those she cared about thought it hurt them, she realized. She had to keep that in mind. But no matter how hard she tried, Telan's expression of worry always floated into her mind.

The Priest leaned over and undid the top three buttons on her dress. She suddenly grew cold and froze, staring at The Priest. She needed to do this without her clothes?

"This is all I'm doing," The Priest assured her, gazing down. "The Shiekita will escape from the area near your heart, that is where we will release it. Then you can put this particular demon behind you." Before Kiadora had time to wonder what he meant about "particular demon," he turned abruptly, and she could hear the metal clanging. Around his back, she saw the flat plate resting in one of his hands, and he was stirring the coals with the other. She could see the panel retreat behind The Priest and heard the metal clank as he let it down on the coals. They were going to brand her after all, like a common steer.

"And what will branding me accomplish?" she asked coldly. The Priest turned back toward her.

"It will create an opening from which the Shiekita can escape. It is commonly believed that they enter through wounds. Naturally, they would exit as well."

"And where will it go from there?" she asked again.

"Directly to the Otherworld; it knows the error of its ways," he said simply. "The Extractor should be heated fully." The Priest turned his back to her once more. Telan started to rummage behind The Priest. He was now holding a bucket and a cloth. The Priest had turned around once again. He was holding the plate that had now turned red-hot. Glowing like the core of an oil lamp, it would burn right down to the breast bone.

The Priest laid the glowing metal plate between her breast, and the searing pain started on her chest and shot to all her nerves. She screamed and thrashed worse than she ever had, but the ropes held her tight.

Her own piercing screams seemed foreign to her ears. The only person she had heard scream like that was a maid who had fallen down the stairs and broken her leg. Only hers was a short, sharp cry. Kiadora kept screaming and screaming as the plate was held in place. Tears started to run down her face, and after a few moments the screams turned into short sobs. She blinked away the tears and dared to look down. She could see her own flesh boiling around the edge of the plate. She started to shriek and sob harder than ever.

"Take it off, take it off!" she yelled, still in a strange, shrill tone. The Priest merely pressed down harder still, and she yelped in pain.

"Please…"

Finally The Priest yanked off the plate. It did not have the intended relief she wanted. The wound still seared in pain. As she breathed, skin around it expanded, adding to the pain. Just when she thought she could not stand it any longer, Telan swept in with a rag, and there was a stinging. It had to have been the genthea liquid. At least they were sanitary, she thought to her herself through ripples of pain.

Telan dabbed around the wound. She could see her blood soaking into the rag, and his pressure only increased the pain. Finally, the wound was let to sit open. They waited for a while, and slowly the pain receded just slightly as the air was let to sit on it.

"Do you feel relieved?" Kiadora only glared at The Priest for such a stupid question. "The Air cleanses and eases all things. Remember the lesson." Good, it was over. But The Priest had turned and was rummaging again.

"No, I thought that it was out of me," she gasped. Of course, that was to teach the lesson of Fire. This was to release it, she remembered. And he brought the glowing plate down once again, in the exact same spot, digging deeper, deeper still. Surly it would be charring the bone. She screamed more, another blood-curdling scream. Through her tears she could see Telan wince slightly before regaining his serene look one more. The Priest continued to push down on the plate, and all she could do was endure the pain, shrieking away. Finally, he brought up the plate and set it down on the table behind him. Telan put down his pail.

The two men joined hands over her open wound, which still throbbed painfully. They began to chant in a strange language again.

It droned on, in angry, fierce tones, like someone kicking a drunk out of their home. At last the chanting stopped.

"We are finished," said The Priest. "It is gone." Kiadora felt a tinge of regret through the pain. Telan brought up the bucket and dabbed the wound with a fresh cloth. After he had finished, he placed a bandage on the wound with tape around the edges. He stooped down to undo the ropes.

"You may sit up now," Telan said as he untied the last rope from her foot. She did, the wound stinging as she shifted positions. It hurt to breathe, as the skin kept shifting places as she inhaled and exhaled. The Priest was walking around the circle, doing his usual waving of his wand, the sanctification banishment.

"What will happen now?" she asked Telan.

"We'll keep you for a few days to monitor the wound, and then you are free to go back to your family. We'll also have to give you instructions on how not to contract a Shiekita again. Although they usually do not inhabit the same person twice, it has been known to happen." If it did, Kiadora would keep her mouth shut next time. She reached up to button her dress over her wound. The Priest had finished deconstructing his circle, and was now walking over to her. He rummaged in a drawer that was in the small table, and brought out a role of paper. He walked around the dais and handed it to her.

"There are a few things you will need to do to avoid another infestation. Be especially guarded round the elements that are not Air. If you feel the sensations again, we will have to do another Termination. Pray often; in the morning and at night. They will not touch someone who is close to God. As you walk through the forest, or light a candle, or even take a bath, think of Air. Imagine the breeze or the sky. Always study the Holy Text and follow the Doctrine. In this scroll is what I just said and a few more minor points. May God be with you." With that, he gave a curt nod and strode out of the room.

"I'll take you back to your room," Telan said. "We have a nurse that will continue sterilization and change the bandages." Telan led her out of the chamber. She had never been more pleased to leave a room in her life. "You may go back to your family in three days time," Telan smiled warmly at her over his shoulder. "I'm sure they are worried about you. Now you can start a normal life for the first time, I imagine. The Priest said he thought you must have been contaminated for a long time."

"Yes," she said. She smiled warmly back at him as he stood aside to let her into her chamber. She tried her hardest to look grateful. "The nurse will be in to check shortly," he said and shut the door.

Back to her family, wonderful. She imagined what it would be like, to be just like them. To go to service, and to adamantly know God. Her mother especially looked enthralled with service, swaying to the music with her eyes clamped firmly shut. Ashila did as well, but Dehlia did not. Her father looked as passionate about it as he could without losing his dignity as a man and a noble lord. She wondered if she, too, would have that same look of pride when The Priest said they were a favorite of God for their royal blood. Kiadora had always wondered why them. Why not the people who lived in squalor in the desert, or another species? Sure she was royalty, but was she not that way because God made her like that in the first place? They had never had to work at it or persevere. There was nothing to be favored for.

Her head always reeled when she tried to consider such things. The throbbing on her chest helped nothing. She looked down. The wound was right where it could be seen when she was in her summer dress. She would have a scar about five inches in diameter. A wonderful souvenir.

She sat down on the bed and looked at the scroll. Dehlia wouldn't have anything to tease her about now. She could sit and gossip about cousins and other sins of those in the middle ruling class. Sitting on her bed, sewing away...

She opened the scroll The Priest had given her. Sure enough, it listed all things minor and petty of what to do to prevent a Shiekita infestation. Focus on Air, pray, study the Holy Text. Then there were some suggestions that looked absolutely absurd: always wear an Air symbol in the forest, brandish the Holy Text before entering a cave. The list went on and on. Even if Kiadora wanted to do these silly actions, she would never remember them all. And was that how it worked now? One false step, and she would be sent back to that chamber? She set the scroll down and lay down on her bed, her wound hurting as the skin stretched once more.

Sleeping would be difficult; she was used to sleeping on her stomach. Kiadora had never slept on her back. It reminded her of the corpses she saw placed on their backs for the departure ceremonies of the dead.

She stared at the ceiling and waited for the nurse to come in.

CHAPTER 7

Three days later, Kiadora walked down the steps of the Church, blinking in the sun. She remembered that fond time in the crate and was glad to be blinded by the sun. The nurse had monitored her closely and deemed her wound safe from infection. Any redness may have hinted at another Shiekita infestation, she had said. The wound now had a thin, yellowish crust to it; the beginnings of the skin repairing itself, the nurse had also said. Kiadora still wore a bandage under her dress and carried a burlap bag filled with clean bandages and a bottle of genthea. She would need the liquid now if the coarse material of the bag kept rubbing her hand so fiercely.

She walked home silently, keeping her head behind the hood of her brown cloak so she would not get the usual mandatory greetings and bowed heads. As she headed toward the outside of town, she wondered what it would be like to walk down a forest path, unbothered, able to keep a quick pace. Convenient? Empty?

Kiadora stood at the outskirts of town, looking at the dirt path that headed into the woods. She took a step forward, and it started. That familiar prickling. Her skin started to feel more and more warm as she walked towards those woods. She grinned. It was still there. Then the edges of her mouth slanted downward. She took a seat on the rock along the path. A man passed, and she pretended to be looking through her sack for something, her head bent low under the hood.

So, the whole ritual really had been pointless for her. And once someone figured it out, that she had not been cured, she would be sent back to do it all over again. Would it be worse this time? The tingling still persisted, worse on the left side of her body, the side that faced the woods. No, she couldn't go back. She had to act normal. But if she collapsed again, they would find her and know.

Yet her family was expecting her, even if they didn't care to pick her up. A noble lord showing up to the Church to pick up his daughter would draw too much attention, the message from her father had relayed. 'They do have an image to keep up,' Kiadora thought bitterly. She hardly saw why she needed to go back. But if she did not return, they would send out a search party. If only there was a way to go around the woods…but there wasn't.

She steeled herself and stood up. 'I've been through worse,' she reminded herself, glancing down at her blouse. The wound still felt raw and tender. She grabbed her bag, the burlap biting into her palm, and walked forward.

As usual, the tingling sensation developed into only warmth. She was already warm from the cloak, but the new warmth seemed to radiate through her, starting from her feet. It was an overpowering heat, one that did not cause her to break out in a sweat. Still, she forced herself forward. Her head began to feel light, but she made herself remain conscious as she had when she was forcing herself to take in air from the vein-sized straw. If she fell, she would need to go back to the chambers. She kept reminding herself of that. As she marched forward, focusing intently on the path before her, she realized she made it through a quarter of the path already. It was the longest she had ever stayed conscious when she became this way.

Her head swam as it had when she was brought up from the pail of water. Still, she forged ahead. The path seemed to be tilting slightly, but she only kept walking. She looked to the side of the path and swore she saw a shape move between the trees.

Oh no, a wolf.

She would never be able to flee from it like this. She looked over and focused on the object she could see running through the trees. The spinning stopped slightly as she focused. It ran under a bush, but no leaves rustled as it went under. It seemed to pass through the bush silently.

She stepped off the path and looked around. The spinning had completely stopped, and she felt entirely normal. If only she had known that all she had to do was fight through it. If only she had known she was strong enough.

Kiadora looked around back at the path. No, no one was on it.

She walked over to the bush under a tall oak tree. She peered under the bush. Nothing was there. As she looked closer, she could see tiny sparkles in the leaves, like the ground up diamonds some of the truly noble women would sprinkle on their cheeks. She was looking at the leaves, but in her mind she could see through the surface of the plant.

Kiadora stared as the small particles seemed to swirl through the leaf. She stood up and looked at the oak tree. Dark particles swirled through the tree in small trails. How could she not have noticed this before? What was it?

Kiadora had the fleeting desire to touch it, but she was terrified of what would happen. Would it burn or overpower her to where she would collapse anyway? Then she looked down at the grass.

She was touching it; the particles were on the grass as well, flowing next to her, through her. She bent down and put her hand on the ground. The small specks, this time bright green, went right through her hand. Nothing, except more warmth. Was this what was causing her sensations?

She stood up and stared at the forest. All through the trees and plants, she could see small particles flowing around them, through them, some white, some blue, green-yellow…the colors were endless. She couldn't believe what she was seeing. She had a feeling no one could ever know about this, no more than they could see this them-selves.

But what if she was hallucinating? She started to move back to the path, which was devoid of the small granules. The Church hadn't cured her at all, only opened new doors to strangeness. She began down the path again toward home. In the corner of her eye, the rainbow danced in her vision. But at least she wasn't dizzy any longer. That had evaporated like her perception of normality. Still, she wished she was incapable of seeing those odd colors. Kiadora thought she would miss her sensations, but now she wished that crate was all she would feel of Earth. No one would catch her staring then.

As the desire increased, the view at the corner of her eye went a stagnant green. She looked over and the world looked as it always did. But now the dizziness returned worse than ever. She fell sideways into the grass, which was still a solid, though spinning, green. She could feel herself losing consciousness. No, she wouldn't allow them to take her back.

She stared at the grass again, willing herself to see those particles once more. The world wouldn't look the same, but this way she could still function. The swirling patterns returned, at first a few, but then the whole world was awash with a these creatures…if they could be called such. Her head feeling normal, she stood up and went back to the path. She would have to do some research on these, someone had to know what they were. But not with the Church and certainly not with Tahn.

Finally, she strode up to the gates of her family's estate. The guards looked at her in surprise, evidently shocked to see Kiadora on her feet without the dreamy glint in her eye. Despite her new, enhanced world, she stared forward as steadily as she could. For the first time outside of the gates, her head was clear.

They both smiled. "M'lady," they both muttered as they opened the gates. If the guards were that happy to see her "cured," she wondered what type of fanfare her family would give. She opened the heavy front doors and found her family waiting anxiously in the entrance hall for her. Dehlia and Ashila were sitting near the back of the room, whispering to each other. Her mother was holding a threaded needle and embroidery, clearly not focusing on it. Her father was pacing nervously. When she shut the door with a wooden boom, the family looked up in unison. Kiadora was pleased to see the décor in her home was not moved by technicolor swirls.

Ashila grinned and Dehlia looked up as if she had just been distur-bed by a servant. Her mother's eyes brightened as she gasped, "Kia-dora." All of this was then obscured by her father rushing to her and embracing her in a hug. She brought her own arms around his bear-like shoulders, his beard scratching her as he drew away.

"You're well, then?" he asked, staring her down. She could almost hear the political ramifications buzzing through his mind if she was not.

"Yes," she said, trying to mimic the earnest look given by Telan all those times. "Completely cured." Her mother gasped and looked next to tears with joy.

"My daughter's completely normal, praise God." But the woman still stayed at a distance. Kiadora hadn't been touched by her mother in years.

"So," Dehlia said, "Normal for now, are you?" Kiadora was about to reply, but Dehlia was pushed aside by Ashila.

"You're well," she oozed. "I'm so happy for you." The two sisters embraced briefly. "What a dreadful state to be in. I'm so glad you're cured, so glad…" Ashila went on about how happy she was, but Kiadora stopped listening.

Yes, cured. Normal. No more pity; maybe Dehlia's snobbery would let up. No more being a political burden, no more fearful glances from her mother. Everything was the way it was meant to be. As long as they never found out.

After her family was done gushing over her wondrous recovery, Kiadora headed up the stairs to her room. She noticed there were no servants about. Probably all sent to the market. Naturally, this would all be kept quiet. She had been told by her father that if anyone asks, she had been at the local theological university that she was considering going to, reading books and taking classes. Kiadora's pulse raced. The family's dirty little secret, kept locked up. As if she would ever consider going to a theological university after that little foray.

She strode into her room and closed the door a little harder than intended. Kiadora jumped as she saw a figure in the corner move abruptly.

"Mistress Kiadora! I'm sorry, you gave me such a fright. I almost leaped out of my stockings." A stalky, middle-aged woman bustled out of the corner, holding a dusty cloth. "Terribly sorry to be in here, my lady." She curtsied briefly, some of her graying, dark hair falling in her face. "Mistress Melanone ordered me to clean up here right away and…"

"No need to apologize, Lisera," Kiadora said. "You scared me just as much." She glanced out the window, a rainbow of sparks flowing on top of the trees. She almost missed to tranquil green instead of the chaotic swirl. She gave herself a mental shake and glanced back at Lisera.

"Is there something you see out there?" Lisera asked. Oh no, the maid had noticed her staring. Kiadora tried not to look flushed.

"It was…it was nothing." Lisera was regarding her intensely.

"You can see it, too," she said in a low tone, leaning slightly toward Kiadora. "I remember when I first could. I went through the same thing. I couldn't keep my eyes off. It's beautiful, isn't it? All the magnificent colors." Kiadora stood stock-still. Not even an hour back, and she had been discovered.

"You can't tell anyone," Kiadora whispered. "No one can ever know. They think I'm cured. I can't be sent back, I can't!"

"Oh, your secret's safe with me," Lisera smiled and patted Kiadora on the shoulder. "You think I want them knowing about this? None of their business how the good God made me see things. I don't need questioning, and I'm sure you don't neither. Your father's been worried sick about how much disgrace a Shiekita would bring upon the family."

"Yes, and that's all he cares about. So what are they, those colors?"

"You're seeing a plant's individual energy."

"How did you find that out?" Kiadora asked.

"I shouldn't say, my lady. I've said too much already…" Lisera wiped idly at a night stand, trying to look innocent.

"Stop teasing me, Lisera."

"But I was shocked that you could see it, too. You don't mistake the awe in a person's face, especially with knowing her history," the old woman prattled on. "Ability's practically burned out of the noble lines. I don't want to be causing you any trouble."

"Lisera, you have to tell me. I can't go on like this. I can't go on the rest of my life being nothing but a disgrace to be swept under the carpet. Tell or…I'll make sure they fire you."

"No need for that, ma'am. I can tell you desperately want to know. You were like me," Lisera said, raising a single hand and shaking her head.

"What happened? Why do you not touch it now?"

"I have no need," Lisera said simply. "Listen, I will tell you where

85

you can learn more and how to get there. We just need to think of how to get you away from here without you being noticed." Both women stared at the opposite wall, deep in thought.

"Where is this place?" Kiadora asked.

"It is a group of people under Shilidek, 50 miles off."

"Under the city?"

"Yes, in a system of caverns, just off the main road."

"Doesn't the city maintenance find them?"

"No, there are ways to watch for intruders."

"What kind of ways?"

"I would explain it, but right now I do not think it would make any sense to you. Suffice to say, if you have the gift, you can get in." Kiadora found it odd to hear anyone refer to what she had as a gift. But still, since the theological university was out, she thought harder. She considered faking her own death for a moment but decided not to put her family through that. Besides, it would be near impossible.

"The Hermetical Order," Lisera said suddenly.

"The what?" Kiadora thought she remembered hearing of them distantly once.

"The Hermetical Order. They are a group of people who devote their lives to the Church's notion of God by prayer and meditation."

"That sounds dull."

"Oh, no doubt. But, if you can convince your father that you are going to learn about God, I'm sure he will have no objections. Having a Hermetic in the line is a great honor."

"I could say that my experiences...um, at the Church have taught me that I would like to search out God." She looked hastily at Lisera, who was not supposed to be aware she had undergone an exorcism. Lisera didn't notice the hesitation, as she was so deep in thought.

"That could work. Look at me, plotting to send away one of the lord's daughters. If he ever found out…"

"He won't," Kiadora said. "But how will I let him know it's legitimate? I cannot just show up at their doorstep. And what if my parents wish to write, and I'm not there? And if I come home, how will I act?"

"The compound has books on Hermetics, you can study those. They have books on almost all of the traditions. And that is just it, you can show up on their doorstep. That is how the Hermetics take in many adapts. They will consider anyone, but you need to pass a test to get in. They also do not permit contact with the outside world."

"So it will be like I dropped off the edge of the planet?"

"Exactly," Lisera said, grinning. Kiadora could not believe this. They had found a way, an almost flawless way. She realized she would need to show resolve, though. As though she knew her calling from God, and she was not some child begging her father to go on a vacation.

"I guess I should start packing," Kiadora said. No need to sit around. She looked around the room. "I wonder if I will ever see this place again."

"That is up to you," Lisera said. "I will pack your rations. Do you know how to get the Shilidek?"

"I've only been there once, when I was very small."

"Very well. You will need to head due west down Cantebury Road. Actually, from there all you will need to do is follow the signs. It's a large enough city. When you arrive, head to the east end of city, along the market square. There is a long lane of market stalls that you will run smack dead into if you follow the road from the east gate. Once you go down the market road, there will be a tavern. Lid's Inn. Give the barkeep this." She pulled a notepad from her apron and flipped over a list of chores. She drew a five pointed star and circled it. She tore off the sheet and handed it to Kiadora. "Tell him Lisera sent you, he'll take it from there."

"How long has it been since you have been there?" Kiadora asked.

"Me? Oh, about 15 years. But I know ol' Lid's still there, don't you worry about that. We keep in touch. I'll go get those rations I promised. Come down to the kitchen to get them, and act like you asked for them."

Lisera looked Kiadora up and down and took a deep breath.

"Good luck. You'll learn much, trust me." With that, she gave Kiadora a broad smile and left. The sun had begun to set and the rainbow of color was dancing across the wall now. She turned around and went to a cabinet for her traveling pack.

"There you are, ma'am. Here are the rations you ordered."

"Thank you, Lisera," said Kiadora, taking the bag. Lisera winked as Kiadora promptly left the kitchen. Although no one in the kitchen was really paying attention, they kept formality in case someone was. She picked up her pack where she had left it outside the kitchen and started up into the main part of the house.

Soon she was knocking on the door of her father's study.

"Come in," said her father's gruff voice. Kiadora strode in.

"Father, I have something to discuss with you." He looked up and quickly glanced at the pack she was holding in one hand, a deep brown to match the plain dress she wore. It was the heavy dress she usually wore for long travels.

"I'm going to go join the Hermetical Order."

Lord Belac blinked as this, evidently trying to soak in his daughter's latest whim. He regarded her for a moment, at last saying, "And what brought this on?" She could already see the slight look of pride in his eye. Lisera was right.

"My time with The Priest. It has changed me." Not a complete lie. "I realized that my time is best spent with my Lord, God, especially if I am to avoid another Shiekita infestation. Prayer is just the sort of thing I must do to keep myself pure. And The Priest said I am especially prone to another infestation since I have already had one." She handed him the scroll The Priest had given her. Her father opened it and skimmed it.

"I think this will be best for you," he said. She knew the argument would work. He wouldn't want to risk another infestation; it was difficult enough keeping it quiet a first time. "I think you'd better say goodbye to your mother and sisters before you go," her father said.

They met in her mother's chambers, an hour later, and Kiadora talked about her experiences in the Church's chambers. She spoke at length about the purity of Air and what they did to her to make sure she knew it. She spoke of the list and the tightrope she now must walk on. What started as expressions of horror turned into smiles of pride from everyone except Dehlia. It was a strange experience for her family to actually be proud of her.

Her mother smiled through tears of joy and loss, telling Kiadora to be safe. Ashila did not cry at her sister's departure; she actually beamed.

"I'm so happy you found your way," Ashila said. Kiadora was too. Dehlia only looked away with an almost threatened expression. Dehlia had been superior for so long, Kiadora could tell that no matter what Dehlia did, how many suitors she had or how beautiful she looked, it would always pale in comparison to having a Hermetic as a sister. Kiadora smiled at her, in mutual understanding. Knowing her own superiority would only be a misconception made it even more rewarding.

Dehlia gave an icy smile back. "Well, good luck," she said in a cool tone.

They followed her to the main doors, and she waved at them as she walked through the front door. With a thud of the door, Kiadora was out and heading toward the gates.

CHAPTER 8

Examining the market stalls next to her, Kiadora strode down the streets of Shilidek toward the inn. The directions that Lisera had provided proved to be non-problematic as she entered the city gates unquestioned and made her way through the market. She kept the hood of her traveling cloak held up in case anyone would notice her, although the chance was slim.

She was pleased with her decision to come instantly as she looked at the curious stalls next to her, enthralled with the slightly exotic selling style. All the goods were placed on tables lining the road under large awnings rather than hidden away in the separate shops that she was used to. She felt like there was more of an actual community as people compared wares and bartered right on the street.

Just as Lisera had said, the stalls ended abruptly and on the left-hand side was a building front with a sign that read "Lid's Inn." The inn looked small and the glass in the window panes was a fogged, smoky color. Kiadora fished in her pocket to make sure she had the paper Lisera had given her. Her finger hit the stiff corner of the folded parchment. For the first time she felt truly nervous, and the fact that she was inquiring about an underground community seemed surreal. She kept running her finger along the parchment, as if it was the only solid thing in her world, her connection back home. But she took a step in.

A small bell rung off as she walked in the door. She had gone traveling a little with her family, but when they did stay over, it was at a family member's estate. She had never seen a common inn and was taken aback at the low lighting and humble wooden tables. Customers of the market sat looking over their purchases or comparing with each other. No one turned a head at her entry. She hovered awkwardly in the doorway for a moment, then looked over to a bar where a large, older man stood ordering a young boy to add something to a stew that was in a large pot on the counter. She walked over to the two.

The old man looked up as she was coming over, peering at her face under her hood. She decided to take her hood down. He nodded at her and winked, an odd gesture for a man who looked so gruff with dark, leathery skin and wispy gray hair.

"What may I get for you miss? Would you like to have a seat over here, maybe a bit of wine?" He pointed to a table to the left of the counter. She nodded and took a seat. He stood next to her, taking a pad of paper out of a front pocket of the apron he wore and poised a pen over it.

"You must be Kiadora," he muttered. "Lisera sent word."

"Yes," said Kiadora. "I have the symbol she drew for me." Kiadora started to reach into her pocket, but...

"Later," said the man.

"Oh, alright. You must be Lid."

"Yep, pleased to meet you." He nodded to her slightly. "I'm going to put you up in room 86." He spoke to her in low tones. "I want you to wait there until about quarter to midnight. That is when all my boarders should be in bed and so no one should be in for food. I'll be waiting for you down here. Until then, how about some stew, eh?" Kiadora shook her head.

"No, that won't be necessary. I still have provisions left over, and I haven't brought any money."

"Consider it on the house. It'll look more normal, like you came in for a meal and board. When you are ready, room 86 is down the left hall." He indicated a doorway off to the side of the dining room. "I have it all made up. See you later, miss." Then he bustled off to get her food.

The candles burned low and the fire in the hearth had all but gone out. As Kiadora re-entered the dining room, after marveling at the rustic level at which some people lived with no mirrors and lumpy mattresses, she could only see Lid's outline behind the bar. She walked over timidly and cleared her throat.

Lid turned around, a plate in his hand that he was drying off. She was already holding out the piece of paper with the star on it. He looked over the bar at it.

"Yes, yes, although I wouldn't have doubted you without the symbol. I'll take you down in just a moment." He turned to finish wiping the last of the dishes. Kiadora regarded his straggly hair and realized she was trusting her treason to a complete stranger. Unlike the doctor, she had no previous reasons on which to trust him other than the fact that the housemaid knew him.

"What makes you do this?" she asked. "I mean, why? Why harbor such as ourselves?" Lid's cow-hide of a hand rested over the plate. He looked up at her.

"When you get down there," he said, his face now solemn, "You'll meet a woman named Uranda. You'll know her instantly, she'll have terrible scarring on the right side of her face. That's my sister, that is. She tried to teach herself to control her gift and tipped off the neighbors. They didn't take too kindly to it. They caught her manipulating fire and deemed her an abomination immediately. This was afore more recent times, when they try and cure you. They tried to use against her what they assumed she would use against them. They got close with a torch, close enough to scar her, but she gained control over the element after she was done being petrified. Burned all of them to death. Naturally, she had to go underneath and that is where it all started. But let me show you." He had put the rag down and she followed him around the bar to where he was holding open a door into the kitchen. She followed him, and they went over to a large door. Lid threw a latch up on the door and opened it.

"This here's our freezer. The law came around asking if I knew where she had gone. I told him the icy depths and wasn't lying. They assumed she ran North." He chuckled slightly, than became sober. "Sad it has to be like this. Figures the only safe place for you people is behind frost and chill." Kiadora nodded, folding her arms around herself, the cold getting to her. At the back wall, Lid pushed a large crate on wheels to the side and revealed an empty space, insulated with a harsh-looking wool. He went over to the wall, and she saw him working at the wool. Soon, a large rectangle chunk of it was pulled back. She looked around his large shoulder and saw a door in the wall with a single lead ring.

Lid pulled on the ring, and the door swung open with a rush of air. Kiadora expected the air to be stale, but it smelled alive and earthy. A warmth hit her in the chill of the freezer.

"They live down there, in a cellar?" she asked.

"Sort of," said Lid. "Follow me." From the floor he had picked up a kerosene lamp and disappeared into the door. Kiadora followed, watching the light glow as a steady dome around them. The walls were made of tightly compacted earth. The steps they took downward were crudely carved out of the earth, and there were narrow stones placed on the top of the levels. And so down they went, never-ending stairs into the abyss, the unknown. Kiadora had several questions racing through her mind, like who had built this, how long had it been here and why was it here to begin with? Was it carved by the group she was about to meet? But something held her from talking. For some reason, she wanted to stay silent so as not to announce their presence. Lid spoke anyway.

"It's quite a journey," he said back to her, like a conversational tour guide at the museum. The wrinkles about his face looked deeper than ever in this light. "We're descending about seven miles underground. When we get there, we'll be in an abandoned heating pipe maintenance area. The area's been developing rather fast and instead of taking the resources to dig it up when the lines were rerouted, the city left it there. The area's full of them from recent expansions." Kiadora remembered the doctor having space because it was forgotten after construction.

"You think they would dig it up or fill in what they left," Kiadora said. "The empty space is being used for all sorts of subversive things."

"Of course it is," said Lid. "But the Church and the law are so convinced that they have wormed their way into everyone's minds so completely they fail to check. Lisera mentioned you had been through an exorcism."

Kiadora's heart sunk at the memory. "Yes," she said. Remembering the experience, she looked at the walls next to them. Small, black particles flowed around the soil that she had failed to notice before. "Oh, good, I'm not fainting," she said, accidentally out loud.

"No, sometimes I need to carry people. It's good you've learned to control your reactions."

"I learned it during the Termination." She laughed. "They helped me get closer to what they were trying to purge."

"But you see, they are so *close* to the truth. They've found a way to rid the symptom and thought they rid the demon. They figure everything is above, beyond, supernatural, it can't possibly be people themselves that's responsible for things. So they assume it's demons who attack individuals, who in their view do not unite. No, they see themselves as quite untouchable."

"Yes," Kiadora agreed, thinking of Dr. Iland's tamed wild that conveniently had not been discovered yet. Down they descended, Kiadora's legs becoming tired and rubbery from taking so many stairs. At last, they reached a large opening, a round hole at the end of the tunnel a few inches off the ground. There was no door, only a light emanating from behind. Lid stepped through the hole before her.

"Hey, Wyland, I have her!" he called out into what appeared to be a large underground cavern. She stepped through herself, careful not to trip on the raised lip, and was amazed at what she saw.

Just as it had seemed, it was a large cavern, the ceiling rising as high as one of the ballrooms back in her home. The walls were covered in a type of steal, the little that could be seen. Someone had draped colorful cloth over the metal, hung by washing pins, apparently to give the area a less industrial feel.

"This used to be the main control center for the heating systems," Lid explained. "At one time this city acted like a large building that is heated from a coal room underneath, and this was the area where the fires were constantly maintained. Worked up into the city and heated the whole place. This was before we went steam and everything was relocated to the surface."

Kiadora looked over to where a single furnace remained. It looked like a large spider, the belly of it glowing red and several pipes for legs branching out around the walls between the cloth hangings, providing warmth under the dank soil. A man sat next to it, looking at a temperature gage every so often, then returning to a book he was studying.

Kiadora looked at the rest of the cavern. Several barriers had been erected, and she could see that they provided rooms, much like the cubicles in the banking office that she had been to. She looked at the walls, and on one side there were a few ladders leading up to several cubby holes built into the wall. A woman was climbing up a ladder and crawled into a hole.

"Is that where everyone sleeps?" she asked, indicating the hole system. It reminded her of a beehive.

"Yes, everyone has blankets and a rustic mattress in there. It isn't much, but it's home to these people," Lid said.

Lid looked over to a woman as she approached them. Kiadora marveled at the way she was dressed. It was unlike the simple clothes many wore on the surface. She had several skirts around her waist, each of varying and bright colors. Her hair was a wild, curly red and flowed down to the middle of her back. Her skin was extremely pale, as Kiadora assumed most skin would be down here. She wondered how pale she would look after a time and looked at her own slightly tanned skin. She had never been one for much of a deep tan, but she looked like she had seen some sun in her time. She didn't dare picture how pale she would be after a few months down here.

The woman came close to them, beaming.

"Hello, Lid," she said, greeting him. She turned to look at Kiadora. "You must be Kiadora. I'm Wyland."

"Pleased to meet you," said Kiadora, who held out her hand. Wyland looked at it apprehensively and made no move to grasp it. Kiadora let her hand sink down slowly, trying to think of something to say to relieve the awkwardness.

"I'm sorry, I don't shake hands," said Wyland, still smiling pleasantly. "It has to do with energy signatures, you'll learn all about that later on." Kiadora frowned slightly, trying to resist the urge to cock her eyebrow in an arrogant manner. Energy signatures?

She looked at Lid uncertainly, but he was looking in the opposite direction.

"You'll have a lot to learn, and in time you will understand," said

Wyland. "Lid told us all about you. When did you know you had the gift?" Kiadora still had trouble comprehending it as a gift.

"Uh, I guess always. Everyone thought I was a freak, because I spent so much time outdoors in the forest. I would light and snuff candles just because I liked to watch the flame."

"Uh-huh." Wyland nodded. "Many of our students have the same experience. That's usually a childish version of trying to grasp your power and affinity. Anything else?"

"Once when I was undergoing the Termination, I made a torch go out." She had tried not to think about it too much; that always make her feel truly crazy.

"Yes, that can happen." Kiadora brightened up.

"So what else can I control?"

Wyland shook her head.

"Don't get carried away. It's only very minor things we can control physically. The current of water, dousing small flames, raising a breeze. Things of that small nature, and usually only under stress. What we typically do is work on a higher level of existence." Kiadora's heart sank.

"Like a religion?"

"Well, yes, in a way. But it's not like anything that goes on with the *Church* up above." She said the word as if she was trying expel a horrible taste from her mouth. "You'll learn all about that in due time. I'm sorry, Lid, we must be boring you."

Lid had been staring into space and looked like he was just hanging around in case any other instructions were shot his way. He looked around quickly at having been addressed.

"What? Oh, no, it's fine. Do you have any other needs?"

"No, thank you Lid."

"Alright. I'm just gonna go visit my sister." He smiled back at Kiadora. "Good luck with your training, miss."

"At one o'clock in the morning, Lid?" questioned Wyland.

"Nah, she won't mind. It's the only time I can slip down here and she knows."

And with that, he turned and disappeared into the maze that lay before them.

"It is, of course, very late," said Wyland to Kiadora. Kiadora didn't feel tired at all. The novelty of the situation was keeping her awake. "We have quarters set up for you. The people who live here stay in those quarters." Wyland motioned to the holes stacked like a dissected anthill. "We found building it like that allows for privacy and saves space. I can take you there, and tomorrow I will introduce you to your teacher." Wyland started to walk through the wooden dividers, and Kiadora followed.

"These usually serve as our classrooms. There is one larger space for a cafeteria of sorts." Kiadora nodded. They were walking along with Wyland holding a kerosene lamp, the shadows reflecting off of the glossy wood, tossing light left and right. As they walked, the dull glow of the lamp started to make Kiadora feel tired. After a time, they came out of the maze and were looking at the cubby holes in the wall.

"We have to be quiet, of course," Wyland whispered. "Everyone is in bed at this time. We have a curfew of midnight." Kiadora wondered why an underground city would bother with conventional time but didn't want to bring it up when everyone was asleep around them.

"Up this way."

Kiadora followed Wyland up a ladder to their left. Kiadora make sure to remember it was the third ladder from the left and then headed to the eighth hole up. Once they reached the hole, Wyland leaned over and pulled the multicolored cloth from the opening and she crawled in. Kiadora followed.

Kiadora had thought the Church was modest, and Lid's downright rustic, but this was like living in the forest. She smelled the strong scent of the soil. It made up the walls. The ground was covered in straw and a single mattress sat on the floor. There was just enough room to stand up if she was hunched slightly. She went over to the mattress and felt it. Straw. There was a single table next to the bed with a pitcher, candle and a bowl.

"It's undoubtedly nothing like you're used to," said Wyland, barely over a whisper. "I understand you come from a large estate." Kiadora nodded. She tried to keep the horror out of her face and look grateful. "Most of our pleasure comes from the pursuit of spirituality and wisdom. We believe we only need the basics, and one of our goals is to live close to Earth and nature."

"You can't get any closer than this," Kiadora admitted. Wyland chuckled.

"It will grow on you, I assure. Tomorrow, we will come by around eight or nine to get you started. Breakfast will be delivered around to your quarters for today. It'll be a simple loaf of bread and water. I will you see you tomorrow." Wyland smiled, backed out of the hole and stepped to the side onto the ladder. The curtain flapped shut and Kiadora was left in darkness.

Luckily she was standing next to the mattress. She felt around both ends for a blanket. Finding it at last, she pulled it back, sat down and covered herself. At least the bedding felt smooth and soft. Even if the mattress had a tendency to poke her.

She put her hands behind her head, staring out into the darkness. So this is how she would live for…how long would she stay here? Until she learned everything? Could she ever finish or was it a lifestyle she had now adopted? She turned over to try to shake away her questions and get comfortable, but it did not seem possible. She was too curious and partly frightened of what lessons they would teach her. Wyland did not really say.

CHAPTER 9

Kiadora jerked awake the next morning, her back aching from the hard mattress. In her half sleep she mistakenly thought for a minute she had been hit on the back with a hammer. She opened her eyes, seeing the soil walls and something shining in at the edge of her vision. She looked over to see the cloth hanging from her doorway, a bright pattern of intersecting colors, much like the way the forest looked after she learned to recognize it for what it was.

Then she remembered they were underground. How was there light? She got up, her back aching less the more she moved it, and walked in a stooped fashion over to the curtained doorway. She pulled back the curtain and looked above. The cavern was lit by a large chandelier of pillar candles, all burning brightly. The enormous thing must take an hour at least to light in the morning.

She looked down and there was a man climbing her ladder with a sack on his back. The bread giver crawled next to her.

"Here you are, breakfast," said the young man cheerily. "You must be Kiadora, I'm Batton. Wyland told me to tell you that she would be up in about 15 minutes." Kiadora took the bread, and he also handed her a cup filled with lukewarm water. "Good luck," said Batton with a wink, and he went up the ladder farther.

Kiadora withdrew into her sleeping quarters and sat down to eat the bread, which tasted freshly baked. She wondered what the wink was supposed to mean. After she finished she waited patiently. After a few minutes, the curtain was pulled back. The outlined form of Wyland peered in, the edges of her red hair glinting, forming a fiery halo.

"I hope you slept well," she said. Kiadora nodded. "Today we're going to meet your first teacher."

Wyland started down the ladder and Kiadora followed. When they got to the bottom, Wyland continued. "To start, you will have five teachers, one for each of the four elements, and your general teacher, who you'll meet now." Kiadora followed the woman back to the rooms. They reentered the maze. They took a left turn, then a right, then another left and stopped at a door on the left. Wyland went in and Kiadora followed. And almost turned out again for what she saw.

They were closed in by a roof in the little room, which she initially thought was all open area, like the cubicles she saw back in the bank. The room was heavily furnished with shelves, which she could barely see under all of the memorabilia. Strange statues glorifying sexual organs littered the room. She blushed at a clear, oblong statue that would have been a joke in any other circumstance.

Drying plants were all around the room. Several live plants furnished the room as well; she could only assume they were plants that needed shade. She could not tell how they grew with no sun.

Vials and jars lined the shelves as well, weaving in and out of various sexual organs like a waltz. Some held powders, mostly green, and others had liquid in them, mostly clear. Large banner-like hangings hung from the wall, announcing not a sale, but various mystical teachings. There were diagrams of stars and geometrical patterns that had several elemental symbols drawn next to them: flames, birds, water, trees. The most foreign part to these was the mixing of the elements in a single chart.

At a desk in the left, far corner sat a woman with long, deep brown hair. It would have been black had it not been for the slightly warmer glow where the fire from the lamps hit. She was looking over with bright, green eyes, her expression serious.

"This is Narissa," said Wyland from behind her. Narissa stood up and came around her desk, offering a hand to shake. Kiadora was pleased not everyone seemed to be terminally afraid of her skin. Kiadora was grasped by a firm hand shake that lingered a little too long, the other woman's handshake like a personal challenge to everyone she met.

"I will be your general instructor." She had a solid, but cool, tone to her voice. "With me, you will learn the basics of meditation, herbs, astral projection, among *other things*." She added an emphasis that Kiadora did not want to think about. Maybe coming here was a bad idea. But she forced herself on with the desire for the truth that had brought her down this far. She had to know.

"I will leave you two alone to get started," said Wyland. And she departed.

"You know, she never told me what she does here," mused Kiadora out loud.

"She's sort of like our main coordinator," said Narissa dismissively, waving a hand. "She's as close to what we will allow as a full leader."

"What you will allow?" Kiadora echoed.

"Yes, we have rankings, but we try to avoid true power as much as we can. At least I do, there are some who are just vying to take over and run the place. I think we should be a little different than the surface. The point down here is freedom. And I think that is where we will begin. Technically, I specialize in Air."

Kiadora shuddered. "You see, and that is just it," Narissa plowed on. "Everyone thinks of the surface, of the Church, and how they have corroded the element itself. That is why we start here, to show you how it really is and to shed all the misconceptions head on. But first, I need to know what you can see and where you are at." Narissa turned and sat down on the floor where a thick, purple rug lay. Kiadora assumed she should sit in front of her. They sat facing each other, their skirts spread over their legs, Narissa's many layers of white skirts a direct challenge to Kiadora's single dark brown. She had stayed in her travel clothes.

"Wyland told me of your ability to see the essence of the elements, and you have already had minor control under stress." Narissa put her arms on her legs and leaned over, studying Kiadora's expression.

"The essence of the elements? You mean those colored particles?"

"Yes, that would be it. Good, we can start somewhere. It's harder

when they don't even know how to view the true nature of things."
Narissa squinted into Kiadora's eyes like she was studying a new bug.

"Do you have an idea of what you saw?" Narissa asked.

"Um...an...energy signature?" It was the only thing that popped
into her mind.

"Yes. Where did you hear of such a thing? I was told you were
very ignorant to our ways." Kiadora wondered if she should feel
insulted, but she was distracted by a look of hope in Narissa's eyes.

"I heard Wyland use it," Kiadora admitted.

"Oh," said the other woman, her bright look fading slightly. "Hm,
I thought you may have the Sight already."

"The Sight?"

"Yes, psychic powers, the ability to view events remotely and know
things purely on intuition alone." Kiadora thought she had done pretty
well with the answer, psychic powers or not. Narissa waved a hand.
"No matter, you are right." Kiadora grinned. Being right was nice for
once.

"What you are seeing is the energy each of the elements emits. You
see, everything has a certain energy signature, each unique to that item.
That plant," Narissa indicated some bright green herbs drying, "is
different from that plant." She indicated another purplish drying herb.

"Why do I not see the particles on those?" asked Kiadora,
indicating the drying plant.

"Because they are dead. You have probably noticed that you
cannot see the particles around stones in a house, or dirt taken from
the earth..."

"But dirt can't die."

"Yet it can be taken away from it's natural state. When that happens, the energy reverts inward as a way to sustain itself." Kiadora raised an eyebrow. It seemed like pseudo logic, the same the Church used.

"You're not getting it," Narissa lightly accused. She stared to the side for a while, her face contracted with the effort of finding a better explanation. "Ok," she finally decided. "You live on a large estate. Has your home ever captured any prisoners?"

They had a dungeon, alright. Kiadora used to sometimes lock herself in there to escape her family when the weather was bad outside. Looking back, it was so fitting.

"Yes, they do. There was a man that was down there for twenty years for squatting on our land. He prayed for mercy but my humble father would never give it to him," she said bitterly.

"Was he sociable or happy?"

"Well, of course not, he was in prison, and we were his captors."

"Exactly. He was taken away from his family and his home," said Narissa, nodding. She got up to get some of the drying herbs hanging from the ceiling. She broke a few leaves off of the bundle and came back. She sat down in front of Kiadora again. "Like I said, the energy retreats. You can no longer see it, just as a prisoner is locked away and will not talk to anyone, nor share his meager food supply with the rats. But touch it."

Kiadora reached out and put her hand to the herb. She could feel it pulsating, like her veins did after running home in the rain. "It feels like it has a pulse," said Kiadora, amazed. "But I've handled herbs before, why now?"

"You've opened yourself to the perception," said Narissa simply. "Each herb has its own pulse rhythm. They vary sometimes slightly, other times greatly. This is sage. Noticed the deep, long pulse?" Kiadora nodded. "As you learn about the herbs, you can learn about the rhythms they carry and why. And you can *use* them." Kiadora balked at the greedy tone in the word use.

"So, we are rats. We demand the prisoner to share his meager food supply."

"But the main plant still lives," said Narissa. "We have not killed it, we have harvested it. It is like one killing an animal for food. It is the darker and harsh reality of the natural world. All things meet death and often die so others will survive and prosper." Kiadora looked absently at the soft rug, considering this.

"Yes, I can see what you mean," she conceded. "To live a life not harming the natural world means starvation. So what is it the herbs are used for?"

"That depends on the herb and the type of energy it emits. Many offer medicinal benefit, as you know. Some nutritional, but there is another aspect of the herbs and plants that few outside of the compound know." Narissa picked up the herb where she had let it drop on the rug. "This, for instance, sage. It can be used to grant wisdom and purify an area. Cinnamon," she motioned back to some sticks in a jar up on the top shelf to their right that Kiadora recognized as the spice she had seen in the kitchens, "can give you power." Kiadora looked puzzled, tilting her head like a confused hound.

" What kind of power? Don't we already have power, and how can *cinnamon* help?" Narissa sighed at the fact that Kiadora knew so little.

"Someone born to power could not understand the desperate struggle to seize it."

"Yes, I do," Kiadora interrupted. "There are neighboring lords disputing land, and we once had a foreigner try to overthrow my father. Claimed my father was a thief and took him into the courts and everything. All over some horses." Kiadora frowned at the bitter memory. She knew all too well of the games of power. "That is why I asked, I did not know what kind of power- spiritual, political?"

She was now having the constant feeling that she would watch what she say, lest she have to defend herself against this arrogant woman. She tried to hide the slight irritation, as her knowledge depended on this woman. She hoped she was not blushing as she usually did when she was annoyed.

"Any kind of power you want, really," Narissa answered, as if she had never really thought about it. "Usually it is used to enhance the energies around you and achieve goals."

"That seems like a stupid reason to beg the prisoner," Kiadora said. She kept holding the image of a rat in her mind. She even lived in a rat hole now.

No, she should be cooperative, these people were nice enough to welcome her and teach her. They knew what this was all about. Just as she had that thought, she felt the side of her face erupt in a strong stinging as Narissa's hand flew past.

"You are not listening, and you will not give me cheek!" Kiadora rubbed her face, leaning back, terrified of a second blow.

"Alright, alright," Kiadora said. "I'm sorry." She looked up into Narissa's eyes, which burned with anger. She would watch it. "So...so how do I use the herbs?" she asked. Just as soon as it had come, the anger dispersed, and Narissa looked calm once more.

"That will come in time," said Narissa. "I am just here to give an overview. But I will start you off with an exercise." She got up from the rug and went to the cinnamon. She took the jar down, pulling a single stick out. She walked over and handed it Kiadora, who took it. The spicy smell hit her nose, and the stick left a red stain on her hand. She could feel a strong and frantic pulse from the cinnamon stick.

"Close your eyes," Narissa instructed. Kiadora obliged. "Feel the pulse on your hand and focus entirely on it." Kiadora had to take a moment to get the dull sting and anger at having been struck out of her mind. One she did, and concentrated on the pulse, it felt stronger than ever. It felt like the stick was changing size; fat, thin, fat, thin.

"Clear your mind and just feel the pulse," said Narissa. "Sit as if suspended, your existence being nothing but the surge and pull of the plant." Kiadora sat and felt the pulse until her very heart rate and own pulse felt in tune with the plant. She didn't know if she was imagining it, but she felt like the plant was taking over her body, mingling with her in some way, although she did not know what.

Soon alien thoughts started to overtake her. Images of success and glory. Herself at the seat of the thrown. It was a damn shame, she thought. If she had not run away, she could easily have the sort of power, the prestige.

It belongs to me, I should have the estate. My sister's don't know shit. I would run the land efficiently, set things right. There would be no Church, and I could do it all, if they did not keep me in this damn sewer of a...

She felt her body hit the ground hard. Narissa was sprawled on top of her, the cinnamon plant in her hand, holding it up high. Kiadora looked down at her own arms, one pinned to the ground by Narissa, the other was outstretched, grasping for the herb. She realized she must have been saying that out loud. She put her arm down and slowly Narissa pulled herself off of Kiadora.

Kiadora sat up and realized they had moved off of the rug; they were on the dirt floor. "I'm sorry, what just happened?" Kiadora asked. Narissa sat down on the rug again, and Kiadora came over and sat down tentatively. For the first time, Narissa looked awed and humbled.

"I should be sorry." Kiadora was shocked to hear the other woman apologize. "I did not realize it would overpower you like that. Many do not feel the pull and essence of the herb that strong."

"What happened exactly?"

"You have a lot of bitterness." Kiadora had wanted an answer, not criticism. "The herb was simply magnifying that, and cueing in on your desire for achievement. It's its nature, it's what we use it for, but not that strongly. We will start on meditation to control that." Narissa looked at her for a moment, as if considering something, and then said in a quiet tone, "but you can use that bitterness. The instructions will come in time." Kiadora just stared. Before Kiadora could question anything, Narissa was ushering Kiadora out the door.

"Right now is the time that the students have lunch and practice meditation. I will teach you how shortly after lunch."

They stood in the strange hallways illuminated by the lights far above, with walls that had no ceiling. The removed lighting cast several shadows in the corridors, and Kiadora and Narissa waded through them like walking through a choppy river.

After a time, they got to a large set of double doors, and Narissa swung them inward. It was a hall unlike anything she had seen. All the tables, rather than being joined together, were separated in a desk fashion, nearly every one occupied by a single person who was pouring over a book or writing in a notebook, nibbling occasionally off of a plate to their side.

"Does anyone here…talk to each other?" Kiadora whispered to Narissa, who was standing right next to her. A few people close to them looked up, smiled quickly, and went back to what they were working on.

"We try to encourage as much study as possible here. Our purpose is to delve into the inner secrets of Nature and the mysteries of the Devine," said Narissa quietly.

"Doesn't morale get kind of low?"

"We have planned social events some evenings," the older woman answered. "Besides, this cuts down on gossip and internal strife," she added as an afterthought. "You pick up your food over there," she indicated a table with several bowls at the front of the room. She walked toward the back and indicated a seat in the second back row a few spots in. "And that will be your seat. Please return to my room after you have finished." And Narissa walked out of the main double doors.

Kiadora hovered awkwardly for a moment and then headed to the tables up front. She picked up a small bowl and looked into the large pots. There was a gray crème soup she poured into the bowl and some sparse, dried fruits and bread sitting out, which she heaped onto a plate after setting her bowl down. She carried them both to her table, walking quietly down the isle, as if she was at a somber, forced wedding. Again a few people looked up and smiled, others kept looking at books and still others just stared absently at their food. One man was chewing with his eyes firmly shut, as if he was trying to memorize the taste because it was his last time eating.

She sat down and looked at all the heads bent over their desks in an eternal exam. This was…cheerful. She looked down at her own food and decided she would brave the soup first. It was a kind of clam chowder and was actually not terrible. The bread was fresh and the fruit was delicious.

She looked next to her at a young man scribbling furiously on some paper and wondered what the rush was. He seemed to be writing an essay, as if timed. He absently jammed some bread into his mouth at intervals. On her other side at a girl with pale blond hair and a lithe figure. She ate quietly and suddenly looked up. She seemed to sense someone looking at her. She smiled. Kiadora smiled back and leaned over towards the girl.

"Why does no one talk?" she whispered. "I know it's against the rules, but why follow it?" A black haired woman in front of her turned around and glared. A few other people glanced at her and went back to what they were doing. The blond girl nodded up to the front. A tall, solid woman was coming down the isle. She simply grabbed Kiadora by the arm and hauled her towards the middle isle, not even stopping in her march.

Kiadora had no choice but to follow, and she was dragged out of the double doors, the doors making no sound as they closed. Kiadora looked up at the woman, and dark eyes glared back down under a strong brow.

"I know this is your first day," the woman said in a deep voice, "so I will only remind you. There is no talking in the mess hall."

"But why, and why do people do it?"

"There is time for talk later. Up on the surface, food is used to bond and meals are a social time, yes?" Kiadora nodded. "Forget everything you know about it," the woman commanded. "Down here, it is a time to know Nature, the gifts of the Divine in their simplest form." Kiadora was shocked to hear the large woman talk in such deep terms. Kiadora had assumed this woman was not above mere grunting.

"And if they don't," she continued. "They have me to answer to." Kiadora nodded again and walked back into the hall. Well, at least that eliminated the social norm of awkward dinner conversation.

After lunch, Kiadora sat in Narissa's study once more.

"Before we break for today, I will teach you meditation," Narissa said. "You will be using it a lot around here. After lunch, and in the early morning and evenings time is set aside for the sole purpose."

"I was told there would be social activities," Kiadora broke in.

"Yes, some nights. But your primary purpose is to understand the Divine. I want you to sit on the rug." Kiadora looked down at the floor where the rug had been and noticed it had been moved next to the wall. She walked over to it and sat facing the wall. "No, the other way," Narissa snapped. Kiadora blushed and shifted herself to face the study. "Close your eyes and breathe slowly."

Kiadora did so, focusing on her breathing. After a time, she felt lightweight, like she was floating. She panicked and snapped to, jerking slightly. She took a sharp breath inward.

"What is it?" Narissa asked.

"I...I just remembered the time the Church buried me alive. It felt like that, the same floating sensation, that nothingness...like death." Narissa continued to examine Kiadora from where she was sitting on another rug, thicker and higher off the ground. Her brow was furrowed and she nearly squinted.

"Yes, I was told of the time. I had hoped no residue from the experience was left over. But the Church always makes its mark." She looked sad, with a touch of spite, as she said this. Kiadora reached up and touched the bandaged spot on her chest before she knew what she was doing.

"Try again."

Kiadora looked at Narissa nervously. There was no sympathy in that hard stare. Then she closed her eyes, but the same peace would not come. She remembered the suffocating tube and the festering flesh wound. She had forgotten to apply the genthea liquid last night. It was in her bag, right?

"Stop," she heard Narissa say. Kiadora opened her eyes once again. "I can see from your expression that you are still thinking about it. It is a hard task to learn, but that is what I am here to teach. Forget yourself." Kiadora looked down. It was like forgetting how to breathe.

"How am I supposed to do that when I am always aware?" Kiadora asked. "I cannot just forget I exist."

"You must understand that to be open, you must put your past aside and behind. You must take whatever is bothering you and learn to release, like you are casting it aside the way you would trash."

"I'm not trash, and I can't forget what I am!" Kiadora's jaw slammed shut as Narissa's fist collided with the underside of it. Kiadora heard the sharp snap of her teeth hitting together. She let out a small cry, feeling her teeth with her tongue to make sure nothing was chipped.

"You're not listening!" Narissa cried again. "I am not saying you are trash. I am saying that for now you will get nowhere if you cling to the past and everything you know."

"So everything I ever learned was wasted, for nothing?"

"You could look at it that way."

"So it is trash."

"Fine, it is trash, if you like. But would you not agree that the teachings of the Church have brought you nothing but misery?"

"Pretty much."

"And you do not want that to carry over into your lessons now. It will poison you and embitter you. And that is far worse than anything the cinnamon herb could do."

"I thought you said I could use that."

"In time, but right now we need to lessen the extent of your teachings so they do not taint the new lessons. You would not again plant seeds that failed to grow last year, would you? Or leave the weeds to choke out the new fruit?"

"No."

"And so you see. This time, when a thought of the past comes, I want you to hold it, do not fear it, and picture it floating away."

Kiadora settled back. She realized she had leaned forward, her arms on her lap while arguing passionately. She closed her eyes and kept her breathing deep. The weightlessness and darkness came back and she remembered Telan standing over her, throwing dirt around her. She kept her face calm, lest she get into another argument with Narissa and have her teeth go flying. She simply remembered it and let it play out. Then she let it flow out, the picture fading away into the nothingness, to where she returned to the darkness once more. Again, she thought of the Church services she attended and her thoughts jumped to what her family might be doing right now. From there she wondered if Tahn knew where she was. She never said goodbye!

"Kiadora, you are not letting it go." She opened her eyes to see Narissa's stern expression.

"Sorry, it's just I never said goodbye to a good friend." She felt like crying. She looked down and noticed her hands shaking. "Will I ever see people on the surface again?" Narissa looked at her, pursed lips easing slightly.

"Perhaps not. Who is it that you miss?"

"A friend. Just a friend." She looked away with tears in her eyes.

"Ah," Narissa said. She looked at the ground for a moment then looked up a Kiadora. "What did you hate about him?"

"Hate about him? I don't think I hated anything about him. He was caring and hilarious. Even if a bit simple."

"Simple in what way?" Kiadora fidgeted. It was like a dung beadle probing for food.

"He was the one to turn me into the Church," she admitted.

"So he did not accept you for what you are?"

"He didn't know!" Kiadora shouted. "He was so quick-witted in Church school, he knew the text back to front. He only did what he thought was right!" Kiadora realized her whole body was shaking now, and she blinked back tears.

"But, you see, that is what he thought was right," Narssia explained, learning close to Kitrara, their faces only inches apart. "That you were an aberration, something to be cured, to be bended, to be subjected to torture. If he really paid attention in Church school, he knew what would happen."

Kiadora remembered the careful consideration he gave, the encouragement, the slight look of remorse. Kiadora nodded.

"He knew what they would do, and he still turned you in to be tortured and given a cure that did not work," Narissa breathed, still leaning in close. "As good as his intentions might have been, you loved a fool."

Kiadora sat leaned against the wall, weary. Narissa sat up, triumphant in her quest to show Kiadora the truth.

"And you see, that is how you will let things go: when you can see the truth and not let emotions cloud you. When you can see reality for what it is, the light and dark, you will be able to pass things away. I want you to do it again, clear your mind, and when the thoughts drift through, I want you to consider the positives and the negatives, as impartially as you can. Become emotionless toward them, and force them away."

Kiadora leaned back against the wall once more and felt the arid darkness return. Her breathing was slow and steady, taking in the earthy scent of the soil-saturated air mingled with smoke. She began to feel like she was floating slightly and then images came. Narissa's dark eyes boring into hers.

You loved a fool, she heard again. She thought of Tahn, of his simplicity and his complete refusal to see past what he had been told.

And she saw an image of the two of them as children playing in a grove, maybe around the age of ten. The pinpricks had been light then, she could ignore them. She was laughing because Tahn had just told a joke. And then it passed suddenly onto Church school where she had heard the joke, but had not laughed. It was funny in the way Tahn had told it, the inflection he used.

A man heard it was to be the end of days soon and walks into a store, looking to buy a small saddle. The shopkeeper goes to get a horse saddle, and the man says, 'No, that's too big, go smaller.' So the shopkeeper comes out with the smallest for the youngest pony, and it is still too small. The man asks, 'What are you going to use this thing on anyway?' And the man replies, 'I am going to ride my son into the final battle with Skira, since he is more stubborn than any mule.'

In Church, Kiadora had smiled half-heartedly at it. It really wasn't very good, but everyone insisted on repeating it. But then she remembered Tahn, who had put in the motions of the shopkeeper. She understood the joke and fable. But Tahn galloping around pretending to ride a small boy was priceless.

The images switched. Now she was the one under the saddle, her father riding her. *Stubborn as a mule.* And she let it go, to return to the darkness. The sweet, vapid darkness. And she hovered there, refusing to admit any more pictures. She started to think of being buried again, but drove it off. No, she did not want to think about that any longer.

After a time, she heard a sharp snapping in the distance. She came to and saw Narissa holding a hand in front of her face, snapping her fingers sharply. Kiadora could feel the gust of wind as Narissa shook her hand in the effort to snap, her hand was being held so close. The hand withdrew a second after Kiadora opened her eyes.

"You've done it. How did it feel?"

Kiadora thought back, trying to remember. It had felt like a dream.

"I kept seeing images. First things I had remembered, going lightning speed. It was like I was an outside observer of my own thought process for the first time. Then I saw an image I would rather not repeat. One that had never happened, something I made up. And then I started to remember the burial and forced it out. I didn't want to think about it. I didn't want to think about anything because it hurt so much. So I didn't." Narissa nodded in approval.

"Good, you're learning. You're going much faster than I expected." A compliment? "But I would like to know what that one image was." Kiadora blushed slightly. She hoped Narissa would not pull anything disturbing from this.

"It was my father, riding me on a saddle. Like one of those strange dreams you get, I suspect it doesn't mean anything. I was thinking about that old joke about the father riding his son into the final battle, and…" Narissa held up a hand to stop Kiadora from speaking. Kiadora looked at her, expecting a harsh judgment.

"What do you think it means?" Narissa asked instead.

"Means? Oh, I don't know. I expect it doesn't mean anything, like I said." Kiadora flinched, as she expected Narissa to bring a fist crashing around again. Instead, Narissa only shook her head.

"That is a sad lie that they tell above. That our own thoughts mean nothing, that all wisdom comes from above and beyond. And it does, but the wisdom can be found right here rather than in the clouds. This is a lesson it takes many students a long time to grapple with, that their own minds have something of worth to tell them."

"'And so what lies in the hearts of men is a lie.'" Kiadora quoted. "It's from the Holy Text."

"Yes, I know," said Narissa impatiently. "Even the most lax Church goer will remember that phrase. It's the first one they teach as soon as children can walk." Kiadora knew the phrase better than the roads that ran through the family's estate.

"Yes," she agreed. "Can I drive it out, like the memory of being buried?" Narissa actually looked sad right then.

"You can try. I think that is all for today. Practice what you learned today. Focus on nothing at all, and we will discuss what happens and what you feel tomorrow. They will call you down for dinner, and tonight there is a social gathering right after."

CHAPTER 10

Kiadora sat in the dining room, looking forward in silence as she had before in services. She had spent the time before dinner drifting periodically through empty space, or so it had felt. It had only been punctured by the words, *you can try*. Would she never leave the surface behind? The more she wondered, the more she lost her appetite and kept listlessly poking the cold meat with her fork. She thought she would come and learn and forget what had happened, but she felt like her past was a colossal fork poking her in the side. She kept thinking of Tahn and actually wished to have her sister's sympathy, or what she used to think of as arrogant pity. It was better than Narissa's lonely arrogance.

She looked around next to her and wondered what it would be like to socially interact with the people right next to her. Kiadora now had been living next to these people for a few days and had no idea who they were. She was distracted from her thoughts by the sturdy woman at the front standing up in front of them.

"Social hour," she barked. Without thinking, they all stood up in unison and followed the woman out of the door. Kiadora followed the throng of people, being carried down the hallways like that river and the wooden walls were an embankment. Soon they came to an open area, and there was a wooden plank on the floor, glossy and smooth, much like the walls. They all flowed around this new sand dune. There was a group of four with instruments on the wooden slab. Kiadora looked over the crowd to get a better view of them, and she noticed a violin, a horn and a lyre. Wyland stood next to them.

"Welcome to the weekly social hour!" she called over the crowd. "Tonight we have a dance planned. Let us direct energy to a bountiful night." Kiadora glanced around. Everyone had extended a hand toward their neighbors and had their eyes closed. Kiadora awkwardly placed a hand on the shoulders of the two people next to her. They were now standing in a large group hug. She closed one eye and kept the other open slightly.

"To our merriment and mirth. To fellowship and fun," Wyland called out. "May we be blessed by the Great Powers." Kiadora glanced around again. Everyone was bent silently, focusing on something. Kiadora looked down at the ground and focused on the floor. The particles sprung out again. They were vibrating wildly, swirling faster than usual. Around some people they flowed in and out of their legs, around the height of the calf. She had some questions for Narissa tomorrow.

Suddenly, in front, Wyland called out, "So blessed by the Great Powers!" The same words thundered out from everyone around her, and the flow of particles stopped and settled to the ground again. Everyone now surged to the dance floor, flooding it. Kiadora stayed back. She had learned how to dance but knew no one who she could dance with. A few others resisted the surge and hung back by the sides.

The musicians struck up a fast, waltzing tune as Kiadora stared.

This was not dancing.

Where were the promenades and separated lines of men and women? Everyone stood in a large mass and swayed with arms in the air. They looked as thought they just made it up as they went along.

"It's quite something, isn't it?" Kiadora jumped and looked around to where a black haired man was standing right next to her. Most people had wild hair around here, but he looked like he regularly at least tried to flatten it back, which made his round jawline more prominent. He was smiling at her in a friendly manner, dark eyes twinkling at her. He held out a hand.

"Regelend. You live right under my cubby hole, I saw you come in the other night." She took his hand and shook it. Kiadora opened her mouth to reply, but he said, "Kiadora. I know you." Kiadora reddened slightly.

"Where do you know me from?"

"Relax, I took a vow. I'm down here for life. I can't possibly tell them where you are. And why would I? I'm down here for the same reason." She studied him for a moment.

"You do look familiar. Have you been to our estate?"

"No, but you were to ours. You were young, but you came with your father to Aethia. He had said you begged to see the mountains, and he had let you come. If he had known what you are, he probably would have thought you would have started the second Bleeding." It was what they had called the eruption caused by the Skira in those parts.

"So, you're…how did you know? And how did you escape the religious fear? It's even stronger out there than by us, what with the eruption destroying half your ancestors."

"The memory runs strong down the lines," Regelend agreed. "But I also knew what I was right away, and I knew how to hide it. I made sure not to show any signs of adoring the natural elements, and I was quick to learn to ward off the fainting spells." Kiadora looked down, ashamed that she had advertised to the world what she was. She would not have lived to be four in Aethia.

"No, don't feel bad." He placed a hand on her arm. "We each come to it in our own way. I was in an area well acquainted with the concept, and your area likes to deny it a little more." Kiadora laughed bitterly.

"Mother was afraid to touch me, and Father said it was something that would pass. All they cared about was keeping it quiet." Meditation had taught her one thing, she didn't need to think about it. "So what is it that they do here, what type of dance is this?" Regelend looked out at the floor, as if shocked that the dance was still going on.

"It's a type of dance they invented themselves. It's supposed to mirror…um, the reproductive cycle." He finished in a dull mumble, and Kiadora barely caught what he said. She looked sharply at him and then started to laugh. Regelend really was from the most conservative area in the country. It was rumored they all mated through cleverly tailored bed sheets. Narissa was right about people not forgetting.

She looked more closely at the dance floor, which had gone from the light prancing and waving to close-quarters thrusting. The horn now dominated the tune and had a strong beat, to which she could have sworn they thrusted to.

"They have rhythm," Kiadora commented, with a half grin directed at Regelend. Regelend turned slightly away from the dance floor with a blush.

"There's juice," he said, indicating a table off to their left. Kiadora nodded and started to walk towards it. She picked up two pre-poured cups and handed one to him. He looked relieved that there was now a slight crowd blocking them from the dance floor.

"I'm surprised they don't force us to join in," she said.

"Actually, they used to." Kiadora felt shocked.

"How long have you been down here, anyway?"

"I sort of lost track. I think it's been about six or seven years. What year is it?" He swirled his drink around in his glass, looking at it more closely than anyone would ever need to. He was clearly embarrassed he needed to ask such a question.

"321," Kiadora replied. "They don't have any calendars down here or keep track of the years? Will I forget what year it is or even what season it is?" Kiadora almost spilled her drink. She had started to wring the paper cup she was holding. She quickly held the cup away as red liquid started to pour down between her fingers through the crack in the cup.

"Here, let me help you with that," Regelend volunteered. He turned to the table and got a napkin. She took it with a quick, "thanks."

"Anyway, you won't forget what season it is. It gets rather cold in winter." Kiadora's expression fell. This just got worse and worse. "No, it's not bad this far down." Regelend waved his hand as if to disperse her distaste. "We're insulated. It's like the fall on the surface. You just need a sweater, which they give you, and an extra blanket, which they also provide. So you can tell the year, I guess. I just haven't bothered to keep track. Doesn't make much of a difference down here." Still, what they had talked about earlier was nagging at Kiadora's mind.

"So, they used to force you participate in *that*?" she nodded toward the dance floor.

"Oh, yes." He had a deadened tone and a bitter twist to his mouth as he relived the bad memory. "I stood there while everyone around me…rubbed against me." She could see the mental shiver travel down his spine. "Eventually they stopped, though, because they could see some people had trouble with it as at first. All those people out there have been here much longer than I have. They say it comes in time. For me, I don't see it ever coming." He glanced awkwardly at Kiadora and looked down at the floor.

She would have taken it as him being enamored with her, but his expression was one of deep embarrassment. She knew the people from Aethia could be extremely charming when they were interested, but they also looked as flustered as a school girl when they were discussing something of deep embarrassment to them. And she had thought all those lessons in customs and etiquette had been a waste. People getting more angry was a local thing.

"This place sounds like it used to be a lot like the Church," she had

Eatheria

now leaned toward him and was speaking in a low voice. Regelend looked more calm now that they had moved on from the issue of sex. He nodded.

"It was and still is," he whispered. "They renamed the god, turned the beliefs on their heads and kept the arrogance. You'll see what I mean after a time. But there is still a lot to learn, if you know how to look." They stood in silence, drinking their juice. He suddenly looked at her and seemed to finally settle on something.

"Do you want to go back up?" he asked, nodding in the direction of the holes. Kiadora thought about it for a moment and decided she definitely was not in the mood to dance, let alone what these people called it.

"Sure," she said. They made their way past the dance floor, Regelend looking at the ground as they passed. Kiadora glanced over at the dance.

Oh, God.

From somewhere they had all produced some cloths that the women had shoved under their shirts to represent pregnancy, and the men were rubbing it fondly. Kiadora and Regelend slipped out of the door. Right as the door closed, Kiadora burst out laughing.

"What was that?" she shouted through tears of laughter. Regelend looked back at her as they walked up the hallway.

"I told you it was meant to mirror the reproductive cycle."

"That was dumbest thing I've ever seen!" Kiadora was laughing harder than she had ever laughed in her life. Regelend started to join in.

"It was pretty stupid," he said through his own laughter. The two laughed their way to the cubby holes. They went to the same ladder.

"Okay, okay. I have to stop or I'm going to fall off this ladder," said Kiadora as she wiped away tears. Regelend stopped laughing as well, and they looked at each other for a moment.

"Why don't you come over to my...uh...place," Kiadora said, looking up at her dirt hole. It wasn't the kind of place you would invite a guest to. Regelend glanced at the ground, looked like he wanted to say yes, but his timid nature got the better of him.

"No, no, it's fine. I really shouldn't go into a lady's bedroom."

"If you can call this a bedroom. No, come on." She waved at him to follow her up the ladder, and he followed her with an awkward, "alright." When they got up to her sleeping area, she walked in and sat down on her bed. He came in next and hovered by the ladder. He looked like a deranged villager begging for scraps, the way his back was bent.

"Have a seat," she said, indicating the bed next to her. He glanced at the floor again, then nodded, settling himself on the edge of the bed as far as he could get from her. "You know, I'm not that terrifying. Well, maybe up on the surface I am." He laughed slightly at the joke. He turned to her to talk.

"No, I'm sorry. It's just that I'm not used to this. At home I would be flogged for several days and made to sit in a jail cell starving for three days for being alone in a lady's room before marriage. It's meant to purge the body of lust. I saw a man go down there once, and the guard said to him, 'since you had your fill, you won't be needing any food for three days.' I know I haven't been at home for years, and won't be imprisoned, but you know..." Kiadora nodded.

"That is what we are working on in my lessons right now. I've only been here a few days, so they are trying to make me forget, to put it all aside. I was met with so much scorn up there, so I thought it would be easy. Why would I want to remember my cowardly mother, my arrogant sister and the friend who led me to my torture? But the memories hang on, and I constantly fight them back. I thought it would get easier after a time. Like the pain would dull, or I would forget those people and move on to new ones. But then I see you still holding on to your old customs. It never truly leaves, does it?" She rested her arms on her legs and picked at a root right next to her bed. The more she pulled, the more it came up, but still held fast.

"Not for me," said Regelend. He looked over at her, sitting stick straight and resting his hands on his lap. Everything about the way he tried to keep his appearance neat, even though he lived among dirt, suggested he was the royalty he had always been, throne or not. Only he had taken it all seriously.

"For you it might be different, it could," he said encouragingly.

"Maybe," she said and sighed. She had kept the curtain propped partway to let some light in, and they could hear the revelers below. There was much talking, and the music played on. She didn't even want to know what they were doing now. Maybe symbolizing the birthing process by chucking fruit at one another underhand.

"What is it?" Regelend asked, looking at her quizzically. She realized she was grinning and shook her head.

"Nothing, nothing. I was just thinking about the dancers." He flashed a grin briefly, but then his face fell into a pale frown.

"What are you thinking about?" she asked. "You look like you're sick." He shook his head and let out a long breath. "It's nothing."

She decided she would change the subject. She walked over to the opening and looked out.

"So where did they get a chandelier that large? Are you ever afraid it'll fall?" Suddenly she jumped and almost fell out of the cubby hole. She had felt a hand touch her back and try to slide timidly down her dress. She looked back, and Regelend had his hand outstretched with a petrified look on his face.

"What are you *doing*?" she yelled. He stepped back, retreating like a wounded bear to the back of his cave. Both were hunched over absurdly due to the low ceiling.

"I'm sorry, I sorry! I didn't want to. My teacher said I needed to experience sexual pleasure more, that I was repressing my inner… beast…or something…" he trailed off.

"Then why didn't she rape you herself? Why me?"

He looked like he was about to cry. She was having trouble staying angry at his earnest shame. And after the dance, she knew that was exactly what they would say here. She looked at him for a moment. He still looked scared.

"Relax. Sit back down," she commanded. He hovered near the wall.

"No, I should leave…"

"You're sitting down. I won't have us leave off on this note. I don't know how long it will be until we can talk again." He nodded and sat at the edge of her bed once more. She sat down next to him.

"She does." Regelend said. Kiadora looked at him, confused. "She does rape me herself. Well, practically. But I never enjoy it. She says I need to go off and find someone else. That once I choose it will become more rewarding." He looked at the ground in disgust. "She says that is the key to being an Eatheria user, that sex is one of the great gifts of the natural world and to know the full Mysteries we need to accept that side of ourselves. Your weakness is to never forget, mine is to never forget and to never live, apparently."

Kiadora's eye was caught by movement at the edge of her vision. She looked down and noticed Regelend was running his finger over a pocket in his tunic. The creased edge looked like the spine of a book.

"What do you have there?" Kiadora asked, pointing down. Regelend jumped, swatting his hand on the bed as if he was doing nothing. His features seemed to relax slightly as he realized what company he was in, his shoulders settling and the frightened deer look fleeing from his eyes. He reached into his pocket and pulled out a pale, yellow book with white writing on the front. Regelend held it out closer for her to see. He wore a sheepish look on his face. As if she needed a reminder as to what it was.

"The Holy Text. Of course," Kiadora said, her voice a whisper. He slipped it back into his pocket.

"I take it with me everywhere."

"But when do you get time to read it? It isn't like reading a book on the surface."

"No, it's not like that at all," he said, shaking his head. He looked at her curiously. "They haven't shown you the library yet?"

"No."

"It's got everything. Books on theory on how to master our art working the elements, mystical writings, musings on every god thought of, and…I'm sure they'll show it to you soon." He said this all in a dull voice, completely unimpressed with it, while Kiadora stared in wonderment. Books of different gods on the same shelf?

"I really wish they had shown it to me before. They didn't exactly give me a tour. I came in late, so they took me right to bed. What else is in there?"

"Like I said, anything you would want to know about. Name a subject, it's there." Kiadora raised a finger and drew in a breath to volunteer a subject that had been on her mind. "On religion and mystical works anyway," Regelend interrupted.

"Oh." Kiadora sagged a little. "I was going to try to look up what the medical community is saying about us. I was told I had an allergy to the woods." Regelend snorted.

"No, we don't have any of that. Are those the nuts over in your city's medical district?" Kiadora nodded. "I've heard about them. Word is, some are starting to say that religious phenomena is nothing but illness and fallacy." She thought of her doctor and his garden.

"Yes, they seem pretty dismissive about the Church. I'm surprised they're not shut down and put out of practice."

"No one on the top knows about them, but a few of the teachers down here keep an eye on them. They like to know what the certain fringe beliefs think of us so that they know if there is an opening for us to emerge. So far, they have not seen one. These new doctors are an even greater threat, apparently, since they think we are lunatics or diseased, rather than just spiritually misguided. At least the Church lumps us in the same spiritual frame of reference." Kiadora nodded, taking in the perspective. Then a question occurred.

"Who is it that keeps track of the doctors and their beliefs?"

"I don't know them all. It's not many. I hear this through, well, eavesdropping, even though I know I shouldn't." He glanced upward momentarily, as if asking for forgiveness. "One is Everanda, one of the fire teachers. Another is Narissa, a mistress of Air." Kiadora looked up sharply at him.

"Narissa's my teacher right now." Regelend looked over at her, unimpressed.

"Why would you want to ask her about it? What does it matter what some doctors think of us? We're down here, they're up there, and that is how it is always going to be." Regelend leaned back, hitting the hard soil with a thud, the empty sound verifying his statement. His brow was furrowed, tightened by his bitterness. "And even if we do have all the doctors' records that have ever been created, and ever are, I still need only one book." He patted his pocket smartly, and Kiadora found a part of herself admiring his devotion. Perhaps she would not be living in a hole in the ground if one book had been good enough.

"But then I would be where they still think I'm crazy," Kiadora muttered under her breath.

"What?" Regelend said, looking over.

"It's nothing," she said. "But I have an interest in the doctors because it was a strange experience when I went to mine with this problem. He wanted to help and listen and learn rather than sweeping it under a chair. He was curious, and even though he understood wrong, he was willing to understand." Regelend looked over at her. She wiped at her eyes, which were starting to feel itchy from the lack of sleep.

"Listen," she said. "I don't want this to be the only time we meet. I think we both need someone we know from the surface." Regelend nodded.

"I think so, too," he said. "I'll see you around. Look for me at the next social gathering, they're held once a week."

"Oh! I thought they were a rarity."

"Not really, but many would consider once a week a rarity." As he was saying this, he was walking to the door and turning around to climb down the ladder. "Practice your meditation," he said with a wink. He stepped to the side and out of view, pulling the curtain with him.

Kiadora smiled and looked down at the floor. Although it had been a joke, she should probably practice. She was afraid a tooth might go flying one of these days. As if confirming her thought, the lamps outside suddenly dimmed. She swung her feet up on the bed and lay down on her back. It wasn't the way she was taught, but she did not want to sit on the soil for some reason. Although she loved the woods, living among just the soil was like living on a lake that had dried up.

She settled her hands just under her chest and tried not to feel like a corpse prepared for a burial. She steadied her breathing and closed her eyes. And kept seeing Regelend's face drift in front of her view and feeling his hand clumsily slide down the back of her dress. *No, let it go, let it go.*

Her eyes snapped open.

She had it earlier. Narissa was right, this would take a lot of practice. She closed her eyes again and focused on Regelend and how much she hated how he had done that. 'I don't want to think about it, I don't want to think about it.' But Regelend, for all his faults, was hard to hate. He had seemed nice enough.

She lay staring into the darkness. She wondered if hate really was the way that this would work. She did not think it would be possible to hate anything as much as Narissa did. And it was infectious. She had convinced Kiadora to despise Tahn, to not want to consider him anymore. Then she remembered what Regelened had said: Narissa knew about the doctors.

Giving up on meditation for tonight, she turned on her side and wondered how she would ever be able to bring it up. There had to be a conversational opening eventually.

CHAPTER 11

A few days later, there was blood. Narissa had brought her hand into
Kiadora's jaw diagonally, which cut the lower lip that Kiadora was
biting. Kiadora let out a cry and tasted iron among the pain that shot
through her lip. Kiadora had had enough, and swung back, landing her
fist in the older woman's stomach, right below the rib cage. Far from
immobilized, however, Narissa brought her hand to Kiadora's throat
and slammed her into the wall. As Kiadora struggled for breath, she
actually saw the other woman grin. Blood ran from Kiadora's mouth
onto Narissa's hand, which was holding Kiadora's throat.

"*Now* you are learning," said Narissa. She let go of Kiadora, who
dropped instantly to the ground, kneeling in the dirt.

"What was that even for?" Kiadora yelled through the blood and
swelling lip. Although not profuse, the blood trickled down her chin.
She wiped it on her sleeve, but more flowed down.

"You were not following my instructions," said Narissa simply. "I
told you to let go, and I see you are not able to let go. It is as simple as
that." She had walked to her desk where she was wiping Kiadora's

blood off her hands with a wet cloth. She did not offer one to Kiadora. "But you are fighting back, that is the first step to letting go of what you hold dear. You just need to direct that rage to the appropriate sources."

I am, thought Kiadora. "And who would those be?" she asked as she stood up.

"As if you need to ask, Kiadora," Narissa said with a mocking tone in her voice as she looked up.

"The ones I left behind," Kiadora said quietly, frowning. She wondered how Regelend was able to walk around reading the Holy Text with people like Narissa on the prowl. Narissa's eyes gleamed as she mistook Kiadora's expression for the subject at hand.

"Yes! They are the ones who imprison us down here, who leave us to rot, who turned us aside." As Narissa said this, she paced around her study, knocking over a plant that was standing in her way.

"Then why don't you do something about it?" Kiadora asked instinctively, regretting the question immediately with a cringe. Kiadora knew enough about politics to know that people like Narissa who brooded silently in the shadows, holding to anger, were some of the most dangerous souls. They were the ones who eventually usurped rulers, who were constantly a threat to her family.

"Do you think I do not want to?" Narissa asked. She had returned to her desk. She now leaned against it, slouching over. "I comb the surface, looking for a gap where we might be made known and be able to take a hold, but there are none as far as I can see. The Church has its hold and everyone is content with the lies they are fed as long as the lies keep them in good spirits." Kiadora's mind suddenly jumped to

Regelend and his constant possession of the Holy Text and how much peace it gave him. Then she remembered another part of the conversation.

"Do you know anything about the doctors?" she asked. "I saw one. Before I came. They are looking into us in a new way."

"The doctors are the worst of all!" Narissa spat. Kiadora had seen her angry, as she seemed to possess a constant simmering rage that boiled in her soul. But Kiadora had never seen her lash out this badly. Although she figured it had to happen eventually, and they had already been together a few weeks. Kiadora gazed down at the floor from where she was standing, marooned in the middle of the room, unsure of how to react.

"They sit up on their pedestals and think they can understand us like we are an empirical science!" Narissa ranted. "If only they knew how deep it goes, but they can never see." She looked up at Kiadora, as if suddenly remembering the other woman was standing there. "That is our curse, Kiadora. Only those who are like us can ever understand. To others, we sound like nothing but mad ravers, screaming at the shadows. It traps us here." Her voice had dulled, as if her anger had finally run its course, and only the sorrow she carried underneath could show now. "Go to your quarters and practice meditation, I'll want you back here in two hours."

Kiadora turned and walked out, looking at Narissa as she closed the door behind her. Narissa had walked around the edge of her desk, sat down and had buried her face in her hands before Kiadora shut the door on her.

Kiadora walked back to her area, now feeling sullen herself. At least the bleeding had stopped. She wiped off the remaining blood with a dark sleeve. As she climbed up her ladder, she remembered her old bed like she had just been in it last night and missed it. She had only been here about a month, and she could see the toll it was taking on some of the people, to live underground constantly. They were not moles.

She flopped herself down on her bed and wondered how she was supposed to meditate and forget now. It *would* be a way to leave the dirt and soil and sorrow behind. She closed her eyes and after a few moments she was floating in darkness. The next thing she knew, she snapped to because of a rustling at her curtain. She looked up to see Regelend poking his round face in the opening between the curtain and door. He retreated as he saw she was practicing.

"No, it's fine," she called out. He attentively peered around again and then walked through the curtain as she motioned him in.

"I'm sorry, I should have known you would be in meditation. That is what a lot of the people do during the day, especially the new ones. It's just, I thought you would be taking a break. Narissa gets moody and sends a lot of people back to their areas from time to time."

"Yes, she was in one of those moods today," Kiadora agreed. "I know she can be a terrible person, but I never thought I would see that side to her. She's so miserable down here." But Kiadora didn't want to think about it. She didn't need to discuss her own misery; she had a feeling that was where the conversation would lead. "I'm getting better at meditation," she offered brightly.

"That's good," said Regelend in a hollow sort of way. She thought he would care more than he did, but Kiadora now realized how foolish the sentiment was. "It took me about three months," Regelend said casually, for the sake of conversation. "You got it down a lot quicker than I did."

"Yes, but I can only do it when I am depressed slightly." Regelend looked over at her confused.

"What?"

"That is how I was taught to do it, you have to have the desire to escape and to distance yourself from everything. Well, the only time I want to do that is when everything is making me sad or angry." Regelend shook his head.

"I don't think that is how you are supposed to do it. I was taught the same way, and that is why I had to fake it for the first...alright, I lied. I never mastered it." He whispered urgently, turning close to her. "I fake it every time. When I said I got good at it in three months, that is how long it took me to learn to pretend. I should not have lied, God will punish me for this, I'm sure." He leaned away from her and sunk his head in despair, running his hands over each other as if to wash the failure in both religions away.

Kiadora rested an arm on his shoulder. "It's fine," she said soothingly. "I'm sure it's a completely worthless skill, anyway. All that ever happens to me is a sort of dreamless sleep. It's nice, but it's not helping anything. And you have to lie in this place to get by, I hope your god would not punish you for that." Regelend looked affronted.

"*My* god! He's everyone's god, Kiadora, even if they do not like it or know it. Don't tell me you do not believe in him!"

"I have no clue as to what I believe," Kiadora snapped, turning on him like a wolf about the jump on its prey. "The Church led me wrong, that stupid woman isn't teaching me anything but escapism and the stupid rituals they have here make me want to laugh. What would prancing around a gigantic stick achieve, anyway?" It had been last week's memorable social.

"It's supposed to be phallic," said Regelend quietly, looking ashamed for using the word.

"Well, good, as long as it's *phallic!* You know something, I think I want to be alone." Regelend stood up slowly, reminding Kiadora of a struck puppy. She was in the mood the kick the brute harder.

"Alright, I'll talk to you later, Kiadora," he said slowly and quietly.

"Fine," she snapped. She flung herself down on her bed and drifted into the place between sleep and wakefulness that she learned as meditation.

A few weeks later, Kiadora sat in the same study, still drifting through darkness. A few days earlier, she had gotten to the point where she felt fully like she was once again in the coffin at the Church and was spinning and falling, though she knew she stayed flat on the ground. Narissa had seemed pleased with the progress. Although no smile had been forthcoming, Kiadora had not been slapped as much. Then, today, a question:

"Have you seen images?" Narissa asked as Kiadora came to.

"No. You told me to banish them," said Kiadora, as she stretched out to gain alertness. It was a habit she had developed when she had spent a few days falling asleep from being so relaxed. Narissa nodded. And then, another question:

"Are you a virgin?" Kiadora looked up, startled, from where she was stretching on the ground, her arms snapping down from over her head. She jumped up.

"What?"

"You heard me," Narissa stated. "Have you ever made love with a man?"

"No! Why should I have?"

"You are female, adult, woman. It is quite natural." Narissa had picked up a pen from her desk and was twirling it in her hand. Kiadora wondered briefly why she was so intent upon it.

"I'm not, I'm only 19. I'm not an adult until 21."

"By legal standards. Here, you are a woman at your first menstruation. When was that?" Kiadora stared at her, resisting the urge to tell Narissa that it was none of her damn business. But Kiadora still had that pale scar on her lip.

"When I was 13," Kiadora said. Narissa still continued to play with the pen, spinning it around on its point on her desk. Miraculously it hadn't fallen, despite the fact that she barely touched it.

"Then you have been a woman for six years. And nothing?" Narissa said accusingly, looking up from the spinning pen; then she slapped it down on her desk. Kiadora shook her head.

"This is unfortunate. So we have little to work with. This will happen with the younger ones, and certainly those with a pious family," Narissa was looking to the side, thinking out loud. "I had thought you and this Tahn must have done something. But no, he was pious you said." She looked up at Kiadora.

"You have not kissed, touched, nothing?" Narissa looked desperate. Kiadora wanted to say something.

"We…we kissed. Once," Kiadora turned red. Narissa looked up at her, eyes narrowed.

"How did it feel?" Kiadora fidgeted where she stood. She dug her toe into the dirt, similar to as she had seen Tahn do often.

"It was…it was nice."

"You lie," spat Narissa. "You're as terrible of a liar as you are a sexual being. Sit in the corner," Narissa ordered, pointing as she got up and came around the desk. Kiadora scrambled to the area that she usually meditated at and sat down again. Narissa stood over her, and Kiadora tried to hide a shudder as she became afraid of what the other woman was about to do. She remembered the relationship Regelend had with his current teacher. She thought she would at least get a male teacher for this.

"Do you daydream ever?" Kiadora had to hold back a laugh. Did fire burn? "Yes, I used to get in trouble for it constantly." Narissa nodded. She sat down in front of Kiadora, no longer looming over her like she was about to jump on her. Kiadora sank back in relief.

"What do you daydream about?" Narissa questioned in her usual short tone. Kiadora laughed lightly.

"Actually, I used to daydream I could fly and that I was swimming." Narissa nodded curtly, looking thoughtful.

"Indeed. But that is not what I am looking for. Never of the opposite sex?" Kiadora had never thought about it. Sometimes Tahn drifted though her dreams in indiscriminate ways that caused… stirrings, but never more.

"*Never* of the opposite sex?"

"No." Narissa glanced to the side, with an expression of someone going out on a limb.

"The *same* sex?"

"Huh?" People did that?

Narissa shook her head. "Never mind." Narissa took a breath, her shoulders seemed to settle and she looked intently at Kiadora.

"Close your eyes," Narissa said. Rather than the snappish order Kiadora was used to, the words came out in a soft hiss. Kiadora did as she was told.

"This is called guided meditation," she heard her teacher say, still in the uncharacteristic, soft tone. "I want you to picture exactly what I am saying. You are in a meadow." Kiadora held the picture of a meadow in her mind. "It is a sunny day, and the light reflects off of several red flowers that spot the tall grass all around you." Easy enough; the red flowers sprung up among waist-high grass.

"Now a man comes to you, weaving gently through the tall grass." Kiadora saw a man walking toward her. She took the liberty to give him shoulder-length dark hair and made him tall. "He comes and lies down next to you. He puts his hand under your shirt." Kiadora eyes snapped open as she remembered Regelend. They had done the same exercise on him.

"What? What is it?" Narissa snapped, that smooth hiss gone in an instant.

"Nothing. I'm just remembering...something." Narissa's eyes narrowed.

"So you have done this."

"No, no not really. It's just...a friend down here tried to...get somewhere with me." Narissa nodded, her lips pursed. She looked disappointed.

"And why did you not encourage it?"

"I didn't know him that well."

"And you know him better now, yes?" Narissa was now leaning on her elbows staring closely at Kiadora.

"Listen, I know where you're going with this." Kiadora stared down, not wanting to look Narissa in the eye. Maybe she would take it less as a challenge. "We do not feel that way about each other." Surprisingly, Narissa had not swung. Kiadora looked up to see Narissa studying her face. Her muscles were tense. Clearly she was trying to restrain herself.

"That is insignificant," said Narissa quietly. "You are the product of the society you grew up in. We all are, but that does not mean we need to be. You have to get past this aversion to physical intimacy." She spoke like a doctor trying to tell a patient to not fear needles, a priest telling her to say her prayers. "Try to take yourself back to the scene I set."

Kiadora closed her eyes, the red speckled grass filling itself in, the sunlight pouring down. It was almost a stretch to remember the gentle warmth after living in a dirt hole for so long. The man with dark hair sat next to her on a bed of shorter grass. Try has she might, his face was nondescript, passive and empty. His dark eyes could have belonged to a scarecrow.

"Who is this man, anyway?" Kiadora asked, still keeping her eyes closed.

"Oh, I don't know," Narissa said impatiently. "The man is who you want him to be." Kiadora imagined him as a local man she had met at the market, a… a jewelry salesman. But his eyes still resembled an object whose sole purpose it was to ease a farmer's fear of crows.

"Now, this time, *you* reach over and unbutton his shirt." Kiadora saw her arms reach over, extend to his shirt and take off the first button. She pictured his facial expression as she looked up. He looked impassive. "You take off his shirt." She slid off the shirt, which he simply shrugged out of. Then he sat there like nothing happened. His skin was pale, with slight muscle definition. In fact, he looked like the stable boys in the summer as they walked around shirtless.

"He finishes undressing himself as you slide out of your dress." No, she would keep her dress on. That was quite alright. She looked over to the man and now that he was undressed there was one problem. Kiadora opened her eyes again.

"Um. What does a man's private area look like?" Narissa stared at her, dumbfounded.

"What?"

"Those parts on a man, I have never seen them. How am I supposed to picture them if I do not know what they look like?" Narissa threw up her arms and stood up.

"Oh, for the love of Eatheria!" she turned around and walked over to the desk, throwing open a drawer with a loud bang. "I know it's restrictive up there, but you are just pathetic. Most people at least have an *idea*." Narissa pulled out a long, oblong object.

She brought it over and threw herself down on the floor, handing it to Kiadora. It was covered with the smoothest leather and seemed to be made of wood. It had a tip at the end.

"That. That is what the males have to reproduce with. Part of it. Damn, I usually have to give this talk to people half your age!" Narissa yelled. She sighed to calm herself down and looked at Kiadora in the eye. "And can you try to guess where that goes to secrete the seed?" Narissa said, pointing at what Kiadora held in her hand. Kiadora looked down and grimaced.

"Age a bit," Narissa snapped. "It's not that bad. It's quite pleasurable actually, as I will show you. Spread your legs." Kiadora shrunk back.

"What, you're not going to..."

"You heard me." Narissa grabbed the object out of Kiadora's hand and was staring her down. Kiadora was pressed against the wall, hugging her legs to herself. She decided to stand up and head for the door.

"No, this is too much," Kiadora said, her voice shaking. "I don't see the purpose here." She was shaking her head. When she got to the door to lunge at it, she noticed it was locked. She turned back to Narissa, who was standing where Kiadora had left her. She was staring over at Kiadora with a calm expression. "You are not going to force me..." Kiadora breathed.

"No, I will not force you. By physical means." Kiadora's eyes narrowed. She took a step back and tried to push on the flimsy walls with the hand behind her back but they were stronger than they looked. Kiadora wondered why Narissa was not hitting her right now for trying the escape. Narissa still stood there, oddly patient.

"This is stupid," Kiadora said. "What purpose could something like this possibly serve?" Narissa was looking down at the object in her hand, spinning it around her fingers like she did with her pen at times.

"You came here to learn, did you not?" Narissa said quietly, not looking up from her hand. Kiadora let out a frustrated breath.

"Yes, I did. But to learn about my abilities and to learn about myself, not have awkward objects jammed in areas that are even more awkward. You people are worse than the Church." Narissa looked up at this, a glint in her eye. Her mouth was set firm and her eyes wild and wide. She started to walk toward Kiadora, moving with a dangerous, cat-like grace, dropping the object in the dust. The next thing Kiadora knew, Narissa was inches from her face. Kiadora could smell the bitter scent of an odd smoke.

"*Don't ever* relate us to that institution. We are nothing like them," Narissa whispered, if only because she was too busy with her anger to generate much sound. Narissa pushed Kiadora against the wall, which held against more force than Kiadora could ever imagine it would. She heard a deep boom that reverberated to her soul as she was struck.

"You are cowardly and insolent," Narissa said in a low tone. "You come down here with the pretense to learn, yet scorn every attempt I make. I see your expressions you think you conceal. And it is not until I force you that you will try anything. If you only knew what you missed *out on*," Narissa gave Kiadora a small shove again at the last two words. Narissa took a step back and looked Kiadora up and down, like she was sizing up a soldier. Kiadora stared back, wanting to run from the room, but unable.

"You have a choice you can make," said Narissa with more force. "You can learn from me, or you can go back up to the surface where you are comfortable with what you know. You can wonder what you could have been and spend the rest of your life knowing that whatever that is, you cannot be that now." Narissa walked around Kiadora, unlocked the door, opened it and held it open, indicating with an arm that Kiadora was free to leave.

Kiadora simply looked at the door, hovering uncertainly. She remembered the cut on her lip that she had received from Narissa. She glanced up, to where she would head if she walked away. Back to the Church, if she had ever left…

Back to Tahn, from whom she would spend the rest of her life hiding what she was. She pictured Dehlia sneering at her as she explained that she did not fit in with the Hermetics.

She would blend…but just blend.

Kiadora walked to the door and looked at Narissa. She expected to see a gleeful grin at not having to force such a dim-witted student through her lessons, but there was only a grave solemnity in her expression. Her eyes rested on Kiadora as though she looked at a dying animal.

Kiadora reached out toward the door and slammed it shut. Narissa actually smiled at this, though her eyes remained distant and cold. Narissa turned sharply and indicated to Kiadora to sit down on the rug.

"Good," Narissa said, as Kiadora sat down. Kiadora tried to regulate her expression to look curious. Narissa looked over at her and squinted.

"Stop," she said, looking at Kiadora, her mouth drawn to the side. "You are a terrible actress. I know you are still terrified. But, you have made the choice to go on. There is hope yet." Kiadora looked down. 'She cannot make me enjoy it,' Kiadora thought.

Narissa walked over to her, scooping up the male representation from the ground and wiping it off on her dress. She kneeled down and looked into Kiadora's eyes. Without the exchange of words, Kiadora knew what to do. She spread her legs and gasped as Narissa slammed the object into her, up her, through her. Narissa started to thrust it into her, and Kiadora felt only pain. She grimaced and had to fight the urge to kick Narissa off of her.

Narissa only regarded her silently, looking into Kiadora's eyes with a detached expression. Kiadora was surprised she was not being reprimanded for not enjoying this. Narissa only kept on, with a type of diligence and patience she showed for little else.

CHAPTER 12

Later that afternoon, Kiadora walked slowly back to her sleeping quarters. She expected to feel more sore than she did, but she still did not feel right. She felt like her body was mending itself, pulling itself back together in those regions, like the way she pulled a sleeve onto a shirt with her thread. She climbed the ladder, wishing she could get the unpleasant feeling out of her mind. Kiadora then flopped herself down on her bed.

Narissa had told her that she needed to meditate on the feeling. Make peace with it, figure out how she felt about it. Uncomfortable. She rolled onto her side, content to merely fall asleep for a few hours until dinner. Just as she was drifting off, she heard her drape rustle. It could only be one person.

"Hello," she called, sitting up to see Regelend hovering in the doorway. She could tell from the way his shoulders were bent in his outline that he felt awkward about being there. He had not stopped by since their fight.

"Is it ok if I come in?" he asked, in a tone that only acted at being casual.

"Sure," she said. The sincerity in her casual tone made him come and sit next to her on the bed. They stared forward for a time, not saying anything. Kiadora wondered if she should apologize for attacking everything Regelend held dear. Her mind made up, she turned to him.

"Listen, I'm sorry for saying I don't…"

"It's fine," Regelend cut in. "I can't pretend I'm home where everyone believes what I do. We're all confused down here." Kiadora snorted.

"I doubt Narissa is very confused. She knows exactly what I have in store and what I would miss if I left. She nearly kicked me out today." Kiadora looked down at her hands that were resting in her lap, studying the blackened fingernails, what with the perpetual dirt under them. "I wondered if I should go; I almost did."

"Many of us would like to. The ones I speak to most, anyway." Kiadora looked over at him. She had never asked who his other friends were. Regelend caught her curious expression and interpreted it immediately.

"I talk to almost everyone," Regelend said. She saw him flitting around at the socials like a bee taking around pollen. "But there are a few that are like me. They are down here because they have nowhere else to go. It's the only place they will not be killed for what they are. Sure, they can hide what they are, but that's an even greater insanity then never seeing the sky again. I go around and visit them a lot. The problem is, we do not meet together that often. We're afraid we'll draw too much attention." Kiadora looked over at him with the same quizzical expression.

"So what if you did? What would it matter, and what would they do?"

"Think about it," said Regelend, playing with a string on her bedding. Kiadora guided his hand away so he would not unravel the whole blanket. He put his hand back on his knee from where it came. "All of us who are bad at our lessons meeting. I don't even want to know what they would do."

"Oh, it can't be that bad," said Kiadora. "They're crazy, but they don't seem dictatorial. Just angry." Regelend shook his head at Kiadora.

"There was something, just a rumor. I shouldn't spread these things in case it's a lie..." he looked down at the dirt floor He looked up to Kiadora's intense stare. She was leaning over and looking at him, waiting for him to go on. She could tell he knew she would not give it up, so he went on.

"A couple of months ago, they say, there was a boy named Eagrade. He ran out of a lesson and refused to do nothing but read the Holy Text. They say his teacher took him to the surface and turned him in to the Church personally. He had already been through the Termination, so now he lives imprisoned in the house of the possessed." Kiadora leaned back against the wall and put her arms on her bed.

"No, they wouldn't. They hate the Church and would never propagate the belief that we're diseased or possessed. I told you, my teacher nearly kicked me out of lessons today. Just held the door open for me to leave. Wasn't going to stop me. I don't believe she would have turned me in."

"Why were you going to leave?" Regelend asked. Kiadora sighed.

She didn't want to have to tell anyone this part.

"It was the dumbest thing," she said, sitting up. "She made me have...relations with a piece of wood. With leather on it." Regelend frowned and looked to the side. He turned a very faint shade of red, staying silent.

"It was mortifying," Kiadora went on. "She told me that I was still a child and needed to accept the sexual side of myself. I'm still trying to figure out what that means."

"Like I said, they hold those...those acts on a pedestal here. It's supposed to honor their god." Regelend absently started to play with the piece of string on her blanket again.

"Sounds like they're just trying to get off here," said Kiadora with a snort. Regelend gave a small smile.

"That's one interpretation."

Kiadora sat up and looked down at her foot, dragging it through the dirt to form a straight line. "I wish it would just end. But it doesn't, does it?" Kiadora remembered the pretense of her first meeting with Regelend. "They just keep pushing you into it."

"Yes," said Regelend simply. He fidgeted like a small boy at Church school on a clear summer day. Kiadora kept looking at him. He seemed far off; obviously something was weighing on his mind. He stared off to the side and then looked back at Kiadora suddenly, shocked to see her staring at him. Kiadora kept on looking at him with a raised eye brow.

"You're probably wondering what I was thinking about."

"Yes." Kiadora looked off to the far wall. "But it's your business, not mine." She stared of into the distance, hoping Regelend would go on but he did not. Instead, Kiadora voiced what was on her mind.

"How do you do it? Get them off your case, I mean. I don't want them doing those things!" She slammed her fist down on the bed, angry for having still more odd acts forced on her.

"You don't," said Regelend hollowly. She looked back at him, disappointed.

"Thanks for the hope." Kiadora frowned down at the bed. "But can't they see it doesn't help, that some people don't want to do it?"

"That's not the way they think. Everything is a learning process and a path to experiencing their god, and I can sort of see where they are coming from there. If you do not agree, you're just a slow learner or not ready for the god yet. But they think you will get there. That is what my teacher tells me. She should be thrilled, I think I found someone I love." Kiadora snapped her head back to Regelend. She grinned at him. But he had the same troubled expression he wore a minute ago, his brow creased and a frown dominating his face.

"Who's the girl?" Kiadora said cautiously. "You don't look happy about it."

"Well, it's not that. It's just…." Regelend looked away, his arms folded in front of him.

"What?"

"If they find out, we're going to have to participate in the Great Union together." He looked up at Kiadora's quizzical expression and went on. "It's a ritual they do once a year. They pick two people who are in love at the time to…you know." Kiadora grimaced.

"In front of everyone?"

"Yes. And I'm not even sure I feel that way about her yet. I always wonder if I am just trying to feel that way because they're putting more and more pressure on me to do it." Regelend stared down, still holding his arms to himself, as if he was trying to shut out the world from his body, or at least his soul.

"This place is crazy," said Kiadora, the obvious floating into the air and hanging there like a dead weight. She turned back to Regelend. "But they never have to know. I won't tell. You talk to enough people so they won't suspect a thing if you go to her quarters a lot."

"Yes," Regelend sighed heavily. He got to his feet and stood as tall as he could under the short ceiling. "Well, I think I'm going to bed. It was nice talking to you," he said, cordially bowing as he turned around to step down the ladder.

"I'll see you," said Kiadora, waving as the curtain fell down once more. She reclined on her bed, looking at the shadowed ceiling. She always hated going to her lessons, but from now on she knew she would dread it. *What you missed out on*, Narissa had said, the words echoing like they came from the end of a long tunnel. She had made the whole place sound like it was a great festival of games and toys.

Kiadora remembered she was supposed to meditate. She had grown lax about it, but if she needed to escape, it was now. Still, she lay staring at the ceiling, having an internal debate lest she face those images again.

Finally, she closed her eyes, hoping for some of that divine wisdom. She steadied her breathing, and just as she had feared they would, images from her lesson flashed into her mind...

"So, you say you are good at daydreaming?" Narissa said from where she was leaning on the front of her desk. Kiadora nodded as she sat in front of the wall on the regular rug, pulling the hem of her dress down around her ankles. It had gone on for a week now, the constant push and pull that Kiadora was sure was a way of plumbing out the human soul. Narissa came to her and sat down in front of her once more.

"You remember the first time I tried to guide you in meditation?" Kiadora remembered the generic figure, if that could count as a memory. "We're going back there," Narissa forged on. "Close your eyes. You are in a field."

Kiadora did so, closing her eyes tightly. She remembered her vow that Narissa could not force her to enjoy it, and so far Kiadora had been successful. Again, the man walked up out of nowhere.

"Where is he from?" Kiadora asked out loud, her eyes still shut tight.

"You're getting distracted," she heard Narissa's voice snap from the darkness. The field was gone. Kiadora opened her eyes.

"I still wonder. I mean, what, this is just a made-up man coming out of the woods? How am I supposed to 'enjoy creation' if this man does not even seem real to me?"

Narissa pressed her lips together, glaring at Kiadora. And still glared. Kiadora watched patiently, expecting a blow. Anything to stall. She was already tired of all the great things Narissa said she would miss if she walked out the door. Narissa finally let out a heavy sigh.

"It's a spirit." Kiadora sat back, her eyes wide.

"Why would I mate with a spirit?" Kiadora shrieked. "They don't even have bodies." Narissa closed her eyes and put the tip of her first two fingers to her eyelids. She groaned a little.

"We're taking this backwards," she muttered into her hands. "The point is to discover that it is a spirit on your own." She broke her face away from her hands. "But I can see you would not come to that conclusion." For the first time it was not a jibe; it was a mere fact. Narissa's eyes bored into Kiadora's, and for the first time, Kiadora knew that her teacher saw her for exactly what she was.

Narissa looked down and broke the gaze she held. "I pity your next few teachers," she said simply, staring at the floor to the side of Kiadora's left knee. "But let's get this going."

"Wait," Kiadora said. "Telling me it is a spirit does not help me with anything. What type of spirit, why does he want to visit me… and…and what could possibly happen to me if I let this thing touch me that way, even in my mind?"

"For one thing, it is not only in your mind." Narissa gave a heavy sigh again, clearly frustrated that she was breaking protocol. "And that is for you to decide, figure out and encounter. You are here to experience, and only experience, at this level. Stop second-guessing and analyzing, you are too far down on the tier system for that yet." Kiadora folded her arms in front of her. Too low on the tier system to think, wonderful.

"Fine, I will live and experience," said Kiadora in a mocking tone. "And damn the consequences." And finally it came, the blinding blow to the side of her head. Kiadora went sideways and caught herself on her elbow, making her arm sting as well. She sat straight back up again.

"Must you fight me every step of the way?" Narissa shouted. "Do you think this thing will rob your soul, that it is a Shiekita in disguise? You see what everyone thinks Shiekita are! They think it is you, they think it is me, and still you fear the spirit realm only because you doubt and fear what you are. How dare you even think I would lead you into that sort of evil. There are good spirits out there; the world is not God and demons."

"All I wanted to know…" Kiadora put in. Both women were leaned in, inches from each other's faces at this point, shouting.

"You seek to analyze, but then you unconsciously filter everything backwards!" Kiadora sat back at this comment, her face burning. Her eyes itched as though tears of frustration would pour down at any moment. As soon as she thought of them, they came. She blinked, as if to force them back in, but they flowed down her face, outlining her deep scowl. Narissa sat up taller, watching Kiadora battle her tears.

"Does it ever leave?" Kiadora asked quietly, looking up at Narissa. The woman gazed coolly down at her. "The old experiences, the shame? I'm skeptical of…all that." She nodded her head upwards. "I've always been skeptical. I thought I'd toss it off."

Narissa gave a small frown, the hard glare in her eyes melting into an uncharacteristic softness. Kiadora leaned forward slightly, eager for an answer or a word of sympathy, at least. But Narissa stayed silent, only regarding Kiadora with that soft gaze. Was it sadness? Kiadora wiped her cheeks, which still had some tears on them.

"Take time to focus. We're moving forward." Kiadora looked into Narissa's eyes as that soft gaze was swallowed by the same hard stare as before. It happened in an instant. Kiadora shut her own eyes and began to breathe steadily. Her eyes still felt wet, but as she kept the rhythm with her breathing, the feeling dissolved.

"Now, you're in a field," Narissa said again, smoothly. Kiadora hated the field at this point and took the liberty to put herself in a crisp forest, with green light filtering down around her as she stood among the trunks of some ancient maple trees.

"The sun is bright, the grass sways in the breeze." Kiadora saw the trees sway and heard the rustle of leaves.

"A man comes to you through the grass." He walked out from the trees, weaving nimbly between the trunks. Narissa paused and the man just stood off in the distance. Then Narissa's voice broke the silence once more.

"He has pale golden hair and is about two inches taller than you." Kiadora decided she could go along with this. He advanced toward her, and she began to notice the pale features.

"He wears a long, blue tunic and has brown riding pants on." And he seemed to grow pants to match the tree trunks and a shirt to match the small patches of sky she could see between the leaves. Kiadora also took the liberty to assume he was a local farmer boy she had met at market. That *was* how she met Tahn.

"As he draws near, you see more clearly a golden buckle on a black belt and his clear, gray eyes." A belt, the eyes. "You now stand a couple of inches apart." He was staring down, and she imagined the slight warmth one feels when someone is standing close by.

"He puts his arms around you." The pressure of his arms on her shoulders. "And pulls you close." She felt the softness on her cheek as she touched his shirt. The rhythmic beat of his heart. Her breathing increased and she felt a pressure in an area that she had not before. She almost jumped out of the trance, but she held the image strong.

"You embrace and he kisses you on the forehead. His lips are warm." Yes, yes they were.

"He puts his arms up to the back of your dress and unfastens the buttons. Your dress falls off." Coolness. She should be ashamed. She chose not to look down; she knew she would only see her own sickly white body, bleached from weeks of no sun, despite the sun that shown down around them.

"Her reaches up and pulls off his shirt." His skin was amazingly a light bronze, shining under the golden hair; a statue glinting in the sun. "He pulls down his pants." And she was throbbing.

"He kisses you on the mouth, his tongue probing, and at the same time you feel insertion." And she did, and it was wonderful. But it was not what Narissa used; it was all her mind, she knew. But felt it she did and the thrusting began. She rocked gently against him. She clung to his shoulders among the waves of heat and ecstasy that flowed through her. She had felt this before, somewhere. The pounding heat, the surge of energy.

The herbs.

The pulsating energy, the force, the desire for more. She opened her eyes and he was looking intensely at her. He had stopped moving and his eyes had gone pitch black. His nose had not looked that triangular before. Ears moved to the top of his head, sprouting and widening, as if to hear her scream all the better. He held her fast, and she still felt him firmly in place. Her vision became a swarm of whiskers and fur.

She looked down and paws clung to her arms, the small nails biting in. She wanted desperately to come to, but he held her tight. She screamed and as she felt her pulse rate increase, she was back with Narissa.

Narissa stared, her eyes wide with shock. Her mouth was open, giving Kiadora a never-before-seen dumbfounded look. Kiadora looked down at the floor, ashamed.

But she knew what it all meant. That is what this all came down to for her: the pleasure-seeking ways of the rat.

"What in the name of Eatheria did you see, woman!" Narissa's voice was a mixture of shock and rage. Her eyes glinted dangerously. Kiadora still looked down at the floor, but her mind stayed blank as to any excuses for what she had seen. How could she possibly talk her way out of it?

"It was…it was the weirdest thing," Kiadora shook her head, trying to stall now. Her voice came out in a hollow monotone. "It was what it was supposed to be, and then I saw the man mutate into a rat." Narissa leaned back slightly, her shoulders quickly squared off. It looked like she was about to go on defense of a physical attack. Kiadora expected to see Narissa's arms fly up to shield her face.

"No, you're lying," she breathed. But the truth of the matter still hung between them, and they both knew it. Narissa shook her head, her eyes narrowing.

"I don't even know where to go from here," Narissa admitted. "This was supposed to be your final day, your final lesson. Most students even enjoy it. No one has ever had to be held back during their introductory lessons." Kiadora's heart sank. Not only was she bad at this, but she was quite possibly the worst. She was a freak even among the freaks.

"Perhaps we should try it again?" Narissa mused. "No," she decided instantly. "We should not progress, not until I consult someone." She looked over at Kiadora, the edge of her lip twitching in the throes of an internal debate.

"Yes, you better come with me," Narissa said at last. Kiadora's face reddened. Would they punish her for this? Narissa got up and walked to her office door, which she wrenched open rather forcefully before she swept out of her office. Kiadora followed Narissa down the maze of hallways, the current sweeping between the stones, pulled by what might as well have been gravity itself.

The two emerged out of the network of classrooms and stood on the far side of the complex. Kiadora had never been over here, and she was surprised to be greeted by a cave-like opening partially hidden behind a rocky outcropping. Just behind the rock, they met a small, pale woman sitting on the ground, gazing absently at the floor. She looked up quickly as Narissa strode up with Kiadora in tow.

"I need to see the Elder of Studies," Narissa said. The woman looked from Narissa to Kiadora with bright, blue eyes that seemed to glow from the shadows. She nodded.

"Very well," she said in a breathy voice. She jumped up to disappear into the cave, her pale hair bobbing in the darkness for a few seconds before vanishing. Kiadora looked over at Narissa, who was merely waiting for the small woman to return.

"The Elder of Studies?" Kiadora asked. "What is she going to do about what I dream up? And what is the problem here, anyway?" As Narissa looked over, Kiadora could see the muscles in her arms tense, and Kiadora was at the point of making an offensive swing before

Narissa could muster up the force. But Narissa's arm relaxed, and she just looked at Kiadora with a clenched jaw and a beady look to her eye. Kiadora looked back to the cave, and the two waited for the white tooth to come bobbing back out.

"You will see," said Narissa after a moment. "That this is very serious business what you saw."

"It was just a hallucination," Kiadora protested, her arms swinging away from her body in frustration.

"It may be more that that, and if it is..." but she was cut off by the platinum-haired woman appearing before them once more.

"She will see you." The woman retreated back into the cave again and Narissa stepped forward with Kiadora following still. Kiadora realized that Narissa was held in high regard. She had not even requested a visit in advance or been asked for a reason for the visit. Narissa was trusted to have a damn good one. Kiadora felt ashamed for arguing with and showing her beliefs to someone who obviously had so much clout.

Ahead, Kiadora saw the halo of the pale woman dance in front of the them and ghostly arms reach up to a torch that rested on the wall. They continued on, making through bends and turns with heavy oak doors on each side.

At last they came to an empty passageway at the end of a tunnel, an opening leading off to the right. They walked through a jagged archway that led into a short, smooth corridor, the torchlight making an orb of flickering orange around them. The three women walked into a cavern with no adornments. In the center of the room sat a woman with shoulder length, steel-gray hair, sitting with her legs folded and her hands resting patiently in her lap. Hazel eyes shone in the light of the torch at them.

Narissa bent forward at the waist, as did the doorkeeper. Kiadora followed as they did, bending about 45 degrees down before rising. It felt odd, after a life spent of bowing to no human. Kiadora found she did not like it. How was it that this woman, who sat in a hidden corner, required such treatment? Kiadora felt her eyes narrow slightly before becoming aware of it and returning them to normal to keep the disdain out of her face.

It was too late, the woman was already staring at her, a calm, observant expression on her face accented by the slight wrinkles around the edges of her eyes and mouth. She looked like she had enough patience to stare at Kiadora for a good part of eternity without passing judgment until she deemed that she had observed enough.

Narissa stepped forward.

"Earia Eledina, during the Consortation, she saw a…a…" Narissa's voice drifted off, at a loss for words for the first time in Kiadora's presence. Eledina held up a hand.

"Perhaps," Eledina said, in a smooth, graceful voice, "we should have Kiadora explain what she saw." Kiadora jumped slightly as she heard a metallic thud. She looked to the source of the noise; it was their guide merely putting the torch into the holder on wall. The woman gave a small smile and left. Kiadora turned back to Eledina, who looked at her with clear eyes and an encouraging smile.

"It was when I was supposed to be taking a spirit as a consort." She now understood what it meant, since Narissa had called it the 'Consortation.'

"Everything was going fine until the most intense part. Then it mutated into a giant rat."

"The size of a man?" Eledina asked.

"Yes, it stood up as tall as a man but was a rat." Kiadora expected the woman to look shocked, but she merely looked thoughtful as she put a hand to her chin, tapping the bottom half of her lip.

"Did he say anything or have any other actions?" she asked at last. Kiadora shook her head.

"No…he just kept at it." Kiadora glanced timidly to the side. "Then I started screaming and came to." Eledina looked over to Narissa, who was standing with a solemn frown.

"And what did you see?" she addressed Narissa.

"Everything was going normal," said Narissa as if she was reporting the crop bounty numbers for the year. "She then started to scream and opened her eyes abruptly."

"And what do you suspect it was?" The top of Eledinda's head tilted toward Narissa.

"It sounds like an Ashilek." One of Kiadora's eyebrows raised. Eledina nodded. She turned her face toward Kiadora, the deep shadows on her face making her calm eyes and passive smile seem more pronounced.

"It sounds like you know what the Consortation is. Many don't; we wish it to remain a secret until afterwards so the experience is unique."

"I explained beforehand," said Narissa promptly.

"Yes, it is where I have relations with a spirit to be their lover, it sounds like," Kiadora said. Eledina nodded.

"And do you know why we do this?"

'Because Narissa told me to.'

"To...connect with the divine?" Narissa snapped her head around. They had not been over that in their lessons. Narissa looked shocked that Kiadora could have caught on. Kiadora was grateful for her talks with Regelend.

"Yes, and the consort spirits that are manifestations of the life force we call Eatheria. Sometimes students will eventually see water forms or fire forms. It is the start of seeing what element they consort with primarily, and that is usually helpful in the next level of training. But no one has ever identified with a humanoid animal as a consort."

"Especially not one as repulsive as that," Narissa cut in.

"Sometimes an animal appears in a deeper, advanced meditation as a spirit guide of knowledge, but never as a consort. They are the Ashilek."

"A rat, where would that even..." Narissa muttered off to the side. She stopped, giving a sharp look to Kiadora. Eledina regarded all of this, her expression attentive, as if she were watching a pleasant musical.

"You still have that notion in your head?" Narissa snapped. Kiadora felt a small smile creep onto her lips. It was all for material benefit, selfish gain. Kiadora believed it, and Narissa knew.

"What notion?" Eledina asked. Narissa remained staring at Kiadora and then her gaze shifted. She looked at Eledina and stepped forward.

"The notion that small animals represent the Earth element. I keep trying to tell her that animals are a completely different energy set, but she still holds on." Kiadora merely regarded Narissa. Narissa looked back with a dangerous glint in her eyes that suggested that if Kiadora spoke, she would not be walking for weeks. Kiadora had no intention of speaking. She knew what Narissa was doing.

Eledina nodded.

"Each path is different, we come to the elements in different ways. I think she is starting the Setting, but it takes a while. I'm glad you could come to the conclusion of what it was. Although I must say, I am shocked at you, Narissa. Usually you have so much more perplexing cases to come to me with." Narissa bowed in apology.

"I am sorry, Earia. It will not happen again. It was just something I had never seen at all, and I thought it might be a spirit guide taking a consort."

"Understood. That would be most unusual. I beg both of you have a good day." And with that, the woman closed her eyes and continued to sit in the same spot. Narissa went to pick up the torch and walked out, leaving Eledina in total darkness.

When they were down the corridor, our of earshot, Narissa spat, "I hope you enjoy your next lessons. I'm passing you on. You're lucky the Elders err on the side of naiveté at times and that Eledina doesn't have the Sight. I've done all I can do for you."

"Hopefully they will be better. I may actually learn something." The two women's eyes met in the dancing flame, which only heightened the hostile glares. Narissa looked ahead.

"They start tomorrow. Your teacher will be around to collect you in the morning, the poor soul."

And Kiadora followed Narissa out of the cavern. Both went in the opposite direction without looking at the other.

CHAPTER 13

"Hm. So she cut you loose."

"Yes. I'm glad of it. I hated the woman." Regelend nodded as the sounds of a turning page rent through Kiadora's sleeping quarters. He sat with his back to the door, and the curtain was pulled back just far enough to allow him enough light to view the pages of an ancient-looking book. He finished scanning the page, then looked up at her.

"Still, she's never passed anyone on out of anger. At least not that I'm aware of."

"Come on, she had to have," Kiadora shot back. "She's an impatient idiot, and the only crime I ever committed was trying to think about what she told me."

"There you have it right there. She hates being questioned. How much did you question her?"

"Not much."

"At every turn," Regelend corrected her, leaning against the dirt wall. "It's not difficult to figure out what kind of student you are," he added, grinning. " Narissa wouldn't like you at all."

"How do you know so much about what she is like, anyway? I thought you said you never had her. Did one of your friends have her?" Regelend looked at her, a shadow passing over his expression.

"I knew her from the surface," he said. "We came from the same area, and she got herself into a situation where she was about to be burned to death. I kidnapped her at the last minute. Well, tried to." Kiadora gasped.

"For what?"

"What do you think? She hates subtly and was recognized for what she was. I had heard because my family was expected to go to her execution. Sort of a night out for entertainment." Regelend looked down to the side as he talked, his expression an outline of disgust against the light pouring in from the doorway.

"I remember so well what my father said when we got summons from the town crier. He smiled and said, 'Oh, good, I haven't seen a roast in ages.' It was like watching a child get exited for a festival. I was on the verge of telling them I did not want to go, and I would have, but I was immediately directed to get my traveling cloak. There was no room for negotiation, and as I went into my room, I figured it would look strange to refuse. When I came back, my father looked even more cheerful. He had that same expression he wore when we went out hunting as a means of bonding. His look sickened me so much, and as we rode over, I pictured it being multiplied by the hundreds in the crowd. I figured if I could find a way to get the person out of this, I would.

"As soon as we arrived, I muttered something about needing the outhouse and left to find this girl. They would, of course, be parading her from the courthouse, so I immediately went there. But it was no good, because that area was swarming with villagers with the same gleeful stare as my father, just as I predicted. Before I could even form a plan, the doors swung open, and out came Narissa with a chained metal collar on her neck with two men holding her at each side. They had bound her arms and held the chains tight. I didn't know what to do, so I just followed.

"They led her down the street to jeers. People threw apple cores and small pieces of wood and stones. All Narissa did was stare forward, her face set in an expression of utmost rage. As I followed, I could see tears fall from her eyes. But she let out no sound as she was cut and bruised by the objects thrown. At last, they rounded a corner and went down a side alley. Yes, I figured, now was my chance. I was stupid, I know." He defended himself to Kiadora's raised eyebrow.

"But I followed them in," he laughed slightly. "I didn't even have a weapon. What was I going to do, attack them with my amazing water powers? Get them damp? Sure enough, as soon as I got into the alley, two other guards rushed up from where I don't know and seized me. They knew I was headed for Narissa. I assume that is a common trap to weed out people who are working with the prisoners or even feel sympathy. I'm sure if I had paid more attention to the politics of the city when I lived at home I would have known that. I'm sure Narissa knew it as well, because when I was captured, she looked back at me with anger and a tinge of distain." Kiadora nodded knowingly. It was probably more than a tinge.

"They grabbed me without so much as a word. We all knew my

crimes. The next thing I knew, my hands were being chained behind my back. Still all the while, Narissa stared at me with that look of anger, her jaw clenched tight. We moved down the alley, as if I had been there since the courthouse. But as we reached the end of the alley, one of Narissa's captors dropped. He had an arrow sticking out of his back. Lightning fast, Narissa took the opportunity to down her other captor with a kick to the breastplate.

"Before I could even think about what to do, one of my captors has a knife to my throat. I still have the scar of where he cut just a bit too deep." With that, Regelend pulled the collar of his shirt away from his neck. Sure enough, right in the middle of his neck was a thin, red scar. Any deeper down, and he would not be sitting here on her bed. Best case scenario, he would be permanently mute.

"Anyway," said Regelend, as he pulled up his shirt collar quickly, "the guard yelled out that if there was one more shot, he would slit my throat instantly. Our city cops never were the best of the best. The next shot downed that man instantly, and the other downed the remaining man who tried to run. Out of a door next to us, three women and a man rushed out and informed us that we were coming with them. I was about to gladly follow, but Narissa stayed back and protested that we didn't know who they were and could not trust them. The only thing we knew was that they were excellent assassins." Regelend shook his head with a sad smile.

"That woman. As far as I was concerned, they had just saved our necks. They could have trapped me for the sole purpose of illegal merchandise trade, and I would have worked for them. Narissa was immediately knocked unconscious and dragged along." Kiadora smiled at the priceless image of Narissa being smacked on the head.

"Apparently, they knew all of the best secluded alleyways of the city and had studied maps of what streets would be deserted. We ran through a few stores and right out the back door, the storekeepers just barely glancing at us, pretending not to notice. A few winked. It was certainly a side of the city I had never seen before, but I knew none of them would show public support, only act as an escape route. It was slowgoing, dragging Narissa along, but eventually we left the city limits and went out into the underbrush of the country.

"As we traveled, Narissa came to, and they explained who they were, how they knew of us and where we were headed, although no specific location, of course, just in case. But we knew they were a society of people like us. They are part of a group down here the makes it a priority to hunt down people like us and gather us. And now Narissa's is on the committee."

"So," said Regelend, "this is how I know her. We traveled weeks together. She was extremely silent and was suspicious of who we traveled with until they brought her down, and she saw for herself what it was all about. I tried to get to know her, ask who she was, who her family was, where she came from, how she knew what she was, but she usually just glared at me. Only once did she reply to say, 'You should have known that was a trap, you idiot.' She then went back to staring at the sky, which is what she did most of the time.

"So I knew she was stern, I knew she was blunt, and from the way she yelled at the society members when we first met, I knew she had a temper. But I never knew she would throw off one of her own students. I thought she had more self-control than that. From what I had seen on the trip, although angry, she seemed relatively self-contained when necessary."

"So is that why you are looking through a book of the society's bylaws?" Kiadora asked. Regelend had left when she had first told him what had happened and had returned a few moments later with this tome.

"Yes, I thought I heard something about it in passing. Arn, one of the people I study the comparative texts with, was worried that his teacher would get rid of him against his will, and a Master was sitting in the room at the time. He informed Arn that he didn't need to worry because his teacher was undoubtedly aware that if she did anything of the sort, she would be exiled from the society." Regelend continued to page through the book, flipping between the index at the back and several other pages. Kiadora didn't know whether to grin or feel ashamed. Narissa had hated her so much she had risked exile.

"Ah, here it is. Yes, the Master was right. It's here as plain as day. 'Any teacher who knowingly passes on a student before they are ready to progress faces exile from the society. Upon exile, the teacher in question must undergo a vow of secrecy for the society upon penalty of death. If such a vow is refused, execution is instantaneous.' Huh. They're really not messing around."

"Well, nice to know Narissa just hated me that much," Kiadora said. Then all of Narissa's fits of rage sprang into her mind, particularly the one about feeling trapped. Kiadora looked over sharply at Regelend.

"You don't think she's trying to get herself exiled, do you?"

"No, that's stupid," said Regelend bluntly. "Why get yourself exiled? You're free to leave when you want, if she hates it that much. Of course, no one ever does, because where would we possibly go?"

"I don't know, you could take up your old life. That's how I got here and heard about this place. My housekeeper, Lisera, was once down here and left. Picked up life again as a housekeeper."

"Alright, so it can happen, but it's not common. In all the years I've spent down here, I haven't known a single person to leave." Kiadora slumped down slightly, playing with the edge of her frayed dress.

"Yeah, I guess, but she might want to leave and is just nervous about doing it. Maybe she's subconsciously trying to get herself kicked out." Regelend only looked at her with a puzzled expression.

"No, maybe not," Kiadora corrected herself. "I'm just thinking out loud. She hates the surface world more than anything. But I got the impression she liked going up to the surface to spy, the little we talked about it." Regelend nodded.

"Yes, I can see why she would. But your idea that she is trying to get herself kicked out might not be so far from the truth. Matrinas of Air usually have a hard time living down here, for obvious reasons. Narissa is even worse than most."

"And she mentioned that she is looking for pockets where the ideas of us have changed. But she says she has not found anything, so why make such a bold move? She has everything to lose by doing this to me. Surely they'll know at the next level that I should not have progressed. The only thing I learned from that last little session is that these practices seem to be based more on greed." Regelend closed the book and looked up at her, his brow knit the way it so often was.

"I don't think that was the lesson you were supposed to learn."

"I know, but I can't help it. All of this is so demented." Kiadora stared into Regelend's eyes stubbornly. He only stared back at her for a few moments, and then,

"I think I know why she let you pass on."

"Oh, you do?" Kiadora shot.

"It's your attitude," he said simply and shortly. "You flatter yourself to think that Narissa is either self-destructive or just crazy to take such a risk on your behalf. It is all where your mind is; you are just going to keep seeing what you want to, and Narissa probably knows that she can drill you all she wants, but you will never grasp it the way you are supposed to."

"It still sounds like she just pushed me off onto someone else," Kiadora interrupted.

"No, that's just it. Experiences at the entry-level only go so far. I know, I was there for a long time. I had a teacher who believed she could drill certain thoughts and behaviors out of me. Of course it never worked. Only until you experience things in greater depth will you understand. No, she passed you on when you were ready."

Kiadora sat and dug her toe into the dirt next to her bed. She rested her hand on her chin and stared at the far wall.

"I don't feel like I'm progressing in any of this. And what about you, you don't accept any of this. What level are you?"

"I'm still a Setrina. I work with all the elements. It's been years, but I stay down because I want to; I don't want to progress to higher levels."

"That's dumb, why not?" Regelend didn't say anything, he only stared toward the opposite wall. Then he turned his dark eyes back to her.

"At the top, they sit and plumb what they call 'the Great Mysteries,' which is their notion of the divine. I don't want to do that, I like my notion just fine. You don't even have a notion, so they figure there is hope to mold and refine you. You'll move further than I ever will. You might not do it in the way they planned, but you'll move." There was something in his eyes. Kiadora looked closer. Sadness...fear?

"Regelend," she chided. "You still believe that all of this is grievous sin, don't you?"

"I'm not comfortable with it, but it is what it is. I hope my God can forgive me." Kiadora only shook her head at him, speechless.

"Regelend, you can't..."

"No, it's something I need to deal with. And perhaps one day I will get over it. Anyway, I should let you get some sleep. Your fire lessons start tomorrow, I assume?"

"How did you know?"

"Because, that is where they always pass the strongheaded types off to first," he said. He turned around with a small grin, which moved out of view as he descended the ladder.

CHAPTER 14

The next morning Kiadora sat at the bottom of the ladder, playing with a smooth stone she found on the ground. As she turned it around in her hand, it left small smudges of dirt on top of the pre-existing smudges. Kiadora tried to keep clean, but there were days when she figured it hardly mattered anymore. She looked up when she heard footsteps muffled by a loud jangling coming from far off. She dropped the stone instantly and stood up, eyes widening slightly.

The woman who waltzed toward her had several skirts on, all of varying bright colors, close to what Wyland had worn when Kiadora had first arrived. But this woman took it a step further with several strings of bells tied around her. They gleamed silver in the light of the chandelier above, rings of them in an orbit around her hips. Kiadora thought she could also distantly see a thick, gold bracelet of bells. And a smaller one around the ankle. The woman positively jangled as if for the purpose of announcing her presence wherever she went. And she walked in such a manner as to announce her presence even more: hips swung, wide strides, arms swung as well. She strutted as if she was making her way across a stage.

But most striking was the bright red shirt, if it could even be called a shirt. It resembled an undergarment: sleeveless, low-cut, clingy. Kiadora could only imagine the outcry it would cause if this woman were stupid enough to appear on the surface in such a thing.

Kiadora looked at the woman's face as she drew closer still. A large smile with larger teeth shone at her between curtains of curly blond hair. The woman finally reached Kiadora, who simply stared, forgetting to greet her. But there was no need, the other woman immediately dropped into a deep curtsy, her many skirts just about brushing the ground. She bent forward, the whole movement swift and like it was out of a dance. But it belonged on a stage, not as a greeting. Kiadora didn't know how to react and settled for nodding her head curtly as the woman came back up.

"I am Sheirkia." Kiadora smiled woodenly.

"Kiadora," she answered shortly.

"Oh, I know, dear, I know." Every word came out with a little too much emphasis. Was it possible to overact your own day-to-day life? "Today you will start your fire lessons." The woman positively beamed. Kiadora still wore her dead smile. At least it looked as though this woman was not the hitting type.

"Follow me," Sheirkia instructed cheerfully and turned on the spot with flair. It was practically a pirouette. As soon as the woman had her back to Kiadora, Kiadora allowed herself a slight smirk.

Kiadora followed in the wake of loud ringing and the bouncing blend of curls ahead of her. She expected to go into the rooms and to this woman's office, but the woman kept on the outskirts of the classrooms. The jangling increased as they made their way into a small passage between two jagged stones. Kiadora's entire head seemed to be filled with the noise, forcing out all else. It was a definite change to the odd silence that usually filled the place. At last they reached a cavern opening similar to the cavern Narissa and Kiadora had entered to meet Eledina, but it lacked a door guard.

Inside to the right was the large furnace Kiadora saw earlier rumbling as it worked, the pipes still rising up. Kiadora could smell the distinct scent of sweat as she watched a man feed logs into the door of the furnace. The crackling of the logs momentarily matched the jingling of the bells that Sheirkia wore. The jangling grew louder as they walked into another corridor past the furnace. This corridor was warm, unlike the ones that surrounded the Elders.

Kiadora quickly realized why as they came into a large room that had a colossal, roaring bonfire in the center of it. Several people sat around the edge, staring into it. Kiadora regarded them with raised eyebrows. It couldn't be that interesting. A man came in from a side corridor with a log, threw the log in and went back out. The flame rose slightly higher as the log hit with a sharp crack. One of the people around the fire, a dark-haired woman, gasped slightly. Kiadora's shoulders sagged. She would need to do this as well.

"This is called the Eternal Fires," said Sheirkia with a drawn-out emphasis on the last two words. Kiadora felt like she was supposed to make some sort of noise that resembled an impressed audience. She settled for a demure gaze at her new teacher. It did nothing to dampen the other woman's enthusiasm.

"As you can gather, it is never allowed to go out. To do so would be something akin to the destruction of us all," she finished in a fatalistic voice.

"They couldn't just...light it back up?"

"No, no, it's not that simple. This fire represents the eternal energy of the afterlife, the eternal life force, the energy that makes us, us." Kiadora squinted at it. Just above the flames she could see the small, red particles that darted in and out of the flames. If she had not been paying attention, they would have just looked like an overabundance of embers. Aside from those, it didn't look any different than any other fire that she had seen, just bigger, and as a result, warmer. Kiadora was beginning to sweat slightly.

"Ok, I understand what is represents, but how does that make it different physically or bring doom on us all?" Sheirkia looked at her with a somber expression, but there was no annoyance there as Kiadora was so used to. She seemed to like questions; it allowed her to play up the conversation.

"To build it up this large, we had to start with two twigs for four months, the number of the elements, of course."

Of course.

"Then, 365 days are in the year, one log on each of those days. You can imagine how long it took for us to build it up to this size and scale. Because it is used as a focus for meditation, it cannot be built too fast. For our fire scryers to work with it properly, we must build it slowly or it will be too overwhelming for their souls."

"Um, alright." Kiadora wanted to douse it with a few buckets of water already.

"Once we tried to build it up directly, but all the scryers ended up going insane." Kiadora searched around for a snappy answer, but this woman seemed impervious to such things, so it seemed futile.

"So why are we here if it will take so long to master scrying on such a scope?"

"I," Sheirkia said, every ounce of self-importance she possessed oozing from each single letter as she placed a hand on her chest, "happen to be a master scryer. I will teach you how to handle it. But make no mistake, it should not be undertaken without guidance. I start off by showing the Eternal Fires to all my students first. It will be a while before we start our scrying, but it will be an integral part of this stage of your studies. It is what we will aspire to do, to experience the Great Mysteries in their depth. Thus I should show you now, is it not wonderful?"

"Yes, sure." Kiadora could not douse a beaming grin like that.

"Now that you have seen, we will go to where the rest of your rituals, or lessons, will take place."

"Are these going to be anything like the group rituals that they do once a week?" The inside of her dress would say scarf-free.

"Smaller scale, more personal." It was the first time Sheirkia seemed terse; she obviously wanted bigger productions. They continued around the fire, passing a young man who was humming directly into the flame. He leaned in so close, Kiadora wanted to pull him back before he fell in. They passed the man as he still sat balancing precariously just before the flames. Another walk down a corridor and a short turn to the left brought them into a small cavern.

The whole area was illuminated by a copious amount of candles, all varying heights, most with a wide width. It seemed a bit less practical than the torches on the wall that Kiadora usually saw. They all sat around the edge of the room on pillars in groups of three, all different colors. In the middle of the room was a round, deep purple rug, sitting just inside the circle of candles. On the far side of the rug was a closed cabinet that hung from the ceiling on a chain. Kiadora had to admit that the setup seemed surprisingly simple for this woman. As they walked over to stand on the rug, Kiadora saw several large, sealed jars on top of the cabinet.

"I know you are a probably wondering what I keep hidden away," said Sheirkia from behind her with a mysterious tone.

"Yes, I was a little curious."

"What is kept in here," said Sheirkia, walking over to one of the jars, caressing one with a finger, "are your items of power." Kiadora stared for a moment, waiting for an explanation. None came.

"So…there is a crossbow in there?" Sheirkia chuckled. She had apparently been waiting for an answer as ignorant as this.

"You misunderstand the notion of power. I feel truly sorry for you, but you will learn." Her finger still played with the lid of the jar. "You understand power in the terms of domination and manipulation, and this is interpreted in many ways as killing. But that is not the way in which you will come to see power. You will come to know it on a deep, spiritual level. It is far above the ability to kill on a physical level."

At that moment Sheirkia reached down into the jar and pulled up what appeared to be a human skull.

"What is it you think of when you look at this?" Sheirkia asked.

"Death," Kiadora said instantly. Sheirkia nodded.

"And what do you think of when you think of death?" Kiadora paused for a moment. She never really thought about death. That was always something that happened to other people. She almost said 'human skulls.' As fun as it would be to loop the conversation and frustrate this woman, Kiadora mostly just wanted the woman to put that thing away.

As Kiadora thought, she remembered she had gone to a funeral once for a cousin, the daughter of a distant uncle. And then there was the passing of the High King when she was four. That she hardly remembered. Plus that stillborn a few years ago in the family. Her mother had been devastated and had prayed in the chapel for months because she thought she had been taken over by a Shiekita. The doctor had told her that these things sometimes just happen. The Priest had blessed her and sent her on her way.

Kiadora had felt indifferent. It was not like she knew the child, and besides, "Is it possible to die if you have never been born?" Kiadora wondered out loud, against her will.

She looked up, and Sheirkia was looking at her with wide smile. She leaned forward.

"What was that, I didn't quite catch it?"

"Oh, um. Coffins, burial."

"Yes, but before that, you said something. It appeared that you were wondering something?" What was the use to lie? "I had a stillborn brother." She had intended to inject some feeling in her voice, but none came. "I was wondering if it was possible to die without ever having been born. If a life never starts, how can it be lost? But we're off topic."

"No, no, we're right where we need to be." Sheirkia cradled the skull in both hands, then put it down on the lid of a jar as one might place a stage prop.

"I can tell death is not personal to you," Sheirkia went on. "You wonder at it the way you would an interesting philosophical puzzle. Nor are you close enough to your family to be affected by such traumatic events." Sheirkia looked at Kiadora and put her hand to her face, tapping her chin. Leave it to this woman to make a production of the thinking process.

"This is good," Sheirkia muttered. "This is good…" Kiadora stood and looked at her for a moment. Sheirkia still was looking down at the ground, but her eyes were not narrowed in the way they were a moment ago when she was deep in thought. Apparently she was just pausing for dramatic effect. She looked back up at Kiadora and smiled.

"Well?" Kiadora snapped.

"*Well*," said Sheirkia with emphasis. "You will do wonders in ritual."

"Because I don't know about death."

"Precisely. You are an empty vessel. I think that ends our session for today. I want you to be back here right as they shut off the main lighting tomorrow evening." With that, Sheirkia stood up, her skirts dropping around her ankles in an inward sweeping motion, as if they were trying to gather all the dust they could. The silkiness of the material allowed all the dust to settle back to the ground.

Kiadora turned and made her way to the door, which Sheirkia held open. Kiadora nodded shortly to her as she made her way out.

"Just be thinking of death and practice meditation," called Sheirkia. Kiadora looked back, her heart skipping a beat. Sheirkia just smiled, pulling the door shut as she turned back into the room in that sort of pirouette.

Kiadora just looked off to the side. "What a horrible thing to say to someone," she muttered, before making her way through the corridor-like cavern, past the bonfire, past the furnace and out to meet a wooden divider. She looped her way back to her sleeping quarters and was almost to the ladder. She looked up and saw Regelend descending. As he hit the floor he turned and walked toward the classrooms, not even noticing Kiadora.

As he turned, she saw half of his face. He had a stupid grin. What in the Otherworld? Regelend never smiled like that. He walked slowly, and she realized there was a slight sweat on his brow.

Oh. She could talk with him later.

She turned to go up the ladder and there was a small, brunette head peaking out in the distance, several rows above and two ladders to the left of her own quarters. She could dimly tell that the gaze was following Regelend since she faced out to where Regelend would now be making his way into the dividers.

Kiadora started to make her way up the ladder again, only to realize that it was Uranda. She had seen her with Regelend, and they had been holding hands. She must have been the girl Regelend mentioned as his love. Of course, Kiadora thought with a smile, swinging herself into her sleeping quarters.

Technically speaking, she had nothing to do that day and the next after she was done meditating, so she almost wanted to stay up late just because she had not been able to. Back at home, she remembered when she would stay up late hours, despite the insistence from Lisera to go to bed and the teasing from Dehlia that she had probably been up all night with those crazy people visions. She never had visions, but Dehlia always liked to take it further than what it was.

Throwing off her shoes, Kiadora felt a twinge of pain, the kind that was emotional, unsubstantial. She had not really thought about home too much since she had arrived. She realized, with a frown, that the people she once knew from above were the reason she was down here, sleeping like a mole. They refused to accept her, so she was down here. Kiadora felt a tear come to her eye and wiped it off with a grubby hand.

This would never do, to sit here in self-pity. It was better than up there, they did not try to chop off her head. But still, even now, Ashila's look of pity would be a welcome. It swam in front of Kiadora's mind as she heard the crunch of her straw mattress, Ashila's gray eyes full of that soft, dreamy look. It was the look you would reserve for a wayward puppy, but all the same.

And one damned retarded teacher after another. Hopefully this one would not smack her. But the pretension that washed over Kiadora felt worse than a physical blow could, in some ways. And through it all, she could not help but wonder what the conversation with Regelend would bring later.

CHAPTER 15

Around lunchtime the next day, Kiadora ambled down the ladder once more. She woke up at her usual time but had no desire to go out to face the public. Just the thought of being around people today was too much. She had drifted in and out of fragmented sleep, still staying in bed even when her heart rate was racing from being stagnant for too long. Or maybe it was the fact that she had a death ritual coming up. Whatever that would entail.

She made her way down to the library, which was where she usually went on her days off. Kiadora was supposed to meditate but didn't feel like it today. Yesterday's had brought visions of funerals. There was a hall designated for people honing this practice, with soft pillows and a lone guitarist playing, but Kiadora preferred the solitude.

As sure as there was dirt under her fingernails, there sat Regelend in back of a tome at a table facing the doorway. He was the only one there. Except he was not reading, but staring at the wall, eyes unfocused. The corners of his mouth twinged here and there.

Kiadora walked toward him, expecting him to look over. He never did. It was not until she sat down square in front of him, not even bothering to find a book to skim through like she usually did. She had exhausted all the ones with pictures, anyway.

Regelend jumped slightly as she sat down and looked over, eyes wide under the mop of uncombed hair. Strange, he usually was so well kept. He continued to stare for a moment and then said, "Hey, I was just…thinking about this book I'm reading."

"What's the title?" Kiadora asked.

"The," Regelend glanced to the side. "Art and science of…" Kiadora reached out at lightening speed. Grabbing the cover before Regelend could, she turned it over in her hands while snapping it shut.

"Wrong. *The Dissections of the Geo-Planes*, star pupil." Regelend looked down at the table, his face red.

"What's wrong?" Kiadora probed. Regelend glanced around. They were the only ones there still. He leaned in.

"Have you, have you…made on understanding of what goes on…"

"Cut it, I know what happened with you and Uranda last night. I saw her on my way in, there's no mistaking a look like that. Even I know it."

"Yes, well." Kiadora could hear Regelend's foot tapping under the table. The tapping stopped. "Hey, wait, how did you know…?"

"Oh, please, we have our trysting areas in our town. I've never used them myself, but I've overheard the whispers. I walked in on a room used for it when I was a kid. Dehlia thought it would be hilarious if she told me Ashila was waiting up there after shopping, taking a rest. Voyeurism was added to my list of insane qualities. Luckily, they still had most of their clothes on. Don't tell me the Northern regions are that sterile."

"The Church never searched?"

"Oh, they searched, but it sprung up again. We just didn't have public beheadings to tell us what was wrong with it, I imagine."

Regelend flinched. "We had prostitutes hanging from our city walls." And, time to return back to the subject at hand.

"So, the stare?"

"No, no, it's nothing…it's just…" Regelend turned his face down toward his book, as if making eye contact would turn him to stone. Kiadora waited.

"It's just…are you familiar with the Summer Solstice coming up?" Kiadora sneered.

"You know I haven't been to those stupid group things in a while." Regelend heaved a sigh. Kiadora had a momentary feeling of regret for not paying attention, just so Regelend wouldn't have to explain whatever he was about to.

"It's where they do the Great Union," Regelend said in a whisper.

"And they picked you? With Uranda?" Kiadora let out a hoot of laughter. "You guys are going to be show players for us! A show I'm sure everyone will enjoy."

"It's not funny," Regelend said, sitting back in his chair with a huff as he crossed his arms and looked off to the side. His face was still bright red. "It's humiliating, it's barbaric, and I'd just as soon go back up to where they can behead me."

"It's simple," Kiadora interjected. "Don't do it," she said slowly, with emphasis.

"It isn't that simple-"

"Oh, and why not? I don't attend group rituals. They don't do anything to me."

"It's one thing not to attend, another to not participate when they ask."

"They can't force you to. A ritual full of unwilling participants… that seems counterproductive."

"There are a couple things working against me. First of all, Uranda wants to. She thinks it's the highest honor. I tried to keep its silent. That's how they chose us. They always choose the newest couple to do it. It's supposed to denote vitality, good fortune, radiance and the resulting new possibilities, longest day of the year and all that. It's like their New Year's here." Regelend slapped himself on the forehead. "How could I have been so stupid to get involved with someone now? I knew that is how they choose, and it's so damn…oh, sorry…" Regelend blushed harder at letting out a curse. "It's so confined in here, these things get out. They told me I was to participate this morning already before I was awake, special messenger and every-thing."

At this he jumped up and began pacing. His speech was becoming more and more flurried. Kiadora stayed sitting, both hands resting on the edges of her chair, her shoulders arched up like a frightened bird, ready to launch.

"I mean, I can't just say no," Regelend said, looking at Kiadora in the eye as he went back and forth. He averted his gaze back to the dusty floor. "They keep us here for free, teach us, feed us, they saved my life, they give us shelter-"

"If you can call it that," Kiadora muttered. Regelend continued, not heeding Kiadora. "Yani said no two years ago, and he's been banned from lessons for a year, can't look at the books."

"Wait, they can do that?"

"Oh, sure. There's a barrier they set up using Eatheria that bars his exact mental makeup. It's highly technical, only one person down here can do it, but it essentially is set up to rob him of mental functioning. Shutting down someone's ability to learn is the worst punishment they can imagine, so they do it. That's an area that if someone refuses, they know that the person is not properly dedicated to their studies and the overall gift. That sort of laziness degrades the community over time."

Kiadora swallowed and stared at the floor, her shoulders still arched.

"I don't do any of the nonsense they make me do. They wouldn't do that to me?" Kiadora wondered if she would enjoy not going to her studies, but to never look at the books, to never at least feel like she could escape from her own mind once in a while, to...

"What did he do all that time anyway?"

"They had him under lockdown. He stayed in his sleeping quarters, except for meals, for a year. Then last year he had to participate in the ritual. He was so bored, he was glad to at least be able to do something. That is how they foster a love for this stuff. They ask that you at least try, but if someone does not even try in their studies and cannot be bothered enough to help others in group ritual, that is what they do." Regelend's expression darkened again. "So I have to do this."

"So how did they even find out about you?"

"Uranda told one of her friends, who is also a Master," he said with a sigh. "I should have known she secretly wanted to be in this thing."

Regelend's pacing had slowed down and now he walked over to a book that was on the ground. He gave it an angry kick, and it went sailing to the wall with a loud thud. Kiadora flinched a little at the sudden outburst.

"This is why they tell us to wait back home!" said Regelend. "What, I come down here, and I think everything they told me was for no good reason? Of course it was! They're robbing me of what I know to be right, what I know to be true."

Kiadora felt an involuntary twinge of a smile. She was remembering back to Dehlia's bragging about her exploits with several men. *He doesn't know, he thinks he's found true love. He doesn't know how we work.* It was always the naive ones she targeted.

"What?"

"You don't think this is happening because…you're a tad bit inexperienced?" Kiadora tried to add a non-threatening smile to the mix, but she had a feeling it came out as more of a grimace. Regelend merely frowned at her.

"I knew I shouldn't have brought this up to you, that you'd never understand. You're worse than the rest of them, everything is a joke to you, Kiadora." He rushed around the table, headed across the library and hit the edge of a table with his thigh on the way out. He staggered for a moment, kept walking and wrenched the door open as soon as he reached it.

Kiadora sat watching him over her shoulder. Before he left the room, he looked back at her, poised in the frame of the doorway. She kept looking at him, waiting for him to speak. He only kept staring. At last, he opened his mouth.

"You need to get some direction, some purpose in your life," he spat. He slammed the door, and Kiadora twisted around to sit and face the table once more. She hadn't even been trying to make a joke. And direction, like these people had it, sitting staring at fires, the bastards.

Kiadora rested her chin on her hand and began flipping through Regelend's forgotten book, reading nothing in particular. What a boring day, anyway. Usually she was in class at this time, but today she had to wait until night. Maybe she should go practice meditation, since everyone was so hot about it.

Her mind drifted immediately to the soft music and people sitting on pillows. Some started to mumble. She wasn't in the mood to be around other people anyway. Plus this book Regelend left was worthless, whatever it was about.

She jumped up and went down the hallways, back to her sleeping quarters. She flung herself back down on the mattress that she had just gotten up from not too long ago. She thought briefly about how nice it would be to never have to rise from it again. She turned over and stared at the dirt floor. No, she would not permit herself to go down that route. She'd have plenty of time to lie in the dust unmoving as it was.

Kiadora laughed bitterly. Sheirkia wanted her think about death. Somehow, this probably wasn't what her teacher had in mind. It had been so long since she had actually reached that point of nothingness in her meditation. She should practice, but she really didn't want to…she had no use for it….

CHAPTER 16

"Kiadora, Kiadora!"

Kiadora rolled over to see dull light flowing into her sleeping quarters. The expansive curls of Sheirkia were framed in the doorway, letting out a yellow sheen at the edges. Almost gold but too dull. Kiadora found herself sitting up.

"You were to be at ritual half an hour ago! Come on, you won't want to miss this." Rather than angry, Sheirkia sounded excited. Kiadora sat up and stretched her back out, then followed Sheirkia down the ladder, around the dividers and through the caverns.

As they walked, Kiadora couldn't help but notice that lack of wild and varied colors that usually undulated in front of her. Sheirkia's dress was now as black as these caverns could get. As they walked in between the torches and Sherikia pashed a shadow, she seemed to take on the appearance of a mass of floating blond curls. The top of her dress was high-cut, and the neckline looked as though it were about to engulf her chin. The skirt billowed out and still managed to rustle wildly. She had only seen the outfit on one type of person.

"Were did you get mourning garments?" Kiadora asked. These were actually regulated the by local government. It was thought that anyone who wore them for other reasons than mourning could attract the afflicted spirits of the dead. They could only be worn in sanctified, holy buildings. It had become a trend for a time for young girls to wear them, either as rebellion or the excitement of having a ghost trail them around.

Dehlia was nearly beaten and kicked out of the house when she came down to dinner in hers one day. During a morbid, melodramatic phase she had been perusing the local death registry and noticed some of the young boys who had died in a barn fire looked cute. Kiadora didn't believe the dresses would attract spirits, but all the same.

Sheirkia held out a pale hand, which looked equally ethereal. "We will only talk about ritual. You must prepare yourself." They were now to the entrance of the cavern, which had a black cloth over the doorway. She saw the head of curls bend down over the slightly darker outline of the billowing dress.

Sheirkia turned suddenly, and Kiadora felt a flood of cold wash over her. She let out a scream. After wiping her eyes, she saw Sheirkia holding a cup that was dripping with water. Kiadora expected her to yell out, "ah, got you," but instead she had the solemn look of someone attending a funeral. Her eyes were down-turned slightly, and she wore a frown.

"What was that for?"

"You'll need to keep your voice down, think of this as you would a funeral. You have attended a funeral, correct?"

"Yes, of course I have." It was for a distant cousin that died young of a wasting illness that the doctors had been unable to identify. First it was her mobility to go, then her mind. The Church had said it was a Shiekita robbing her soul one piece at a time.

Kiadora had spoken to Dr. Iland at the funeral. In muttered tones he has said it was most likely a degenerative birth defect, but he wasn't supposed to think that. It was how she had known to go to that certain doctor for her little problem, how she knew he thought differently and openly. She had looked over and seen a certain gleam of amusement in his eye when the eulogy was given and they spoke about a Shiekita robbing the girl's soul.

Her thoughts were interrupted by Sheirkia pulling back the black curtain to walk though a passageway with a second black curtain at the end. Kiadora followed. Sheirkia went to the edge of the corridor and rummaged around in a large wooden box that was standing there. She pulled out a high-cut, black satin dress that rustled in the dark. Part of it darkly glimmered in the torchlight, the rest forming a sort of blacker state of space in the corridor.

"I need you to put this on," Sheirkia said, turning to Kiadora and holding out the dress. Kiadora's hair was still dripping, and she was ringing it out onto the dirt floor.

"You never answered my question about the water." Droplets splashed down as she pulled.

"Coldness," she said simply, "Now please, the dress. Let me know when you are finished," said Sheirkia, whisking over to the second doorway. "And don't forget to secure the veil tightly," she said over her shoulder as she disappeared behind the dark curtain with practically a skip.

Veil?

Kiadora held up the dress, black and plain as ever, cut up to the neck with long sleeves. The only decoration was some black lace trimming at the top of the dress, right at the neckline. And on top of the wire hanger was a veil with a piece that was meant to be secured into the hair. Kiadora sighed and started to take off her now raggedy dress. She wondered how long she would stay in it before it became complete threads. It was a part of home, after all.

After her dress was off, her skin feeling the worse for absorbing the chilly, damp cavern air, she pulled on the silk dress. The refined smoothness felt good after worn-out cotton. With the dress now around her waist, she jammed her arms into the two sleeves and brought the high neckline almost up to her chin. Although it figured, the lace was cheap and coarse. As she brought the zipper halfway up her back and pulled the rest up with an awkward arm over the shoulder, the cheap lace dug into her neck with a harsh intensity. It felt like she was being stabbed in the neck.

Kiadora looked down at her body, the dress rustling around her as she stood. She looked back over at the wire hanger she had placed on the box and at the veil. She picked the veil off the hanger and looked at it. She had always been terrible at figuring out how to do her hair; Lisera had always been there to do that.

The hair piece the veil was attached to was basically a felt loop with a comb clasp over the loop. So, she figured, you put your hair though here?

She put the piece on top of the wood chest and pulled her hair into the simplest of ponytails. She had always managed to be able do that much. She forced her hair through the loop, and the comb neatly dug into her hair at the base of the ponytail. The veil simply hung over the back of her head. Kiadora wished she had a mirror; she must have looked like the bride of an undertaker.

Kiadora turned and called out the Sheirkia, "finished!"

In an instant, Sheirkia swooped out of the curtain. She smiled solemnly, although Kiadora got the feeling from Sheirkia's excited gleam in her eye that she wanted to clasp her hands together and squeal. Instead, she merely instructed Kiadora to flip the veil over her face, which Kiadora did.

The dark passage went ever darker with a distinct sheen coming off from the torch to the right. Sheirkia faded into nothing more than a dull outline. Kiadora saw the darker area where the curtain would be hanging sweep aside and enough light came through for Kiadora to make out Sheirkia's figure again as she stepped aside to usher Kiadora into the chamber.

As Kiadora walked in, there was enough light to see plainly through the veil. Large, black pillar candles outlined the wall, half melted and leaning. The majority of the room was encapsulated in a smaller circle of candles, slightly smaller pillar candles on the floor. The circle of candles was not perfect; the candles were placed deliberately in a sort of zigzag pattern. They were placed far enough apart were Kiadora could walk into the circle and not catch her expansive dress on fire.

She glanced around, quietly counting the number of candles. Knowing Sheirkia... yes, there were 13 candles. Lighting this exact amount was sure to bring doom to everyone, they said. Kiadora heard

Sheirkia rustle in behind her. Kiadora turned to look at her.

Sheirkia did not wear a veil, only putting her hair in an intricate updo with strands of hair flying everywhere from the back. Kiadora grinned at her.

"13, huh? Plus you put me in a funeral dress. I guess this is our bad luck for the decade?"

"Ah, but down here, 13 means luck," said Sheirkia, brushing past her into the center of the circle.

"Of course," Kiadora muttered, regarding what was actually at the center of the chamber for the first time.

As she walked forward, the first thing that hit her was the vile smell of rot. She looked down at some bowls placed on the floor in a zigzag pattern forming a circle, and there was an assortment of blackened fruits and vegetables in the bowls, eroding away to their heart's content. It was a subtle smell; Kiadora hoped she would get used to it.

Kiadora looked up and there was a funeral pyre. A raised wooden platform was surrounded by sticks of kindling. Kiadora knew right away she was to lie on it.

"I know I'm a bad student, but this is a little harsh, isn't it?" Kiadora said, flashing a grin. Not that Sheirkia could see it through the veil.

"You know I'm not going to light it, come, come," said Sheirkia in a soft tone, almost a whisper usually reserved for speaking around the dead. "This is much deeper than the consumption of the flesh."

Kiadora walked forward and recoiled as she felt something snap on the ground, and a sharp object pocked at her foot. She looked down, her gaze falling directly below the veil, to where her foot was resting on a bone. Next to that were a few smaller bones and several winter twigs. A dark substance glimmered next to that on top of the dirt. She stared at it a little more intensely.

"Blood, Sheirkia?" Kiadora nearly shrieked. "Isn't that a little much?"

"Please, keep your voice down," Sheirkia urged. "It's to call the energies of the end times."

"Yeah, ok. It's not people blood, is it?"

"It's from a chicken slaughtered for a meal," Sheirkia hissed, now her annoyance starting to show through. "Now please lie down." Kiadora jumped over to the pyre, stepping in between the debris on the floor. She threw herself onto the hard wooden surface, a welcome to her back after months on a lumpy straw mattress. 'Maybe I'll just ask to sleep on one of these,' Kiadora joked to herself.

Kiadora looked up at the dark ceiling of the cavern, the light around her shining up in a ring, as if it was tunnel that led to nowhere.

"I once heard," Kiadora said, "that the sky can be the limit to my dreams. What happens when you live underground like this all the time and you really no longer have a sky? Does the ground become my new sky? Is the limit to my dreams nothing but ground level now?"

Kiadora was amazed at herself; she never spoke this much, esp-ecially when in session when all she wanted to do was get out. She felt like giggling, sprawled here on a funeral pyre surrounded by chicken bones. She chuckled slightly, then looked over at Sheirkia, who was standing there regarding her with the same stoic gaze of someone watching the dead be buried. She was waiting for Kiadora to finish, not looking in the least bit surprised that someone would behave this way.

Kiadora looked at her, and Sheirkia just looked back. Kiadora's face fell, and she just turned her head to the underside of the earth again, her eternal sky. At last Sheirkia spoke.

"Have you figured out the purpose of this ritual?" Sheirkia asked in that same quiet tone, although somehow her voice had become more expansive, her speech slower, as if years of tradition and people saying these exact words echoed through her vocal cords alone and she needed to take the time to reflect that.

Kiadora stared out at the dark expanse. "To... make me think about death?" she said, taking a stab at an answer. "Oh, to remind me that we're all mortal." That sounded high-end and impressive.

"No. You are about to be introduced to rituals that the followers of Eatheria practice. You will be changed, transformed into a new person. For that to happen, we will symbolize the death of the old self." Kiadora shifted uncomfortably. Her current self was fine, thank you.

Kiadora saw a silvery flash in the edge of her vision...was that?

"Wh- What are you doing with that thing?" Kiadora had sat bolt upright, throwing her legs off of the edge of the pyre. Sticks went flying everywhere.

Sheirkia was holding a double-sided knife in her right hand, its sleek blade glinting in the light of the candles. By the break in the sheen, Kiadora could tell it had been sharpened.

"It is an integral part of the ceremony," said Sheirkia, still in a whisper, waving the blade with flair. "I must made a small incision-"

Kiadora recoiled, putting an arm up in front of her chest at a 90 degree bend, as if she would need to knock Sheirkia flat at any moment. Her other hand leapt to her chest where the burn scar still resided.

"It's not more than a pinprick, just a way to draw the energies-" Sheirkia's voice was pleading now. Gone was the scripted quality.

"And what if I refuse, what then?" Kiadora was now shouting. Sheirkia winced, clearly upset that all of this was disrupting the mood.

But then her face fell, and she glared at Kiadora through the veil.

"You do not have to if you do not wish to," she said, now in her quiet tone, trying to do what she could to keep the faux funeral setting at its best dignity. "But are you aware of the penalty for not participating in ritual?" It was not a threat. It was an honest question. Kiadora nodded, staring at Sheirkia for a moment, weighing the two options of being locked in eternal boredom, worse than she already felt, and pointless pageantry.

She extended her arm out to Sheirkia. "Do what you have to," Kiadora spat. Sheirkia nodded, her facial expression returning instantly to a solemn one. Kiadora expected Sheirkia to slash her palm with the thing, or at last jab her finger, but she turned the handle of the blade to Kiadora and laid it in her hand. She felt her arm sag with the unexpected weight of the thing.

Kiadora bent her fingers around the black handle, which had a silver skull at the bottom. Sheirkia looked her square in the eye.

"Plunge the blade into your chest."

Kiadora grimaced with incredulous defense.

"Only enough to draw a drop of blood. The blade itself has been well sterilized, as was the fabric you are wearing. As you do so, I want

207

you to imagine a dull gray light exiting the wound." Kiadora looked at Sheirkia for a moment, then down at the glinting blade. It was this or entrapment. But there was one problem.

"My veil drops to the floor, am I supposed to plunge through it?" She was stalling now.

"Throw it over your shoulder while keeping your face hidden," said Sheirkia with that quiet patience. Kiadora did so, the mesh pressing against her face oppressively. She glanced at Sheirkia once more, hoping her hatred would show through. She looked down at the dagger.

"When you say 'plunge…'"

"Or as soft as you want," said Sheirkia, a tone of disappointment seeping in. It was probably more dramatic the other way.

Kiadora brought the tip of the dagger to her chest and exerted enough pressure to break the skin slightly, wincing at the sting of the prick. She looked down to see the front of the dress turn slightly wet, too dark to be able to see the red of the blood. She brought the dagger away, a touch of her blood on the end of it. Now what…oh, gray light.

Kiadora paused, debating just pretending, but for some reason a vague fear of doing something so solemn incorrectly persisted. Kiadora chalked it up to the superstition surrounding the funeral dress, 13 candles, pyre and blood as she closed her eyes. It couldn't hurt, at any rate. In her mind's eye, she saw something that oddly seemed like black smoke fly out. She opened her eyes to feel no different, except that the weight in her hand was relieved as Sheirkia took the dagger back.

"Now, I want you to lie there and clear your mind, as you would for meditation." Kiadora closed her eyes. She immediately wanted to start bopping her foot, but resisted the urge. Suddenly she remembered that she was miles underground, wearing a dress that she spent her childhood hearing would attract spirits. In spite of herself, she hoped that their little cavern world wasn't near a cemetery.

Kiadora heard a low, melodic chant come from Sheirkia, the sorrowful tones sweeping over her. It was the funeral dirge sung whenever someone passed. It didn't actually consist of any words, it was only a series of hums and oh-like intonations. The idea was that words were never enough to express the grief felt, only raw music straight from the soul could do that. It was completely ad-libbed and took much skill to do right. It was usually sung by trained vocalists called the Sorrow Singers.

Sheirkia had such a skill with her perfectly low voice that held the tremble they knew to keep. Kiadora settled back and felt the tones wash over her, marveling at the fact that the people down here were probably the only living souls to have the music sung just for them. As she lay there, she didn't quite know what she was supposed to be thinking about, however. Was she supposed to feel like she was dying, see some great vision that would herald a rebirth?

She continued to lie there, but all she could see was an intense darkness, one that seemed to flow into her thoughts. The only thing she could think about was the way Sheirkia's singing seemed to repeat itself after a few minutes, not doing anything truly new, the same tone weaving in and out, with the same quavering melody. Kiadora started to see why the tone was not sung very long traditionally. There was not much one could do within the form of the singing; it had to keep quivering as much as it could and could not loop too fast. It also had to keep a slow lilting rhythm, which restricted the variety. How boring; Kitrara jokingly missed having a hot plate jammed into her. Well, maybe not.

And on and on it went. Until it stopped suddenly, and Sheirkia was commanding her to sit up. Kiadora did so, opening her eyes, realizing she was shaking off the sort of drowsiness that can only come from being asleep.

"Rise reborn," said Sheirkia in her usual expansive tone, arms in the air. Kiadora merely looked at her and stood up. Sheirkia threw the veil up over Kiadora's head to reveal her face. Somehow the candles had gone out and were all now white. Before she could puzzle about it too much, Sheirkia was handing Kiadora a white lit candle.

"Light these, and as you do, think of yourself being reborn into the Mysteries." Kiadora merely nodded, still thinking that the only mystery here was why she needed to do this. She walked around the crooked candle circle, lighting the candles while wondering if Regelend was still angry with her. He'd get over it, he'd have too.

Kiadora finished lighting the candles, then returned to Sheirkia standing in the middle of the circle and handed her the candle. Sheirkia promptly sniffed it out and put it down on the ground next to her.

"Now, what did you see while you were asleep?" Sheirkia asked, sitting down cross-legged in the middle of the circle. Kiadora figured she should do the same and sat next to the woman.

"See? Uh, I didn't actually see anything. Was I supposed to see something?" Kiadora ran her index finger along the lace at the edge of her collar and then glanced over at Sheirkia. Sheirkia frowned earnestly now, the creases by her mouth deeper than when she was just doing it for ritual effect.

"Nothing, nothing at all?"

"No, I think I fell into a dreamless sleep, though." Kiadora mentally kicked herself. She should be making up grand visions right now, she just realized. Maybe the others were quicker to fool her; that was why Sheirkia was so upset.

"Nothing at all," Sheirkia muttered, her stare drilling into Kiadora's gaze. "And what do you think that means?" she said abruptly. Kiadora glanced quickly around, trying to come up with some answer. Nothing offered itself up.

"How can nothing mean anything?" Kiadora asked.

"How can it indeed," Sheirkia echoed back. Her voice was now soft and vague. She continued to stare Kiadora down with those wide eyes.

"I think," said Sheirkia, her tone growing ever softer, "There's been a true death. You may exit the circle as you please." Sheirkia waved her hand vaguely at the door in a diagonal motion. Kiadora looked at her, eyes narrowed.

As she got up, Kiadora figured Sheirkia really had witnessed a sort of death. It was the death of something. Logic maybe, thought Kiadora as she passed through the black curtain, pushing it violently. She reached up to the zipper and pulled it down, letting the black dress fall off of her, not thinking about the mourning that it connoted at all.

She threw the dress in a heap, it nothing more than a mass of silk. Yes, that was it: the death of meaning.

CHAPTER 17

A couple hours later Kiadora was rummaging through the library again, looking for anything to page through. Several books on metaphysical theory yielded nothing to her, and now she was going through the history of the formation of the Church. Nothing interesting, she'd already paged through it all. Damn this place. They didn't know how to have more fun than this? She had just turned towards the section on monarchical politics when she heard some footsteps behind her.

She turned, and sure enough, there was Regelend looking down at the floor. She was right, he wouldn't stay mad for long. Kiadora had been surprised he even knew how to raise his voice to another person. He looked down at the ground for a while longer and then finally found the nerve to bring his eyes back up to her.

"Kiadora, I, I'm sorry. Can you just come with me? I need to introduce you to some people." Kiadora felt her eyes narrow slightly out of confusion.

"Some people? Who?"

"Just come on, we can't really talk about it here." He glanced to the side, as if someone else would have spontaneously popped into their section of the room. The library was deserted except for two people going over a large book in the far corner out of ear shot.

"No one will..." Kiadora started, but Regelend still gave a hurried glance to the right and beckoned Kiadora to follow him before he turned and started to head out of the library. Kiadora rolled her eyes slightly and followed Regelend out of the room and down the outside corridor. She glanced at Regelend, who walked in a calm, assertive manner in front of her, quite the opposite of his usual slow meander.

They kept going, and he trailed off into one of the many caverns on the outside of the offices and classrooms. This one she had not really paid any attention to; it seemed like no one did. It was the smallest of crevasses, just big enough to admit an average-sized person. Both Kiadora and Regelend turned sideways to scuttle in through the narrow space, the coolness and dampness of the rock pressing against Kiadora's back. She grazed her arm on the way in as she ducked and pivoted to avoid a narrow outcrop. She was a little annoyed that Regelend had not thought to tell her to mind her head.

"You could have..." Regelend turned around, and she could only see one eye and the half of his mouth that he held a finger over in the small column of light. She could hear his tunic rustle slightly as he reached into a pocket for something, and she saw a flame erupt near a rough stone. Regelend brought up a match to light a torch. He held it up and she saw the narrow pathway widen and further down turn off toward the right. She followed him down the corridor, glancing back at the narrow strip of light that flowed in, looking smaller as they walked away from it.

They made the bend, and there was an open cavern about the average size of one of the classrooms, with several flat-surfaced stones in a rough circle. Five people sat on some of them, each looking up and smiling.

"It took us forever to get them in a circular formation like this, hard to push rocks that size and try to do it quietly," said Regelend. "And Arn's thumb never did set correctly afterwards." One of the boys to the right, a kid that must have been about 18 years old, held up his right thumb with a grin. It was cocked at the joint to the right.

"Luckily I'm left-handed," he said.

"So what is all this?" Kiadora said, not really caring whose thumb pointed which way at the moment.

"These are the people down here who are still devoted to the Holy Text," Regelend said with a smile. He pointed to a thin girl of the left with straight black hair down to the middle of her back. "This is Reena," she turned a pale face to Kiadora and waved. Regelend continued to point at the others.

"Torren," a man who looked to be in his early 30's with light brown hair waved.

"Aela," a woman with dark hair streaked with gray nodded and smiled.

"Wellian," a man who must of have been in his 20's with light hair that seemed to point in every direction smiled. And, of course, Arn, who smiled with a, "hello."

"This is Kiadora, whom I've spoken to you about." They all nodded. Kiadora turned to him. "And what have you been saying exactly?" she said in a low tone.

Regelend brought himself around to Kiadora so she could only see his face. "I told them that you have been having trouble grasping the teachings down here. I think there might be a reason why you have not been so successful with yours studies, it might be the same reason I've been having. Somewhere, you still hold on to the old ways of doing things. And there is nothing wrong with that. In fact, it may very well be the right way, that's why we can't let it go."

"Regelend, I didn't like it when I was up above. I never wanted to go to services, not once. Just because you hold it dear doesn't mean we all do."

"Maybe you experienced it in a shallow way, didn't give it a chance. Just give it a shot, you're struggling down here and this can help. You seem like someone who just hasn't found your spiritual home yet, and what they teach down here isn't it."

"You're damn right it's not, but this is what I grew up with, and it didn't fit either. Damn it, they're the reason I'm down here. Them and that stupid book."

"We look at it slightly differently, could you at least try?"

"Fine, I will *try*," said Kiadora. "But I can't promise I'll like it."

"That's fine, we can't force you to stay and there's nothing keeping you here, not like this whole place. But stay or leave, you can't tell anyone about this. If the Elders knew what we were doing, I don't even want to know what they would do." Kiadora rose an eyebrow.

"For studying the Holy Text? They let you guys do that in the library all the time."

"Yes, but they don't let us do anything else. We can't pray over it, we can't talk about what we read in it and we can't worship. They say that is the old way, we need to move on and we need to embrace what we are now. They're convinced the Holy Text will only hold us back." Regelend turned back to the others and called for Torren over the slight murmur in the cavern; everyone had started to chat with each other when Regelend turned toward Kiadora. Torren looked up.

"Tell Kiadora what happened when they caught you with the Holy Text in your quarters." An annoyed expression passed over Torren's face, and he stood up to join Kiadora and Regelend where they stood.

"Those idiots," said Torren as he came over, shoving his hands into the pockets of his tattered, brown tunic. "I was bringing it back to my quarters with me, and my teacher at the time came up unannounced and caught me mouthing prayers out of it to myself. I won't give up my God for them, I won't do it," he said with a deeper scowl, looking off to the floor. He looked back up at Kiadora jerkily, as if willing away the frustration. "There's been talk about banning student access to the Holy Text."

"Torren is on the Matrina level and attends the Master monthly meetings," Regelend explained to Kiadora.

"Right, this was a while ago they caught me with the text. Haven't given them a reason to distrust me since," said Torren, looking from Regelend and back to Kiadora. "But they don't want to fully become what they hate. They figure that as long as they keep it open to us to read on a theoretical level, they are still open-minded people."

"So what did they do to you when they found out that you were practicing the old way?" Kiadora asked.

"Well, they denied my access to the Holy Text; I am still not to be found reading it to this day. And as far as they know, I have no interest in touching it. That is how I have moved up as far as I have, same with Aela over there," he said, nodding his head backwards.

"I was resigned to my quarters for two months," Torren went on. "You ever see the bars go up on some of the sleeping quarter doors?"

"Yeah, once," said Kiadora. "There were bars on one about three rows above me for a couple weeks. It just came down a few days ago." Torren nodded.

"That's to keep people in. Two months is torture when it is just you, the dirt and a day's rations that they pass into you in the middle of the night. They don't tell you when they will take you out, either. They expect you to learn what to say to them, what they want to hear, before they let you out. It's for you to learn your own lesson.

"If you are there for longer than three months, you are brought before the Elders and you have a guided meditation, which is really just them relating images to you when you are in the Second State, a type of hypnosis where they make you figure out what they want you to learn. For me it was a series of images of what the Church has done wrong to people like us. What they wanted me to learn was that the Holy Text cannot possibly benefit us, since it led to those actions. And I did learn it, as far as they know."

Kiadora suddenly glanced back toward the doorway, as if she would see the Elders marching in that very second. "And what if they catch us? We'll be locked away for years."

"Not years, three months tops. And Aela and I will be knocked down to the level of student again, of course," said Torren. "That's a risk we care to take. What are they going to do, rob us of the one thing we don't get anyway?" he said, pulling a smaller version of the Holy

Text out of his pocket. "Besides, they can try, but they won't get my faith. So it's up to you Kiadora, if you want to risk it."

"How long have you been meeting?" Kiadora asked Regelend.

"Five years." Kiadora shrugged. If it had gone this long...

"And I think it will really help you," said Regelend.

"Why not?" Kiadora made her way to one of the rocks and threw herself down on the cold, slightly jagged stone. Things had started to get too boring down here, she figured. Might as well listen in.

The rest took their seats on the stones and they all faced each other in a tight circle. Rather than going on about their usual business, as Kiadora expected, they all turned to look at her, as though she was there as a guest speaker. Torren looked over at Regelend after a moment.

"So tell us, why did you bring her to us?" Torren asked.

"She's fit in here poorly since she got here," said Regelend, who frowned as Kiadora shot him a glare. "Well you have," he added, turning to her. "I figured this would be best, that clearly Eatheria does not seem to be the way for you. Maybe you need the true way."

"The true way?" Kiadora asked, a little more shrilly than she intended. "Hasn't the way we were treated up there taught you people nothing?"

"It taught us everything," Aela said. "I was sentenced to death for what I am, was broken out of prison by some Matrinas. I owe them everything. Torren was beat senseless his whole childhood, his uncle was a priest."

"Tried to knock in straight out of me," said Torren, holding up an arm. In the dim lighting, Kiadora could make out some twisted scarring on his forearm, and his arm had a slight crook to it at the elbow. "But after we got down here, we couldn't give up God, blessed his name be. This doesn't feel right. None of it does. Staring into fires, odd rituals involving…ehck…Regelend, tell Kiadora what they're making you and Uranda do."

"She knows," Regelend muttered into his lap.

"But the point is, it's not right to us. It's not the truth, it's just some game they play down here to rebel against what they think is evil." Kiadora thought of her current teacher with her swishing skirts and elaborate productions. But a game, a lie? It seemed more real to these people than that. Why else stare into a fire for hours? Kiadora kept her mouth shut, but it didn't help.

"You look confused," said Torren, leaning over slightly and staring into her face.

"It's nothing," Kiadora hesitated but they all just kept looking at her. "It's just, to be convinced that this is a game? There seems to be conviction here, too."

"You can have conviction in lies," said Wellian harshly, with a slight curl to his lip.

"The point of the matter is," said Torren forcefully, "We can't give up on God just like that. We grew up with him, many of us learned to love him. What, we have to hate him just because we're something that his people don't understand?"

"Yes!" said Aela, as if letting off a rally cheer.

"I don't think I ever learned to love that god," said Kiadora in a small tone. "Regelend, why did you bother to bring me here?" Wellian's sneer somehow managed to increase in depth. "The only thing

you showed me is that I don't fit down here, and I don't fit above."
Kiadora was ready to jump up and go. Regelend lunged out and
grabbed her wrist before she could get up. She remained sitting.

"Has it ever occurred to you that maybe you never fell in love with
their version of god, that maybe there is another way to go about
things, other ways to look at the text?"

"The truth," Wellian said, Aela and Torren nodding. Kiadora
looked around and noted the various copies of the Holy Text sitting
around the circle next to their owners.

"But that thing says we're evil. We caused the Great Fires, or
something."

"It says Skira caused the Great Fires," said Regelend, finally letting
go of her wrist. "Do you feel like a demon or like you have something
besides your own mind riding around with you?"

"No, I never did, not once."

"Ok, then we're something else entirely. It doesn't lock us away
from God. All I ask is that you give this a chance. You seem lost.
Too many people around here have let their bad experiences with the
people of God mess with their relationship to God. I was almost
sentenced to death, too. That hasn't stopped me." Kiadora looked
over and Regelend was staring into her eyes. The others around the
circle were watching her closely as well.

"Alright, what is you do at these things anyway?"

"It's a lot of what we did in Church." Kiadora wrinkled her nose at
this.

"Church, I hated Church."

"No," said Regelend with a sigh. "It's not the exact experiences we had in Church. It's a lot more intimate. You'll get a lot closer to God. You'll see, you'll fall in love with him." Kiadora rose an eyebrow.

"He's not going to be my lover." Regelend threw his hand halfway up in the air and looked up at the ceiling briefly.

"It's not that way, you know what I mean," said Regelend. "I see it in you. You want something more, that's why we're all here. This will give you a chance to get closer to God, to get what the Church could never give to you."

Kiadora looked at him for a moment. His earnest enthusiasm positively shone out of his eyes. They looked bright, yet glassy, as if he was about to cry with emotion for what he was talking about. That smile was too much as well. She didn't want to dash such an honest love, especially with how she was behaving toward him these past couple of days.

"Alright, lead the way. What is it that happens here exactly?"

"Prayer, reading of the Holy Text, a few songs." Kiadora grinned slightly.

"Well, that doesn't sound so bad." Not as weird as what she was having to do in her courses, at any rate. Regelend beamed back and sat down on one of the flat stones. She looked around as everyone picked up their books. She noticed one sitting on the rock next to her and picked it up.

Wellian stood up, spreading his arms.

"Welcome, everyone, to this week's meeting of The Children of Sky's Dominion." Kiadora groaned inwardly. 'Ah, damn this place.'

She looked over at Regelend, who she had never seen look happier. Usually he had a habit of trying to look serene when he was walking around, but it always just sort of faded into a dull, muted look of boredom or sometimes despondence.

His face was lit up now. Although he did not have the stupid grin of a minute ago, he had a genuinely happy smile, his teeth shining out as the torches reflected off of them, forming their own beacon of light.

Kiadora looked at the others. They also seemed to have the same eager smile.

"Let's open with the passage of our savior." Wellian opened the book with a pompous flourish, every bit of the priest that Kiadora grew up knowing. Regelend leaned over next to her.

"Page 676," he whispered. Kiadora opened the book and turned the pages as fast as she could. When she found the page, the yellow-edged pages fell into her lap and the dancing black bugs of the words in the torchlight wriggled before her. She could feel her eyes go wide in shock. The book of Jayalla?

Kiadora remembered it well from her religious classes in youth. It was one of the few books that she even bothered to pay attention to. It was a book of stories recorded by the earliest settlers that had come out of the deserts. They had come to fertile land at last, only to find it was under a massive volcanic mountain. Kiadora remembered being captivated by that book and that book alone. She liked the idea of landing somewhere new, of a fresh start and new experiences.

What she hated about the book was that it contained some of the most bloodthirsty stories she had ever read: detailed accounts of the settlers clashing with the small tribes of Earth worshipers that resided there beforehand. Those tribes were all wiped out now. Those parts were glossed over in her classes, being deemed unnecessary for children. Kiadora still found it funny how that was unnecessary, but the Church physically almost drowning her to death, burning her and burying her alive couldn't be avoided.

But what she did remember out of the book was some of the greatest descriptions of the new surroundings. Looking back, Kiadora realized it was probably a child's self-centeredness that drew her to those stories. The area settled was her country before it had been tamed into farms and villages. The book recounted lush forests with ferns as tall as three men. Monster-sized oak and elm trees created a homelike dome over the soil that had been enriched for centuries with volcanic ash. At that point, the volcano hadn't gone off for hundreds of years, Lisera had said.

Kiadora loved the book so much she had come home talking about it to her maid that night. She had walked home, imagining the trees she passed to be five times their size and seeing in her mind massive ferns she could hang off of. Kiadora had mentioned to Lisera how much she would have loved it if the ground hadn't been tampered with, if she could still see those magnificently large trees. As Lisera looked down at the sheet she was folding, Kiadora remembered catching Lisera's bitter smile. From the side, Kiadora could also see a hard look in Lisera's eyes.

"What is it?" Kiadora had asked.

Lisera turned around and stared at Kiadora. Kiadora stared back, waiting for Lisera to speak. Lisera seemed to be caught in a battle as to whether she should say anything to a superior about her own religious views. "You can tell me," Kiadora had urged. Lisera smiled.

"Sorry, miss. You know I am not used to being able to speak sofreely. You're not like the others," she trailed off in a despondent tone. Kiadora nodded. Dehlia had a habit of hitting Lisera at any opportunity.

"I was just remembering what I had read in that book, years and years back. Not to be condescending, but it is refreshing to hear the book retold with the innocence of a child's eyes. You have a certain wonder for a version of the book that was not there when I had read it. Have you read the whole thing?"

"Just the parts about landing and right after that, so far." Another sad smile from Lisera. Kiadora didn't like those forlorn looks. "And about the setup of the early Church and the fertility that God provided. Oh, but the ferns, as tall as three men, they said. Wouldn't that be wonderful?" said Kiadora in a spirited tone, desperately trying to rid Lisera of her foul mood. Lisera only put the folded sheet she had been holding in a drawer, slamming it shut.

"I would urge you to read the rest, miss. That is when Skira rose up out of the mountains and caused the Great Fires." Kiadora shuttered. She hated hearing about him.

"I hope I never have to meet him, I don't think I would survive. He doesn't just kill you, he steals your soul for all of eternity. I really wouldn't want to live with him, he seams mean. Like Dehlia but with a lot of fire." Lisera chuckled briefly, then the mirth faded as fast as it came.

"Well, it wasn't really a demon, miss."

"No? But we were always told…"

"I'm well aware of what they told you. Don't forget, we all have to attend the spiritual education when we are young. It was actually a simple volcanic eruption. People were just too primitive to know that."

"What's a vol-anic eruption?"

"Volcanic. That is when a large amount of melted rock spews out of the top of an active mountain, a volcano. However, very few people know that. Many still think it is simply a demon." Kiadora leaned forward, eyes wide. She had wished Lisera could be her religious studies teacher.

"Where did you hear that?" Kiadora asked.

"Around," said Lisera evasively. "There's more information out there than the Church wants you to know." She shook her head and turned toward the door, then looked back. "Look at me, sitting around being so critical. I trust this won't make it into other ears?"

Kiadora shook head and slapped her hand over her mouth to signify silence. "You know me, Lisera," Kiadora said upon removing her hand. "I don't talk to anyone around this place, not really. And Tahn wouldn't even understand."

Lisera laughed. "Good, and I would go back and look at that book again. You'll be surprised."

Right as Lisera left the room, Kiadora reached over to the edge of her bed where she had placed the Holy Text. She opened it to the book that they had studied and began to read.

Looking back, if there was a time Kiadora had to pin where her innocence took a nosedive out of her life, it would have been right then. She had read the book, despite how hard it was to keeping going after what she was all reading. In between the wonderful passages of fertile land and God's gifts to his chosen pilgrims, there was another story of the volcanic eruption, the fear and the murders that had ensued.

The eruption had brought forth belief in a terrible, bloodthirsty being that was out to destroy the prosperity of the chosen and devour their souls so that man could not reach the eternal afterlife with God. They would simply blink out of existence upon death. The belief ran that those killed in the eruption no longer existed because they had been consumed by the beast, who they just referred to as the "Great Demon" at this point.

Upon the eruption, it was described that red, glowing blood had blown out of the top of one of the mountains. It was said it was a self-sacrifice that the demon had to make to consume them. It was also recorded that the face of a creature with slanted eyes and a gaping mouth could be seen at the top of the mountain during the eruption.

The red blood had rained down on the settlement's main village, annihilating everyone there, soul and all. About a third escaped and set up camp farther from the mountains. Most went down into the plains, where less fertile but still livable soil was abundant. Many stayed out of desire for the fertile soil that had not been consumed by the demon. They were convinced that once they found how they could repel the demon, they could live out the rest of their days in prosperity.

But the question remained for them, how to repel such a mighty force? The highest holy men of the day were put to work to find a way to keep it away for good. The most obvious answer that came to them was to avoid all fire. They knew that where the demon's blood hit, it would burn. Around the same time, several rains hit and caused severe flooding. They thought this was a way for the Great Demon, which they named Skira, to rally a second attack. So water was avoided. Extensive dams were built to control the flood waters. Several died during this endeavor as they tried to contain the raging waterways. Earth had already been avoided because of the severe sandstorms back from where the pilgrims came. Further, under the earth is where Skira resided, where he had come from. Over several centuries, a new god was brought to the people.

The way the book read, it was made to seem like this god made himself apparent, as if he was waiting in the dark somewhere for a group of people to just pop up and need his assistance. It spoke in terms of God showing his grace to his people through the rejection of what was false. Kiadora remembered one passage particularly well. She was forced to memorize it in the higher levels of her schooling:

"And God came down out of the sky and spoke to the three priests. He said to look up if ever they were in need of him. He would be in the air they breathed and the rolling blue vista. He would be in the flying birds and gentle breeze. All man needs to do is look up, look up, look up."

To this day, Kiadora had no idea whether God came and spoke to those three men. She had never known God to speak to anyone, and those who heard voices were usually just suspected to be possessed. She increasingly began to wonder if those three men were even real.

Then there was where it had all begun: "After the priest lost his mother, God came once more to him when he was out on a lonely cliff looking for a sturdy wood to hold the waters. He told Olleil, 'You who wish to find solace must hunt down those who run with Skira. They can be found in the water, with the fire and looking too hard at the earth. They are the possessed, they are the ones who allow HIM to come to the earth. They are his gateway, they must be destroyed."'

Now, in addition to the manhunt that lasted for hundreds of years, that was why Kiadora was sitting on a rock a good 30 stone throws under civilized man.

As she surveyed this happy group, which was now singing a traditional hymn in hushed voices, she just didn't know how they could return to this. She caught a glint off of Reena's face in the torchlight and looked closer. Sure enough, the woman was crying. But with a smile: tears of joy. Tears of joy for a god who had told them to hunt people like them down.

The book of Jayalla didn't end there, either. Kiadora remembered, as she looked at Reena sobbing in supreme pleasure, the book went on for 40 more pages of brutal recounts of stonings, hangings and the torching of entire houses of people thought to be possessed. Kiadora had thought it hilarious that they were playing pyromania with people thought to be a little too fire happy.

'But we're a more civilized, refined society, aren't we now?' Kiadora thought. There was the Termination for more minor cases that popped up 200 years later (why God had not thought to slay the Shiekita before then, Kiadora didn't know). And now for extreme cases there were homes. For the worst cases, there was a quick, humane execution that involved a simple toxin injected into the veins. The injection site was even numbed first so that there would be no chance of pain.

And here these people sat and sang about God's triumph and glory. Kiadora caught a line, "And He will rise above all else," before refusing to listen again. She looked over at Regelend, who was singing, but also looking at her with a worried expression. Her bitterness must be showing. She looked away and started to mouth the words. She would never sing these words again, not when she lived in a damned dirt hole for fear of death.

At last, the singing stopped. Next to her, Arn let out a little louder "praised be!" Aela nodded in agreement. Wellian stood up once more.

"Again we want to thank you, God, for bringing Kiadora to us. We hope that she can live out your plan as much as we do, maybe more even." Kiadora went red as everyone watched her again. "We hope that she can spread the word of the Ollox and be taken to paradise with us all." Kiadora jumped a little and looked around sharply at Wellian.

The Ollox was another wonderful story out of the book of Jayalla. Kiadora realized that was why they must have been reading on page 676 when she was off in her thoughts. At the height of the demon scare, there was a Shiekita (a possessed human) that supposedly was about to destroy an entire town by raising Skira's blood out of the ground once more. Right as the woman was raising her hands, a large bald eagle came and scooped her away. The bald eagle itself was seen as an embodiment of God, who at this moment, had decided that he *didn't* want his people destroyed by killer spirits. The woman was never seen again and neither was this wonderful eagle. It was said in Church a number of times (later when she was of an age where it was deemed non-scarring for her to hear such dreadful things) that the Shiekita was taken off in the direction of the volcano. It was assumed that she was sent back to her master.

"Um, sorry, but why would I go around talking about the Ollox? Much like everything else, I thought it was out to kill us."

Everyone in the circle exchanged amused glances, and Regelend spoke up.

"No, you're thinking of the Church's version, Kiadora. You see, we see it as a sign from God that he will eventually bring us, his chosen, to paradise."

"But it went in the direction of the then active volcano, what else would it have done but kill that woman?"

"That's an assumption," said Regelend. "We're much more inclined to believe that there was a paradise awaiting that woman. The text says that she was dropped to her origin. The Church believes that because she was evil, that means the fires of Skira, or the demon's blood. However, it commonly is stated in the text that man originates from good. It is the world that turns us evil. In the book of Elita…"

Kiadora held up a hand.

"No, I don't need a long string of text quotes, I know what it says. So you think this 'origin' is some sort of paradise? And what exactly is in this paradise?"

"Oh, it's different for each individual," said Reena quietly, in a breathy tone. "In the book of Illent, Rentis was being tortured by God. Each torture for him was different for what his individual worst fear was. So you see? God likes to make our reality into what is in our own heads. For me, I always liked to hang upside down as a kid. It was just comforting. So I think that my paradise will be one where tree roots grow into the sky and the flat surface of rocks face upward."

"Eventually," said Wellian, "the Ollox will come to pick us up. We even know the date and time." Kiadora just stared for a moment.

"A giant eagle… is going to come get you?" Kiadora glanced at the doorway. She had to get away from here. But Torren was already pulling up a stack of papers about as high as his knee.

"You see, I set out the text in a certain matrix. It's the third letter in all applicable words in the Holly Text matched to the place in the alphabet it appears. A is one, B is two and so on. I multiplied that number by nine, a common number of God. There were nine great priests, nine Shiekita killed in the book of Jayalla and nine times God spoke directly to man in the text. I then took each of those numbers and divided by three, another common number in the text: three great priests in the beginning, three pilgrimages and three times God saved man from a disaster. When I do that, keeping them in the order found in the text, every ninth page has a major date that something happened in the Holy Text, including when the Holy Text was done being written. The pattern deviates one time, a date that is about a month from now. That's too unlikely to be a coincidence. Here, see."

Torren leaned over and handed Kiadora a sheet of paper. It was a block of what looked to be random numbers. Some numbers that came out to be 17/1/322 were circled in red near the center of the page, right under a descending line of threes circled in blue. Well, at any rate, is was nice to know it was the seventeenth cross-section of the year, although they had now lapsed into the next year since she was down here. Damn, she longed to see the surface. As she stared at the page, something dawned on her.

"So, the Ollox," Kiadora said slowly. "Where will it come? If it is a giant bird, it can't possibly make its way down here."

"Oh, yes, we know where it will be," said Torren, now dividing his stack of papers in two to where a longer sheet of paper stuck out as a marker. "You see, on this sheet here is a list of coordinates that comes out to where the Ollox was seen first, surrounded in a set of three nines." Torren handed the sheet to Kiadora. More circled numbers.

"It's about twenty miles east of here," said Regelend. "We're going to go meet it." Kiadora nodded, pretending to study the sheet of paper.

"So, how will you get out? They have all the exits guarded, I hear." Kiadora's eyes didn't leave the papers. She didn't want the desperate look in her eyes to show, although it may have helped to make her look more convincing. She looked up. 'Please have this well-thought-out.'

"That's the trick," said Wellian. Kiadora's heart fell slightly. "We found an exit that is not guarded. It leads behind a waterfall and it looks like it ends, but instead it takes a sharp twist to the right. It's a walk, it's about three miles off from here. We've been combing for it for a year now very carefully so we don't get caught. Reena's been in charge of it. She's been telling her Masters that she is looking for some underground wind tunnels to practice her craft better. She's going to be a Matrina of Air soon."

"Underground wind tunnels? Are those real?" Kiadora asked Reena.

Reena shrugged, expressionless. "Doesn't matter, I found what I was looking for. A lot of this place has been relatively unexplored.

We don't need a lot of it, our numbers are limited, and most of the High Masters, the Earia, are too busy with their dreams."

Kiadora had to stop herself from laughing. She would get out of this place. But once she escaped, would she come back? Where else would she go? And there was another matter.

"You mentioned me talking to people about this."

Wellian exchanged a glance with Regelend. Regelend looked over at her with a tense expression.

"You see," said Wellian. "We don't believe this paradise is just for us, we want to spread the word to as many people as possible."

"Then why don't you do it?" Kiadora snapped.

"That's just it, we're all known for holding to our old ways. That's why we need a fresh face to go and tell people about it in a way that does not scare them into thinking this is all about their old experiences with the Church." Kiadora frowned.

"But it is about that."

"Well, yes, in part," said Wellian. "But don't you see? This is a new era in the old beliefs! People will finally have happiness in the most final and ultimate sense."

Kiadora didn't like the expansive grin on his face and the glint in his eye. It was a look of rising mania. The only time she had seen anything close to it was when she had passed the house of the possessed. Maybe it was a similar type of madness.

As Kiadora regarded this look of sheer enthusiasm, she wondered about finding the exit herself. There couldn't be too many waterfalls down here, could there? Then again, the caverns were so expansive she would probably get lost or caught wandering. She knew from far-off sounds of running water that they only occupied a small portion of the area; there was no way to possibly find what she was looking for in a small amount of time. And what if her torch she would have to carry went out? No, she needed these people as much they thought they needed her. Although, she still felt a slight twinge of anger at having been let in just to be used for their propaganda.

"I understand," she said, trying her best not to sound as if she was being put through the most grueling chore of her life. Now that she thought of it, that might be the case. She wasn't exactly outgoing. "What is it you want me to do?"

"Basically what I said," explained Wellian, though rather insufficiently, Kiadora had to admit. "Spread the word of the coming Ollox to the people." Kiadora laughed slightly.

"And how do you think I should do that? Just walk up to people, 'Hello, have you heard of the great Ollox who will come to take us to paradise?'" said Kiadora with a laugh. No one else laughed. They just looked at her with the utmost seriousness. Wellian nodded, without even a flinch of his lips.

"Yes, that's essentially the idea." Kiadora looked sharply off to the side.

"Alright.... Are there certain people you think that I should speak with?"

"No, just whomever you can spread the word to, although I might steer clear of the higher leaders and teachers." Kiadora laughed again, although this time more internally so it came out as a smirk. She pictured herself walking up to some old crone on a throne in some cave, telling her about a magical eagle that could come and take them away. Then her smirk faded. She imagined doing this to someone at a nearby table in their dining hall, of sorts. That is what they were asking her to do. What was she supposed to do? Lean out her sleeping quarters door and call through at the curtain next to hers until the person poked their head out? Did you hear the amazing news of the Ollox? Even now, she knew she wouldn't be able to say it with a straight face.

Was going to the surface worth it? Was it really worth that sort of humiliation? Then she looked over at the damp, oozing cave walls and remembered what is was like to be in a forest, an actual forest. It would be more vibrant and lively now that she was more in tune with Eatheria. Another twinge of anger surfaced as she realized that these people wanted to be in touch with that force, but one of its greatest reservoirs was kept separated from them. And what she wouldn't give to see the sky and maybe watch a skilled street performer. No, it was worth the humiliation.

"Ok, I'll go spread the word as best as I can," said Kiadora. She was met with wide grins and a small whoop from Arn. "When did you say it would be coming?"

"In exactly 45 days," Wellian went through and looked at the bottom of the pile of papers and pulled up a dog-eared piece of parchment. "We've made a calendar of sorts," he said, handing it to her. It was just a descending group of numbers starting at 50. 50 through 46 where crossed off. Number 35, 25, 15, and 5 were circled.

"Keep a tally of the passing days. We meet in the same place on the days that are circled, and after the one, we go to the surface," said Wellian. Kiadora nodded. Not too long for having to walk up to people and talk to them about a bird, really.

Yet as she thought about it, she remembered other people coming up to her with odd and strange messages, mostly delivered to them via their meditations. People she had never seen before would wander up and tell her universal truths that they swear they had discovered after staring into a fire for three days straight.

One woman who had looked like she had not washed in days, her plain, tan dress covered in an extra dark layer of grime, informed her that she needed to start preparing for the arrival of the Bangan, a race of kin-slaying monsters disguised as people. Another woman who had a myriad of colored flowers tucked under the sleeves of her dress informed her that they were all going to be absorbed by a universal being of love and should prepare by loving more expansively. The Ollox seemed tame in comparison.

And Kiadora thought the Regelend and Uranda ritual was going to be enough to deal with.

CHAPTER 18

Kiadora walked along the outskirts of the wooden classrooms, then passed by the furnace and bonfire on the way to her teacher's room. She had just been summoned by one of the runners, students charged with rounding people up for classes after extended breaks. Kiadora had started to get nervous. Far be it from her to not enjoy missing class, but Sheirkia's long absence after their last little mishap seemed a little foreboding, even to Kiadora.

Sheirkia must have been debating something, perhaps even taking it up with a boss or two, Kiadora figured. It had to have been a few weeks since she had found Sheirkia's door shut and a note taped to it telling her to take the time to meditate. She was beginning to wonder, with a tinge of fear overshadowed with large indifference, if she would be allowed to stay. She feared she might be sent back to the lower stage for not progressing. Back to Narissa. She kept mentally kicking herself for not just making up a grand vision while lying on that funeral pyre. She chalked it up to the absurdity of the situation acting as a distraction. It wasn't every day people pretended you were dead.

Still, Kiadora didn't mind the time off. She spent it in the library or trying to figure out how she was supposed to go about convincing people to believe in a giant bird, or at least look like she did. She was worried that to do nothing about it would mean that the Children would assume that she was not devoted to the cause and any hope of getting some fresh air would then be out of the question. If no one had even heard of the Ollox, they might get word.

For a group of people who spent most of their time in intense spiritual study, word travelled fast around this place. The whole compound seemed to know about Regelend and Uranda in a flash. Kiadora heard two people she didn't even know talking about it in a hallway. No, best to find a way to fake a love for this bird.

Kiadora made it to the door where Sheirkia performed her various antics. Kiadora stopped abruptly before the door. An intense wailing came from behind it, not unlike the wailing Sheirkia did when she performed the death ritual. Kiadora shuddered at the thought. She still didn't know what that smokey stuff that came out of her wound was. Part of her expected to feel like there was an alien presence released from her, like she imagined it would feel if she were really exorcised of a demon. But she felt exactly the same as always, disappointed and irritated.

Kiadora waited outside the door for Sheirkia to stop, but after a minute it kept on going. If Sheirkia couldn't be ready for her... Kiadora forced open the door and went through the curtain, stopping at the entryway.

Sheirkia sat in the usual circle designated by candles. The candles formed a perfect circle this time and were green and purple, alternating color with each candle. Sheirkia sat among fruits, herbs and nuts that littered the floor. The leaves appeared to be maple and there were triangular formations of purple stone sitting around. Kiadora knew it to be amethyst from the jewelry stores.

The woman sat in the middle, draped in many brightly-colored skirts and a green, sheer shirt with no sleeves. She sat cross-legged and her torso went in circles as she continued her wail. Kiadora realized that this must be how the woman practiced meditation. As Kiadora walked closer, she realized that the woman sat in a slight indent in the ground. The dirt seemed to have been dug away by half a thumb's depth, and in front of Sheirkia sat a bin with what looked to be the displaced dirt. The bin had pressed hand marks in it.

Sheirkia's eyes suddenly snapped open, looking straight at Kiadora. She didn't seem the least bit surprised to see Kiadora standing there. She had a livid look in her eye and shook slightly. Sheirkia then jumped up and pointed at Kiadora.

"You," she said, practically yelling, "will go through the Fires."

Kiadora didn't know what to say to this. She simply jumped back from the woman's finger.

Sheirkia came forward, waving her hand at the circle before she passed and leapt over the candles. Kiadora looked down. It was amazing none of Sheirkia's expansive skirts caught flame.

Wait, there was smoke rising from the base of the woman. She seemed to not notice, as she still had the same livid look, grabbing Kiadora by the shoulders.

"I have been immersed by the powers of Eatheria for days and days, seeking guidance, supplicating the spirits. It's drastic and dangerous, especially for one so inexperienced as you, but it's the only way. Fire is the greatest purifier." She spoke at a rapid pace, sweat falling from her brow.

"For you it won't be! Your clothes are on fire," Kiadora shrieked and spun around the woman to where the flames were visible at the bottom of Sheirkia's skirts. Kiadora stomped out the flame. Once the fire was out, Sheirkia spun around, beaming and grabbing Kiadora's shoulders.

"It's a sign. I'm correct, this must be done!" Kiadora's shoulders started to hurt where Sheirkia was digging in her fingers. Besides the pain in her shoulders, Kiadora felt her heart stop.

"Fires?" She backed up rapidly. "I won't be scorched again, I won't!"

"No, no," said the other woman, advancing. "This is different. You will remain physically unharmed, but your spirit needs intense cleansing. The only thing that will provide that so quickly is fire. You've had the darkest Eatheria flow out of you that I've ever seen, and so little of it."

"So that was Eatheria that I saw?" Kiadora asked. Sheirkia cocked her head to the side slightly. "You saw?" Kiadora glanced at the floor and brought her eyes back up to meet Sheirkia's bright gaze.

"In my mind. I saw the...substance...go out of the cut. What was that?"

"Negative Eatheria." Sheirkia's hands finally stopped shaking, but she spoke fast. She glanced out the door, as if she was losing time by explaining. She looked back at Kiadora, studying her face. She apparently decided Kiadora deserved an explanation.

"Humans have Eatheria flow through them. Everything living does. Over time, that energy you hold on to can become tainted with your own resentment and hatred. I didn't see all of it leave, either. You held onto it and hold onto it still. Usually a greater amount of negative Eatheria is released, and when it is, it is not nearly as dark. I didn't know what to do, so I kept going. I was in the flow of things. You still have that blackness and you won't release it. I only hope you can see the higher energy, the pure path." With that, Sheirkia swept around Kiadora, passing through the curtain as she expansively swung the colorful cloth.

Kiadora stood there, watching the ripples of brightness in the cloth, a patch of yellow and red violently moving at the level of her gaze. Sheirkia seemed to be leading up to the last little pronouncement before she whisked off, probably to see an Elder.

Kiadora frowned as she realized Sheirkia was trying to be helpful, trying to heal her scars from her last major spiritual exploit. Kiadora wished it hadn't come out so damn condescending. Higher path, indeed. The people in charge always had a higher path.

Kiadora heaved a sigh. No sense in staying here. Sheirkia had made no comments as to when she would be back. 'Honestly,' Kiadora thought, 'if you're going to be preoccupied, why send a messenger?' The dolt probably forgot she sent one and then got distracted. Kiadora headed out the curtain and heaved open the heavy wooden door, letting it hit back with a thud.

As she walked back to where she came from, passing the familiar stony outcrops, she remembered what was bothering her on the way here. There was still the matter of making everyone believe she had some higher message that had come from a group that wasn't supposed to exist.

Higher message…of course, the wisdom Sheirkia had just seemed to glean from the dirt. That mania, that enthusiasm, that conviction. Kiadora would look like she had just come out of meditation as well and had just received the clearest message of her life. She might be able to look crazy enough so that no one would believe her. The Elders and Matrinas would just think of her as a misguided novice for talking of such a bird and her peers would probably not be inclined to go on the fool's errand. Part of Kiadora's problem was that she did not want to drag more people into this madness and look like a liar when nothing came. The last thing she wanted to do was spread false hope.

But Kiadora wondered if she could even manage a look even close to what Sheirkia had. She would have to develop a glint in her eye, a wild smile and be shaking with energy. Kiadora was never much of a performer. She would need something reflective to practice in.

She mentally kicked around various objects like a pool of water, some metal and ideally a mirror, or course. Mirrors were hard to come by down here, for some reason. It was as if everyone had collectively decided that the vain act of staring at yourself was unnecessary. At any rate, her best bet would be her bowl of water in her quarters that she usually used to clean up.

Once she reached her quarters, she headed straight for her

makeshift vanity table. Kiadora wouldn't have gone so far as to even call it a vanity table. It was more of a squat stool. She lit her candle with one of the matches provided. In the technicolored haze that streamed in through the cloth, the wick burst into flame, bringing a truer light to her quarters.

She looked into the bowl that she could now see the bottom of. She poured in some water from the pitcher and her face leapt into view, rippling with the water. As the water stilled, she looked down and stared for a moment.

Kiadora had not taken the time to really look at herself since she came down. Her skin was so pale, it looked whitewashed. She had picked up lines under her eyes from the poor sleep. It was the night-mares of priests with hotplates and stories of death trials for people like her. When she woke up, she did her best to forget the panic and images of hateful stares. Sometimes, during her half delirium as she came to, she woke up to see the sod walls and think she was in the casket the Church put her in. In spite of herself, she almost hoped this cleansing by fire would work. She had not realized that despite her best efforts to forget, it had all manifested in her appearance anyway.

She kept looking. Despite the morning washes, somehow the dirt always made its way back onto her face. It would probably aid her in her struggle to look like a madwoman.

Kiadora summoned the image of Sheirkia back into her mind. That livid look, that fervent energy. Kiadora doubted she could ever look so energized about anything, but she had to try.

She tensed all her muscles to the point where she was shaking and opened her eyes as wide as she could. She increased her breathing and felt her heart race. If she were to talk, she knew she would sound fevered and rushed. Her face started to flush and she felt as if her blood was flowing as strongly as it could.

And then her candle exploded.

It was a blinding spark accompanied by a loud pop. Kiadora threw herself to the floor, letting out a small scream. She was prepared to scurry out the door if the table caught fire, but as soon as it had come, the flame returned to burning on the wick just as it always did.

Kiadora tensely returned to the table. Nothing looked singed and her water sat peacefully unaware. So that was how she controlled it. She stared at the candle, which flickered innocently enough. Should she try it again? She realized she had a grin on her face; she did it, she actually managed to control an outside force. But she didn't relish an explosion and as her giddiness faded, she realized she wasn't consciously trying to control it. So it might not even count.

And the flash could be dangerous to what she was trying to do. She needed to look livid without exploding things. Kiadora looked into her bowl and widened her eyes. The glint she wanted in her eyes automatically appeared.

'You have to see it, you have to know,' Kiadora mouthed into the bowl, quickly as she could without stumbling over the words. She did her best to keep her breathing at a moderately fast pace. Perfect. She looked appropriately crazy.

CHAPTER 19

Three days later, Kiadora got the message from her teacher. She would be resuming her regular schedule of going to her lessons right after the first meal. She nodded to the young man hanging in the door off of the ladder. He disappeared with a quick thanks for her time. Time, all she had was time down here.

She mentally reprimanded herself. What she hadn't used the time for was to spread her own little message of this bird. She wanted to, she thought about it, but her own lack of nerve held her back. Well, maybe that wasn't it, she had faced worse. She had plenty of nerve. Her own…lack of interest, probably. She didn't believe in it. Any of it. She would just as soon go to the surface to tell the Church about Eatheria and see how that flew. She would think about it later. Always later.

After her breakfast, she wandered over to Sheirkia's quarters, not sure what to expect. As she passed the alcove from where the heat from the Eternal Fires blasted her arm and the side of her face, she remembered one thing. She needed to ask about the candle. Kiadora knocked on the door and went in after a loud "come."

Sheirkia's room was unusually bare with only one large, orange candle on a table in front of a stool. No rug was out, and Sheirkia wore a comparatively simple, red dress. Her skirt billowed out only slightly and the top of the dress was cut higher than normal and had half sleeves. Sheirkia simply gestured to the stool. A dull look in the woman's eye told Kiadora that this was not the way Sheirkia would be going about things if it were up to her. Kiadora took a seat.

"No fabulous stage or grand costume?" Kiadora asked.

"The higher-ups," said Sheirkia in a stifled tone, "want us to hold off on that with you for now. It is just your physical self and your spirit, as basic as we can get so as to better focus on energy and cleansing. Just as much energy, if not more, can be focused with the items of power, but the Elders want this to be more intensely elemental. Highly unorthodox for one who has not matured with the items yet, but I have no say in this."

"Oh. How will they know?"

"They will know. They will know," was all Sheirkia said. "Now, we're going to be working with fire gazing to start. I will light the candle-"

"I made a candle explode yesterday," Kiadora blurted out. Sheirkia looked at her sharply from where she was searching her pocket for matches.

"And how in Eatheria did you manage that?"

"Well," Kiadora paused, looking for a lie. The Ollox wasn't the woman's business. "I was worried about the firework. I've been burned before by the Church's cleansing; I still didn't know what to expect." Not entirely false. She had sat awake at night wondering what the fire cleansing even was. She still doubted the lack of physical harm. It wouldn't be the first time she walked away more harmed from a ritual than let on.

"So my heart raced," she continued. "The more I thought about it, I started to shake. Then the candle popped violently and returned to normal." Sheirkia bit her lower lip in thought.

"That's impressive," she said after a pause. "It seems you're manipulating Eatheria unconsciously. Most students at your level need to be in the most extreme stress or have dire need to control it. But it seems that you can do it already by just raising your emotions alone. Interesting… interesting."

"So what causes it, what am I doing exactly?" Kiadora asked. Sheirkia was bent, leaning on her arms against the table. Her blond hair was covering her face. She lifted her head, to where Kiadora could only see one steel eye.

"It's simple. You're reaching out your essence, your spirit, and combining it with Eatheria of other elements."

"That doesn't sound simple. I don't understand," Kiadora said, shaking her head. Sheirkia stood up and came to kneel in front of Kiadora. She extended her hand and put it on Kiadora's chest. From where Sheirkia's hand was, a warmth spread around Kiadora's heart.

Kiadora leaned back abruptly, toppling the chair along with herself. As she scrambled up, the area in her chest slowly returned to the point where it felt like nothing had happened.

"What did you feel?" Sheirkia asked, standing up slowly.

"Warmth in my chest. Why? What did you do?"

"I was extending my spiritual energy to you. Everyone has it, it's part of the Eatheria that flows through everything, making us one. Those predisposed to sensing it can control it and manipulate other forms of it. The particles you see and what flows through us are the same substance, all Eatheria, so it makes it possible to bond with outside sources and control them. I suspect in your agitation, you lost control of that spiritual energy and it expanded past your physical frame. The first other strongest form of Eatheria it hit and bonded with was the flame. Hence the explosion. You can do a lot more with it," said Sheirkia, bending and moving in a soft spin, her less expansive skirt still swinging wildly as she bent for matches on the floor and lit the candle.

"One thing I can't do," said Sheirkia as she put out the match with a sharp wave of the hand, "is summon Eatheria from where it does not already exist. However, I can add to it and condense it at will." Sheirkia put her hand close to the flame, and Kiadora watched in fascination as the flame grew, then shrank down to almost an ember. Then it grew again to where Kiadora thought it would start to travel down the candle and engulf the table. But then the flame shrank down to the original size and continued to flicker just as normal.

Kiadora couldn't believe she was seeing such a thing, but she still felt let down that she could not summon fire. All this talk about controlling the elements, and she couldn't be a god herself after all. But this was pretty interesting. She tried to wipe the dopey grin off her face, but she couldn't help it. Now here was something worth sticking around for. None of this universal oneness garbage. Here was something she could use.

"But," said Sheirkia, pointing at the chair. "Now is not the time for that."

"Oh, come on," said Kiadora, sliding into the chair as expected. "Then why even show me such a thing? That was just neat. I should work on that." Sheirkia leaned on the table with a hand on her hip. Her eyes were narrowed and she had a frown. Was Sheirkia mad that they couldn't work on it, too?

"Later, later. Right now, I want you to stare into the candle," said Sheirkia, whisking around the chair and leaning over Kiadora's shoulder. "Watch the candle. Watch the flame dance around, back and forth, up and down. Notice the bright center, the weaker edges."

Kiadora watched the flame. It looked like any other flame, and she had seen many. She certainly didn't feel like just sitting by and watching those. What she wanted to see was the flame rise with the placement of her hand. That she had not seen. The control must be gratifying, to watch the flame rise only because you wanted it to.

"Watch, just watch," said Sheirkia, almost in a whisper. Kiadora watched the flame still just be a mundane bit of fire. It was so small she could barely see Eatheria particles around it. Two particles danced by touching the flame and rising again. Touching, rising. There were undoubtedly more in the flame, invisible under the brilliant flicker. And Kiadora vowed to control them with her hand as well.

Kiadora found herself focusing on the two particles. They continued to dance and roam. One disappeared into the flame and came out in the same spot on the other side. She watched as it moved down the flame and did the exact same thing again. In, out, now on the other side where it started.

She wondered if she could guide it. She focused on it and thought with all her mind. 'Move up, move up.' It moved farther down and danced into the flame. Damn it.

Then she thought of how she made the flame move in the first place. She tensed her muscles and started shaking...

"Stop. You're just to watch," Sheirkia snapped. Kiadora was almost reminded of Narissa until she glanced at Sheirkia, who had a hint of an amused smile on her face.

"Oh, really? You want to teach me this," Kiadora stated.

"You're a doer, not a watcher. I like that," Sheirkia admitted, "but you have to learn the ins and outs of the elements before you can willfully control them, before you can combine your own soul's energy with them."

"Didn't I do it already?"

"Yes, and look what happened. You had a reaction you didn't expect, one that could have injured you and countless others." Kiadora didn't like the fatalistic tone at the end of that sentence. "You merely wound up your essence until you lost control of it and allowed it to hit other particles of Eatheria. The two hit then bounced off of each other. That is not what we are looking to do here. Now watch the flame," Sheirkia finished, with a violent gesture at the flame. The flame danced to the side out of wind pressure rather than the impressive feats with Eatheria that Kiadora wanted to see done, but she knew better than to ask.

She turned towards the flame once more. The particles kept it up, in and out, in and out, that same rousing dance. As Kiadora watched, she realized there were three particles she could see. It became obvious which one passed a certain area, as they seemed to move in a half orbiting, looping pattern around the outside of the flame, then in, then out again.

"What causes them to maintain a straight line like that when they move through the flame?" Kiadora asked.

"No one quite knows for sure," said Sheirkia in a distant tone, looking off into space. "Several theories exist, but they are nothing more at present. We've only been down here twenty-two full solar rotations. We spend much time studying, but that is a comparatively short time when we are dealing with forces of such a magnitude. Some have their pet theories and hold onto them as if it is fact," Sheirkia finished with a bitter tone.

"What are some of those theories?"

"One is that they can build the most force by speeding through the element and it can fuel their movement on the outside, the part you are evidently seeing. Another is that they just want to get out of the element. Something about their charge means that they want to save as little energy from the element as possible, or only as much as they want to use on the outside. The rest is a waste. In the case of fire, some think they take the energy from the air and can give that energy to the other element, going fast in a straight line gives them the time and friction they need to release all the energy without being destroyed. And we have no idea why some step outside their element, why some stay encased. But I'm glad you were able to pick up on that pattern.

Some students take months to even see that." Kiadora felt a bit startled. One of her first compliments around this place, of sorts.

Sheirkia came around the chair. "I think that about does it for today. Don't be surprised if your candle has been removed from your quarters. We don't need to add temptation to the students first learning firework. Otherwise, same time tomorrow." Kiadora jumped out of her chair as Sheirkia blew out the candle.

"Aw, how am I supposed to see when I wash up?" Sheirkia turned with flair.

"You'll just have to put your bowl by the doorway and pull back the curtain. It's only temporary. Now off," said Sheirkia, waving both hands at the door.

Kiadora walked out of the door and back to her quarters, wondering if she could beat them to it and hide the candle somehow, but it was already gone when she got back. How did they communicate so fast around here?

As she was fiddling with her curtain to see how she could possibly secure it back while she was washing up, Regelend was making his way up the ladder next to her doorway and stopped.

"Did you start your studies project?" he said with a wink. He leaned over and secured the curtain to a loop that was attached to the side of the entrance. Odd, Kiadora had never noticed it before. Handy.

The curtain in place, Kiadora leaned on the opposite side of her doorway and said in an undertone, "Oh, yeah, I talked to a few." Regelend only looked at her with a half smirk.

"Sure, I know you. I also know that you're a terrible liar." Kiadora jumped to the other side of her entrance and leaned past the curtain.

"Regelend, I don't know who to talk to. They could be a Matrina who sees it for what it is. I don't want to get dragged before the Elders for this. And who do you think you are?" she suddenly half shouted, shoving Regelend's shoulder. He teetered slightly on the ladder, looking down as if he were contemplating his chances of continuing life if Kiadora was to shove him off.

"Can I...?" Regelend said, gesturing toward the door.

"Fine." Kiadora took a resolute step backwards as Regelend took a grateful step off the ladder.

"Regelend, why did you bring me to those people?" she said in an whisper. "All they wanted me to be was be some message running stooge."

"I didn't know they were going to ask you to do that. Do you think I would have put you in that spot, especially knowing your stance on all of this and being so new? I know you better than that. I also know that you are just going along with it to get to the surface."

"You're damn right I am. And I've been trying. I've been trying to think of a way to bring this up to people innocently, and I think I have it. It's unconventional, but it will allow me to go undetected by the Elders."

"This is something we believe in, Kiadora, and you're just tagging along."

Kiadora felt her heart miss a beat. This is what she had been afraid of, that they would know and she would be stuck down here. But still.

"Listen," said Kiadora, a breath away from Regelend's face. "You need a sales person, and I need to get out of here, at least for a little while, or I'm going to lose it. I'll spread your message the best I can, and you keep your mouth shut as to why I am going along. You guys don't seem likely or in a position to find someone else. Your days are numbered, and most of you are blacklisted by the Elders, anyway."

Regelend threw his arms up, then spun and threw himself onto the edge of Kiadora's bed in a lump. He clenched his jaw, looking like he was keeping from yelling. Kiadora just stood at the doorway, her hands on her hips, regarding him.

"All I wanted to do was help," said Regelend in a controlled tone. "I didn't want to send out a nonbelieving prophet on behalf of us, and I didn't want to force a friend into something she didn't want to do." He pressed his thumb and forefinger to each side of his eyebrows. After a pause,

"What did you have in mind?"

Kiadora came and sat next to him on the bed.

"Well," she said in an even tone. She was touched that Regelend counted her as a friend after all that had gone between them lately. "I walked in on my teacher after she came out of one of her meditation trances. She was livid. She had wide eyes and shook because she was so energized. She had just received what she called wisdom from Eatheria. She was enthusiastic and positively radiant with her realization. I figured if I could look the same, look touched by a message from Eatheria, it would be plausible." Regelend reclined, looking into the distance.

"Yes, yes, that could work."

"But the problem remains, who do I talk to about this? I don't want to walk up to a Matrina or an Elder and announce our trip to the surface." Regelend laughed slightly.

"Wellian doesn't think things out that clearly in his enthusiasm. I have been thinking about that same problem as well. I'm glad you didn't start, but I figured you'd put it off." Regelend shot her a disarming grin.

"Do us a favor, mark down the people who seem interested in the message of the Ollox without mentioning the trip. And make sure not to call it the Ollox, that will only raise suspicion. We will find people later and pass them the information of what our plan is. Otherwise, I had a list of people who might not squeal and seem to fit poorly with their ways down here. Granted, not as much as you, so be careful."

Regelend reached into an inner pocket and pulled out a piece of parchment, handing it to Kiadora. Kiadora opened it and frowned as she saw a list of names.

"Regelend, I don't know most of these people. In fact, I don't know anyone on this list. People can be pretty secluded here, and I'm no social creature myself."

"Kiadora, most people appear secluded to you because you look like you would rather be dead than be where you are. They have a tendency to pass people up like that because they assume the person doesn't want to talk. Yes, this place is a somber study environment, but other people make more than one friend."

Kiadora sat in silence for a moment. Then,

"Sometimes, I'd rather be dead than down here."

"Then talk to the people who I wrote down. Here." Regelend took the piece of paper from Kiadora. "I'll write down any distinguishing features."

Kiadora got up to get a pen from her table drawer and handed it to Regelend. She sat down on the bed and looked over Regelend's shoulder as he wrote. She saw comments like, "mole on right cheek," and "fiery hair with a limp." At last Regelend handed the piece of paper back.

"You remember that Belina has more freckles on the left side of her cheek than her right?"

"Yes, it's quite distinctive. People are very unique when you take the time." Kiadora shook her head.

"Alright. I'll give this a shot. I'll hunt people down and give them a talk."

"I don't know how aware of this you are, but it is only 10 days until the Ollox arrives."

"Like I would know anything about the sun, I've been down here so damn long. Time is weird down here. Weeks feel like days, days feel like weeks. But I'll get going. I'll return this piece of paper with a yes or a no marked next to it." Regelend smiled.

"Perfect. And I'm not trying to get mean about it, but make sure you're convincing and sound like you care. The others, and especially Wellian, will not be so forgiving of the fact that you are in it for the day trip."

"Sure, I'll make it look like I love the great bird in the sky," said Kiadora with a grin. Regelend nodded and made his way to the door.

"10 days, Kiadora," said Regelend, as he turned and stepped out onto the ladder. Kiadora looked down at the list of about 15 people. All these people to talk to. Regelend had made sure she couldn't mistake these people either. Hair color and height were added in addition to the odd physical quirks.

She was glad for the extra light as she scanned Regelend's cramped handwriting.

How could she not have noticed that hook hand?

CHAPTER 20

That night at dinner, Kiadora sat at her individual table eating a brown beef and potato concoction. She knew Lid handled much of the cooking, but his prowess consisted mainly of every casserole dish it was possible to make. She sat eating, glancing down at her lap. There she had placed the list from Regelend. It was hard this way, as she was sitting at the back of the room, but it beat constantly turning around to scan the crowd and this was the largest regular group gathering. She would use the large social gathering in five days to find the ones she could not find otherwise. Now was her best chance at identifying them initially so she would remember who to talk to.

She had already spotted one far off to the right side of the hall- a tall, lanky man with the shortest black hair she had ever seen. It was practically fuzz. She had also found a woman with drooping eyes, another woman with a long scar on her nose named Corminda and the woman with more freckles on one side of her face than the other. It was like one side had been in a freak brown paint flinging accident. Now she sat at the back watching people sit down. She had come early for this purpose. She scanned those who were already seated based on half profiles. By the end of dinner she had nine of 15. When she got up to leave nine became 11 with a man who had no eyebrows and the woman with the mole. She now had enough people she recognized to approach.

In the evenings people usually meditated, something about the darker aspects of the sunset. Whatever the case, no one was out for Kiadora to approach so she went to the library to go through a book about 200-year-old artistic styles of the desert dwellers. Odd, lots of prophets with glowing bodies. She looked at her own pale hand in the shadow of a bookshelf.

"I have to tell you," said Kiadora in an urgent undertone, grabbing the droopy-eyed woman by the shoulders at the perimeter of the classrooms, "about a savior." Kiadora made sure to keep her eyes wide and shake slightly, but not enough to set off any explosions, just as she had practiced in the mornings before several hours of dully staring into that orange-white flicker. It had been half an hour before the blue spot in her vision had faded.

The woman turned around and looked at Kiadora, her eyes going slightly wide, the characteristic droopiness fading slightly.

"Savior?" Her voice came out in a soft tone to match the wispy blond hair that fell to her shoulders.

"Yes, it came to me, I know it to be true. From Eatheria, it has to be," Kiadora carried on in a rapid tone. "I have to tell as many people as I can. Just a few days from now, our savior will come as a great eagle to take us to paradise."

The other woman, Merrina, the list said, actually reached out and patted Kiadora on the head. Kiadora's eyes would have gone wide if they weren't already and the shaking stopped.

"You must be in the water stages, it happens to the best of us." Then Merrina smiled and continued on her way.

Kiadora followed the man with the short hair out of the library later. He only politely smiled without a word and kept walking. Kiadora let him go. She still didn't want to drag too many people into this madness.

The third, the man with the hook hand, also parted ways immediately with an amused smile and a, "that's alright."

The fourth, the woman with the freckles, actually stopped. "A giant bird?" Then her eyes went wide. "The Ollox," she breathed. "You saw him in a vision?"

"Yes, yes, and he is our savior, not our destroyer." The woman scratched her chin as she thought.

"I guess for our kind he might be. Interesting." And she continued on her way. Kiadora pulled out her piece of paper and marked three "no's" and a "yes." On to the woman named Corminda.

The rest of the day Kiadora wandered around in futility, failing to find Corminda or anyone else. Eight more days. Only 25 percent of the people she talked to had said yes. Still, she looked like she was trying, without putting too many people at risk.

The next day, Kiadora sat looking into the candle. The last time she had done this she had pretended to gaze while her mind ran around and wondered about this business with the Ollox. She had worried about it all morning and yesterday as well. The woman, Belina, recognizing it as the Ollox meant that Regelend was right about her, her mind was still with the Holy Text enough to outwardly associate the two.

But this also meant that word could get back to the Elders that there was a woman rampaging around with ideas about the Ollox, the being from the Holy Text and their oppressors. All Kiadora could do was hope that these people who recognized it were so devoted to the text, or apathetic enough, to not go to the Elders. If she was caught, she could just say that all she saw was a giant bird, it wasn't she who had said it was *the* giant bird. And were the Elders really that in touch, anyway?

Kiadora couldn't stand to think about it for another moment, so she just let go and decided to watch the flame.

It was the same as before, the tiny particles going in and out of the flame in straight lines, however this time there were four instead of three. Kiadora watched each particle go in and out, in and out, switching between the four.

And then it happened in an instant. It was as if the flame itself became transparent. Rows and rows of the particles, white, yellow, orange and red, now made up the outline of the flame in lines, some parallel, some intersecting. The flame was no longer hard to look at like before, no longer possessed that blinding incandescence. Kiadora resisted the urge to leap backwards. Instead, she kept staring as she had before.

Around they went, passing through the wick and up to the top regions of the flame, bending and swaying with the flame, caught in their own elemental dance. Somehow, Kiadora knew it was as old as the very first days of existence and as new as this very moment, changing, shifting, but sustaining man for ages. Kiadora vaguely wondered how she was capable of thinking such a profound thing.

But right now it didn't matter. None of those endless questions mattered, just this dance of Eatheria. She watched until she swore she was captured in it, the dance engulfing her. It seemed to encase her world, her peripheral vision only seeing this scene.

And then she felt a rough pull backward and the world returned once more. She was in the hard wooden chair on the stupid purple rug. Sheirkia's hand was on her shoulder. The flame twinkled, closed off and distant, as if it might as well have been the flame of a light-house, shining to her from a distant coast on the horizon. She longed for that closeness and felt a depth of loneliness that she, in all of her years as an independent outcast, assumed that she was immune to.

For the first time since she was a small child, she broke down and wept. Sheirkia bent down and hugged her, her wild hair falling in Kiadora's face. The enclosure of yellow only reminded her of the flame and she wept harder out of sheer loneliness. It was as if she was a young woman in all of those ballads she heard on the surface. Women would wail at their guitars for lovers lost to the sea, war or to other women. They sang about how isolated they were and how they just wanted the comfort back. It now seemed Kiadora knew how these women felt.

This went on for about five minutes, Kiadora sobbing rivers into Sheirkia's hair and Sheirkia rocking her as if she were a child. Finally, Kiadora pulled herself back as she gradually felt the pain go from an immediate burn to a dull ache. She reached up and wiped her eyes as

Sheirkia sat back on the balls of her feet in a squat.

"What was that?" Kiadora asked in a hoarse voice. "I don't cry, I never cry."

"That was your first time touching your soul essence to elemental Eatheria for a prolonged time." Sheirkia had an awed tone in her voice and shook her head. "You latched on remarkably fast. My intention was to just have you observe it for a while. You were at first, and then you started to connect." Kiadora stared at her.

"How can you tell?"

"When you get more advanced, you start to see the flow of others' energy. I can see lines of sorts that are people's energy and yours were flowing right into the flame."

"Is it like that every time?" Kiadora played with the edge of her dress. She was starting to feel awkward and just downright stupid of crying over a candle. But that connection…

"No, no, goodness no," said Sheirkia, shaking her head. "It's just very intense for those who aren't used to that sort of closeness. Were you loved as a child?" Kiadora furrowed her brow.

"Yeah, I think so."

"No, you would not think so, you would know." Sheirkia put a hand on Kiadora's knee and looked into her eye. "Were you loved?" she repeated slowly.

"I, I don't know. Everyone made sure I was healthy, but Dad was always busy with politics and Mom, well, I never knew what she did. It didn't involve us. Dehlia and Ashila, my sisters, thought I was deranged. Lisera, the housekeeper, was nice. She was the one who recognized what I was and said I should come here. But she was still distant because she was so busy. Dad didn't like to pay too many housekeepers. Why?"

"You seem to have an isolated background."

"Not completely," said Kiadora defiantly. "There was my friend Tahn."

"And how often did you get to see him?"

"Well, once a week, if we were lucky. And I never could open up to him about what I was, and when I did he turned me in." Sheirkia nodded and Kiadora sat back with a sigh. She remembered what Narissa had said about hating him, despising him in order to let him go. Narissa was right in a way, he was essentially her betrayer, but somehow she wanted to believe that there was hope between them, even if it was because he was all she had from her past, she knew.

"I don't want to completely forget about my past," Kiadora said. Sheirkia leaned in.

"Sorry?" Kiadora jumped when she realized that was out loud.

"My..my last teacher said to leave it all behind, to despise it even, so that I could move forward." Kiadora had been looking straight ahead. She turned her head slowly to look Sheirkia in the eye. "Are you going to make me do that?" Sheirkia paused for a moment.

"I think," Sheirkia said in a deliberate tone. "The answer is that you will get to a point when you see it as necessary." Sheirkia stood up and turned her back to Kiadora as she started to gather up her candle and the rest of her materials. "You may leave," Sheirkia said, as if to the table.

Kiadora stood up, watching Sheirkia, now with the items in her arms, walk over to the cabinet and open it with a free hand as she balanced the candle, the holder, the snuffer and the matches in her arms. Inside was what Kiadora expected- all the shiny metal objects one could find: daggers, swords, incense burners, a large copper skull. That last one she hadn't expected. But there were candles galore, about three shelves of them, and another shelf stuffed with dark jars. Sheirkia made herself busy arranging the candles on the self in an exact position to the left. She seemed intent on stopping today's session, her back still to Kiadora, as she started to rearrange the third shelf as she carefully put away the snuffer. Kiadora let out a breath and walked out the door.

As she walked past the numerous gaping caverns, her mind reeled, trying to make sense of what just happened. It was just flame, like the millions she had seen during her lifetime. But she felt close with it, as if a second jigsaw puzzle piece had been wedged into an empty slot in her soul. She still felt the gaping emptiness, even if she was past being reduced to tears over it.

Kiadora felt jilted over what Sheirkia was implying. Sheirkia had never said it, but Kiadora knew what she was getting at. Kiadora had a history of isolation and loneliness, and her connection to Eatheria, her first true, direct connection to it, filled in that emptiness and made her that much more likely to bond with Eatheria.

And somehow, as she rounded the bend and felt the heat from the Eternal Fires she passed, the knowledge did not matter. She felt herself being drawn to the warmth and headed over to the fire, gleeful at the sight and sound of the crackling flame and that inviting orange flicker on the wall from the fire. And then she couldn't help but grin when she saw the roaring fire that measured about 20 arm lengths in diameter. She didn't know how she could have been so unimpressed the first time she saw it. Watching the flames interact was paradise. More fire particles than she had ever seen danced wildly among the flames, in and out, in and out. Her grin widened at that sight of the merry particles. Her breathing became still and she could feel herself being pulled toward the fire. Any moment now, those flames would open themselves to her and she would see that elemental dance, like a lover opening his heart to her.

And then a hand came down firmly on her shoulder again, stopping her in her tracks.

"I knew I shouldn't have let you make your way back on your own. This is just too much for most students, and you especially." Kiadora shook her head, coming to. The rest of the world seemed to come flooding back, and the flame didn't seem quite as large as life. Kiadora turned back to see Sheirkia standing behind her with her arm out-stretched to Kiadora's shoulder and a frown to match her stern tone. She took a step closer and put her arm fully around Kiadora's shoulders, steering her around.

"Come." Kiadora had no choice but to follow Sheirkia. Her steps slowed as she looked back towards the flame. Sheirkia forced her on with added pressure, and Kiadora felt a dull ache somewhere around her chest as the warmth of the fire receded and the dampness of the caverns returned. The intricate heating system seemed to take care of most of the dampness, but what was left seemed exaggerated now.

Then her thoughts shifted back to what she was considering before.

"I'm like this because I wasn't terribly close to anyone. That's it, isn't it?"

"Yes," said Sheirkia bluntly, her arm still around Kiadora's shoulders, as if she expected Kiadora to bolt at any moment. "You easily have one of the strongest affinities to Eatheria, and especially fire, that I have ever seen. And I don't think that's a coincidence, given your background. We've all had a certain amount of isolation, given what we are. Many of us have never been particularly close with our families, like you. However, few of us have been betrayed by a good friend. Still, no one has been tortured in such a prolonged way and survived coming down here. Most decide they are cured, others die, some go insane. Only one made his way down here."

"And what happened to him?"

"He committed suicide." Apparently Sheirkia had no sensibilities about sparing the emotions of others by withholding the truth, Kiadora thought. Her heart felt like it had stopped. Take out the rituals, and apparently you were left with the woman's blunt truth.

"What?"

"He hung himself from one of the ladders with a bed sheet. He couldn't handle what he was, thought he was an abomination and that he had deserved the torture in the chambers of the Church. Also couldn't handle being forced to engage in what he had been made to believe was evil."

"Wow, I never once thought of this or myself as evil…"

"I know," said Sheirkia, staring straight forward. "You have too strong of a personality to think otherwise. But either way, you have been betrayed, isolated and tortured, mentally cut off from the creative forces as a result. It's natural to latch on to a connection to something other than yourself so strongly."

"Something that isn't a failing human or an imaginary creator. Something that just is," Kiadora spat. Sheirkia gave a thin smile.

"But that is why you are to have a guard. He is to meet us at your quarters."

"A guard," Kiadora shrieked. How was she supposed to do this prophet work and get the Hell out of here? There was this new pleasure of the fires, but nothing could compare to the trees and the forest, and she imagined the sunlight would take on a whole new level of enchantment.

"Yes, I think it is best so you are not tempted. People have walked straight into the Eternal Fires before."

"I wouldn't do that," Kiadora protested.

"You almost just did," said Sheirkia, rounding the corner out of the caverns. A man with brown hair and a beard going down to the center of his chest stood waiting for them. Through all of that hair, Kiadora thought she could glimpse a friendly smile.

"This is Broean," said Sheirkia. "He'll be your guard." Kiadora gave a thin smile.

"And how long will you be watching me?"

"As long as it takes," said Broean, that smile further manifesting itself in a twinkle in his pale blue eyes. He was a large man. Something about the way his muscles bulged under his plain, tan tunic told Kiadora that the friendly smile could disappear fast were she to try anything.

"We will move the curtain back farther from the entryway. Broean will sit on the outside and you can still have your privacy." Sheirkia walked forward and led Broean and Kiadora up to the quarters as if she was showing Kiadora the place for the first time. She stopped on the ladder right by Kiadora's doorway and leaned over. Her hand touched the end of the pole that held the curtain up. She simply yanked the end of the pole out of the sod wall, which automatically retracted in the middle. Kiadora saw the end was nothing more than a sharp spike, which Sheirkia jammed about two long strides farther back from the doorway. She got off the ladder and did the same to the other side.

'Great,' thought Kiadora. 'Now I can feel more cramped.' Sheirkia stepped back onto the ladder, moved farther up the rungs and motioned the other two to step in front of the curtain. She kept climbing and after a moment returned with a chair hanging off a leather harness she had strapped around her shoulders. She stepped over, slung the chair off her back and set it in front of the curtain, farthest to the right, facing the ladder. Broean gave a quick thanks and Sheirkia nodded as she folded the harness up and placed it in a pocket in one of her skirts.

"Kiadora, Broean will accompany you wherever you go. And if you try anything, we will know," Sheirkia said, giving Kiadora a stern look in the eye that further implied that Kiadora didn't want to know the consequences of disobeying. "Same time tomorrow, then," said Sheirkia as she stepped onto the ladder. She offered a thanks and a goodnight to Broean and was gone.

Broean smiled at her once more and took a seat in the chair Sheirkia left.

"Do as you wish, ma'am, just no funny business with Eatheria. I'll be watching."

Kiadora just stood, looking at the man. She felt strange, standing outside her shut curtain, looking out onto the massive compound. She looked at the labyrinth of open-topped corridors and the spots of brown, blond, black and the occasional red moving through them.

She looked back to Broean, who stared back into her eyes boldly. Kiadora went back into her quarters with a simple swish of the curtain. This would take some thought.

CHAPTER 21

Kiadora walked along her usual way to her session, studying the rocks as she went as if she had never seen any formed in quite so interesting of a pattern. Broean was trailing behind her. He looked relaxed and had a pleasant expression, but he watched Kiadora with an intense gaze. Kiadora looked back at the rocks, not wanting to incite conversation. The night before the man had swept open the curtain when she was in the middle of washing up and started to make small talk by asking where she was from and what brought her down here.

She had answered with, "Where I'm from is none of your business, and what do you think brought me down here? The same thing as everyone else. Now I'm going to bed, close the damn curtain."

What had bothered her was his expression had not changed a bit. He still had that pleasant smile and had a soft, but deep, tone. He had closed the curtain with an, "alright, goodnight," and had left it at that.

He had followed her down to the first meal, cheerfully voicing his hopes for an egg dish, had sat directly across from her at her table (no one seemed to think this was odd) and was now escorting her to Sheirkia's room.

"Are you going to watch the lesson, too?" Kiadora spat.

"Of course not," he said in a pleasant tone. He reached into an inner pocket of his tunic and pulled out a small brown book. Borean sat on the ground next to the door and proceeded to read the immensely small type in the flickering torchlight.

'I hope you develop blurred vision,' Kiadora thought as she entered Sheirkia's room.

The same candle, table and stool sat out. Kiadora had dreaded having to deal with the flame again. She had spent too much time before she fell asleep dwelling on what had happened yesterday. She had loved the sensation, but dreaded getting sucked in more. The worst was the sense of being so dependant on the flame for her happiness afterward. She had always stood on her own. Why the fire made her feel so lonely was still mostly beyond her. It didn't matter that she wasn't close to her family. Sheirkia had made it sound like she needed a substitute in her loneliness, so she latched on to the fire's energy. She didn't need that connection, she never had before, just that control Sheirkia had forced on the flame with ease.

Nevertheless, she walked toward the chair and took a seat. Sheirkia turned her head and smiled to Kiadora from where she was rummaging in the cupboard. She came forward with the same box of matches.

"Have you thought about what happened yesterday?"

"Too much."

"Do you feel any different?" Sheirkia put the matches down and leaned on the table slightly.

"Not really, just ashamed." Sheirkia rose both eyebrows.

"Ashamed?"

273

"I cried. I cried because of a candle."

"It was more than that."

"I almost walked into a bonfire because I was that enamored with something. I shouldn't need other things like that. I was always fine mostly by myself." Sheirkia gave a thin smile.

"You'll see differently." She bent down to light the candle, and Kiadora watched warily as the flame jumped back to life. It seemed more sinister today, turning around violently, wanting to draw her in. And still she watched it because she knew that was what she was expected to do. Sheirkia stepped off to the side without a word.

Kiadora wasn't in the mood to cry today. She was aggravated enough. She needed to get rid of Broean. The usual less ethical ways of disposing of someone in the high courts leapt to her mind: poisoning, "hunting accidents," simple abduction. But as much as she wanted Broean out of the way, she knew she didn't have it in her to dispose of the man. That was the frustration talking.

No, the only thing that came to her mind was slipping away when he wasn't looking, which seemed to be never, or the hope of knocking him unconscious, despite the fact that he looked like he could take four of her at one time. And then there were the unspoken consequences. It was probably three days of confinement for slipping away, and that would only set her back on her work for the Children, if she was even free in time to get out of this place.

As if returning from another realm, her thoughts surfaced to the candle right in front of her, like it sprang up from nowhere. That thing got her into this mess. Would it be possible to prove she didn't need this person hanging around if she were to show them that she could manage the presence of flame on her own? Would it be that easy, could she do it in a matter of seven days?

No, she would need more time to play prophet some more to get rid of suspicion. She hardly had anyone convinced. If she couldn't finish her task, would Regelend then be so forgiving still? She knew he wasn't malicious, but she was walking a tightrope as it was. The others already had little reason to trust her. Could she do it in one day, two? Kiadora didn't know what other choice she had.

"About this business of getting my connection to Eatheria under control, I'll do it in two days," Kiadora said. She looked up sharply at Sheirkia, who looked back with an expansive smile.

"Ambitious. Two days, you say? You should know it can take up to several moon cycles."

"I don't care, I don't like being watched. I feel cadged." Not an entire lie. "It'll take two days, and you're going to help me." For the first time, Kiadora heard Sheirkia laugh. It had a tinkling, musical quality to it.

"I like that spirit," Sheirkia said. "I certainly can't guarantee anything. I once had to work with someone for 11 moon cycles."

"What's the shortest you've ever had?" Kiadora asked, leaning forward with her elbows on her knees. Sheirkia looked off, shifting through her memory.

"Two weeks," she said, looking back at Kiadora. Kiadora leaned back in her chair, her elbows now placed on the backrest. Two weeks. She didn't have two weeks.

"And they were very eager and skillful with this Eatheria to begin with?"

Sheirkia nodded.

"Oh, yes, crashed through the lower levels like a charging bull. She's now a higher level Matrina of Air, Delandea is her name. She'll be an Elder by age 45, they say. She would be the youngest Elder the council has seen." Kiadora nodded slowly, frowning. She doubted she could ever be that skilled and move that fast through here. But she had a small glimpse of freedom on the line, that had to account for something.

"I'm still going to do this quicker and faster," Kiadora said, leaning forward in her chair once more. She had her elbows resting on her knees again, as if to get closer to the candle to take it down head-on. Sheirkia cocked her head.

"You really hate being watched that much?"

"I don't like being controlled, I don't like feeling like a prisoner and I don't like being around another person all the time. I value my privacy, it keeps me focused. Now let me watch this candle." Sheirkia retreated about a body's length away from the table while Kiadora marveled at her own directness.

"Anything I should know before I go at this again? I want to be successful. No crying."

"Unfortunately, the process is so individualized to the practitioner, all I can do is supervise." The other woman had a bitter look. Clearly she wanted to do more, far more. Kiadora already knew enough about the woman to know she wanted to be center stage. Kiadora focused on the flame.

"Alright, but if you think of anything, offer it."

And Kiadora watched the flame, this time counting four particles flowing around the outside. Again the pattern: in, out, in, out, as quickly as possible. This time it seemed to happen almost instantly. The flame seemed to shoot open, and she could see the rows of particles flowing, surrounded in a bright material that almost looked like molten lead, but white. It was light in liquid form. Although the miraculous substance took a background to the particles of orange, red, yellow, and at the center, a creamy white that barely stood out against the pure white of the background.

Although she knew where her body was, she seemed to leave it behind as her peripheral vision faded. She was surrounded in particles that danced along certain highways. The vision had a 360 degree surrounding view, and she knew that somehow she was in the flame, touching its essence, its primal energy.

Kiadora looked closer, and the tiny particles seemed to be clusters of even smaller dots of the same color. And still smaller particles danced among these. The smallest of the particles looked only like the tiniest pinpricks of light, as if she was viewing the farthest star in the night sky, except instead of inky darkness they hung in a background of purest white.

She seemed to sit in this substance, but did not feel warm or cold, wet or dry. She realized she felt physically nothing, as if she had escaped that part of her being; somehow she knew it had been left somewhere else to deal with her physical needs. She had no needs at the moment. There was Eatheria and nothing else.

Somewhere in the back of her mind she felt a love for what she was viewing grow. Eatheria would provide; it would make whatever stupid thing she was worrying about not matter anymore. She could stay here forever, just watching these images of pyrotechnic splendor. The way the particles seemed to dance around each other... The biggest, the medium and the smallest formed infinite patterns. It was the most miraculous thing she had ever seen. Some formed octagonal patterns, other formed diamonds and spiked patterns, only to disappear instantly. And she watched as those patterns formed and faded, as if it was happening solely for her amusement.

And then in an instant, Kiadora was sitting on the chair in Sheirkia's room. It had happened as if Kiadora was in the flame one moment and then had teleported back to her chair. Sheirkia had her hand on Kiadora's shoulder again, and by the way her shoulder ached, she could tell Sheirkia was shaking her hard. Kiadora wanted to think it would take more than shaking to get her out of such a trance.

Kiadora looked back at the flame and saw it flickering once more, a typical lit candle. She felt saddened at the distance of the flame, regretful that she could not spend her whole life within that entity, but she did not feel the same earth-shattering separation and loneliness.

"Good, you've undergone the Separation." Kiadora looked up at Sheirkia, who finally removed her hand and went to blow out the candle. With a huff the flame was no more. Kiadora felt a twinge of pain. It was how she imagined it would feel is someone close to her had died. She took a deep breath, willing herself to move forward. She didn't have time for this.

"The Separation?" Kiadora asked. Sheirkia stood up and faced Kiadora, leaning on the table.

"Yes, that is when you mentally shift from your body to the element. You allow your spiritual complete essence to flow into the candle. Your mind and all of your perception flow with it. Your body is nothing but an empty husk at that moment."

"I didn't feel anything physically, even when I expected my heart to race or even see my body. But none of it was there," said Kiadora in a pensive tone. Sheirkia nodded.

"That's why it's called The Separation."

"And all it took to get me back was a shake?"

"A little more than that. You may notice a bruise on your arm in the morning. At this stage, the only thing that can bring a student back is a slight trauma to the body. There is still a connection there, like a small string holding your spirit to your body. The spirit will recognize the threat and come back instantly. Later you will control this on your own."

"I don't feel like crying," Kiadora stated. "Why?"

"Again, that has to do with the Separation. The mind is experiencing Eatheria separate from the body, so the body does not crave the connection *as intensely*," said Sheirkia, putting emphasis on the last two words. "This is why you still need to be watched."

"Still, I'm doing better than last time. I'm not a weeping mess."

"Yes, but you are still vulnerable." Sheirkia came around and put an arm around Kiadora's shoulder. "You're doing much better in a 10 hour period than anyone. You're moving at a rate none have seen." Kiadora jumped out of her chair.

"Ten hours?" She already lost a day. Six more days now.

"You need to relax, these things take time."

"I want to stop being watched, stop being held prisoner," Kiadora nearly shouted. Sheirkia glanced at the door with a worried expression. Kiadora remembered Broean was sitting out there all ten hours.

"At any rate, I think you had better get going." Kiadora walked to the curtain and turned.

"I'll walk past that fire and not give a damn, you'll see." Kiadora went past the curtain, out the door and looked down to where Broean was. He sat cross-legged, looking out at nothing in particular, somehow as bright and attentive as ever. He looked up at her with that ever-present smile, as if he had been sitting out in the hall for two minutes, not ten hours.

"Why have you been out here all this time, anyway?"

"In case you bolt past your teacher, it happens," he said in that deep tone as he jumped up nimbly. "How did your lesson go?" he asked as they started down the corridor.

"Fine, just fine." She meant it to come out more harsh, but it just sounded weary. She didn't expect to feel as tired as she did. It only felt like she was in there for not even a few minutes, but ten hours had apparently knocked it out of her.

She felt the warmth coming up from the fires and felt a twinge of longing come with it. She would prove to them she didn't need to be watched. As the warmth hit the side of her arm and her face she dearly wanted to turn in, but she was able to resist this time. She chalked it up to The Separation thing Sheirkia was talking about, but there was the fatigue. She was not fighting it off nearly as well as she wanted to. Her steps wobbled towards the flame, but she was able to steer herself back.

They reached her quarters, Kiadora stepping off the ladder. Broean followed and made his way to the chair. Tomorrow. Tomorrow he would be gone. Broean called out a cheerful, "goodnight!" to which Kiadora made no response.

Kiadora splashed water on her face and threw herself into bed, the coarse straw mattress actually welcome to her leaden body. What she didn't understand was that if she was separated from her body all day how she could still be so tired physically. All her body did was sit.

Yet despite the intense drowsiness, she couldn't fall asleep. She lay there, looking up at the mottled surface of her ceiling, light playing over the crevices. The main lamp that hung from the giant cords was turned down already to about of third of its full capacity, just enough to see to get around, but not enough to read by.

She was just about to fall asleep, feeling the drowsiness finally flood over her and take control. Then her eyes snapped open. Kiadora's foot bopped and her finger tapped. She felt panicked and her heart raced. She needed something. Something. Yes, that was it. She didn't know quite how she knew, it was as if it was calling to her.

Time to pay a visit to the Eternal Fires.

Kiadora got out of her bed, never feeling more sure of anything in her life. It was time to visit the fires and nothing was going to stand in her way. She walked to her curtain, threw it open and took a step forward.

And was immediately tackled to the ground. She let out cry, her right cheek hitting the compacted sod floor.

"Get off, I need to go!" She struggled against the mass that held her down, her arms pinned behind her back. What she thought earlier was right. Broean could take four of her at once. Broean held her silently, his knee digging into her back. She could not see his face, just the outline of his wild mane of hair. Kiadora glanced past his head.

The chandelier, if only she could get there and feel the warmth that amount of candles must produce. She felt a tear leak down her cheeks as she realized that she would never be able to reach it, nor the Eternal Fires. Her shoulders started to ache from the awkward position that she was being held. An idea came.

"Can you let up? You're hurting me." Her voice came out with a sob attached to it. She was still crying. But Broean kept his unusual silence and held her as tight as ever. She had no choice but to lie there, that hurt and odd feeling of abandonment growing. If she could just get to the fires, she wouldn't feel that way. She lay and sobbed silently into the dirt as Broean held her, apparently afraid she would bolt if he moved. She felt a prick in the side of her arm. If she could just get to the...

CHAPTER 22

The next thing Kiadora knew she was lying in bed. The lamps were turned all the way up again, and her shoulders still ached slightly. Her arm hurt a bit worse, and she pulled her sleeve up to see a blue bruise had formed. She stared for a moment and remembered being pushed to the ground and held there. But she wasn't tossed that hard. No, she remembered what Sheirkia had said. Sheirkia had been the one to call her back to her body, to express an apology for putting the bruise on her arm.

Kiadora swung her legs to the floor and glanced through the curtain to where she could see the outline of Broean sitting as stiff and straight as ever on his chair. She didn't want to face him on the way to breakfast. She remembered clearly the sobbing and that resolve that no one would stop her on the way to the fires. And that loneliness… Kiadora knew her face must be going red out of shame at that moment. She was supposed to be stronger than that, especially after telling Sheirkia that she would show them, that it would be done in two days. She was now down to one and still reduced to tears. But sitting here wasn't going to change any of that.

She stood up and went to her bowl on the little night table. Her face must be a mess after having it planted into the ground like that. Kiadora reached up to touch her face, only to find that it was perfectly clean. Broean must have…Kiadora let off a small groan. And to be washed off by someone else like a child... She turned, heaved a sigh and headed out to face Broean.

He looked over with his smile and said in a friendly voice, "Good morning. Did you sleep well?" As if nothing had happened. Kiadora stood looking out at the labyrinth, the sounds of people chatting softly, making their way down the ladders toward breakfast. In the distance she could hear the sounds of pots hitting tables as they set up in the dining room. The distinct smell of bacon wafted up, no doubt part of some conglomerated dish. Still, Kiadora realized with a rumble of her stomach, she hadn't eaten in a whole day.

She looked back at Broean, who was starting to get up. She felt her face still burn with shame, far from being distracted by the prospect of bacon.

"Sorry about last night," she muttered, looking off in the direction of the ladder now. "I thought I was stronger than that." Broean waved one hand dismissively.

"No need, no need, it's what I'm here for. They don't just stick me here because they want to bother you. These things happen all the time. Did you sleep well?" he asked again.

"You know, as a matter of fact, I did, better than I have in years, if ever." No waking up from the nightmares, no inability to fall back asleep. It was bliss.

"Good, I administered the serum correctly, then. I'm still new at it, we just started using it." Kiadora snapped her head around.

"Serum?"

"Yes, it's a natural sedative that goes right into the veins via injection," said Broean pleasantly, as if discussing a sunny day. He reached into a pocket and held up a syringe.

"You put that in me, and you're still new at it?"

"Guarantee you didn't feel anything from the elemental withdrawal, and the sedative helps with the people who have the most trouble adapting to the connection with Eatheria. Many have gone mad in the night, craving that connection like a drug. This should reduce it by almost 90 percent." Kiadora closed her eyes for a moment and let out a breath. She was going to throw this man off this ledge, no matter how painless the drug had been or how much it helped.

"You mean to tell me, you injected me with a drug without my permission to counteract what you see to be something akin to a drug craving?"

"Well, yes. It helped, didn't it?" said Broean brightly. "A close cousin to it is also being tested to see how it can help with visions and higher spiritual connections. One to stop the connection and one to help; interesting what we can do with herbs, isn't it?"

Kiadora took a slow breath. 'I can get out of here, if even for a little while,' Kiadora told herself silently. She was starting to wonder if she would even come back. 'I just have to find a way to harness this. Today.' She started down the ladder towards the first meal.

Later in Sheirkia's room, Kiadora sat in the chair looking at the ceiling, her arms hanging down on both sides and her legs out. She had mulled over at breakfast how she was to stop the nonsense of craving this element. But the feeling was so intense she didn't know how she would stop it, how to control it. Her brain felt like it was going to split in half with all of the possibilities she ran through since she just woke up. She had run through everything from causing herself physical pain every time she thought of Eatheria to not crave it as much, to requesting a miracle brain surgery to stop insanity. At one point she had settled with, 'Well, I should just stop being like that. It's as simple as that.' But it wasn't.

She again remembered Narissa telling her she had to hate something to let it go and later thought about the connection between her and her body being somehow severed while in the trance. She didn't hate her body, did she? She truly had no idea what she was dealing with or where to go with it.

It had been another day, same as the last, with no progress except for that same awe and the feeling of remorse she was fighting back. As soon as she had realized she spent another day like this, losing yet another day that she should be spending playing the prophet, she had returned to her thoughts of what she could possibly do to speed things up. Sheirkia stood in front of Kiadora, watching her warily since she had thrown herself back in her chair shortly after being shaken out of the connection.

"Did you see something?" Sheirkia asked.

"See something? No, it was the same as yesterday. I'm just thinking. Well, I'll see you tomorrow. Thanks for the extra time you're spending." And Kiadora jumped up out of her chair and headed for the door. Kiadora could somehow feel Sheirkia's eyes on the back of her head.

Out in the caverns, she looked down to see Broean hastily shoving something in his pocket. Once he slipped his hand out of his tunic, he turned and smiled to her. It wasn't the same alert smile, but one of someone who looked like they were close to sleepingwalking while drifting through a magnificent dream. His eyes were half closed and not quite focused. Kiadora leaned in to peer at him.

"Broean?"

"Yes?" he asked in a slow voice.

"What's wrong?"

"Nothing, nothing, couldn't be happier," he said, ending the sentence an octave higher than its beginning. He hovered there, looking at her with what looked like one eye. The other was drifting off to look at the wall behind her.

"We should…get going." It would have been the perfect time to give him the slip, but Kiadora didn't feel right about leaving the man like this. Broean jumped up and followed her down the corridor, weaving slightly as he walked. Kiadora walked along to her quarters, looking back occasionally to see Broean following her with a glassy gaze out to nothing in particular.

They finally made their way to the ladder, and Kiadora continued up to her doorway, the one opening that looked to be missing a curtain; it was a dark, gaping socket in the midst of all the colorful fabric. She looked down when she did not feel the ladder shake slightly with another person's movement.

Broean was standing down by the ladder, looking at it as if it was a strange beast that he had never seen before and had no intention to ride.

"Are you coming?" she called down to him. He looked back up to her, a confused expression marring his features.

"I'm sorry, I don't quite understand." Kiadora let out an exasperated sigh.

"What is there to not understand?" she shouted down to him. "How often have you climbed these damn things? You put your foot on one rung, your other foot on the next above it and keep walking up!" Broean looked down at the bottom most rung quickly, as if just noticing that it was there. He let out a childish bark of laughter.

"Oh, right, right. Alright, I'm coming, hold on!" He put out his foot on the bottommost rung and his other foot on the rung above it, unsteadily like a child just learning how to walk. He still had not put his hand on the ladder. As he fell back, he grabbed the ladder with two hands, looking up at her. Kiadora shook her head and kept moving upwards. What had gotten into him?

"Hey, this is pretty easy, isn't it? You can go really high on these." Kiadora looked down. Broean had a grin on, as if he was on some sort of carnival ride. He looked out. "I can see the top of the classrooms from here! Look, there's Lilliana. Hello Lilliana!" Broean lifted up his arm to wave and swung around wildly before he regained his grip on the side of the ladder.

"Would you get up here, you fool!" Kiadora spat. She was now just outside her quarters. Broean looked back up at her, his gaze still unsteady. He continued to stagger up the ladder. Kiadora jumped to the side and with halting steps, Broean was now in her doorway.

"That was fun, now what do we do?"

"I'm going to bed, and you're going to do whatever it is you do. Sit over there," she instructed, pointing over at the chair. He gave her an expansive salute and tossed himself into the chair. He immediately put his head back and started snoring. Kiadora watched him for a moment, her brow creased.

What was this, some kind of test? Kiadora thought about bolting but leaving him like this just felt heartless. She went back into her quarters and sat on her bed, Broean's snoring echoing back past the curtain.

Kiadora had once seen some of the stablehands act in a similar fashion. Word was that they had gotten into some cleaning alcohol. Kiadora was not so sheltered as to not know that chemicals did some strange things. The use of them was never outwardly condoned, so such chemicals could certainly not be found in legal beverages and foods. To partake in such things was to bond oneself to the earthly pleasures. As Kiadora thought about Broean's ladder escapade, it was no small wonder that the stuff was banned.

But that was another world. Would they care as much down here? Was he just enjoying something that they had decided was a way to get closer to Eatheria? She thought back to the drug that Broean had administered, which had infested her veins in a way a silent poison might. And they were using this to induce visions. *Interesting what we can do with herbs,* Broean had said.

She looked out at his slumped silhouette and thought again of sneaking down. She had work to do. And then Broean rose out of his chair and went to stand at the edge of the doorway. He was laughing and teetering dangerously close to the edge. She jumped up and ran through the curtain to find Broean tottering on the ledge. He looked back to her.

"Look, I can see more people," he exclaimed, pointing down. As he spun to look at her, his foot scraped the edge of the doorway. He lost footing and teetered over. Kiadora ran and caught him, holding him right under the arms. His legs dangled over the edge. She pulled him back and let go of him when he was back on solid ground. He just lay there laughing.

"Ah, that was funny! I'm so clumsy, you know that? Clumsy, clumsy." His words blurred with hysterical laughter. Kiadora frowned. No, there would be no going anywhere tonight. She got up and put her arms around his shoulders and gently led him up and into his chair.

"Just sit there," she said sternly. "I'm going to watch you. Don't try anything." In spite of herself, she gave an ironic grin at hearing herself echo back Broean's role. She went and sat in a corner, slightly behind Broean. He sat in his chair, still laughing for several minutes until he was out again, snoring away.

Kiadora later woke up with a jerk, not even having realized she had drifted off. She looked up to find Broean rummaging loudly for something. He kept jerkily banging his arm against the back of his chair as he searched in one pocket. He seemed not to notice the large thumps to his elbow that would have sent another person into convulsions.

Kiadora blinked at him, trying to figure out why she was not in bed, and then Broean nearly falling off of the edge of her quarters came back to her. Before Kiadora could say anything, Broean pulled something out of his pocket, small and glinting in the light of the chandelier. She stayed still. He did not seem to notice that she was awake.

Kiadora saw him raise his syringe in an arch and plunge it into his arm. As he did so, he was shaking badly and tears were coming out of his eyes. Kiadora jumped up immediately, and Broean snapped his head around at her, the shocked expression of a caught criminal on his face.

"Hey, what do you think you're doing?" She marched toward him, reaching for the vial in his arm. His thumb was already holding down something on the end.

"You don't understand." His voice came out rough and haggard, quite unlike his usual cheery, deep voice. She almost took at step back at the change. "I...I need it for my own studies."

"You don't see what this stuff does to you." She looked closely at his frightened expression. "Or maybe you do. I think you know exactly what is going on with this."

Broean looked down at the syringe, his hand still badly shaking.

"There are days I try to stop," he said gruffly. "But I need it for ...my studies." He was getting that far away look in his eye again. Any moment he would start to babble like a mad man. Maybe fall off the ledge.

Kiadora shook him violently. The syringe fell to the ground, a dull thud on the soil with a hint of a clear ring after.

"Broean, you need to take control of this. You can't live this way, it's not life being that attached to something." Broean started to get a hint of a twinkle to his glassy eyes; it was that of a man lost to her in a state of delirium. Kiadora felt her heart race as he started to fall deeper into that euphoria. His smile grew. Who would she even take him to? They seemed to condone this sort of thing.

She didn't want another night and day of making sure this man did not fall off the ladder. She had precious little time as it was to do what she needed.

As Kiadora pressed up against him, she started to feel her arm getting damp. She looked down to see her sleeve was indeed wet. She had been touching Broean's sleeve, which was soaked through where he had been injecting the needle. Kiadora squinted at it.

"Wait…" She grabbed his arm and pulled back the sleeve. Broean made no resistance.

The arm was entirely clear, no needle marks, no blood. It was only wet. There was no scent, it appeared to just be water.

"You didn't even put this in your arm!" Kiadora looked up into his face to see a broad grin and a steady focus, his eyes calm as before.

"Why?" Kiadora demanded, throwing his arm down. "Why would you do this?" He only still stared at her.

"Forget it, you bastard. It's time for class, anyway." She looked down to the dining area, which from here she could see was empty already. "And no breakfast, thanks to you."

When she made her way over to Sheirkia's room, she felt her joints aching as she walked, like a seized up old spinster. Sitting on the ground all night had not been kind to her, and she was now worried about being able to accomplish what she needed to, much less stay awake.

Sheirkia lifted her head from where she was arranging the candle on the table yet again, and Kiadora knew from the other woman's look of concern she must appear in every way to have been up all night.

Kiadora self-consciously reached up to her hair, which she knew she forgot to comb. Sure enough, it was full of knots as she ran her fingers through it. It was rather oily; she had been too distracted to pay much of a visit to the large wooden tub of tepid water that they called a bathing area. Her eyes felt heavy and gummy, and she knew she must have had terrible circles under them.

"Rough night?" Sheirkia asked.

"I don't want to talk about it," said Kiadora, throwing herself down in the chair. "And it wasn't because of the…cravings, or whatever," she added in a rush.

"Well, nevertheless, are you ready?" said Sheirkia, brandishing the match she held.

"I don't have much of a choice." Sheirkia lit the candle again, and Kiadora gazed at it. To her surprise, she didn't want to drift off to sleep at all. Just watching the flame, she felt more energized than ever.

It came in a rush today. The alien particles surrounded her in an instant, like a parted lover running for the embrace. She felt the bliss and wanted to get even closer this time. She reached out her hand but it was a strange phantom limb, clear for all intents and purposes. She was able to detect it by a slight distortion of the background, as if she was looking through a magnifying lens.

She didn't worry too much about it. It seemed nothing here in this other plane would surprise her any longer. She continued to reach for the nearest stream of particles, the image of streams behind her "arm" bending rapidly as she passed.

Kiadora hesitated for a moment, jarred out of her sense that she needed to touch the rivers of energy. What would happen when she touched them? Would it help? She searched her memory for why she needed to know this, which at the moment seemed to be at the bottom of a deep ocean for how easy it was to access her memories. There was something…something major that had happened, something that was just a shame, but confusing at the same time.

And it came back; Broean falling off the ledge, stumbling about like a loon and his gruff intensity that he *needed* whatever was in that vial. The rest of the memory floated up: the wet arm, the lack of needle pricks, the return of that calm demeanor. It had been nothing.

But it had not been nothing. She had believed that he needed that drug, that he was its true servant, had feared for him, panicked when she couldn't shake him out of it and had told him to take control. She remembered Sheirkia shaking her till she was bruised. Would she be able to be pulled out once she went even deeper?

Not unless she took control, until she lived by her own words to Broean. But she still hesitated, looking at that living, malleable glass that was her own limb. How would she even go about it?

She looked at her arm and watched the particles appear to bend around her arm as they passed behind. But it was an illusion, wasn't it?

She tilted what she imagined to be her head. At any rate, her view shifted, and she felt if she had vocal cords at the time she would have gasped.

The stream of yellow particles that rushed past her arm maybe a foot behind actually bent in flow toward her arm. The entire flow of particles went in a straight line, except for the small rise where her arm hovered over the stream, like it was a river bubbling over a rock.

Kiadora moved her arm back and forth and the small rise of the stream followed her arm perfectly. This was it, she had control! She could have cried, in joy this time.

She moved her hand closer to the stream… The stream started to bend in a large arch to flow right under her hand. Should she try to move it away?

Looking at the arch, she thought of it flowing away from her hand, like letting a tight rope go limp. She briefly wondered how she would make this happen, then the stream bent away from her hand as she had exactly imagined it.

Kiadora imagined the arch widening so that it flowed in a circle rather than a line. It widened still to the point where it was that circle, flowing around her. Still, it widened and hit another stream, a red one.

And the world started to crumble.

Streams that flowed one way reverted their flow so they were perpendicular to other streams. Some streams dissolved and new ones arose out of the distance. She shifted herself, pulling her arm back as an orange stream came flying at her and rushed past her view by mere inches, a roaring noise echoing where she had previously heard nothing.

Then she was back in the chair and Sheirkia was rushing to the table, the top of which was now burning. The woman directed the palms of her hand to the flame, which blinked out in an instant. Sheirkia turned back to Kiadora was a large grin.

"I have to say, I'm impressed. You didn't do it in the two days you desired, but three is a high achievement, the fastest that anyone has managed it."

Sheirkia came over and embraced Kiadora in a light hug, her blond curls enveloping Kiadora's vision like the flame. The heady scent of some oil dabbed on the woman's skin filled her nostrils. Kiadora was painfully aware of the other woman's breasts squeezing too tightly just below her chin. Kiadora laughed slightly, pulling back out of the cloud of hair and perfume.

"Um, thanks. Sorry about the table. So what did you see?" Kiadora asked. Sheirkia stood up, whipping her hair around her shoulder with a flick of her hand.

"You gave the flame quite a push. It shifted to the right and grew to the point where it was able to ignite the table. You even pulled yourself out when things were too large to handle. It was a flight response. There are other ways to break the connection that I can teach you, now that you have the basic gist of elemental control. Brilliant, just brilliant." Sheirkia shook her head at Kiadora. "How did you realize your control, and so fast?"

"I don't really understand it. I was there in the flame, like always, seeing those strings of particles, and then I tried to move them and could see a clear...sort of outline of my hand and arm. The closer I moved my hand to the strings of particles, the more it pulled the string towards me. I realized I could control the stream and started to warp it. Then everything shifted, and the strings flew in different directions. One almost hit me before I dodged it, and then I was back here."

Sheirkia nodded, an odd gleam in her eye. She had that same broad smile, but Kiadora now wondered if she would start shooting sparks from her eyes from excitement.

"And how did you control the stream?"

"I still don't understand," Kiadora repeated. "It was like I just knew what to do. I just wanted it to go a certain way and it would do it. And I don't know why I had a body. I thought I was separated from it."

"Your ethereal form," Sheirkia said simply. Kiadora waited for her to go on, but she seemed to think this sufficed as an explanation.

"My what?"

"The form you take on the spiritual level," said Sheirkia patiently. "It all works on the subconscious level. Somewhere you knew what you had to do, and your mind bent your spiritual awareness to view what you needed to view. In your case, you wanted control badly enough, so you were given an image to focus your awareness on for that control; for you it seemed to be a hand. A typical choice, hands are usually the instruments of material manipulation and control in this world. From there it is all about the will the individual has. You dearly wanted that stream to move, so you were able to move it." Kiadora's head spun with the abstraction of the process and the myriad of questions jostling her mind. "But why was my body clear? And how does me willing something alone make it happen?"

"Your will directs your spiritual energy and that combines with the energy of other entities. 'The will is the all.' It's a standard spiritual phrase for a reason." Kiadora frowned. Nothing about this seemed standard.

"And the other question. Why clear?"

"That is also typical at this stage, though as I said, it does not usually happen this fast. The ethereal form appears clear because it is still new, the practitioner uncertain. We theorize that a clear form is the most generic, so it is what the ethereal form settles into. It will not take on form until later. Do you have any more questions?" Sheirkia finished in a chipper tone. She was like a tour guide who was asked about a historical monument.

"Um, no, I think that does it for now, thank you."

"Until next time, then," said Sheirkia, waving toward the door. Kiadora headed out and wondered if Broean would even still be there. She half expected him to just know that she achieved her task somehow.

Yet she found him waiting on the floor patiently, as still and stoic as ever.

"I did it." Kiadora couldn't keep the smile off of her lips.

"I know," said Broean, with a hint of a civilized smile through that ragged beard.

"How do you know? You're bluffing."

"Think what you want, but you did a great job. And in three days!" He got up and shook her hand. She stared down at such a mundane act of greeting. It seemed so out of place around here that she laughed.

"You think you're meeting a new person, do you?"

"Why, yes. I am." He let her hand drop, and they looked at each other for a moment.

"So you're not going to offer an explanation?"

"You're no doubt referring to the Yalla?"

"Excuse me?"

"That is the name of the drug that I pretended to use. Very perceptive of you to have caught me faking it." He had an amused twinkle in his eye.

"Knock it. You wanted me to find it. Why else soak your sleeve? But that doesn't answer my question. Why?" That's the only word she felt like she was using anymore.

"Why ask when you know the answer?" Of course, he wanted her to know more about control, but that wasn't the heart of this.

"I want to know why you even took the time to teach me about control. You're my guard, nothing more. Or did you just want to get off of duty faster? Do you do this for everybody?"

"No," he said in a bright tone and turned to walk away. He looked over his shoulder as he strolled towards the warm glow of the fires ahead. "You'll know eventually. Right now, you wouldn't understand the explanation, not to be condescending. You're just not at the necessary level of study. Till we meet again." He let out a small flick of two fingers over his head and was around the bend.

CHAPTER 23

It had been a couple of days spent taking her message to the corridors. Kiadora had stood in that rigid pose, shaking slightly; wild-eyed and deeply convinced. Kiadora found the woman with the mole on her cheek, who looked utterly amazed, then claimed she had been seeing something similar in her dreams. It had been enough for Kiadora to stop for just a moment and wonder if what she was spreading was real before she stopped herself and realized that a bird was a common enough figure to begin with. That woman was a "yes," and Kiadora marked it on her sheet of names.

Kiadora was shocked to find that the man with the fiery hair did in fact have *fiery* hair, like his head had been converted into a torch. It stood in stark difference to the light browns and blonds back home. He just kept on limping past her, smiling as he passed, as if determined to get where he needed to be and off his leg as fast as possible.

Corminda stood pensively, the long scar on her nose luminous since the smooth, pink skin was angled towards the chandelier while she was considering. She then turned her face down to Kiadora and merely asked, "And what will you do with it? Where will you let the vision take you?" Kiadora had stopped for a moment and caught herself as she was about to start stuttering about a trip to the surface. No, not to be mentioned in public. Still, a handful of others continued on their way, not like this woman.

"That's the great question, isn't it?" said Kiadora, her voice still shaking, hoping her eyes had stayed feverish the whole time. "The visions will guide me." And Kiadora walked off, still trying to understand if that sounded appropriately devout or not.

It wasn't until later that Kiadora heard an odd, uneven *thump thumpthump thump* travel up the ladder towards her room. Thinking it would pass to someone more interesting, the noise stopped right outside her curtain.

"Hey! Hey," said a gruff voice. "It seems you're in there. I have a way of telling these things." Not wanting to particularly know what that way was, Kiadora jumped up from where she had been lounging on her bed simply daydreaming about seeing crisp, white clouds again. She yanked back the curtain, and there was the man with the limp, his head looking more like a torch sticking out from the wall. His slender, pale features seemed too flimsy to hold such a gruff tone.

"I've been thinking. My leg is acting up, so it took some time. Heh, maybe that is why I keep on thinking. Anyway, this bird, what about it again?" Kiadora regarded him for a moment. She just wasn't in the mood to get the act up at the moment, and it would look odd if it just overcame her at the mention of the beast, anyway. Kiadora laughed awkwardly.

"I caught you earlier after one of those visions. I've been having them, and they just take over. It's always the same, the Ollox, taking me into a corridor of light. There's always a feeling of escape, of salvation. Like everything that was bothering me just melts away. It's always almost too much for me to handle." As Kiadora spoke, it was hard to keep the smooth, slightly melancholy tone out of her voice. She was beginning to like telling the tale of something that would just take her way. It was a nice dream, really. Then she realized she mentioned the Ollox by name, but it seemed so safe with him.

Kiadora shook her head. A dangerous road, dependence and closeness to a separate entity, something so strange it almost existed solely as an idea. Not that again. She looked up to the torch of a man, still looking at her for answers.

"You want that too, don't you?"

"Of course. Don't we all at times?" He had the darkest eyes, as if they were specifically made that way to hide something. She couldn't remember his name off of the list for the life of her. And it would have looked strange to know it beforehand, she figured.

"I'm sorry, what is your name?" Kiadora asked.

"Best you don't know, talking of this as we are." Kiadora tried to not let her pulse rise. She felt a little jilted by the lack of trust and secrecy.

"Anyway," the man went on, "they talk so much of interconnected spirituality, but when someone combines the two, below and above, there is fire to pay. It was interesting, I thought maybe you had read something on it, that was all."

He looked at her for a moment more, his eyes looking heavy

among the pale exterior. She imagined he was probably one of those types who was pale even on the surface. Except maybe when his skin matched his hair after too much sun. But there was not a freckle. And rather than looking sunken, dead and faintly drug-addled, like she felt they all did down here, his skin had an ageless, pristine look to it. It was like fine china that had been used time and again, but kept to top standards by the pickiest of dish cleaners.

"No, just a vision, that's all," she said. She felt uncommonly compelled to keep him talking. She never even really saw him around. Where would he disappear to, anyway? She got up and leaned on the side of her doorway, trying to make it look like she wasn't going anywhere, like this conversation was far from over.

"It's the most vivid dream I've ever had, usually I get it every other day." Suddenly she became aware of just how many conversations, first contacts and first impressions she was making based on a complete lie. Was it right? At the moment, it seemed to matter for some reason. She wanted to go on about it, to keep talking just to keep those eyes on her, but she faltered. She didn't want to keep the lie up. He just kept staring at her until she felt like she had to say something.

"Usually my visions fade when I'm not in the heat of them." No, another lie. "But like I said, I feel an intense…retrieval. As if I'm just accessing something that can just…take me away." He smiled. It was a tight but oddly kind smile, lingering in the two distinct worlds of empathy and aloofness.

"Once you come out of it, find me. I want to hear more." He

hesitated for a moment, looking at her, then looked at the ladder as he descended down.

"I will," she called down to him. Dare she do it, try to look frantic and summon another act? She knew that she would not be able to around this stranger. She could barely even go through the falsehood to describe it, much less act out the mania again.

With that torch of a head finally out of view, the lasts wisps of hair bouncing as he descended unevenly, flickering like flame itself, she abruptly turned back into her quarters. She lifted the rough straw mattress and pulled out the list. She ran her eyes down Regelend's neat, typist print and found, "fiery hair with a limp- Astrian."

Astrian. What a name. She wondered what his family name was and then caught herself, confused as to why she would care. She slumped back down on the bed and considered running wild through the compound screeching about the Ollox, just to get his attention. Kiadora shook her head, a hint of a smile at the absurdity. This was stupid. She put the piece of parchment back and flopped onto her bed.

The next she knew she was dreaming. In it was a large bird sent to deliver her home. She didn't know where home was, but it didn't matter.

Kiadora sat in her session with Sheirkia the next day, still trying to rouse herself from her dream. That joyous feeling of flying away from all of it had been replaced by a bitter regret when she awoke from feeling like she was falling off the bird's back into her bed. As if taking the extra effort to mock her, life had decided to stick her with a large piece of straw in her back when she awoke. The feeling of regret intensified when she did not see Astrian anywhere. He had been flying in the background all night.

"I'm still amazed," said Sheirkia, arranging some small logs on the ground with her back to Kiadora. Kiadora started as she remembered there was another person in the room. "Three days, that's all it took. You might just be destined for the top around here." Kiadora scowled.

"What's this about a bigger fire, anyway? I thought you said with the Eternal Fire you had to build it twig by twig. Since when is a log a twig?"

"This won't have the same type of power," Sheirkia said vaguely, arranging the third and final log over some parchment so they pointed towards the center and upward at a 45 degree angle. She turned to see Kiadora's look of confusion.

"The Eternal Fires are imbued with the energies of hundreds of scryers over the years. With that act, they leave their own unique signatures with it. When you put out a flame that energy is dispersed and dissipates. When you keep one going like that, it becomes more powerful, in addition to the sheer size of the element held active. That is why it stands as such a useful and unique tool in the first place; it's the sheer power of the element as well as collected energy from fellow spirits, the internal flames of hundreds of individuals. That is why you must work up to it." Kiadora only nodded.

Sheirkia took a match out of one of her skirts and struck against the circle of stones that the logs were propped against. She threw the lit match onto the parchment in the center of the logs and the flame leapt into a high state of being. Kiadora could feel an odd sense of warmth around her chest leap into life as well.

"Wait, I won't get pulled in the way I just did? Bigger fire, more, whatever, Eatheria to contend with? I won't get addicted to it and have to have Broean sit outside my sleeping area?" What a disaster, then she would miss her escape.

"I presume not, you have grasped the feeling of control. It's a little different at a scale this large, but not by much. What we can do, as you know, is fairly limited to begin with so you won't light my rooms on fire under my watch. For instance, you could never hope to gain control over the Eternal Fires. It would be like trying to single-handedly control the sails and steering of a freight ship. After some time, you just have to go along for the ride."

But that seemed to imply she could have a little control over this. Fun. The flame had caught to the logs and was flickering up in a way that reminded her of Astrian. Kiadora looked up a Sheirkia, who had whisked to the side and nodded.

It wasn't like being pulled anymore. It was like she was just falling in from her chair. An illegal swimming hole of flame. Strings of the particles sailed faster in every direction. Where she was only in a country town before, she was now in a metropolis. Before she could easily have counted the strings, but now she would have been hard-pressed to keep track of them all. In the Eternal Fires, it must be impossible, if you could even sense them individually at that point. That is what Sheirkia must have meant by needing to go along for the ride. She looked down, possibly for the first time, and there was a vague outline of a body, clear as glass. It was as if an artistically challenged child wanted to draw a figure, but could not quite figure out the details because of its complexity and had settled for outlining his friend.

And there was that clear hand, ready to do business. She held out that vague hand and just as she wanted, a strip of red particles bend towards her. It was an ever so slight gradual arch, not much to the eye, but Kiadora could feel herself grin even though she highly suspected that she had no mouth in this form. It was more than just the control; it was the feeling of being so intimately united with the flame that it did what she willed. And, yes, she had to admit to herself, it was the feeling that even if she didn't have too much power in her life, and she never had despite being of a higher family or maybe because of it, she could at least control the seemingly irrepressible flicker of this flame.

In the back of her head, she held an image of what the fire must look like outside. She saw it bend to the right and the strings of particles in her view seemed to lean to the right, the world tipping as if on a rocky sea. Certain strands went in other directions, others reversed without her say so. It saddened her that she couldn't make it do more…could she?

Kiadora thought about the flame growing bigger and bigger, of adding strings until it was as great as the Eternal Fires themselves, as big as the sun. But then she stopped abruptly. Best not to engulf the compound. Cursed as it was, it was home for now. But to just add to it a little, to feel that power of creation? She saw the flame grow ever so slightly in her mind.

Everything stayed the same. She pictured the flame growing more and more. Until it engulfed the room. Sheirkia could protect herself. Still nothing. The luminous highways kept their course.

A panic spread. Maybe she lost it completely, that control. She saw the flame go to the left in her mind's eye and strings reverted; the world tilted to the left. Best play with what she had. She saw the flame whipping around and around. The streams reverted themselves in a Marionette dance. She wanted to cry in joy, but knew she had no vocal cords. She had something better. She could control what was outside of her, with her mind alone. Kiadora remembered what Sheirkia had said about the spirit combining with the element. Well, maybe not just her mind. But it was connection and control.

Little by little, she felt more powerful, strong, fierce. She would have engulfed mountains if need be, if she had the strength. But somehow she felt she had all the strength she needed. As she moved those puppet strings around, controlling a hot, dangerous puppet, she couldn't possibly want any more. She had it all to begin with.

As she moved the particles, images began to arise in the back of her mind. Strong images of battle, blood, conquest and destruction. On one level she saw the strings moving around her faster and faster. On another she saw men being slaughtered by the edge of a sword, horses riding into throngs of people, their riders raining down arrows, and she heard a cannon shot going off somewhere.

She had never witnessed a war. Kiadora had only heard tales from a great uncle, who spoke of the experience with valor. The proudest moment of his life, he had said, was when he took the head off the leader of a clan of desert people for their nonbelief.

"That had shown him what to believe in," the old man had said with a chuckle.

"But Uncle Felend, he's dead. He doesn't know what to believe in if he's dead," Ashila had said (most subtly was lost on her, especially the gruesome kind).

"That will teach him for the afterlife," their great uncle had said, as he stumped off to do something involving food and a nap, as he usually did.

So how she could possibly know these images, Kiadora did not know, but they kept coming. Making the particles shift was something of a compulsion now. She did not want to let go of that control, but she was also horrified by what she saw. A wagon full of children was now being set to flame. She heard the screams and saw only smoke and flame rise out of the canvass. Before she could see more, she only felt a brief chill down her back, as if cold water were being dumped on her head and running down her spine. She even felt slightly wet. The images ceased, and she took the time to release control of the particles. They now stopped and resumed a steadier course, as steady as the elemental particles in a flame could be. Strings still reverted here and there and particles flew at top speed, but the world did not spin quite as fast.

She knew it was time to go back to her body, and no sooner than she had started thinking it, she was in her chair looking at an average fire, like ones she had seen in a fireplace a million times in her life.

Kiadora looked down at her dress and was shocked to see she was not drenched. Kiadora had figured Sheirkia had broken out a water bucket to stop the unsteady flame. But she was bone-dry.

"You didn't dump water on me, did you?" Kiadora asked. Sheirkia just looked at her, puzzled. Then she gave off her bright laugh.

"Clearly you are not wet."

"I don't know, maybe you…dried me." Kiadora felt her face go red at uttering such stupidity. It had made a sort of odd sense a moment ago.

"I felt wet. And saw war. What in the name of the Otherworld…"

Kiadora shook her head; it was like trying to rouse herself from a nightmare.

"I can guarantee I did not use any sort of water," said Sheirkia with a playful little smile. She tried to wipe the smile off her lips, but it was too late, Kiadora saw.

"You did something."

"No, far more fascinating." Kiadora just frowned.

"Fascinating or not, it was still uncomfortable. And what's with the disturbing images?" Sheirkia cocked her head to the side like a bemused puppy.

"Has no one taught you the associations of the elements?"

"No, why should they have? I didn't know there were any."

"Fire," said Sheirkia, ushering Kiadora out of her chair and to the door, "is associated with war."

"War? Why war?" But they were at the entrance, and Sheirkia had slammed the inner door shut. "And what was with the damn shower?" Kiadora yelled through the door.

Sheirkia popped her head out into the small, crude atrium. She still had that annoying smile. "That you will find for yourself. No one else can do that for you." And the door was shut once more.

CHAPTER 24

Kiadora had not been in a true, social crowd of people for so long that she forgot what it was like and how much she disliked crowds and noise.

People had managed to procure outfits that were not dull and mangy for the event, sporting simple but vibrant dresses of the most radiant reds, shocking yellows and gaudy oranges. Thankfully, there were some pale greens that had been available from a man at a table in front of the dining hall, something about spring and the first grasses. Secretly, she loved the red but didn't want to draw attention to herself in such a bright color because of what she was going to try to talk to people about tonight. Looking around, she now realized what a mistake that had been since she was one of the only muted, pale ones.

Kiadora stood off to the side of the large room, scanning the crowd among the hundreds of candles hanging from the ceiling in chandeliers a little too low for Kiadora's comfort. It made it harder to not want to stare at the candles all night long. She thought momentarily of how thrilling it would be to make certain numbers of the flames dance a certain way.

She shook her head. That was stupid, she was here for something else.

She continued to scan the crowd for people on the list, but no one appeared. She figured all the better to look like she had tried to contact everyone. Kiadora only needed five people still, and she was under enough suspicion. That was what she told herself. Whether she wanted to admit it directly or not, it *was* good to be out of her little cave.

For some reason, some people had come sporting animal-themed masks so it made the search feel impossible.

And then there was a man in a mask next to her.

"I would never have expected you to be here. Getting lonely?" The tone was friendly, where usually the comment would have been mocking in others. And there was an earnest quality that made you just want to trust it. Regelend.

"Cut it, I'm scouting. This is what I have so far," she said, passing Regelend the paper with names marked on it. Regelend looked at it and nodded, handing it back. He had a purple mask on shaped into the face of an eagle, the beak scooping down almost menacingly.

"So why the masks? And I never pegged you for a demon bird."

"The surface tradition of wearing masks started as a way to scare off Shiekita, so they do it as an empowerment symbol down here."

"Interesting," Kiadora lied. "So why you? You big on political statements now?"

"To keep a low profile."

"That also doesn't sound like you." Regelend heaved a sigh. It sounded hollow and far-off from behind the mask.

"People keep approaching me about the Great Union." Kiadora just stared at him for a moment.

"So is it official then?"

Regelend looked down at the floor. His ears had turned red and the edge of his face behind the mask burned like a scalding iron rod. He slouched forward and looked like was trying to make himself as small as possible, as if that would just make everyone forget.

"I don't know who needs to see that," Kiadora commented idly.

"It's a celebration here," said Regelend, his voice low and defeated. "It's what generates everything, creates you, me and it's a…pleasurable act they see power in." Regelend sounded like he was going to be sick.

"I don't know, my sister Dehlia seemed to like it well enough, she did it with loads of people. Or so I assume, I only saw the illegal herbs around her room, you know, the ones to stop a child. She was so stupid, left it labeled and everything." Kiadora laughed at the memory. Looking back, she should have used that as blackmail. Then she looked over at Regelend.

"Sorry, babbling. So speaking of which," said Kiadora. "Where is your little love princess?"

"Not here yet, she's usually late to things. There she is now."

Then she saw a face drifting through the crowd towards them.

Looking closer, something didn't look quite right about it, but Kiadora couldn't tell what it was in the distance. Then Kiadora could see the web of light scar tissue on the right side of her face, nearly missing a dark brown eye and running to the side of her mouth, narrowly avoiding her lips as well. And it clicked.

"Lid's sister?" Kiadora asked.

"Lid tell you about her?"

"She burned a bunch of people, she's a murderer, Regelend!"

"Naturally, I would have wished to avoid the incident," Kiadora jumped and looked around to see Uranda standing right beside her. "I didn't have full control over the power then. To this day, I practice with the element to control it with the best ease I can. It's not easy for me. I see it as a type of atonement. This as well," she said, indicating her face.

Kiadora marveled at her deep brown eyes, chestnut hair and darker complexion, despite the lack of sun. She had to be from the desert region. Her beauty could have started wars, had it not been for the scarring.

"I, I'm sorry, I didn't mean anything by it...I, I spoke too harshly," Kiadora stammered out.

"There is much misunderstanding and misconception around here." Uranda spoke in a grave monotone. Kiadora didn't think she had the capacity to laugh. Who would anymore? The three of them stood there, all looking off to the crowd, the silence heavy between them.

"So...are you two looking forward to the Great Union ceremony?" Before it was even out of her mouth, Kiadora mentally smacked herself. Regelend gave her an embarrassed glance from the side. Uranda's features didn't change in the slightest.

"We will do what we must."

"You don't think it's…demeaning, even a bit of shameless voyeurism?" Kiadora asked in a low tone. She glanced around, knowing that it would be her luck if an Elder was standing right behind her.

"I don't believe they see it as such here," said Uranda. Her dull monotone had changed to an even tone of seriousness. Was this the closest this girl ever got to excitement? "They see it as a great honor and a thing of beauty." Kiadora glanced at Regelend, who had gone even redder.

"It doesn't seem right to make someone go through with this if it is against their will," said Kiadora, knowing she was crashing into the murky waters of slander.

"If people don't want to participate, they have their priorities set the wrong way. It is a beautiful thing. They need to learn to accept it." Kiadora thought Uranda was going to give a meaningful glare at Regelend, but she just let the comment hang there for whoever would take it in.

Kiadora mentally kicked herself now. She had spouted out a belief against the Elders in the presence of someone who honestly believed in what she was doing. But would Regelend get sucked into this? As the three stood there, Kiadora tried to think of a way to change her comment against the rules but decided that trying to fix it would just bring more attention to the situation. All she could do was leave it and hope this woman wasn't a snitch as well as a maniac.

"I'm going to leave you two to do whatever it is you do at these things. Dance, or something. Anyway, have fun," Kiadora said as she broke away from them and deposited herself into the crowd. The masks would make it impossible to hunt anyone down, that she knew.

Any other members of the Children here would have to understand, if they even came to these things. She tried. She headed for the door and then someone passing bumped her shoulder a little too roughly. She turned around to see a man in an eagle mask in flowing yellow garb. She marveled at the obviousness of it as she remembered the man's towering height.

"Wellian?" He leaned in, the beak almost taking a chunk out of her cheek.

"Tomorrow after the evening meal, same place. We need to plan." He abruptly straightened and was moving through the crowd. Kiadora went on her way out the door.

"You will be passing on," Sheirkia said. Kiadora looked at her abruptly. She had just come in for another lesson, had a seat and was met with this comment. Her mind jumped to that old euphemism people used for someone who had died. "Passed on to their Maker." She thought back to the death ritual she had to do and hoped there was not a part two. And then she realized Sheirkia had to have been talking about the lesson structure. She felt a pang of sadness she had not expected to experience. All in all, Sheirkia had turned out to be fairly tolerable as teacher, and Kiadora didn't want to leave the element behind.

"Fire will be with you every day, you just need to practice with it. Light a candle," said Sheirkia, apparently reading Kiadora's expression.

In spite of herself, Kiadora said, "But don't I get to look into the Eternal Fires?"

"These are just introductions, there will be time for that later."

"Right, later."

"You may not realize it, but you've done scrying of sorts on a smaller scale. Those war images? That was not just something that popped up for no reason." Kiadora looked down at the floor, thinking.

"Were those someone's memories?"

"Close, their feelings. People who are torn on the inside will manifest their feelings in troubling images. I have no doubt you know what that is like; everyone has had nightmares. That's how it starts, you can pick up images from another's mind, but they come fragmented. Emotions are the strongest and easiest to pick up. Eventually, there will be actual events." Kiadora grinned.

"So does this mean I can eventually read minds?"

"Not unless they want you to." Kiadora slumped slightly in her chair. "People are too guarded. You'll only pick up the most severe of emotions from the most unguarded." All this new power, and it turned out to have more inner limitations than not having it in the first place.

"So whose emotions were those?"

"We don't know. We've been trying to pin it for months, but it keeps getting more severe and that adds another level of complication. The person starts to throw the signal around without realizing it, projecting it onto others. We'll probably never know, but they need help." Kiadora only nodded.

"So when do I start these new lessons?"

"In a couple of days, your next session is the element of Water. And your teacher is currently on a sabbatical of sorts." Kiadora didn't want to know what *of sorts* meant, but if she knew this place, it seemed like a code for "complete loon." Kiadora looked around the room for what might be the last time and realized she was actually going to miss her time learning the element, mastering control. She also realized that nothing was set up.

"So this is it, I'm just passed off like a lame horse to the butcher?" Sheirkia actually gave one of her musical laughs.

"You have a way of putting things sometimes, Kiadora. You don't realize how much you have progressed in the short time we have had. It's up to the next teacher to continue the milestones." Sheirkia frowned slightly and crossed her arms. "Normally we would have a larger banquet ritual, but the Elders have been expressive in stating that someone who has undergone what you have needs deeper training. The rituals will just remind you of the torture, they said. I don't see them as entrapping you thus, but they are the Elders, and they know what they are talking about."

Kiadora put her hand to her chin, thinking. As far as this went, it seemed like they did. It was the one and only move, Kiadora had to admit, that made them seem like the wise beings everyone regarded them as.

"But why everyone else?" Kiadora asked. "My friend has to be in a ritual, the Great Union, and if he doesn't do it he's basically stated that it's confinement for him. He's had rough times, too."

Sheirkia smiled and looked off, a sweet memory apparently coming to mind. "That's more of a magical act than a flat-out ritual, though they do usually blur. It's difficult to explain. Just promise me you'll go and watch. You'll see. Consider that as your great transition from session to session. And now," Sheirkia said, dipping into a graceful bow, "we must part ways for the time being."

Sheirkia stood up and started to walk towards the door and held it open. "Give Aeliean my fondest wishes, someone will be by to collect you in a day or two. I'd tell you to keep practicing with Fire, but I don't think I need to remind you," she said with a wink.

Kiadora walked through the door, rustling passed that multicolored curtain. Then she was out the door and now in the rustic atrium. She gave a short good-bye as Sheirkia closed the door, and Kiadora was left among a dark entryway.

Still dazzled from being passed on so suddenly, Kiadora meandered back to her quarters, now realizing that she had a full afternoon to kill before she met up with the Children. She knew exactly what she would spending it doing.

CHAPTER 25

Kiadora came out all on her own right before the evening meal. The candle flickered peacefully, and it felt like it had only been five minutes of moving those bright streams around. She felt peaceful, content and energized, more than she had in the whole time she was down in this dump.

As she looked around, the Earthen walls seemed to look less damp and dingy. They looked like a deep, rich brown that seemed to just sort of warmly glow around her. She looked closer and realized the particles were held in place: no movement, just a uniform pattern of infinite squares. So that was how these quarters never collapsed, controlled Eatheria held them in place. And why had she never noticed before? The particles were so still.

Kiadora shook her head. She didn't know how she had been able to come out just in time for the meal. She heard pots clanging below. Everything was all starting to flow so naturally, it all just seemed to happen without effort. Like she just knew what to do when it came to this element.

She stood up, threw back the curtain and swung herself onto the ladder. She headed down to the hall to grab dinner.

Tonight the food tasted better, even though it was the same old salmon and rice concoction she had ingested countless times. She didn't think anything the Children could say could ruin her mood. She didn't know if it was the afternoon spent doing Firework all on her own or the prospect of getting a little trip away from this place.

Kiadora went to the small corridor where the Children had met and remembered she had forgotten a torch. She hovered uncertainly at the small crevice before Regelend came up behind her.

"Only a day away," Regelend exclaimed as they headed in. She raised one eyebrow at him.

"If you think you're going to be taken away to paradise, why have you been so worried about this Great Union? You're supposed to be off in super happy happiness paradise land or something," Kiadora whispered as they reached earshot of the small fissure through which they would all meet. Regelend slowed slightly, and stopped, considering. Kiadora came to a halt in front of him.

"I think it's just the idea of having to do it," Regelend said.

"You're doubting this, you don't know if it will come. Good, you always struck me as being more sane than that." Regelend heaved a sigh and stepped to the side behind a small outcropping, motioning Kiadora to join by raising his chin abruptly.

"You've read the Holy Text. These things rarely meet expectations. People think salvation is going to come in the form of rain and they get a flood. It happens all the time. Yes," he said in a harsh whisper. "I have thought of 'what if.' What if it doesn't come? What if it does and

321

we all stay where we are but just become more enlightened spiritually? What if we have our day wrong? Yes, I've thought of it. Now let's get in there or they'll wonder."

Kiadora followed Reglend, smiling at the fact that Regelend still had it within him to question. Here she was worried that her good friend was just a zealot. Instead, here was a man who could admit that what he was waiting for might not happen. Kiadora knew for certain he only just dearly wanted it to.

As she followed Regelend through the fissure, she saw the Children all sitting in the same circle, in the same places, like wolves that had staked out territory.

But standing outside the circle of stones was Corminda, Belina, the woman with the mole on her right cheek and, her heart stopping slightly, Astrian. He smiled at her, his red hair flickering along with his torch. Four out of the list of 15 people wasn't so great, but she had more success than she thought she would, which was none.

There were three other people she had not spoken to, a dark haired, thin man, a shorter pale woman (paler than everyone else around here) and an extremely nondescript man. He was someone you could pass on the street every day and not know that he was there. He had mild medium brown hair, mild light brown eyes and extremely average, symmetrical features. She would forget he was there in a second. Must be secondary referrals.

She took a seat where she had sat before, deciding whether or not to respect that these people were creatures of habit in the extreme.

Wellian stood up with a smile.

"And that is everyone. You all, of course, know why we are here.

Tomorrow is the holiest of days, the time when the great Ollox comes to us all…" Wellian was cut off by a, "blessed is the Great Ollox," from some of the regulars, their heads bowed and hands folded over their hearts.

"For it is written that he will come to grant us eternal paradise. For when he carried away the Shiekita, he went East, the place of new beginnings." It took every ounce of Kiadora's willpower to not roll her eyes. The tale's certain edge of stupid had not managed to recede for her. Instead, she managed a smile as she thought of just one day in the sun.

The meeting went as she thought it would. It ran like service. There were several of the classical hymns, all about how great the creator was and how she personally needed to be saved from human temptation. One whole song was devoted to repeating the refrain, "from this, our earthly body, be saved." The newer people all looked at each other questingly and then happily began in. The singing was in a hushed whisper again, despite the fissure being jammed with cloth by Aela at the beginning of the meeting.

Finally the hymns ended, but only to be followed by a twenty minute prayer to the Ollox to see them safely to paradise, rephrased a different way every couple of moments. And then they got into what Kiadora wanted to hear, that they would meet tomorrow morning.

Astrian asked, in his deep voice that gave Kiadora shivers, what they would do about the courses they needed to attend. Wellian explained that there would be an intricate system of messengers explaining various reasons, from fatigue to illness to a desire to spend the day in meditation. Everyone was granted a few of these days, though Kiadora never used hers because she felt so bored, she figured she might as well go. She lost track of this messenger web they had set up, only remembering that Regelend would go to Sheirkia and request that she wanted a day alone with the flames. Kiadora perked up at this comment, again amazed at how oddly astute Regelend was, but told him that today was her last lesson. Regelend would still go to Wyland, who was charged with the dull task of regulating teachers, room assignments and the requests for any messengers to be called off for the day, although a next day messenger was uncommon after a student had progressed.

With a final notice that everyone should cover as much skin as possible because sunburn would be particularly bad with this much time underground, the meeting let out, with Kiadora still wondering who the new people were and if the raptured should really be caring about sunburn. The new names were never mentioned, but Kiadora figured with the "big event" leading to something more, dull pleasantries like introductions were probably moot.

Kiadora pulled away the cloth in the fissure and slipped into the corridor, relieved that nothing had been said to her about not getting enough people. Wellian had been distracted, his face constantly marred with a far-off stare the whole evening. She left the corridor, the first person who would sneak out so that no one would see a large group just emerging out of nowhere, remembering how deep Astrian's voice had been as he sung.

The next morning dawned with Kiadora in bed, staring at what she had come to know as a ceiling. She had vague memories of drifting in and out of sleep every hour or so, but despite the estimated three hours of sleep, she jumped up, excited as ever. They had said not to go to the morning meal. It was supposed to look like they didn't want to be out among people at all.

Thinking that this thing wasn't planned out as well as it should have been, Kiadora climbed down the ladder as fast and as quietly as she could, desperately hoping no one would notice.

It was after the bustle of the morning meal. Everyone was off doing what they would be doing for the day, whether it was taking lessons, teaching lessons, just sitting around a fire for the day or whatever else people did down here. She passed no one on the way to the meeting area, the same place they had all been last night. They had said that the way out was in the same direction.

Kiadora arrived at the crevice, wedging her way in. She was immediately met with a hand holding out a wide-brimmed hat. It looked every bit as comfortable as jamming your head into a sac of oats. She took it from Aela, who smiled widely and explained, "for the sun." Kiadora didn't want to ask who made them, but it looked like they were made in the back of someone's quarters at the last minute. At least they could go up together looking like a group of poor farmers.

Kiadora sat on a different rock than normal, figuring no one would be thinking of that sort of thing today. She looked around to see about half the people there, some sitting around praying silently with their hands folded and held to their hearts. Corminda, the pale woman and Regelend just stared at the ground, oddly disconnected, deep in thought. She looked around and noticed Astrian was not there. She didn't know if she wanted to see him here or wanted him to be safe, off doing something that was not sneaking out of the compound.

Others arrived, taking the hats and looking around apprehensively, as if an Elder would jump out from behind a rock at any instant and haul them off. The area remained in a hushed near silence, however. Only Wellian's flickering torch made a sound.

People kept coming, and at last, Kiadora could see two red points shimmering in the distance. It was the first time she saw him walk for an extended period of time and his limp seemed more pronounced than ever. Despite the pain, he kept a calm expression, not looking worried in the slightest that they were doing something considered to be illegal in the compound. Kiadora had been bobbing her foot and Cormina kept biting her nails.

"Thank you for coming," Kiadora heard Wellian say. He was beaming from ear to ear and holding out his arm that wasn't holding the torch, as if to embrace the whole group. "I'm sure what we will receive will be a bounty beyond what we can imagine. Our texts have spoken of this for a long time and today is the day we finally meet our salvation. Has everyone put on their hats? Let's get started."

Wellian turned and they continued into the cavern, along a narrow passage that just kept getting so narrow that Kiadora had to remain straight so that the rough edges of the cave would not take the skin off of her shoulders. She wondered how Astrian was doing with this limp and turned to see that he kept himself clear of outcroppings by placing one foot in front of the other and lunging forward awkwardly. She turned to hide the smile for the somber man with dark eyes lurching so sporadically until the passage widened again.

What was the matter with her? The man had obviously been injured or born that way, it wasn't funny. No, endearing somehow.

Kiadora shook her head. Why did she care? She was going to see the surface damn it all, she should be thinking of the beautiful clouds and the sun. She had a momentary startle as she wondered if it would be raining or sleeting or if it would be cloudy and bitterly cold. All of that planning and there would be nothing she was interested in seeing. She just remembered the sky as if it was always that pristine blue and the trees were just always that wonderful shade of green.

No, it couldn't be winter. They had just done a spring ritual. But how would the Children know it was nice out? Maybe they had a scout?

Soon Kiadora could hear the distant rush of water, echoing against the walls. It sounded like it was coming for all around them, as if the water would rush toward them at any moment. How much did they really know about this way out and this part of the caverns? The group remained dry but the walls kept closing in until they all had to turn sideways again, doing a sort of crab walk. The cavern walls began to feel more damp and she was eye to eye with rather foul-looking, green fungus.

The torchlight ahead widened and expanded, and she could see it glinting off some falling water ahead. They emerged into a large cave housing a waterfall pouring down into an underground lake. She wondered if this pool ever just filled up, but it looked to have a steady height. It had to trickle elsewhere.

"Welcome to our water supply. It feeds into a stream closer to the compound," said Astrian from behind. She looked back and he was looking at her. "You looked curious about it," he said in that gruff, quiet tone. She looked around and everyone else didn't seem to give a thought about the waterfall. The members of the Children she had met at the first meeting all looked like they were far off from where they were, imagining something that had the last thing in the world to do with waterfalls. The others just looked apprehensive still, as if that mystery Elder was now hiding behind the waterfall, waiting in a spot to give them just enough false hope.

Wellian led them around the underground lake and everyone followed in a single file line, the "shore" of sorts, Kiadora thought. It was only a thin strip of slippery rock. She glanced back at Astrian, who only gave her a smile as he touched lightly against the rocks with his injured leg and deftly stepped with his uninjured leg.

Kiadora could feel mist now as they came near the waterfall. They went up a steep incline next to it, Aela slipping above and nearly sending the whole line crashing down. She regained herself just in time and the group continued on. Kiadora looked to the right now to see the water cascading next to them. She had seen a waterfall as she went through the woods back home, a small one on her family's estate. She never even thought to go behind it. The near darkness made it look like this was not water, just an endless stream of emptiness creating an eternal echo of noise. Only small glints could be seen in the torchlight.

And then there was the light. It looked like all the great chandeliers above the main area of the compound had been multiplied thousands of times, that intricate structure nothing but a dull imitation. Kiadora could feel her heart race as she knew this would be the real deal. Something she had taken for granted all her life and now that she did not have it, she felt like she was being admitted into her own vision of paradise. She wanted to be away from these people, to just feel that warmth and brightness that was right in front her…growing and growing.

And then they were out. Kiadora squinted, her eyes actually watering. She moved clumsily forward, not sure of where she was or what she was walking on. She must have been on grass, it was soft and yielding, better than the solid rocks and trampled soil below. Slowly her eyes adjusted and she saw they were coming out of a cave in the forest. It took everything she had to not break down and weep.

The trees were a beautiful green, doing their eternal dance in the breeze. And the sky through the leaves…blue as she remembered, with white clouds floating past. She smelled soil and the fresh, sweet scent of what must have been a nearby apple tree in blossom. She would know that smell anywhere. It was far from the damp, moist nightmare of below.

Kiadora glanced around at the group, none of who looked impressed. Some still squinted and she noticed the woman with the mole look back at the cave, as if wondering if it was not too late to go back. She looked over at Regelend, who had a soft smile and she beamed at him. She hoped he got the message of sincerest thanks. It was at this moment that it was not about getting her to believe or not believe; not anymore. It was a favor for a friend. She wanted to hug him and just sit in the grass staring at the clouds, like she would for hours as a child.

But they kept moving. Wellian called back that the spot was a mere five miles away, a short way to travel for eternal bliss. Easy, too easy.

They went through trees and fields, Kiadora taking in every last detail. She normally wouldn't look twice at the top of a cattail, but today she wanted to pet it, as if it would purr its approval at her.

And the sun. It warmed her shoulders and she felt like she could sit in it all day, trying to see the particle strings it could create. But she blocked the thought out before she actually sat down and tried such a thing.

There was no reason to let them know how she felt, what she was up here to do. They might just get angry. And when they did go back down, because she knew they would, she didn't need a group of people angry enough to blackmail her against the Elders at any moment.

As they traveled, she started to sweat. They all were. Living in a confined cavern and not being used to the sun would not be easy on them for a five mile hike, Kiadora knew from the start. She became more grateful for the hat they had provided, as having the sun beat down on their heads would be more of a pain, despite how glad she was for the sun.

No matter how tired she became, however, she could not stop staring at the grass and the trees they passed. Even the weeds looked beautiful.

And then they stopped. They were in another field, away from the farming areas.

"These are the coordinates. We have about an hour," Wellian proclaimed. He promptly dropped the burned-out torch, fell to his knees and stared up at the sky. The original members of the Children did so as well and everyone else just looked at each other. A few dropped down to their knees, still more hesitated then shrugged. Astrian was the last to carefully lower himself to a sitting position, as kneeling didn't seem possible. Kiadora was left standing and then threw herself down on her back.

At last she got her wish. She lay among the long grass, staring up at the sky, taking in the light consistency of the clouds and the warm, but no longer overbearing, feeling of the sun that she couldn't just find anywhere these days. It wasn't long before she forgot entirely about their deliverance to paradise. This was enough.

After a time, and what felt like no time at all, she heard a pleading from up ahead. "Wellian, we can't have been mistaken?" It was Reena.

"No," Wellian snapped. "It will come. Are there doubters among us?" He yelled back to the group. Everyone just stared, a few shaking their heads.

"But it is passed the time," Kiadora could hear from Arn, in a shaking voice. He sounded next to tears.

"He will be here," said Torren, "the Ollox will not forsake his faith-ful." And they waited. The time seemed to stretch, and she could actually hear sobs eventually.

"This is a test," said Wellian. "He will come and we will..." Wellian was cut off as Aela shouted out, "look!"

Off in the distance was a flying figure, wings flapping, coming towards them. Whispers passed between the others as the original Children jumped up.

"Deliver us, great Ollox," shouted Wellian. The others stood up, looking into the sky as it came closer and closer.

As it descended, Kiadora did not see the deep brown of the Ollox mentioned in the text, but a light brown body and a black head. It dropped farther and farther, and she could see Wellian and the others start to weep tears of joy.

And then it was before them, but it was not a giant eagle.

"It's a goose," said Astrian. The five at the front only stared as the bird landed on the stone. It hopped down off of the rock and waddled over to them, letting off its characteristic broken court bugle sound.

"I think it wants food," said Kiadora, her eyes watering up with tears of laughter. She was shaking to keep it back.

"No," said Wellian. "This is also a test. Very rarely in the text are things as they appear. This has to be it." Wellian walked over and dropped down to his knees.

"It is I, great Ollox, your faithful servant. I am ready for the paradise you promise." Kiadora could hear stifled chuckles as Wellian addressed the goose. Aela and Torren went to stand next to him and kneeled. The goose waddled in place and then turned to leave.

"Where do you go, mighty Ollox? Do you bid me to follow?" And the five original members started to follow. The goose spread its wings.

"He will take us with!" It was Torren, who lunged out and grabbed the leg of the poor thing. The goose started to cry in broken tones. Wellian and Aela also lunged, meaning to just touch it, apparently assuming they would be transported that way. Aela, however, tripped and came crashing down. The goose cries were replaced by Aela's screams as she jumped up, blood and feathers on her right shoulder.

The rest gathered around to see the still goose, blood on its head and unmoving. Its neck sat at a 90 degree angle.

"I killed it, I killed the Ollox!" Aela moaned, dropping down, hugging her arms to her middle and rocking back and forth. Wellian and Torren just stared.

"That wasn't it," said Torren after a moment. "It would not lead us up here just to die. It would not die, period. It is eternal."

"Yes," Wellian said, nodding. "We have obviously miscalculated. It will come, it will come soon. This was a sign that we are gravely mistaken and are not yet perfect enough for paradise. We shall all need to study more."

Without another word, Wellian began heading back. With several confused glances, the group followed once more. Kiadora relished in the fact that they headed toward the sunset so she was able to see once again the hues of yellow and pink and finally orange and dark blue. They made it back to their entrance with just enough time to see by the faded twilight their hidden cavern amongst a band of honeysuckle bushes. As Kiadora passed, her hand touching the delicate flowers to her left, she decided this would not be her last time passing this way.

CHAPTER 26

"Ma'am!"

Kiadora looked up from where she was vigorously scrubbing her face with cold water and a citrus scented soap. She had figured it would wake her up as she tried to get last night's dreams purged from her mind. Kiadora had dreamed that rather than destroying the bird, it had been large after all and had grotesquely decapitated most of them. She was relieved to wake up with her left arm still attached.

Not that the actual memory of the event had been too much better. As she called out that she would be done in a moment, she shook her head to clear out Aela's shrill cry.

The joy at seeing the sun had been replaced quickly by a dread of what would happen if someone else had been there on a lark and decided to alert the Elders as to what had happened. Now, the cold of the caverns just felt colder, and she now resented being down here more than ever. The small taste of freedom had made her feel most desperate, like a bird that had been captured and put back into captivity for a second time. Then she had to shake her head to get rid of the image of the bird's bent neck, poor thing.

They had silently crept back to their normal meeting place and thrown off their hats. They nervously checked for signs of sunburn or tan, but there had been nothing they could detect in the dull torchlight.

Wellian had given a rallying speech about the need to reconsult the texts and look for further guidance and other clues. Word would come when the process was complete, but in the meantime everyone was expected to pray. Kiadora didn't think many would be back. Torren and Aela had nodded enthusiastically, Aela clearing her tears as she did so. Arn and Reena had a distant, lost look. Regelend looked oddly unfazed.

Kiadora had been the first to leave; she was starting to feel panicked about the prospect of someone spreading the word of what they had done, so much so that she ducked to the side and waited for Regelend to pass out of the entryway to the cavern.

"So what happens if someone tells?" Kiadora had said abruptly, falling in line with Regelend.

"Kiadora, we're not supposed to group up like this as we leave."

"They don't know where we're coming from. I'm serious, what if someone tells and how do we stop it?" Regelend looked at her and nodded to a rocky alcove several paces away. They stepped inside.

"We're not going to need to stop it. Are you going to tell anyone?"

"No, the whole thing was an insane embarrassment. And they'll know I was involved enough to be aware of what happened."

"Right, you answered your own concern. No one will risk being thrown in with this. And besides, the council will know it could all just be rumor. Despite how harsh they may seem, they do need proof before they go throwing locks on people. And you underestimate how accepting people are around here. Many people will just see it as a spiritual mishap that needed to be made to learn." Kiadora heaved a sigh.

"I see. So what will happen to the Children?" Kiadora said. "Will they go again?"

"No doubt. It's hard to shake that kind of hope. Although I think some will find a way forward." Regelend started walking around the outskirts of the classrooms. Kiadora followed, catching up to be close to his ear so she could keep her voice down.

"And you seem like one of them." Regelend gave a small smile.

"I can't spend my life waiting for something with an uncertain date and an uncertain time. I have something else here." And then he started to go that characteristic red again. Then he had a shocked look. "Not that I've let my belief in my creator go. He's still important. There's just…things I need to think of here. I think that's what he wants."

"Whatever you need to tell yourself. Give Uranda my best," said Kiadora, winking.

Kiadora threw open her curtain. There she found a thin, tall man with the squarest jaw she had ever seen leaning against the side of her door, as if he was waiting for a carriage.

"Your lessons are to start today, miss." He had a high voice for someone that looked to be well over twenty, as if everything else had hit and passed puberty but his voice. Kiadora nodded and followed him down the ladder.

Her heart was pounding more than she thought it would. She remembered Narissa and how much she had hated Sheirkia when they first met. Kiadora wondered why she couldn't just stay with Sheirkia. The woman had to know enough about the Water element to teach introductory lessons.

But Kiadora knew she did not have a say in it, so there was no use to wish and hope for what couldn't be. Otherwise, she would just be a legitimate member of the Children.

The two passed down yet another outcropping in the crags Kiadora had never been near. It was eerily close to the passage they had taken to the waterfall, and Kiadora could feel that same dampness, although it did not feel as oppressive down this way.

Behind a royal blue curtain and another door stood yet another classroom. The messenger freely pushed into the door and motioned toward a chair on the edge of a trickling, underground creek no more than two hand lengths across. Kiadora took a seat, which was slightly unstable against the jagged creek's rocks. With a high, light, "she'll be in shortly," the messenger was gone.

Kiadora marveled at the tapestries of intricate needlework that hung next to cabinets and shelves full of various bowls and canisters full of liquids, all jammed onto the narrow bank of this creek. The tapestries looked new as ever, despite the ever-present dampness. They had the most intricate patters of flowers, geometric spirals and a few detailed lifelike half human, half animal figures. It was clearly from the mind of someone who lived in a world of fantastic visions and images. And knew just how to capture them forever in a physical medium.

Kiadora had always been envious of people who could do that. Her mind's images faded and mutated in her hands before she could even do anything with them. Years of lopsided drawing attempts had proven that. Except the memories of the Church basement, the goose and Astrian; those seemed etched on a mental stone that not even her inept hands could corrupt.

As she reflected on the dark eyes of Astrian, Kiadora hugged her arms to her chest and wondered if she would catch her death in this area. But despite being cold, she felt just fine. In fact, Kiadora realized, she hadn't been sick at all since she had come down here, not so much as the sniffles. She remembered Broean's comment: *interesting what we can do with herbs.*

Kiadora heard the door open and a wisp of a woman came through. She had the same pale brown hair Kiadora had, although it looked like it had the natural waviness Kiadora always wanted for her lank, straight hair. The woman had wide, large eyes. They were a pale, almost crystalline blue like the waters of the dark creek to Kiadora's left. Her skin was, of course, pale.

What she lacked in a natural vibrancy, she made up for in a thick dress that had needlework to rival the tapestries. Interweaving patterns of purple and blue played about her deep green dress in dizzying arrays. Up and down her arms were linked symbols Kiadora couldn't begin to identify. There were waves and spirals and what Kiadora could swear were the outline of fish.

The woman seemed to flow deftly over the slippery rocks by the creek and smoothly offered a hand to Kiadora. Taking a hand that had a large spiral made of small circles painted on it, Kiadora nodded a hello.

"Kiadora, we have much to do," the woman announced in a light, airy voice. "Are you familiar with these waters?"

"I'm sorry, I don't think I caught your name?" Aeliean was it? Kiadora remembered she was supposed to pass on Sheirkia's best, but something about this woman made it seem like it would pass right through her.

"In this life I am known as Aeliean, but that is but a facet of the gem."

"Alright." 'Not another one,' Kiadora thought. Where they all like this at first?

"Now, these waters," Aeliean said again. "Do you know them?" Kiadora immediately thought of the racing waterfall.

"No."

"Most people don't. It's the one thing that sustains us above all else. We die even faster without water than food, and yet few people take the time to look at where it comes from. It's just always in a bucket, isn't it?" She did not say that accusingly to Kiadora. She was actually looking off to the creek, speaking in a distant tone as if she was addressing no one. Aeliean kept staring at the water, and then as if realizing there was someone else in the room for the first time, snapped her gaze back to Kiadora.

"This is our main water supply," said the woman, gesturing slowly and almost lovingly. "It flows through us every day, so it should not be hard to acclimate to it. It is not from without as much as some of the other elements." Kiadora didn't know how true that was, but she wasn't too concerned about it one way or the other.

Aeliean turned and drifted to a cabinet, took a small rug out and set it down next to the rocks. Without a word Kiadora knew what she was to do. She sat down on the rug in front of the creek, grateful for the dry, smooth square as her ankle touched the damp, jagged rocks. Aeliean stood behind her, and Kiadora could see Aeliean's rippling reflection in the water.

"You will learn things about yourself you never knew you had the capacity to know, glean the darkest secrets and understand your highest triumphs in this life and others. You will begin to know what makes you tick and the deepest emotions in others. It is not complicated to do in itself, only complicated to understand and work with it once achieved." The reflection continued to move and bend. One moment Aeliean had no head, the next she seemed tall as a mountain.

"You have learned the basics of scrying," Aeliean continued. "You just need to feel the element within yourself and give over to it. This is a little different than Fire. There is less will, more raw experience. You will just view and you will learn. Now gaze and give in." Aeliean stepped back, and Kiadora looked right into the running water. She took a moment to consider how stupid this was, but then remembered she thought the same thing with fire scrying.

She watched the ripples like she did the clouds drifting in the sky the day before or the flame dancing on its wick. The ripples drifted in their own eternal dance across the rock, and Kiadora suddenly realized how different that rock was now because of that constant small trickle.

Then shadows started to move in the water. She thought that they had to be warped images of dark rocks that the stream passed, but then as if someone has moved them with an invisible hand, they now danced at the back of her mind.

It was the strangest thing. She still saw the water, dancing, flowing, entrapping her. Her heart rate moved more slowly than it ever had before. But she also saw the images play in the back of her mind. Shadows danced, turning into the images of dogs and birds, man and flame, prey and hunter. The images shifted and kept shifting. She couldn't tell a certain story from it, only that she kept seeing the out-lines of things half recognized, half known. There was a bird. It could have been the goose from yesterday, it could have been one she had never seen. There was a stallion. It could have been the one she was afraid to ride back home, or it could have been a wild one from eons back. There truly was no way to make sense of any of it.

Then there was only the stream. Kiadora looked up to see Aeliean's hand on her shoulder. She did not feel a sting or any muscle strain like she had been shaken or hit. The hand had just been placed there and that was all that was needed.

"I've been out for a while, haven't I?"

"The whole of the day," said Aeliean simply. This was common, Kiadora was beginning to realize. And that was why you never saw too many people out and about, why people just starting their training had so much more free time and why there was not too much organization about the place. People spent their time doing this, or at least most of their time. Kiadora knew she could lose her life in these waters, if she chose. Or maybe most felt as if they were gaining it. She desperately wanted some meaning to those images, those shadows that she knew she could not have created all on her own, could she? When had she seen the outline of something that was half cat and half bird? Or possibly the images had just blurred together.

"The shadows," Kiadora said. "What were the shadows? There were animals, people, things I had never seen or maybe I did." She felt so confused she wanted to cry. And she was the type of person who hardly ever wanted to cry in her past life, so why now?

"Ah, the outline phase," said Aeliean, retracting and falling down into her chair. "That is common. Soon they will take substance and grow. You will recognize things, others you won't but you'll still know what they are. Right now your mind is just acclimating and practicing with what you are able to pick up. It's like when you begin to read or draw. Short words like cat will begin to generate more complex words like feline. Circles will become heads and tottering steps long strides."

Kiadora stood up, her bottom sore from the rocks. She bent down and picked up the rug, which was not soaked through thanks to a waterproofed hide on the bottom, she noticed. Kiadora just stood, holding the rug, considering.

"You said 'this life' when you introduced yourself. Are you saying that what I see could be from another existence? Like there's more?"

"The soul never stops trying to learn. It takes several lives," said Aeliean. Kiadora just cocked her head. She had never encountered such a belief before. "You are but in one stage of your soul's journey through its various lives."

Kiadora just went and silently put the rug back into the cabinet from where Aeliean had taken it out, still thinking. Kiadora didn't even know what to make of this life, much less several others before and after. She started to head for the door, about to say good-bye until tomorrow, but Aeliean stopped her with a comment.

"I was a king back in the Before Times." Kiadora turned around sharply.

"A king? There were no kings in the Before Times. That is why they are called the Before Times. That is before we had rule and order and we knew of God as strong as we do now. Clans just had family leaders. There were no kings and queens, no lords of the land, no territories as we know them now to even rule over. It was war constantly." Kiadora was now almost shouting.

She had grown up being told her family was a figurehead of rule and order in a time when they had the luxury of such concepts. The Before Times had been a time of bitter feuds and constantly shifting borders based on who had killed the most people and stolen the most cattle that summer. It was the time when their ancestors from the desert had just come, and the Earth worshipers defended the land before they were assimilated into the new religion. There were no written rules, no treaties dictating peaceful negotiations and times when acts of war were permitted, and certainly no families to manage all of this, so naturally war just had a habit of erupting constantly.

"Do you think that nobility would prevent such a thing?" Aeliean said. Again, it was not accusatory, just a simple question.

"We do now," said Kiadora, a lifetime of reassurance that her noble line had a positive place in this world spewing out of her mouth.

"You hold your established threats and resources," said Aeliean, gazing at her mildly and holding a tone to match, as if they were discussing how breakfast had been that day. "The kings of those days had the gall to move and take what they knew was theirs, and I was one of them. I really liked to pick fights with the lords on the coasts. They had such great fisheries." Kiadora let out an annoyed groan.

"We have carved stone from those days, word-of-mouth stories passed down, and as if that wasn't enough for you, we have relics of the heads of families that were honored because they were the heads. It says so on them- special plaques placed on doors, shrines dedicated to family elders. These were families that were set up in a clan structure. The oldest did what they wanted and feuds erupted because of centuries-old murders. Did you mean you were a family's head of household?"

"No, a king. Designated by the Earthly Holy One of the time to rule over a bordered land. And we were the worst of them." There was no regret and still no outward signs of confrontation. Aeliean had the same tone and expression Wellian had when he was explaining that everyone needed a sun hat on the surface to prevent sunburn. Aeliean's statement carried an air of common knowledge and internal logic; it might just have been forgotten because of the length of time since the Before Times. There was no arguing with her, Kiadora could tell.

It *had* been 3,000 years ago, anyway. The current calendar started 322 years ago as a political stunt by the High King to reconsecrate the years to God. It was a poor morale booster in a year of failing crops. The knowledge was courtesy of Lisera, of course.

"I'll see you tomorrow, Aeliean," said Kiadora, shaking her head, almost just to show Aeliean that she knew that she was a lost cause. As Kiadora walked, trying to push the insanity out of her head, she smiled as she remembered the pact she made with herself to work with her candle tonight.

CHAPTER 27

It had been a good night of losing herself in the flow of particles, the incandescence of sheer life and the feeling of control at being able to bend the element to her will. And now Kiadora was restless. She wanted to do something, be somewhere else; she just didn't know what or where. She felt energized and charged, rather than drained after the long days of struggling with the element at the beginning.

She wandered in and out of corridors and into the caverns, looking at the large groups of scryers at a large pool of water that she was shocked she had not noticed before. Calming music played from a guitar somewhere as everyone just stared down at the pool. She went past classrooms with shouting coming out from one, loud groans and grunts coming from another and a third had pleasured voices coming from it that she didn't even want to think about too hard.

She then wandered into the main eating area where people lounged about talking, and some had a few card games out. Were people always this sociable? And then she saw him. The bright red hair bent over a book, sitting right behind a group of five people laughing about something or the other. Despite the bright hair, Kiadora would have missed him behind the group of people with loudly colored shawls and louder laughter. It was like hiding a street performer among a group of clowns. He looked dull in comparison.

She hovered at a table and had a seat, wanting to look like she had a purpose to come here, but sitting stupidly by herself with nothing to occupy her only made her look more like she did not belong. Still, as Kiadora looked over at that uncommonly pale skin, she knew where she wanted to go and what she wanted to do.

She looked down at the tabletop and let out a fast breath. Here she was, just lounging, like those court damsels who would gaze at men at the far side of the banquet, just willing them to come over and not actually making a move themselves. After all, ladies didn't make the first move in matters of love. Kiadora looked back over. He looked to be engrossed in his book. Did he even want to be interrupted? She squinted around a woman in a blue headdress waving her arms wildly as she spoke. Kiadora tried to see what he was reading, but the book cover was down on the table and she could only see the tops of the pages.

Kiadora got back up and headed out the door, unnoticed. Someday, just not today. It was probably time for bed anyway.

The shadows swirled at the back of Kiadora's mind, still just barely shapes today. She saw the stream and its undulations. But somewhere in the back over her mind, like she was remembering a distant, bygone time she could only half grasp.

Aeliean hadn't even said anything to her as she came in earlier. She was puttering with something in a large, wooden crate on the far left side of the room. The woman had only gestured to Kiadora to sit at the creek. The small rug as already there, and Kiadora knew what to do. The shadows had come just as easily as yesterday, a fluid and constant stream of their own. And they had kept coming all afternoon.

Here and there she thought she could see birds, turtles and something that looked like one of those bins they used for churning butter, but she could tell she was just associating things to shapes, not the other way around. It was like seeing bunny rabbits in the clouds. The Church sometimes used those as omens of good fortune, being from the sky and thus Air. But Kiadora had a feeling she could look at an oddly shaped rock and do the same exact thing.

And then the images stopped. Kiadora blinked and realized she had lost focus. Somehow she had decided to look up at the rocks. She shook her head, her eyes starting to feel heavy, and she looked back down at the stream and let her mind go. The images came again.

On it went, and then she saw it.

In the back of her mind, as clear as anything she was looking at right now, was a small, white lizard with dark eyes. It was all she could see, as it scurried across a burning log, like she was asleep and this was a dream. But somehow more vivid than that. Then it was gone, and she was sitting in front of the creek, the same bubbling echoing off of the walls.

She looked up to see Aeliean sitting and rocking back and forth in her chair. Aeliean didn't seem capable of sitting still.

"I think I just fell asleep," said Kiadora.

"No, you didn't," Aeliean said quietly, as if in awe. "You had your eyes open and your breathing increased. You had your first vision." She leaned forward on her chair, arms on her knees and was bopping her heals up and down. "What did you see?"

"A white lizard, with the darkest eyes I've ever seen." Well, almost the darkest.

Kiadora stood up, feeling her knees popping as she did. She stiffly bent down and picked up the rug. Aeliean smiled warmly.

"Yes, your first vision. Many of the first carry connotations of deep significance to the viewer. Any idea what yours might be?"

Kiadora stood, holding the half wet rug away from her body. It had the same dark eyes, but a salamander? Besides, strange things seemed to happen when teachers knew about matters of love. She mentally shuttered as she thought about the Great Union and banished the idea from her head before she started to picture herself before everyone.

"No idea." Aeliean only nodded.

"It will come, it will come. Please put the rug in that cupboard, and I will see you tomorrow." Kiadora went to put the rug away in the cupboard Aeliean was motioning towards, shoving it under some shelves full of jars filled with pale pink liquid and what looked like roses floating in them. Kiadora only took a second to wonder what they might be used for before heading out the door and wondering what she would do for the night. She wanted to go back to the dining area, but decided it would look odd two nights in the row.

She figured she would just work with her element again, but then Kiadora wondered why she had not been back to the surface. It had been almost a week. It was her ultimate ticket to freedom, and still she stayed down here.

As she hovered where the end of the caverns branched off to the hallways leading to her quarters and those to the exit, she realized it was because of the threat of being caught. She couldn't guarantee that no one would recognize the constant patterns of her walking that way.

And she did not have her sun hat, which she had given back to the Children. The only thing she could do would be to swelter under her cloak, which she still had from when she first made her journey down here. It would look odd to walk around the compound with one, as no one needed them thanks to the heating system. Her only option would be to go up at night to avoid the appearance of a gradual tan. There were also no clocks down here, everyone seemed to run on instinct as to when to be somewhere. The lights went bright and it was morning, they went dim and it was night. It was remarkable when Kiadora considered it.

So then that led to the question of when it was even night. Was the lighting synchronized with the rising and setting of the sun? It seemed to be, as the lights were fully on when they went up the first time, and they were dim shortly after they got back.

Kiadora knew she had been wandering as she thought, but before she knew it, she was making her way around the perimeters of the classrooms to the same cavern entrance that the Children had used. It was decided then, but it would have to be later tonight, when it would be dark outside. She took a turn and headed to her quarters for now. No sense in not having the best of both worlds, and she went to practice with what she realized she was fondly referring to as *her element*.

CHAPTER 28

It was still as slick and precarious as ever, this path behind the waterfall. As Kiadora scaled it, she realized she was glad that there wasn't someone ahead of her to slip and send her tumbling down. On the other hand, if she were to slip, there would be no one there to catch her. She might lie bleeding and broken at the bottom of the pathway for an indefinite period of time. It wasn't like the area was used at all; that's why they had traversed it the first time. Or she could tumble off the side of the path, meet with the waterfall in midair as she descended into the pool, hopefully not hitting any rocks that might be lurking under the surface of the water.

Kiadora took a deep breath and made a mental note to take the utmost care and not rush her way up and out as she had wanted to. All the way over she just wanted to be out of the place, lest someone see her leaving. She finally hoisted her foot off of the last slick rock and was walking towards the exit, the sound of the waterfall echoing behind her.

She emerged to a perfectly clear, still night. Again, she had been afraid of adverse weather, but it seemed to be close to the time of the year when the rains held off. At least the "misread" date from the Holy Text had been convenient. She blew out the torch she had been carrying and trying to scale the slick rocks with. She walked forward onto the slightly damp grass, again reveling at the soft yield under her feet rather than the hard, rigid stone. She was thankful for the light provided by a full moon. Kiadora put the torch down in a bush besides the cavern entrance, not wanting the burden of carrying it around. It was time for a little freedom.

She considered walking in the direction they had gone to see the bird, but she decided against it. Kiadora already knew what was that way, and it was time to stick to the main roads for once. She was in the mood for a little civilization tonight.

The problem was remembering which way the main town was. And she would have to make the mental note to stay away from Lid's bar, lest he see her wandering. Although she questioned whether he would even remember who she was. Better to keep it safe, or as safe as technically being a fugitive was. She was completely turned around, knowing she could not be too far from a main town, but still not knowing which direction she came out or how far she actually traveled underground. She had never been the best judge of distances or directions.

Kiadora just set off to the right. There might be some road sign. And a little way down the silent, moonlit path there it was: a sign pointing to Shilidek. She followed the path along through a half wooded area, woods to her left and fields to her right. Kiadora had some time to marvel at finally being able to pass by a wooded area and not faint or just lose track of time. She had been too excited the other day to even notice.

She rounded a bend in the path to the left and there was the main gate to the city. Kiadora slowed a bit, remembering who she was. She had almost forgotten that she was the daughter of a local noble. She mentally shook herself, wondering how she could even forget such a thing. She might as well have forgotten her own name and gender. But somehow that didn't seem to matter anymore, not that she felt it mattered to begin with. Her special "gift" had seen to it that she was still less than nobility, even if she bore the family crest by birthright. But the problem remained as to whether these two gate guards playing a game of cards would know who she was. She was supposed to be out roughly hundreds of miles away at the Hermetical Order.

Still, she had come this far. If anyone even noticed, she was out on a trip. Kiadora made a mental note that she would somehow have to procure a hat, bonnet or smuggle the hooded cloak. She certainly had no money. Maybe they kept the hats in the Children's meeting area. As long as she didn't run into any of them…she truly didn't want to face any of them again.

Kiadora strolled through the gates, trying to look as natural as possible. One of the guards glanced up from his hand of cards he was studying and nodded. Kiadora nodded back, and muttered, "visiting my aunt." The guard nodded again and turned his head down. They apparently didn't pay him enough to care about strange wisps of women walking into a city at night. It wasn't exactly like these were war times, though. Security across the country had been complacent as far as Kiadora could remember. There had not been a major war since the Before Times.

The kings of today wanted surface peace for the sake of prosperity. They now knew how to wage war in the shadows for what they needed. Good to be civilized, Kiadora thought.

She strolled into the quiet little town. It seemed like a painting she saw in one of her old story books about a talking statue. The entrance led right into the center square, depicting a statue of a large eagle. The air smelled distinctly of frankincense; incense burned in a tray right underneath it. Benches surrounded the area, obviously for devotions and a large clock tower stood right behind it. The cobblestones, an alternating cream and gray color, formed a checkered pattern. It was the perfect setting for a good citizen to be devout and orderly. No one even stood in the square this late; they were undoubtedly off elsewhere having dinner or already in bed after a long day of humdrum activity.

Kiadora put her hands on her hips and surveyed the perimeters. There had to be something interesting going on somewhere. Life couldn't be all massive clock faces and perfect geometry. She headed forward and set off down a random street, store signs on this road reading "closed" and the resident apartment windows above them glowing softly.

She headed down another street, this time all homes, mostly with shut curtains. Those opened revealed people reading by fireplaces or eating dinner at tables. Kiadora hurried on, heading past a couple just out for a stroll and another woman out walking a small dog that could have had a spacious bed made out of her shoe.

And then, just as she got out off the long streets of residential boredom and was about to give up hope and head back, she heard it. Noises of shouting, of laughter, drums and guitars. Ah, here it was, the nightlife Dehlia sometimes snuck off to.

Kiadora had heard the stories of drunken passes by men who smelled of sweat, drink and dirt. She had heard the stories of people who would be tossed into the streets for pinching waitresses, and she had heard far more than she needed to know about the women who would take money for their favors and the dramatic shows they could put on when they got stiffed by a poor man who didn't want anyone to know he was there in the first place. And through listening to all of this, Kiadora had sworn that she would never want that, would never go there, had better things to do with her time. But that was before she lived the clandestine life of a mystic and wanted for one night to just not dream about those Church chambers deep underground.

Kiadora rounded a corner and came to a brightly lit street with candles in every window. Bright signs boasted titles to places with odd names the The Jack's Ass and other names that clearly arose from too much illegal drink. Groups of men stood on the sidewalk laughing, and at the end of the street was a grand building with posters and large pillars with feather patterns chiseled into them.

Not wanting to look like a stunned country girl come to the city, Kiadora turned into the nearest door she could find. As she passed, she saw a sign that read "The Royal Bizarre." She walked in to see a mockery of the court world she had spent her entire childhood in. Jesters wandered two-and-fro between tables of jostling patrons. Square banners with tapered ends, fashioned to look like court banners during festivals, hung everywhere. Where in the courts the banners were mostly colored gold and bronze, these were all different colors. A large painting of a king and queen was on the back wall but not the kind of royalty that Kiadora had grown up learning about. Instead, the two had their tongues hanging out and were cross-eyed, false cartoonish versions of the monarchs who kept a false peace. Kiadora marveled at how this place was even kept open. Maybe the king and queen had more of a sense of humor than she thought, or maybe it was just a closely kept local secret.

A court jester slapped her on the back of her shoulder.

"Hello, m'lady, and where will ye be sitting yourself this eve?" He had the old way of speaking that existed in the Before Times, when there was true chaos. Kiadora realized the place was set up to be a long-running joke about the life of the nobles and the "order" they stood for. Kiadora liked it here.

"I'll take a seat over there," Kiadora said, motioning to a table in a corner practically behind a large podium fashioned like the octagonal ones that stood outside the main court's doors. She was beginning to feel self-conscious about being here. She stood in an establishment that seemed bent on the parody of her class and with little in line of a disguise, someone must know who she was. But the gangly young man who nodded and led her to the table seemed not to notice or care. She seated herself in the sturdy, wooden booth.

"And what will ye be partakin' in line of beverages?" And suddenly Kiadora nearly let out a gasp. She had no money on her. These places didn't want you if you couldn't pay.

"I, uh, could I have a moment to think about it?" Kiadora

stammered, her voice coming out louder and more panicked than she intended. The man gave an overly dramatic flourish of a bow and was off to the counter. She looked toward the door. Well, best to leave and hope no one noticed. So much for getting out.

Then Kiadora jumped a little when she heard someone slide into her booth across from her. It was Lisera, who had not even changed her clothes. She was still wearing the same old pale, blue dress and red bandana on her head she always did, dark locks flying down.

"I never would have thought I lived to see it. You escaped the compound. Gone rogue so soon? I would have thought they had some things to teach you." The words did not come out as accusing as they probably should have, Kiadora realized. Here Lisera had risked her job, and maybe her life, to tell Kiadora about this place, and it looked like she was a deserter.

"No, I still live there. I just...found a way out," Kiadora ended in a whisper. "I needed a break, you know?"

"Hm, not many people down there feel that way. They get trapped by it all." Lisera had a light in her eyes. Kiadora couldn't tell if it was from amusement or whatever was in the mug she had her hand around. "So where did you find it?"

"Find what?" Kiadora asked distractedly as she watched a juggling show on a low stage. This was more activity than she had seen in months.

"The way out, I thought while I was there every way was sealed off. Not that I ever had the boldness you have to go looking. You better watch yourself, the Elders don't look too kindly on such a *misdeed*."

Lisera put an emphasis on misdeed that made it sound like a joke of a concept.

Kiadora looked up to see the waiter standing there. "A decision on the drink, m'lady?" Before Kiadora had time to stutter about leaving, Lisera jumped in with a smooth, "She'll have the honey wine," and the waiter was gone again.

"But Lisera, I don't have money." She felt more like a naive rich girl than ever at the moment. Other people had always provided the money; it had never been her concern.

"Don't worry about it, the drink's on me." And other people were still providing it. Not living at home, it didn't feel right.

"Somehow, at some point, I'll pay you back," Kiadora said. And then another thought. "But...I didn't think the staff got paid." Lisera chuckled.

"Oh, we do. It's a pittance. Hardly worth the groceries I buy, but there's at least enough for this every so often," she said, holding up her drink. "And we get lodging, it's not so bad." Kiadora felt ashamed for her family. The money they did give out hardly got the staff anywhere. She would pay Lisera back. Somehow.

"So what brings you out here?" Kiadora asked.

"Lid," said Lisera simply. "We still see each other. But it's peak time at the inn right now and with having to feed all of you, he doesn't have much time tonight so we got together earlier. I thought I would stay for a little longer out this way, and I do like this place. Good thing I did, with you blabbering and jabbering at the waiters. You have a lot to learn," Lisera said with a wink.

"I like this place, too," said Kiadora, and they fell silent for a moment, each awkward at admitting their own derision for their loyalties.

"How does this place get by?" Kiadora asked. "The high courts don't find out and get offended?" Lisera laughed.

"Heavens, no. They don't even know about this place. It's an area of commoners. And truth be told, the staff doesn't know too much about the higher courts. Not as much as you think they would with how critical they are. You don't see anyone actually recognizing you?" Kiadora shook her head.

"I still like it here," Kiadora said.

"Me too."

"So what if I wanted to come back? I doubt the compound has some sort of hidden cash reserve they give students to go and drink. And I couldn't ask you to put me up."

"They have tabs here, but that's nasty business, getting into that sort of debt. They have ways of calling on that."

"But they have no idea where I live."

"They take portraits, and they find you. There's a rather large industry and profession to find bar tab dodgers. And they are not friendly." Lisera spoke in low voice, as if she knew from experience. The waiter came by and put Kiadora's drink in front of her and was off again. She looked down at it like it would cause her ruin.

"Oh, one won't hurt you," Lisera said. "I'm talking about the people who are out every night of the week drinking their brains to putty." Kiadora hesitantly picked up the glass and put it to her lips. The cool liquid delivered what it promised, that sweet taste of honey, but on the other end it had a bitter aftertaste and stung slightly on the way down.

"It's alright at the beginning, but I don't think I'll be getting addicted to it," Kiadora said in gruff voice, hoping her throat would feel better after a few seconds. Lisera let off a chuckle.

"It takes some getting used to. This place is known for its harsh drinks. This is the most tame in the establishment." Kiadora nodded and pushed the drink to the side.

"So you seem to know this town pretty well, what is there to do? That doesn't burn my throat and incur eventual debt."

"Hm, it's fun you're wanting. Meditation and the inner ways of the soul not completely covering it?" Lisera let off a grin, but Kiadora suddenly felt horrible again, ungrateful.

"It's not like it's horrible. I've learned some great things." She leaned over and in a low tone said, "I can actually control flame. I mean, not a lot, but enough to be just amazing. And I think they're teaching me to...what's the word?...Scry?" Lisera nodded, looking impressed.

"Control over an element in such a short time," Lisera said it a tone of pure wonder. "That is very amazing. It took me years, and even then I was never very good at it. I'm surprised you'd even want to leave, if only for a little while. You seem to be getting on great." Kiadora let out of huff.

"I can't get my head around the belief system. It's archaic and foreign. People care about rank too much. And there's always the threat of punishment from these Elders no one ever seems to see. It's like they're the shadows themselves, dark and terrifying. You have a feeling they're not going to truly hurt you, but they scare people so much they might as well just get on with it." Lisera laughed.

"That's sure a way of putting it. No, I don't miss those days," she said, leaning back. "It's why I left: the rank, the politics. And you're not even out of the Sitrina level yet." Lisera looked into Kiadora's eyes. The maid had been staring into her jug much of the night.

"But I shouldn't discourage you. Lots of people have fulfilling lives down there, just because it wasn't for me. And you have a lot of mental scarring that won't make it easy."

"People were a little more tactful than to say mental scarring, but so I've heard," said Kiadora with a lopsided grin. It was great to see Lisera so open. It was a side Kiadora only saw hints of at home.

"You know I didn't mean it like that. It's just something you'll have to live with and work through." She leaned forward again. "Not many people live through the Church's curing process. Some infections, lot of suicides." Kiadora let out a sigh and just looked into that pale, yellow liquid, thinking of the yellow banners that she saw hanging in the Church. Then she looked up.

"So, what's fun around here?" Kiadora asked again. Lisera looked off to the door, thinking.

"Have you seen the playhouse?"

"No." Lisera grinned and poured the last of the liquid in her mug down her throat with one swig and got up, motioning for Kiadora to follow. Lisera threw some coins down on the table, and they walked out, leaving the honey wine abandoned.

"It has to be the greatest one on the south end of the continent," said Lisera, as they set off, winding past groups of people and weaving in and out of street lights. "Granted, I can't get in by myself too often with all the work I have. The shows should have started a long while ago by this point, but I know some people I need to introduce you to."

Just as Kiadora had expected, they were soon walking up the steps and between the pillars decorated with feathers of all colors, the paint and sculpture breathing life into the stone. As they passed by, Kiadora thought it looked as if the feathers were moving.

Rather than walking through the main doors, they took a sharp turn to the left and were walking up what looked like an access ramp to the backstage. Lisera knocked four times on the door in rapid succession and the door swung open. On the other side was a man who was tall enough to nearly bang his head on the top of the doorframe. He was dressed in black and had the longest hair Kiadora had ever seen on a man, a wave of dark brown that went down past his shoulders and was only slightly under Kiadora's length, right in the middle of the stomach region. He looked stern for a moment and then flashed a big smile.

"Lisera! It's been a while, old girl." He glanced back. "I can't talk long, but what brings you here so late in the night?"

"I need to introduce you to someone. This is Kiadora, she's staying in the area for language studies and wants to get into a few shows. You can tell them it's a favor for Lisera." The man nodded.

"Sure thing. You'll love it," said the man, addressing Kiadora. Kiadora had to practically strain her neck to give the man eye contact. "Just tell everyone you know how great it is, no mentioning the free rides, though. You're lucky, not everyone has given as much to this theater as Lisera has." Kiadora nodded. Who would she tell? Just then the man looked back, and Kiadora could see a lantern light up.

"Back to the curtains. Just knock rapidly four times just as Lisera did, I'll be seeing you around. Lisera," he said with a nod in Lisera's direction, then he closed the door. Kiadora just stared in amazement at Lisera as they went down the ramp again. She had no idea the nice cleaning lady held so much clout in other areas of the country.

"So if you have such an in at this place, why clean our bathrooms? I mean, the theater, what a life!" It was out before Kiadora could stop it. Kiadora mentally slapped herself. It sounded so dismissive.

"It's not as rosy as it sounds, Kiadora. My son is one of their greatest actors, and he had to beg and plead with me to let him join. It's an odd life, being an actor in these times, Kiadora. Playwrights have disappeared for being too dismissive of the Church, actors even more so. The playhouses attract a lot more attention than a small pub. The only reason this place stays open is because of the certain...tips I give them. This is their fifth home under a different name. Right now, it won't make a whole lot of sense. But enjoy the shows," Lisera said, smiling back at her. "It's getting rather late. I best get back to the estates."

"Yeah, I suppose I should head back. Speaking of which, do you have a match? Otherwise my torch won't light again." Lisera passed her a small copper box. This woman's generosity never ceased.

"Just flip the small lever on the side, a match tip dispenses and hits a coarse surface. It's not enough to keep burning, but it will get your torch going." Lisera stopped and turned towards Kiadora. They were now on a quiet street corner on the edge of the residential area.

"I don't know when I'm going to be in these parts next, much less if we'll meet up. Keep yourself safe. There's some odd things that go on down there, so keep your ears open." She hugged Kiadora, all social status of servant to master gone in a strange town in the night. Lisera then fumbled in a front pocket on her skirt.

"Here," she said, holding out a few copper pieces.

"No, I couldn't Lisera, my father doesn't pay you enough…" Lisera then grabbed Kiadora's wrist and forced the copper pieces into Kiadora's palm.

"I'll have more coming, you won't. Daresay you'll need it with what's ahead." Then Lisera gave a smile and was heading down the street. Kiadora sighed, pocketed the coins and headed back to the country, trying not to think about Lisera's comment about what was ahead.

CHAPTER 29

Kiadora was in the dampness of Aeliean's room once more, but today there was a large tub. Kiadora stood by awkwardly as Aeliean poured in steaming water. When Kiadora had asked what was going on, the only thing Aeliean had responded with was, "ritual bath, you'll like it." A bath didn't seem so bad, but a bath also meant no clothes and gauging by the special level of openness that there seemed to be down here, there would be no robe she could sit in soaking wet.

After the water sat steaming in the tub, Aeliean went over to start rummaging through the cupboard and brought over several jars, large and small. Out of the small jars she poured several drops of heavy liquid with pungent flowery and herbal aromas. Kiadora thought she smelled some lavender mixed with a sharp mint smell. Aeliean scooped her hand into the larger jars and cast some dark green powder over the water, muttering something under her breath. Kiadora was motioned to step in.

Kiadora stepped forward to see if she would be told to take off her clothes. She didn't mind getting them damp. She had a spare set back at her quarters. But Aeliean motioned at her own dress to indicate that

Kiadora's should be removed. Marveling at how adept the woman was at communication with so little words, Kiadora heaved a sigh and slid the thin brown dress over her shoulders. Sometimes she wondered if she should look at something more vibrant at the monthly clothes exchange, in which they were allowed to exchange old clothes for new ones. Not the highest quality, certainly nothing she would have worn on the surface. But she had come down in a nondescript brown to not attract attention, and she still was not terribly interested in attracting any attention to herself. 'Except for one person,' she thought, and she blushed as she put the clothes down on a nearby chair. Maybe a change of clothes would be in order. But she looked over at the brown and realized it just felt like her. And she wasn't even sure why.

She stepped into the bath, glancing at Aeliean self-consciously, but Aeliean just watched her get in as if she were watching a man cross the street: completely average, everyday activity.

As Kiadora settled into the steaming liquid, her skin turning pink at the touch of the near-scalding stuff, she realized that the bath felt like bliss, the warm water like a luxury from another world. Kiadora felt her bottom hit the smooth porcelain and looked up at Aeliean for instructions. There had to be more to this. And there was:

"I need you to do a similar exercise to what you were doing with the stream. This time, you will need to close your eyes, but just focus on the water around you. Breathe the scents of the oils and just view whatever you then see." Aeliean flowed into a chair next to the tub and bopped her leg soundlessly as Kiadora turned her head to rest it on the edge of the basin. The smell of summer flowers and mint- was it spearmint, peppermint?- wafted into her nose. It felt out of place down here. And just like that, the shadows were back, wavering, but this time color grew and she was surrounded in green. She was in the forest, real as though she stood there now.

She started to walk forward, the scope of the trees changing from scarlet maples to a fall orchard bearing apples. As she walked, the leaves fell to the ground in a swirl of crimson, orange and yellow confetti, finally turning bare and the ground turning to mud.

As she watched the scene change she knew exactly where she was; she would know it even if she were in the memory-addled years of old age. The orchard stood in the same orderly rows it had for decades, the maples to the west. And over there was the footpath leading to… where? It was, of course, her family's estate, but something was wrong. She knew the path should be heading back home, but as she walked down the path, it took her around the orchard instead.

Kiadora continued to wander, not really knowing why. She knew this place, there was nothing left to explore, but everything still seemed new, out of place. Snow started to fall at a rapid pace and now she was wading through a foot of snow and starting to shiver.

Now she was walking out over a pond at the bottom of the hill next to the orchard, still kicking snow as she went, taking it slower so she would not slip and fall. Strange, the pond was not this close to the orchard. But it was the right shape. There was the old oak tree, standing skeletal and white-bearded in the winter.

She had always been told to stay off the ice, why was she out here now? She looked back at the orchard, but it was gone. She looked in every direction, only to find the barren maples. Kiadora wanted to yell.

Where was she? Even the oak was not where it should have been. And here was a pier. No, this wasn't right, there was never a pier.

And she had been out here for three seasons. Why had no one come to help her? Where was everyone, did they care? She kept kicking snow and sliding. She had to get back home, somehow.

Then, what she was fearing worst of all, she heard cracks beneath her feet, a sharp snap that jarred her heart. No, this couldn't be happening. No one would know where she was, no one would help. Why wouldn't they help? Was Father too busy in the courts again? Was Dehlia too busy doing her makeup, her mother and sister sewing again?

Kiadora felt the surface under her legs give way and now painfully cold water was rushing up to meet her head. She was submerged in the bitter cold, she could feel her skin lose feeling on contact. She had just enough strength and feeling to flail her arms until her head was above water, and she could suck in air that seemed colder than the water, chilling her innermost organs.

She barely felt the large chunk of ice hit her arm and looked over to see the limb was a purplish-blue. Why had no one been here? Kiadora began to feel her strength fade, and she sank down under the water, all feeling in her muscles lost. Her last thought was of the estate that no one could be bothered to emerge from.

Then she was back in the tub, the water around her a soothing lukewarm and no snow in sight. She took a few minutes to remember why she was even bathing before a stranger, the mint and lavender as pungent as ever. Aeliean was sitting silently in her chair, the alternate leg swinging. Apparently, Kiadora had come out of it on her own again without the painful jarring or touch she was used to.

"What did you see?" said Aeliean in a smooth, calm tone.

"I died. I was on a frozen lake when the ice broke, and there was no one around. I was close to my home, and there was no one there to help. I just froze and drowned to death." She very nearly started to cry but held it back with a deep breath. "But it was odd," she continued after Aeliean stayed silent, a prompt to go on. "It was the estate, but everything was turned around. I was lost, and fall passed into winter. I roamed and was out on the thinly frozen lake, even though I knew it was a stupid thing to do. But there was no one there, no one looked for me for all that time." Kiadora leaned forward and hugged her knees to her chest, shaking her head. "But just a stupid dream right?" she said, looking hopefully to Aeliean.

"No, you most likely are remembering a past life. You may have died that way, but your mind is still mixed into this world so the two lives are combining. I suspect that is why no one looked for you, you were not yourself in this vision. You were from another life. You will start to see more pure visions as time goes on." Kiadora swirled a large chunk of dried leaf around her finger that floated by.

"I didn't feel like a different person. I saw my hair, my arm looked like it always does, except blue from the cold water."

"Again, both of the lives are combining. This is all you know now. You will be able to glimpse what you were more clearly as time goes on." Kiadora nodded slowly. She had always been raised to believe there was only one life, that nothing came before, but everything came after.

"What would even be the point of having multiple lives?" Kiadora asked. "Isn't one enough to have to put up with?"

"The reason varies from person to person," said Aeliean, looking into the water. "Some people don't even have past lives yet, some are in what they think is their hundredth life, some are in their last and can feel it. I'm in my 82nd to be exact. Some people believe it is so they can get the gamut of experience to learn from and become stronger. Others think that it just is and cannot be explained. I believe it is so I can become a god." Kiadora looked up suddenly.

"A god?"

"Yes. Once you see everything and are everything, you have supreme knowledge and with that comes supreme power, as in a god. My Ashilek confirmed this." Kiadora nodded slowly again, not sure what to say. She had no interest in becoming a god, much less living hundreds of lives. She felt if she thought about it for too long her head would explode. She had enough problems figuring out this life.

But still, what if she had once died that way? To be able to view something like that would be rather extordinary, and she did once think that a bond with a simple flame was beyond imagining. Still, multiple lives....

"Can I have towel, or is there still more I need to do?"

"No, that concludes everything for today," said Aeliean, rising gracefully from her chair. She moved back to a wooden bin, the intricate silver needlework on her blue dress glinting in the torchlight. Spirals today, Kiadora noticed for the first time. She had been too preoccupied with what the bath would be used for.

Kiadora gratefully took the thin but soft towel and wrung the bottom half of her hair out with it over the edge of the tub. Kiadora dried off her top as she stood up and dried the lower half of her torso as she stepped out, trying to ignore the other woman behind her. The dampness of the cave hit her in a bitter chill as she slipped her dress on. She tried not to think about the frozen pond as she dried off her legs and feet to slip into her shoes. With a nod towards Aeliean she was out the door, still trying to shake the panic of certain death off all the way down the corridor.

She headed through the main classroom corridors, looking to the left at the main eating area where three people idly waited for dinner to start, by the looks of it. She walked past the library, scanning the crowd and not remembering why. When she saw him, she remembered why. There, just as before, diagonally behind a group of people studying was Astrian, reading a book. He held the cover up today. She couldn't read it from where she was standing so she casually went over to a shelf near the table he was sitting at and pretended to browse while she glanced back at the cover.

Atonement and Grace. Odd title for someone who always looked so calm. Usually more of a topic for the generally panicky and the retribution fearing, Kiadora mused. Kiadora mentally cringed as she wondered if deep down he was one of those people who feared the afterlife, thought he was vile and doomed for torture. That might explain why he had been so interested in the Ollox. But he didn't seem like that kind of person. He seemed too...composed, assured.

Whatever the case was, Kiadora was tired of hanging in the shadows and speculating. She realized she was doing it for two weeks now. Some women did it for years, longing for the day they would strike up a natural conversation and instantly connect, heart and soul. Two weeks was still too long for Kiadora.

She put whatever dull title she held back onto the shelf and walked over to take a seat next to Astrian.

"Why a book on atonement and grace?" A simple question, but infinitely more complex than a yes or no answer.

Except that Astrian offered a shrug. And by way of explanation he gave, "I've just always been interested in it." Kiadora nodded, lost. She realized she hadn't planned this out very well. Now what would she say to this quiet man with the dark eyes?

"I don't really have a favorite reading topic. Well, I look through enough stuff, but not enough to really read anything in depth." She looked down at the ground, her confidence quickly fading.

"Maybe you should," he said evenly. He was staring at her, his book resting flat on its cover. "You've seen a lot of trials at the hands of this stuff." Kiadora cocked her head, feeling more like a confused chicklet than she wanted to.

"How did you know about that?"

"Regelend told me." Kiadora nodded. Man of thousands of words for a million people. "Look up *The Nature of Suffering*. It's a favorite of mine. You might not find all of it completely practical, in fact a lot of it is rather outdated in thought, but it's an interesting book."

"I'll do that, I'll do that right now," said Kiadora, and she went over to the selves under "N" and pulled out a dark book with ancient, blocked scribbling. There was an engraving of a man being splayed by a demon with a spear on the inside of the cover. Cheerful. And an odd thing to find such a representation of in this library, she thought. But there was a fair share of works by all religious thinkers from the surface, some even put to death for their words and their books barely rescued, Regelend had said once. It made her feel terrible that she used one to steady a table she was sitting at once and even more so that she never seemed to have the attention span to read through a single one all the way. She had a feeling she might with this one. As she headed out with the book, she gave a passing nod to Astrian as she held up the book.

CHAPTER 30

Kiadora sat at the edge of her quarters, legs hanging over the doorway as she leaned over her book and read by the light of the chandelier. Her candle had burned down long ago, but she didn't feel like breaking away to get a new one from the storage area where someone always sat behind a desk all day looking like they were about to jump over the desk and strangle someone, just so something interesting would happen.

The book was full of theories of why bad things happened to good people, or even moderately decent people. And in some places, some who downright deserved it all. It covered everything from ideas of making up for past wrongs, to suffering to build character (Kiadora hadn't understood that one- she felt a little set backwards herself), to the nonbelief that these things just happened and people needed to just live with it. Some wrote that bad experiences were tests to attain a more glorious afterlife, some just blamed the Shiekita for generating a lack of faith and the resulting struggles.

Kiadora had perked up when she read that pain was to atone for wrongs in a past life. Not that Kiadora had decided she believed in them, but she thought her teacher might find it interesting. Aeliean probably already knew. If Kiadora had indeed drown to death in a past life, she wondered if that would make up for past transgressions, unless she was a twisted soul who had made many errors.

The book had said, "The nature of suffering has been theorized to exist within the natural turn of the lives that one leads again and again. The necessity of atonement for deeds can pass over to other lives if that deed was so heinous that it cannot possibly be made up for in a single life. It is in this way that balance of deed and balance of soul is attained."

The book spoke much about balance, as if life existed on some great scale that constantly had to line up in terms of morality and that somehow, someway, everyone got what was coming to them, whether it was from a god, some intangible force that made it so or just cause and effect.

But it wasn't the desire to understand any of this that kept Kiadora going through the dense language and high ideas that alluded some of her understanding (what was "transcendental moral equilibrium," anyway?). It was the fact that Astrian thought this was important enough to go over again and again and recommend it to her specifically.

She wondered what he could have possibly seen in his life to make him wonder about what the causes of his pain were, what ate at him so much that he needed to find a rationalization for it all or some religious code that would somehow make it all okay; that is what this book mostly turned out to be all about. Whatever happened, there was always another cause, a deep cosmic reason that made it alright that it had happened. Whatever was the plague to mankind (and it covered everything from death to torture to disaster of every size and variety), it was just that it was atonement for past misdeeds, the fault of a supernatural being or, "the simple phenomenon of transcendental moral equilibrium."

Kiadora had, of course, been angry about her torture, distrustful to the point of being glad she would possibly never have to see her family or Tahn again and other feelings she didn't even really understand. But it was a passing transgression made by some people who had tried to mean well, she realized as she read. Their unshaken beliefs just got in the way.

Had Astrian, on the other hand, lived a life where the suffering was never fleeting, just a constant struggle that needed to be made alright? And what did he think of her if he felt just fine lending out his favorite read, and subsequently, a glance into his soul, if there ever was one?

As Kiadora looked out over the compound, she saw a hand waving to the side and at the bottom end of the ladder. "Miss, you're late for your lesson." Kiadora looked down and realized the man was looking at her.

Her lesson already? She looked down at the book she was three quarters through and realized she had been up the whole night plowing through this thing. Today would be a fun lesson. Kiadora let out a weary, "alright." She put the book on the bed and made her way down the ladder.

As she pushed open the door to the classroom, she saw Aeliean sitting in a chair by the creek. "Lost track of time, did we?" Again, from anyone else that comment would have been accompanied by a tone of deep irritation, but for Aeliean, it came out even, smooth. Friendly, in its way. Kiadora closed the door behind her.

"Do you know anything about transcendental moral equilibrium?" Kiadora asked.

"Ah, you've been reading, good. And about past lives. I'm glad this is making an impact on you enough to seek out further information on it." Kiadora nodded and looked to the side.

"Yes... I was curious about it..."

"You'll learn very quickly that your past lives are never regulated just to the past. They often have consequences for your present life, subtly make you who you are and still guide your fears and your dreams to this day. Otherwise, there would be no point in living all those past lives, would there?" Aeliean looked off into the distance as she spoke. Kiadora was beginning to realize that Aeliean's speeches never came out as lectures, she spoke more as if from unadulterated reflection.

"That is where transcendental moral equilibrium comes in," Aeliean went on. "The deeds you do in past lives sometimes cannot be atoned for, or paid for, by the time you die, so you must continue to suffer for them in however may future lives it may take. It's an older idea, one that comes from before the times of the Church.

"I'm still surprised it was written by a man on the surface. He must have had it secretly passed down the family lines and was the unlucky one who felt the urge to record it. Or he possibly learned it from the desert dwellers, many tribes of which still have strong beliefs in the ways of the recycled soul.

"But back to this idea of moral equilibrium. It comes from the idea that everything has to be repaid in some way. If you were to rack up a huge sum of monetary debt for instance, more than your yearly allowance makes, you would probably be paying that back until you die. It's the same with misdeeds."

"So there's some amount of suffering you have to do to pay back for what you did wrong?" Kiadora asked. "Like if I killed someone, I would have a tree fall on me at a later point as part of some cosmic payback?"

"Yes, that is the basic belief behind it."

"Is it possible that my death in a past life was an atonement?"

"It's hard to say, Kiadora, but it is possible. That last thing I want you to do this early in things is to sit around and wonder about your past misdeeds and how that works into was is wrong with your life now. Your job is just to experience these things for right now. The knowledge and the whys of what happened will come when you have all the facts of your past lives."

Kiadora nodded and looked around for the first time. A table with a black basin on it and a chair sat in the middle of the room. As Kiadora walked up she could see the liquid glint in the torchlight. Floating in the liquid were several fresh flowers: roses, small lilacs, apple blossoms. She sat down in the chair.

"It is the same principle as the creek, really," said Aeliean, coming up behind her. "You just need to gaze in and let your mind see what it sees." Aeliean stood just so her reflection would not hit the water. Kiadora could only see the smooth black surface, a shimmering field of pure nothing supporting the flowers.

Kiadora gazed and soon the shadows in her mind started. But they hardly lasted at all, only a mere blink before the actual images started, as if her mind was simply learning to bypass these formless creatures.

It was the white salamander again, eyes as dark as the surface that supported the flowers. It crept between flames on a log. Kiadora could have sworn it was playing, almost for her amusement. It kept weaving in and out, and that had been the day.

CHAPTER 31

That night Kiadora dreamed about someone she never really expected to think about again in her waking moments. Tahn drifted in and out all night. She was back at the bar with Lisera, and he was the waiter, looking timid and uncertain as he went from table to table, out of place in this sinner's drinking establishment.

Later he was the stage attendant at the playhouse who guarded the door, speaking in a low tone about how they could not get in, looking still more uncertain about having to guard anything. She never remembered the words after exactly, just the fact that he stammered out something about a lack of entrance.

He was a teacher, instructing a student in the ways of Eatheria. She saw, as she passed in the hall, the door was left mistakenly open. He looked resentful for having to even be aware of such a thing and turned red at having to utter such blasphemies. She didn't know how she knew how he felt, but it was as much of a fact of the dream as it was that she was walking through the compound, which was darker, as if the massive chandelier had been put on some sort of mood setting:

not as dark as night, but not as bright as day.

In the same dream she saw him at the Eternal Fires, looking passively at it. He looked away from it and up at her with an expression that seemed to plead for something, and Kiadora knew it was to come home, to just come back from all of this nonsense. It wasn't what he had intended for her when he had mentioned her issue to the Church. The last thing he had wanted was for her to get caught up in this dark business away from God. He never said a word of this, but somehow Kiadora knew that was passing through his head.

And then she woke up in a cold sweat, Tahn's face swimming before her and that desperate plea in the look he gave. Kiadora sat up and shook her shoulders, rolling her head, trying to shake off the dream.

As she splashed water on her face, she tried to think of the last time she had actually thought of him. It had been with Narissa. Narissa had said to let certain things go, but she half admitted that she had loved Tahn, he had only wanted what was best. Now that she wanted someone else, had her mind drifted back to Tahn? She blushed as she realized she was consciously admitting it to herself for the first time.

But Tahn had been a major part of her life for years, she remembered, as she descended the ladder. You didn't just leave something like that behind. Still, she wanted to see Astrian today.

She kept her eyes open during the morning meal, hoping that she would see him, but he did not seem to be a breakfast person, or even a morning person. She had never seen him before the afternoon meal.

Kiadora went off to class, where she sat before the same flowered bowl, gazing in. As if to taunt her, she saw the salamander all day. She also now saw a great green dragon, which she didn't know what to do with. It was the green lizard variety, like the ones she saw painted on the murals of old tales from the Before Times. There was much doubt that these mighty beings once had been slayed by the old tribes, but people seemed to like to draw them nonetheless and tell the tales of the men who were fierce enough to slay them. It was thought that the dragons were a mere metaphor for the evils of the elements of Fire and Earth, and the Church had accepted this and encouraged the tales.

Kiadora saw fire come from a cave. The flame caught the surrounding wood as it passed. The white salamander scurried past and was nearly trampled by the massive talons of the dragon as it left the cave. And that was the end of it.

Aeliean questioned Kiadora on what she saw, and Kiadora merely reported the dragon. Aeliean had only nodded.

"Little do they know, dragons were a reality in the Before Times." Kiadora rose an eyebrow.

"Dragons? Come now."

"It was true, there are many reports of past life viewings with dragons. I was also a dragon slayer in another life." Kiadora had to choke back a burst of laughter.

"You'll see that through this process, you will learn and unlearn what you thought you knew," said Aeliean, carrying away the bowl and scooping the flowers onto a towel, pouring the liquid into a jar.

"Alright. See you tomorrow," was all Kiadora could say before she got into the hallway safely behind the closed door and let out audible laughter. She chuckled all the way down the corridor, looking into the major scrying areas for Astrian. The library, dining area and corridors yielded nothing as well.

Kiadora hovered near the ladders of the sleeping quarters, still thinking of that dragon and her dreams of Tahn. Kiadora decided it was time to reap the benefit of the theater that night. She was tired of thinking of this stuff for the time being. And she went up to her quarters to work with the flame until dark.

Kiadora knocked rapidly four times in the succession that she was shown. She struggled to remember, hoping she was getting it right. What was it, four short raps? As the door swung open, she realized her memory deserved more credit than it got.

The same large man looked down at her and nodded as he stepped back to let her in.

"You stopped in for a good one tonight," he said in a deep, yet soft tone. "Take that way down to the seats and tell the usher you know Lisera." Kiadora smiled and followed a walkway down past some curtains and large crates. She came out to an arena with padded seats and found a man at the end a row. Kiadora mentioned she knew Lisera, and he sat her in the middle towards the front, what Kiadora suspected were ideal seats. It wasn't quite balcony seating, either, but she would take it.

As more and more people settled in, she was grateful for the hat she was wearing, which she pulled down as low as she could to her face without obscuring her view of the stage. Kiadora had retrieved the hat from the Children's quarters early one morning, deciding to risk it with them. She knew she was the only one wearing a hat; social mores usually dictated taking off hats in any setting like this, but it wasn't tall and the brim pointed downward. People behind her would see just fine.

People around her, wearing deep colored evening wear- rich blues, reds and purples- settled in. She became painfully aware of the drab brown she wore. It was all she had. She hoped no one would question what such a ratty person was doing in the theater. "People who look like her *can't* afford things," Dehlia's haughty tone echoed in her mind. That was the phrase she had heard as Dehlia commented on the ill-dressed throughout society, a far greater evil in Dehlia's mind that any other prevailing social problem.

But Kiadora instantly forgot all of this as the curtain rose.

The scene was a hillside, or as close to a hillside as a wooden stage could get. A painted backdrop showed hills and trees under a rainy sky. Trees glistened with dew here and there on the actual stage and in the left corner was the opening of a cave, which Kiadora suspected was made out of what looked like papier-mâché.

Kiadora had seen elaborate plays before and could tell this was a local production, made with a low-budget and an even lower profile. From where she sat, she swore she could see nails sticking out of one the stage "trees," she now realized. Still, she couldn't be picky. How many from the compound were able to even watch a show?

Then a narrator stepped out from the side and stood at the edge of the stage.

"For many long years the town of Abergale had been tortured by a fierce dragon," he said. "There had been a total of 34 villagers to date who fell to the beast's flames since it first arrived in times before the

villagers could even remember. The town saw it as a necessary sacrifice to the dragon. Until one rose up, a boy from a local farm village." Kiadora could have started laughing. How appropriate, and it
was one of the most famous tales.

The story progressed with the boy trying to fight off a dragon that
was little more than a few actors with a cloth thrown over them. Two
people at the front held a wooden head that was painted green and
carved with too many teeth to count. The fight went on for a good ten
minutes, the small boy dodging and rolling. Then when she thought
they would just end the damn fight, a burst of flame actually came out
of the wooden head. Kiadora jumped back in her seat in surprise, marveling at the level of choreographic planning and technical skill that it
took to ensure safety. She hoped that it took.

The boy then dodged and ran off. Kiadora knew what would
happen next. The boy's mother went missing in the night, a loud cry
issuing from the boy to the side that the village was assumed to be
from. A tense scene with dark lighting progressed as men searched
the forests and the hills. Kiadora could tell it was going to be one of
those plays with no scene changes. She rather liked to see the stage-
hands work deftly and to be mentally transported to a new area
with the dimming and brightening of stage lights.

But Kiadora remembered she couldn't be choosy at the moment.
She felt ashamed that her inner rich girl was showing herself again.
The last thing she wanted was to be as snotty as Dehlia, critiquing the
finest plays in the land as if they were put on by some children in a
romper room.

"We did better plays than that when we were five and pretending to be princesses," Dehlia had said. Kiadora had always been the evil monster or the bumbling old fool.

Kiadora shook her head, wanting to return to the play. She had hoped the play would take her mind off these things. And with that, she made the effort to focus on nothing but the play.

The search worked, as the villagers heard cries from the boy's mother within the cave. Kiadora now felt like she was sharing in their apprehension. None of the villagers wanted to venture in. They all had families, obligations, so the boy was sent in. Bright red lights erupted from the cave and loud, tense music played while roars were heard. The boy was suddenly thrown out from the cave, covered in ash and soot. And his left arm was missing. Kiadora did not even take the time to think that it would be tucked in his shirt, safely hidden away. She began to worry that they would not get him care until infection set in, even though she knew the story.

Another day, the lights bright, the boy was back in the woods with a party of men on their way to hunt down the now missing town's sheriff. On their search, they found something startling in the cave while the dragon was away. It was the possessions of everyone the dragon had captured. Sure, there were plenty of things the boy did not recognize because he did not know everyone that had gone missing, but there was old Jillean's walking stick, and Margarine's flute that she loved to play, he yelled from the cave (or side stage). Then the sounds of flapping wings and roaring flame chased them all back to town.

"Margarine, my daughter?" the mayor asked at mention of the flute. The boy told him of the toys of children and silverware around the cave. He recognized his mother's mug she always carried around, not too certain about how clean the cups of other establishments were, much to the great offence of others, the boy remembered with a fond smirk.

"What are saying, boy?" the mayor said in a rough, loud tone.

"They're in there, they're really in there!" The boy tugged on the mayor's sleeve. "We have to get them out." The mayor questioned the boy, wondering if he did not want to accept that the boy's mother was dead after all. Kiadora marveled at the twist. This was never part of the tale, they were always certainly eaten. After all, how could a creature of Fire and Earth not consume everything it its way?

The mayor looked at the boy in dismay, but Kiadora could tell he was wanting to believe it all by his soft stare and long pause.

"But did you see any of them?" The boy shook his head.

The mayor bent down to the boy and told him he was about to send him on a very dangerous mission. The boy needed to sneak in at the dead of night and see if he could find the lost hostages. The boy nodded bravely. Anything for his dear old ma.

And with the dimming of the lights, and a few shadows moving some trees and throwing up blankets in the darkness, the lights came back on to find the boy in the cave, much to Kiadora's joy. She wanted to see if the hostages were alive.

The boy walked through, slow and cautious. From offstage she could hear a flame roaring, or what sounded like a flame. As he went forward a blanket was torn down to signify a progression forward, and there were about five people in a heap. They were darkened by soot, many had red wounds and looked next to death. One woman sat up, tending to a small girl's burn wounds.

"Ma!" the boy let out and ran over. The woman gasped and held out her arms to her son. Kiadora almost cried.

"What are you doing just sitting in here, Ma? We have to get out!" His mother hushed him and told him he would alert the dragon. He pulled and pulled at her but she would not budge. He pleaded with her to come but she would not. She only shook her head.

"I can't, my son."

"But why?"

"I cannot explain, it is just something I cannot do. If I leave, where will I go, what will I do? I may be punished."

"By who? We can slay the dragon, we can Ma, you have to come. You can come back home with me and Pa, we miss you." But the scorched and tattered woman only shook her head.

And then the dragon came, Kiadora no longer seeing the long line of human feet under the blanket. No, it wasn't a blanket, it was dragon, and it was chasing the boy. He ran and swung his sword at it but it dodged. It dove at him, trying to take him down, and then he ran out of the cave. Right as he left, the dragon swooped over the group of people, doing an odd dance around them, tighter and tighter, and settled them in a strange hug. It let out of contented snort. Kiadora could see flame from behind the back of the dragon and then there was a cry from the mother before the lights went down.

The lights came up and the boy stood on the edge of the forest with a group of people holding pitchforks, shovels and a few hunting rifles.

This part of the tale Kiadora knew. They got to the opening of the cave and stood there, not sure they wanted to try to kill the damn thing. What if it became more angry? What if a worse fate met them after they killed it? It might have friends in faraway places. What would they do and where would they go after they killed it? They've known its fear and stronghold for so long.

"We'll live in peace," the boy shouted. "We'll finally stand on our own, secure in our own merits! If you want to stay under its shackles, than go, leave now. Another dragon will come and you can worship that with your own unwilling sacrifices. It's time to throw off the rituals and the games, the fear. Come if you are with me!" And then Kiadora had a sudden inkling that this was not about a dragon.

The men looked at each other, their nerve renewed. All the men charged at the cave entrance, and out came the dragon, swerving and breathing flame. Men barely dodged out of the way. Several men attacked at the back of the beast, others came at the sides. The dragon toppled over, flames flying as it fell. The boy stood beside its neck and drove his sword into its head. It jerked then moved no more.

Then out of the cave came the hostages, some being carried, barely conscious. The boy met his mother and who was assumed to be the father, and they fretted over a large red welt down the side of the woman's arm. They all turned to head back to the village.

The play ended with another dragon rising from the edge of the trees, a yellow one, and settling into the cave.

The curtain then fell and the actors came out to take a bow. Kiadora clapped furiously. She had expected subpar acting, no scene changes and no change in the plot of the original tale. She wanted to jump to her feet and start cheering, but she needed to not draw attention to herself, so she kept to her chair.

Kiadora headed back through town, out along the country trail and back to her own cave, her mind swimming with images of the dancing dragon and the boy seeing his mother again, and most of all, what it meant that they needed to stand on their own merit. She now knew why the Church hunted the troop so relentlessly and hoped they could stay around at this new location.

She picked up the torch, lit it with the match contraption Lisera had passed along and went back into her own cave she had recently learned to escape. At least for a little, she thought, with a heavy sigh. As she followed the path downward, she saw a human shape at the edge of the pool right below the waterfall. Kiadora instinctively jumped to the edge of the trail and lost footing on the slick slope. She let out a cry as she fell and dropped her torch, which went over the edge and down the waterfall. There was still enough light from the torch the person carried below to see the rock she had clutched to avoid falling. Still, she knew she had attracted the person's attention. This would be it if it were an Elder or a Matrina.

But she would know that double flame anywhere, one from the torch and the other from the person's head. Astrian looked up at her and smiled, his eyes darker than ever in the cave.

"You need to be careful this far in. Especially on rock this slick," Astrian called over the sound of the rushing waterfall.

"So I've noticed," she called back, tempted to tell him he was the reason she slipped. She got up slowly and edged her way down. He hovered at the bottom of the path as she descended, leaping stones.

He looked at her apprehensively, like he was waiting to catch her on the way down.

Astrian hesitated for a moment and then held out a hand for her to grasp as she leapt the last stone. She blushed as she took his hand.

"So what brought you out to the waterfall?" Kiadora asked, letting her hand fall to her side, trying to steady her heartbeat. Astrian just gave a lopsided smirk.

"I don't know if I should tell anyone this, but I've been going up into the town. And by the looks of things, so have you." Kiadora took off her hat that she was starting to get warm in, despite the dampness.

"I know a way out now, how can I resist?" Kiadora said. "Even if I don't have anywhere else to go permanently, as of yet." Astrian looked over at her with a solemn expression.

"Thinking of leaving?"

"Nah, don't know where to go. I still have my dragon." Astrian looked at her with a confused frown.

"Sorry, it was a play I saw tonight. Have you seen the playhouse?"

"Yes, that great feathered building?"

"That's the one. You should come see a show. They're really talented, and I have an in." Astrian nodded.

"That would be nice," was all he said.

"It's settled then," said Kiadora. Astrian just gave off a hint of a smile. She wondered if he was happy about it or just trying to look amused. He was so hard to read.

They walked in silence for a little while, Astrian's uneven footsteps echoing off the walls as sporadic thuds. Then Kiadora remembered what she found so curious about him.

"I'm almost finished with that book you loaned me."

"Oh, really? You like it?" He sounded pleased that she had taken the time to read something he found interesting.

"It's fascinating. I never looked at suffering like that before. But I have to ask, why is it your favorite book? I, I mean, I'm probably being too blunt here," she stammered, "but why a book about suffering? What happened?" Astrian stayed silent, just walking unevenly for a moment.

"I saw a lot of death growing up," he said in a low tone at last. "You get that living in the mines." Kiadora made a small gasp.

"The mines? That must have been a terrible way to grow up. And you're so...socialized," Kiadora said before she could stop herself. Kiadora knew only the lowliest in society were sent to the coal mines: murders, thieves, the worst of the insane. Usually prisoners were used as cheap labor, and because they did not live long, it was a cheap way to also execute the worst of the worst without being too wasteful about the whole thing. That explained his gruff voice, with the dust and the fumes.

"I was born there," Astrian said. "Most of those down there are these days. The whip and constant fatigue teach the rest the manners necessary for life in close quarters. The...uh, *gift*, if that's what you want to call it, ran in my family line. Some ancestors weren't too quiet about what they were and we ended up down there. When I was found by a group of Matrinas at the age of ten, I was happy to go because it meant that I stood a chance of living past 30." Kiadora nodded, realizing she was walking behind him so he couldn't see.

She was glad she stood behind him, maybe he couldn't see her sudden embarrassment for living such a pampered life compared to the miners, where 16 hour workdays were the norm and little was done in the ways of ventilation.

"I'm sorry," was all she could say.

"It wasn't like you put me down there."

"My family runs the education system," Kiadora said in a low voice. Astrian glanced back at her.

"You're from the noble families? I never would have thought it. It's still not your fault." Kiadora smiled. They both knew it was a compliment. Lords and their kin were renowned for their fussiness and inability care about anyone but themselves. Even the rock hounds knew it, it was joked around Tahn's family. Rock hound, such a miserable name for someone who seemed more capable of deeper thought than her.

"My family has a say in who is educated and who isn't. The original idea was for it to be everyone. By and large we've achieved it, with the help of the Church of course, but…"

"But being taught to read the Holy Text after a 16 hour day in the mines doesn't work?" She could tell Astrian was trying to keep the bitterness out of his voice.

"I never did anything to stop it. I never thought about it. I just thought my life was so damn miserable because my sisters are bitches, and I had this fainting thing outside."

"Most people don't think about that stuff. It's a lot to take in. There were people born who were executed at birth because their family was supposedly a more dangerous form of Shiekita than us. They figured our blood was diluted. I never thought much about it. I still try not to." Kiadora nodded again to the back of Astrian's head, realizing there wasn't any more she could say.

They came out to the main corridors and the chandeliers were turned down low. Kiadora balled her hat up and stuffed it under her arm. She walked faster to catch up to an even pace with Astrian. She didn't want guilt to be the last thing Astrian remembered about her for the evening.

"Anyway, I'll see you for that play." Astrian smiled, and Kiadora was amazed that he would still go with her.

"Let me know how you like the end of the book," he said. Kiadora told him she would, and they both headed up their respective ladders.

The next morning, Kiadora was trying to shake off a dream once again. It had started nice enough, with her and Astrian up in the town. He had told her he was having a good time and was starting to lean in. Then she woke up. When she went back to sleep there was a dragon burning her arm.

It was with these thoughts that Kiadora sat down to the cauldron of water and flowers. She had skipped the morning meal and was thinking that even the flowers looked like a decent morning snack.

At Aeliean's instruction she let her mind go blank. The shadows happened for a single moment and then were gone in a blink. Then the vision of the dragon and salamander sprang up, the two outright sparring against each other. The salamander dodged nimbly. If it was possible for a salamander to even break a sweat, this one wouldn't have even come close, while the dragon swerved desperately trying to hit its prey. After a time, the salamander dodged through a random bed of roses, the dragon breaking through thickets of apple trees in full blossom like the ones on her family's estate, causing them to explode with a blizzard of whirling petals, some charred and burning as they fell.

It happened for what must have been all day, because Kiadora was back in her own line of vision, and Aeliean said it was time to leave. She looked at the bowl for a moment, seeing the flowers still floating there looking wilted and soggy for having sat in a pool of water all day. Then the apple blossom sank. The rose stayed floating at the surface, hardly wilted or watered down at all.

CHAPTER 32

Kiadora sat in her quarters on her mattress, the candle in front of her bed. Months ago she would not have dared put the candle so close to her bed, but she was able to direct the size and shape of the flame so nimbly now that she had no issues with putting it this close.

Something interesting had happened during her firework. It was like having a split vision that had come so suddenly and felt so natural it was like she had always seen that way. On one level she could see the particle stream and the flow with perfect clarity, a dance playing out in her mind like the visions she had. But unlike the visions, she did not completely lose herself. She could see the shape of the flame in the traditional sense dance and flicker.

It had been thrilling to be able to see what she was doing, see the flame warp as the particle streams changed direction. But she still remained frustrated that that was all she could do with the damn flame. Spontaneous generation of a flame seemed impossible, and try as she might, she could never make the flame grow too much. Once she shrunk it, it would never return to its original size. She realized she could put out a flame with perfect control, just a single thought was all it took now, after weeks of having to strain and will for minutes for it to go out.

Today she had only been working with the flame for a couple of minutes before she let it go out and just sat back in the semidarkness, dull colors flowing in from the light behind her curtain.

The visions from her Water scrying had started to become worse and worse. The dragon's fire had turned into a tactile sensation that left her skin stinging for hours afterward, like how her chest wound felt after several days of healing. And guilt, the dragon left her with such guilt. She had picked up the nasty habit of tracing the circle of scarred tissue under her dress again.

And the drowning vision, or hallucination, had become longer and more painful. The other day she had wallowed in the pond for hours before she sank, watching her skin turn from a pale blue to a sickly purple and then black. A nail had fallen off. Still no one had come. Still the same isolation.

The worst of it was that was all she seemed to see, just those two images: burning or drowning. She rubbed her eyes, tired from not sleeping well the night before. The images had become dreams, no longer confined to her classes in the day. It had become one loop from class to dreams with the same drowning and large lizards that breathed flame. And that damn salamander.

The only sanity she felt like she had was from working with the flames, but the nights of waking up in a cold sweat were hindering her concentration with the flame. It would just snuff out more often than anything. Not only that, but she knew she could only move a flame to the left and right for so long before it lost its novelty. It was remarkable, she could control something outside of herself by will alone, and she was getting bored with it.

And the flame didn't help her get rid of these damned visions, and it didn't change the fact that she had to slink around town under a ratty old hat.

To the side, she saw her curtain stir, and Regelend popped his head in.

"It's been a while," said Kiadora.

"I've been busy." Regelend had a slight smirk.

"With Uranda. How are things?"

"Good." The smirk was now framed with red. "Anyway," he said, trying to bring the smirk down with only moderate success, "how are you holding up? No nightmares about the bird?"

"No, I have my own issues besides that. You?" Regelend nodded and shrugged. He looked to the side as he sat down on her bed. Kiadora just looked at him, waiting for him to go on.

"I had wondered and even hoped a little," was all he said. "It's hard not to think about it, but it's not like I hate being down here now. There are things I'm glad I'm not missing out on."

"I'll bet. Speaking of which, isn't she going to get jealous, you coming to sit on other women's beds?" Kiadora asked with a smile.

"Uranda? No. She knows how it is. I would never." Kiadora nodded.

"You've got a rare woman. It's a good match."

"What's that you're reading?" said Regelend, purely to change the subject Kiadora could tell. "You don't normally read. *The Nature of Suffering.* Of all the things, Kiadora."

"You don't know whose favorite book it is? You know everything about everybody." Regelend just shook his head with a lost puppy expression. Astrian was more silent than she thought. And it looked like she was one of the few people, if not the only person, to be let in on such personal information.

"It's from Astrian. I just finished it a couple days ago. Ending part's real weird, all about how we'll pay dearly at the end of days. The whole book's quite a trip, actually. It got me thinking about past lives. I'm on the Water lessons right now." Regelend threw his head back against the sod wall.

"Those. They'll have you believing anything. Delusions, false-hoods, lies. It's all real and sacred to those Water folks. Don't get caught up in the mess of past lives. I doubt they exist." Kiadora stayed silent, staring out at a section of the curtain that morphed from yellow to green.

"I've wondered about them a lot," Kiadora admitted after a moment. "Who's to say that they haven't happened? What I see is so real. And I see it all the time. I don't know, maybe it's a message of what I have to atone for." Regelend just scoffed and shook his head again.

"Kiadora, you don't know what you're thinking about. I'm sure Astrian passed that book on to you because he thought you might find it interesting, not because he wanted you to mentally beat yourself up. Besides, what would you have to atone for that would matter now?

You think what happened in the Church was just that, you making up for a past sin?"

"It could be, I don't know. It would make my life make more sense." Regelend turned towards her, staring her down.

"If there is one thing I know, it's trying to find sense in this life. I spend a lot of time looking for that in the Holy Text. Truth be told, even after what happened up there," he nodded his chin up to the ceiling, "I still do. I don't look as hard because I'm starting to realize there is more to life than just looking for meaning everywhere but in what is going on right now. I hope you can realize that too, Kiadora." Regelend put his hand on her knee. From anyone else it would have been a romantic advance. From Regelend it was just a plea.

"You don't want to go that way, Kiadora, looking for meaning in the shadows." Kiadora just let out a sigh.

"I can't stop thinking about it." Regelend just looked at her. Something in his expression seemed to change from desperation to a dull resignation.

"I guess everyone has to work these things out for themselves. Just keep your head above water. And I'll be around," he said with a meaningful look before he got up and swept through the curtain.

Kiadora just sat back again. *Keep your head above water*, he had said. She hoped she didn't have that drowning dream again.

Kiadora stopped short in the entrance of the classroom. There was a large crate.

No, she wouldn't get in one of those again. She considered running out the door, but where would she go that they couldn't catch her? What, run for the surface, then go where?

On some level, somewhere beyond the fear, Kiadora marveled at how strong the reaction was. This sort of thing should have been cleared up by now. She thought it had. Kiadora had not thought about it for a long while. She had been too preoccupied with other horrors she could neither understand nor explain.

Kiadora kept looking at the box warily as she advanced. There was water in there, not so bad. Not dirt.

Aeliean came over from one of the cupboards holding a dark cloth. A darker cloth than Kiadora had ever seen. It wasn't just black, it was the level of black that looked like it was itching to drain color from its surroundings as well.

"No need to be alarmed," Aeliean said smoothly. "I've been given instructions to not lock you in completely. I'm aware of your past." She put the cloth down on the chair that sat by the tub. "You will have the blanket over the top, which blocks out all light, so that should keep things feeling a little more open. Usually we seal people in with a heavy lid for sound control. It will still be dark and all sensory input should be cut off, aside from the water. I'll just have to make sure I remain more quiet than normal." Kiadora nodded and slowly stepped forward. Aeliean just looked at her, motioning at Kiadora's clothes. Of course, it would be another one of those days. At least she would be under a dark cloth. As Kiadora let her dress fall to the ground, she asked,

"And what is the purpose of this exactly?"

"It's sensory deprivation. Once the mind and soul are released from the distraction of sensory input, it opens a new level of visions. You do not feel any pressure, you will see and hear nothing, and taste and smell are a moot point altogether." Kiadora gave the woman a raised eyebrow as she stepped into the water. It was neither hot nor cold this time, only a gentle lukewarm. No scents lingered, there were no herbs. It was just clear water in its simplest form. Even the porcelain was black.

"We used to wrap people in cloths and hang them by their feet," offered Aeliean helpfully. Kiadora ignored the comment as she settled down. "Lie flat and let your body float," Aeliean instructed. "Oh, I almost forgot." She reached into her pocket and brought out a small bag, from which she pulled out cotton and a small jar. "Put these in your ears and spread this over them."

Kiadora looked at the jar. It was labeled beeswax. She put the cotton in both ears and opened the jar. It was less tough than the beeswax she was used to. The kitchen staff had bars of it for strengthening and waterproofing cord that bound the meats. This felt like dipping her hand in jelly. She spread it over the cotton in her ears and lay back. Aeliean drew the cloth over the lid, and then all was darkness.

Kiadora floated there, feeling awkward. Aeliean had never said it, but it had been the same for nearly every exercise. She let her thoughts settle, feeling oddly comforted by the feeling of weightlessness. Kiadora had expected to feel trapped and panicked, but this was rather nice. Although she realized she was doing a poor job of stopping her thoughts today.

She simply floated for what could have been a second or a week. Out of nowhere a bright, white light came in a flash, and she was drowning again in the frozen pond. Today, the images stopped with her flailing and went to a feeling of being thrust into a cold bucket of water, again and again, not allowed to breathe. The water stunk and she saw the yellow robes of the Church staff to the side.

No, she was supposed to be past this. But it didn't stop. Rather, it shifted.

Kiadora was the one forcing a woman down. She did not wear the robes of the Church as it was today, but some muted gray color. She was in the same chamber, but Kiadora forced a woman twice her size down into the bucket. Kiadora could only see the woman's gray hair and hear several shrieks. She rather enjoyed it.

Kiadora threw the woman back onto the large dais and strapped her down quickly and efficiently with large, frayed ropes. The ropes turned the woman's skin a raw red almost on contact as the woman struggled, but she was no match for Kiadora's swiftness and sheer force. It was like strapping a mouse to a wooden doorstop.

Kiadora felt giddy as she reached down for her bucket of toys, as she referred to them. The first was something that looked like a nutcracker. But Kiadora knew it was not for nuts. Well, it could be, but that didn't apply right now, did it? She let out a laugh, and the woman let out a scream.

Kiadora brought the clamp down on the old woman's knuckles and relished in each bone-shattering pop and pained scream. She walked to the other hand now. Why save the fun for just one hand? More screams, more pops as the left hand became as much of a bloody, deformed mess as the first.

Kiadora looked down at her little toy chest. A saw, perfect. Kiadora brought it out and walked around the edge of the table.

"So many uses for a saw, when you think about it," she said to the woman. "What needs shedding off of your heathen form? Well, everything, but why rush the fun?" She brought the saw down to the woman's left ear just to see her squirm. She'd move on to something more painful and debilitating in a moment.

Then Kiadora looked over the woman's face. Strange, she had Kiadora's hazel eyes. And there was something familiar in the round shape about the jaw that she could still make out, despite the amount of wrinkles around the neck and cheeks.

Then Kiadora was splashing and waving her arms around. For a moment, she thought she was back in the drowning vision, but she felt her bottom hit porcelain. She reached for light as her hand moved the blanket away, as if she'd never see it again. Kiadora started to shout at Aeliean, only to realize her voice echoed right back into her own skull. She pulled out the cotton from her ears, the beeswax leaving a sticky mess.

"What in the Otherworld was that supposed to be?" Aeliean looked at her calmly.

"See something strange? Most people find it to be a relaxing experience. They see a lot of colors and report feeling at peace with the world, at one with it, almost."

"I don't need to hear about your latest drug trip." Politeness was for people who hadn't just had fun torturing what could have been their own grandmother. No, fun was the wrong word. Kiadora had loved it. Not that she had ever met her grandmother, who had died some ten years before Kiadora was born. "I didn't even know I was capable of imagining something so horrid. What is the matter with me?"

Kiadora slumped forward and ran her hand through her hair, ready to yank it out by the roots. She discreetly kept her front covered by the infinitely dark cloth.

"What did you see?" Aeliean asked again, still as calm as ever. Kiadora took a moment to let her hand fall and collect her thoughts.

"I was drowning, then back at the Church, being forced into the bucket of water, hardly able to breathe. And I wish that was the worst of it. Then I was torturing someone, breaking their knuckles. I was in the Church doing it. Right where I was when I was held there. I was about to cut off a woman's ear, or maybe something even worse, I don't know. Then I looked over and she had my eyes, my facial features, but she was old."

Aeliean nodded and sat back in her chair, her foot swaying at a steady pace again.

"Maybe you were a torturer in a past life," she said at last. Kiadora shivered at the thought.

"But I loved it for the sake of the pain. It wasn't just a job or something I did because I believed in some cause. And that woman could have been a relative." It would explain why Kiadora was tortured in this life. Moral equilibrium.

And then Kiadora had a towel in her face.

"Dry off, it's damp and cool down here." Kiadora nodded and ran the towel through her hair, scrubbing some of the dampness away. "It will be hard for a while," Aeliean said bluntly as she sat back down, picking up Kiadora's clothes and holding them while Kiadora dried off.

Michelle Lovrine

"It's never easy to see a past misdeed in another life. You feel like you should go back and fix whatever it was, but all you can do is wait and see if it affects you now in this life. I once killed an infant bother-in-law because I feared he would ascend the thrown. Not a day goes by where I don't wonder what would have happened if he was alive, what kind of brother I would have known."

Kiadora only took her clothes and put them on after stepping out of the tub, too troubled to worry about another woman's past mistakes. As Kiadora walked to the door, Aeliean came up behind her and put her hand on Kiadora's shoulder. Kiadora looked back.

"You will work through it, you are strong. But if you need anything, send a messenger." Kiadora nodded, a little shocked at her teacher's openness. None of the others seemed to have the time for that sort of thing.

"Ok," Kiadora said.

CHAPTER 33

Just as she was afraid, this vision, too, had interwoven with her other ghastly, reoccurring dreams. It was always that grandmotherly face, always the broken bones, always the saw. Her visions in her class had not been any better. They had gone back to water scrying in a cauldron for a while, as if to try to give Kiadora a break, but no break was coming thanks to the same visions in her cauldron scrying as well.

A couple nights later, she decided it was time for another trip to the surface to try and forget it all. Remembering her agreement with Astrian, she wandered the compound trying to find him. They had never set up any formal agreement on where to meet. But it was not hard. Sure enough, she found him in the library reading next to a group of people who sat aruging over an old scroll.

Kiadora came up to him and nodded her head towards the door. Astrian nodded and put his book under is his arm. Kiadora caught just a glimpse of it. *Thoughts on Worlds Hereafter.*

"Always something cheery with you," she said with a smirk, motioning towards the book. Astrian looked down and actually turned a little red.

"It's something I always thought about. A lot of…well, you know the situation." Kiadora nodded.

"I'm not much better right now." She leaned in close to his ear as they walked, feeling herself blush. "That's why tonight's the night. Are you up for it?"

"I wouldn't be walking next to you if I wasn't," he said with a hint of a smile. She grinned.

"Let me get my hat," she said right as they approached the outside of the wooden classrooms. She fled to her quarters and balled up her hat under her sleeve. "Issues with being from the damn family I come from," she said as she came back to him.

"I understand," was all he said in a quiet tone. They walked silently out of the compound and out through the cavern, a crescent moon following them as they continued down the country path.

"You mentioned that things are not going well?" Astrian said at last.

"Hm?" Kiadora had been watching the moon in the starry sky, transfixed. "Oh, yes. I'm in the Water lessons, and I keep seeing some on the strangest images, gruesome things, stuff I thought I could never even imagine."

"It's an odd time in the studies. You have to look within yourself as much as seeing what else is out there."

"You see other things? Real things from this life?"

"Yes, that is the goal." A pause.

"I saw myself torturing an old women. In the Church." Kiadora let it hang there, waiting for Astrian's scorn, words about what a terrible person she was. He remained silent, walking calmly, his skin almost translucent in the moonlight. "I think I was a torturer for the

Church," she added. "Or a Shiekita exorciser, as they would put it. And I enjoyed it. In a past life, I mean."

Astrian's brow creased and he frowned, deep in thought.

"I mean, you read about these things all the time, don't you? You would know more about it than I would."

"It is a possibility," he said after a moment. "To be truthful, I don't know what to believe in the matter. For every idea in these studies, there is another one to contradict it. You can question these things for years and not move a step. I know. But I do find it interesting. I thought you might as well." Kiadora stared at him, shocked.

"You're the first person I've met who doesn't have their mind made up on these things. I mean, it would explain why I was tortured. Transcendental moral equilibrium and all."

"It is a convenient explanation," Astrian agreed, as they passed through the town gates and walked past a sleeping gatekeeper. "But I would ask yourself, can you now or even in the distant past see yourself doing something like that? Much less enjoying it, as you put it?"

"No. No, not ever," said Kiadora without a moment's hesitation. Kiadora dodged past a group of drunk young men near the curb as she led Astrian to the playhouse. One hooted at her. Kiadora noticed a momentary look of anger pass over Astrian's face and had to keep a smile back for how flattered she was.

"Then you probably have your answer as to whether that was a real vision or not," Astrian pressed. Kiadora shook her head.

"But that was a past life, a different time. I could have been a whole different person; my soul could have changed and grown in that time. That was one of the theories, wasn't it? We go through these things so we can change and become more whole and pure as the lives pass?"

"Yes, and in such a case, wouldn't that change designate a different time in your soul's journey?" he said conversationally. "So now you are in a different moment, and it should not matter. Even if you were tortured for the sake of retribution, you are past that now."

"And you are past the days in the mines, but still you read morbid stuff. It doesn't have an impact on the now?" said Kiadora, climbing the stairs towards the feathered pillars. Astrian was quiet for a moment, considering.

"I suppose you are right; I do still think about it. But I do not beat myself up over it and let it consume me. That is where the line must be drawn." Kiadora stopped and turned in the middle of the access ramp Astrian had followed her up unquestioningly.

"You'd be a good teacher down there," she said. Astrian only smiled his little smile.

"Hey, Kiadora's back," said a deep voice from behind her. She turned to look and there was the large door guard, still in black. Kiadora said hello and mentioned she had brought a friend. The door guard stepped to the side.

"Anytime, just don't be bringing masses of people. We need our wages, you know." Kiadora nodded a thanks.

Once inside they settled into two seats and looked at the large gray curtain.

"What's the play about?" Astrian asked, leaning to the side. She suddenly felt very shy at having his shoulder touch hers. Their knees almost touched.

"I, I'm not sure, now that I think about it." Kiadora shuddered, mentally shaking herself. It was stupid to act like a nervous schoolgirl, even if that was what she still technically was. "They do a good a job," she forced herself on. "Their plays border on the subversive; the person who got me in said this is their fifth stage because they're always on the move. People have even gone missing, I've heard."

"Subversive? Nothing we're not used to," said Astrian with a smirk. Kiadora nodded in agreement. The play started just a moment later, the curtain going up in a smooth motion. Kiadora marveled at her own sense of time. It wasn't like she had a traditional watch to work off of. She had worried that she was going to miss it.

The stage was not anything like the last time, a pleasant forest grove. Now they were seeing the dissection of a prison cell, all stone, chains, shackles and a single barred window. Kiadora decided all prison cells must be the same. This one looked like the ones they had at her family's home, which was only used to house the occasional drunk or thief they found on their property before they transferred the prisoner to the town jail.

In the early days, she had learned through Lisera, it had housed everything from petty thieves to murderers to people the head of the family just plain didn't like, such as the poor.

In chains, his arms hoisted above his head by shackles, was a man on stage wearing nothing but a tattered pair of loose shorts and an even baggier tunic. He had a long, black beard streaked with gray and bushy hair that ran past his shoulders.

He was weeping, but tonight Kiadora felt oddly removed from the man. She didn't want to mentally associate with him. She had been there, stuck in a basement made of stone. There were no shackles, but she still didn't want to relive it.

The man pleaded out for someone to hear him, for anyone to listen to his words. The same plea went on for some time, punctuated by bitter sobs.

Then a booming voice from somewhere off the stage, possibly above the stage for how loud it was, answered.

"What do you wish to say?" said the voice. The man looked around for the source of the voice, as if expecting to find a warden at the door. But he appeared to be alone.

"Who are you?" asked the man. The voice thundered a reprimand at the man for even having to ask.

It was a lengthy, melodramatic play, Kiadora felt. Or at least it seemed lengthy. The man on the wall begged and begged the being to tell him why this had happened. Sure, he had never been the most devout of men. Sure, he had never been too active in the life of his god, but there was no reason to deserve this. He had been wrongfully accused of a murder, he insisted over and over. It was not he who had killed the neighbor. The man had never said who it was or why they did it. It just wasn't him.

It went back and forth, the voice reprimanding him for being cowardly, sick, weak, not having enough faith. The man defended himself, poorly, saying he had always been faithful. The voice said he was never at services. The man said he believed in his heart.

"I *see* the hearts of men! No lie you say can touch me," the voice boomed. But still they argued, as if the source of the bodiless voice just wanted to see how the man could defend himself, whether he would see the truth that he was the murderer and how he could justify himself if he could see the truth. After a time, Kiadora started to wonder if the man was indeed innocent. The man couldn't even accept that he was the murderer. Perhaps the man had blocked it out?

Then at some point a prison guard had come in to feed the man. The voice from nowhere had stopped, but the guard had caught the man saying it wasn't him over and over. The guard asked the man how he could legitimize the bloody shovel in his shed and the body in the backyard. The wife had found it all, had shown the police the makeshift grave, had shown the shovel she found stowed away. Further inspection had revealed the land dispute. The neighbor had died for a mere two extra inches on one side of the creek.

The man on the wall shook his head the whole time, saying that no, no it was not him. Further proof had been unearthed when the dead neighbor's watch was found in the prisoner's pocket upon arrest. The man still shook his head back and forth. No, not him, certainly not.

"Was it a sick souvenir?" the guard asked, mocking him now, shoving a spoon of mush roughly into his mouth. "Did you need a tangible object to know the man existed, to know he fell by your hand? Is it your temple, your shrine to your bloodlust?" The prisoner still just shook his head, openly sobbing. With the rough feeding done, the guard spit in the prisoner's face and left, muttering about murderers being the worst sort of breed.

The voice came back, more angry than ever. The being said he knew what the prisoner did, of course, had witnessed it. The man did not question it, seemed to know who it was and how this could be. The audience did, too.

Not as a mercy gesture, the voice said, he was going to grant the man his freedom. The man still sobbed, tears of happiness now for being able to see his family. Would they remember anything, the man asked. Of course they would, replied the voice. No one should forget something like that. Still, the man assumed that if they could not forget, they could forgive.

And so the guard came back and released the prisoner. He did not say why, he just let the man go. There was no mention of his innocence, no mention as to whether the guard would remember. As if to tempt fate, while the man walked toward the door massaging his wrists, he turned to the guard.

"Do you know what I did?" the man asked.

"I know what you did," said the guard. "The higher-ups know what you did, too. But these things happen, and we're sure you had your reasons." The man shook his head. This was not good enough. He wanted the belief erased, but this would have to do, the actor conveyed with a single shake of the head as he walked toward the exit.

The lights went down and came up in a small cabin. A woman looking worse for stress, deflated and beaten, sat hunched over some food with two children eating ravenously. The former prisoner came through the door, and she looked up, jumping out of her chair in sheer shock.

"But how?" she asked. The man couldn't explain it and didn't try.

"I'm out, isn't that all that matters?"

"You killed him. You were former business partners, he attended our wedding!" the woman screamed. She lashed out and the spoon in her hand went flying to the floor. The two sons just watched. One looked ready to run to his father and hug him, but he stayed in his chair. The other looked at the man as if he had never seen him before.

"Get out!" the woman screeched. "Get out, and don't come back! I don't need the boys learning that killing is any way to behave." The man stood in the doorway.

"Boys…" he said. One returned to eating, the one who looked like he wanted to hug his father ran out to another end of the house.

"Get out!" the woman repeated. The man hovered in the doorway a moment longer and was gone. "And don't expect me to not turn you into the police!" the wife shouted after him.

The lights went down again and came up on a forest scene. The man stumbled wildly through the woods, pleading for the disembodied voice to hear him once more. But the voice did not come back.

"You got me into this mess, get me out!" the man yelled. The voice still did not return. Not watching where he was going, the man stumbled into a river. The sound of rushing water could be heard as the man tripped and fell behind some rushes on the stage.

The lights down, the lights up, another scene. The wife stood at the door of the small cabin. A police officer stood just inside, explaining that her husband's body was found on the side of the river, probably tried to escape prison, did a bad job of it. She asked if he had been wrongfully pardoned. The officer shook his head. The wife said good-bye to bad business. And it was time for the cast and crew to line up and bow.

Kiadora looked over at Astrian as she clapped politely. Astrian clapped as well, that small smile on his face. On anyone else it would look smug. On Astrian, it managed to look like true joy. In was a smile that touched his eyes, twinkling and dark.

As they walked out and down the stairs, Kiadora said, "I'm sorry, the last play was more cheerful. More action to it," she felt terrible for dragging him out for a fun night and that had been the play. She wanted to bring back a schedule of plays but didn't want something like that lying around the compound, even if she would just shove it under her mattress. You never knew.

Kiadora drew in a breath of the fresh air, trying to shake the depression. It smelled of smoke and drink on the street, but the night had an underlying crispness. It must be early in the summer season, not late enough in the year to shake off the night coolness.

"I'm not much for stories where the main character dies in the end," said Kiadora conversationally.

"I'm afraid I'm not able to offer much in the way of a play critique. This is my first play," Astrian confessed. Kiadora put a hand to her mouth.

"Oh, no, and it was so grave!" The first play she had ever seen was about a boy who couldn't control his puppy. It had been children's day at the theater. But, Kiadora remembered with that jarring sense of reality sinking in, other people were trying to avoid mine collapses.

"No, don't feel bad. I enjoyed it. The man was an analogy for God, did you catch that?" Kiadora looked off to a far street lamp, remembering.

"Yes, a human god liable to something even greater. His watch, the guard mentioned it was a shrine to bloodlust." Astrian nodded, smiling.

"He committed a murder, but was not about to admit responsibility. Not even in the face of every fact in the book. Then he carried the watch as a reminder to who fell for him, and when he was released, he expected everyone to be alright with what he did. But no one was, and he basically fell off the face of the planet. Do you know how many holy wars there have been just since the calendar switched, although they will never be called wars?" Kiadora shook her head.

"Two. They exist in the books we have. You won't find it on the surface, but in my town there have been the descendents of survivors. I was lucky to find a written record to fill in the gaps of mad raving.

"In 114 there was raid against the desert people, in 220 the Church marched against a settlement that had erected a statue to a sun god. Practically the same notion, a sky god and a sun god. But the whole town was slaughtered nonetheless. A famous temple now stands there, a watch as a trophy, if you will." Astrian spoke in a low tone so Kiadora had to lean in as she walked, his breath warm against the side of her face.

"I wonder what would happen if we didn't forgive God for his crimes," Kiadora said.

"He would fall off the face of the planet and be washed out of history," said Astrian in a tone most people reserved for describing a draining tub. Kiadora smiled at the thought.

"Does that make you happy?" he asked, looking at her.

"Yes. All the pain gone. No more rationalizations for why people get tortured." Astrian picked up the torch from the bush that they now stood next to. Kiadora gave over the lighter Lisera had loaned her, and the torch burned once more.

"Another god would pop up in his place," said Astrian, his voice echoing in the caverns over the sound of the waterfall. "As long as people can wonder why we are here, there will be gods. Gods are a conduit for human curiosity."

As they made their way behind the waterfall, something occurred to Kiadora.

"The book you gave me, the one about suffering..."

"Did you finish it?"

"Yes, it was amazing. I never thought that way before. But something about it bothers me. Most of it insinuates that suffering is for a reason, it's not just something that is."

"That it does," Astrian agreed.

"Well, the man in the play, he suffered for a misdeed. It's like it's always a continual chain of events. My suffering can't just be because the Church is there. I must have done something." They were now at the edge of the compound, and Astrian turned to her.

"Even so, what is done is done. We better get back before they think we're out doing something that would warrant participation in the Great Union." Kiadora looked at that hint of a smile, then decided that it was indeed a joke and smiled as well. They got to the ladders and bid each other good night, Astrian saying that he would see her at a later point.

Kiadora got to her bed and lay down, throwing her hat under her mattress before she did so, pleased that the evening had gone so well. Still, the play nagged at her as she fell asleep, tossing and turning all the way.

That night she dreamed about torturing the old woman again, who turned into the prisoner on the wall and then lost several bodily organs to a knife that Kiadora didn't know she could be so creative with.

CHAPTER 34

"Kiadora, I just wanted to...oh, no, sorry."

Astrian had just thrown open Kiadora's curtain. She squinted at the sudden light, throwing her arm up against her face like an unearthed monster. She had only slept half the night, waking up with images of organs strewn around and the pale, dying face of the prisoner from the play. She was still in bed.

"Something has to make this alright," was the first thing out of Kiadora's mouth.

"We can make this alright," said Astrian in a clam tone. He came forward and saw that etched into the wall were images of chains and shackles, as crude and hectic as the ones they found in the old caves depicting trees. He looked down at Kiadora's hands to see that they were bloody. He grabbed her wrists and looked over at the book he had loaned her, which was her sitting on the nightstand.

"No, this isn't what I had wanted at all," he said, releasing her and putting the book into a deep pocket in his tunic. "Come, we'll make this alright." Kiadora had started to sob and nodded as she followed Astrian down the ladder and over to another. They went up about eight stories, and Astrian called out for Uranda.

Uranda stuck her head out. "Yes?" she asked, still in that dull tone. Then she looked down and saw Kiadora wiping at a flow of tears with the back of one hand, the other hand holding on for dear life to the ladder. Uranda stepped back and held the curtain open without a word. Astrian and Kiadora came forward to see that Regelend was there making use of Uranda's small mirror and bowl of water to clean up. He turned around and blushed slightly, but his embarrassment quickly turned to a look of worry as Kiadora walked in sobbing, blood still on her fingers. Kiadora realized that blood marks must be all over her face now.

"By God, what happened? Here." Regelend emptied the dirty water into another container, then put clean water into the bowl and shook a bar of soap in the water until it lathered up. He came over to Kiadora, put a hand on her shoulder and ushered her over to the water. Regelend instructed her to wash her hands. She nodded and began scrubbing her fingers in the cool water. They stung as she ran the soap over them.

She still sobbed, letting the tears flow into the water as she scrubbed, wiping her face with water as well. She could see her fingers were clean, but she kept scrubbing.

Slowly her sobs slowed, and the tears became more manageable to see through. She caught phrases from behind her of, "Well of course she would feel guilty if that is what she thought she saw," and, "I just gave her the book because I thought she would be curious."

Eventually Kiadora's breathing slowed, and she brought her hands up from the brownish, reddish water. Regelend rushed over with some clean pieces of cloth and tied them around the tips of her fingers and left thumb. They were slightly damp and a strange smell of strong herbs met her nose through the stuffiness from crying.

"Thank you," she said quietly. She just sat down on Uranda's bed, staring at the floor, her mind gratefully blank for the moment, her body feeling limp.

"Uranda's great with treating wounds. She took a liking to the herb crafts. That should stave off infection."

"Learning to heal is my atonement, it's how I make this better," said Uranda from the side in that monotone voice. Kiadora looked up and saw Uranda was sitting on the bed next to her. "I don't scratch things into the wall, I don't lose sleep and I don't injure myself," said Uranda, motioning to Kiadora's bandages.

"It's no less than I deserve," said Kiadora. "After what I did to that lady and probably countless others. I keep seeing it, in dreams, in visions. Aeliean says it's probably from a past life. How can I live with myself, knowing that is what I did, awaiting a just enough of a punishment?" Kiadora paused for a moment. Everyone was watching her, waiting to see if she needed to say more. She felt suddenly ashamed that she was disturbing them this early in the morning. And just like that, that gravity of the situation sank it.

"I don't know why I was carving chains. It just seemed like the thing to do, I can't explain it fully. It was like I thought if I could get the images outside of my head, I could somehow expel all of this." She remembered feeling like she was purging herself by the release of blood into the drawings. "It was insane," Kiadora said, shaking her head, her voice wavering. "I lost myself there for a while, I went mad. Astrian, I'm so sorry, you must think I'm an idiot. You lend me a simple book, and I lose it." Kiadora laughed bitterly. "I guess that will show you to be nice to me." Astrian shook his head.

"No, there is nothing simple about any of this. These are deep, complex ideas and deeper, more complex emotions you are dealing with in these lessons. I was careless."

"I nearly drowned myself during them on purpose," said Uranda. "It was then that I had to face what had happened. I still can't understand what was going through my head. As if my dying could bring those I burned back to life. The Water element and the teachers have a way of bringing out your past traumas. It is then that you have to face them or die. The will is the all with these things. But it was what led me to become an herbalist." Kiadora nodded, another single tear falling.

"I hope I can become stronger, though after this, my will isn't exactly lacking," said Kiadora, holding up her bandaged hands.

"And that is why you will become stronger," said Uranda, staring into Kiadora's eyes.

"Plus, you're able to think about these things," Astrian added. Kiadora smiled at the compliment as she heard the clatter of the pans below. She walked to the door of Uranda's quarters.

"Damn, they're taking them away. I'm sorry you missed breakfast."

"We'll manage," said Regelend. "This was more important. We should all probably go to lessons. Let us know if you need anything." Kiadora felt a reassuring squeeze on her shoulder, and she smiled at

Regelend behind her. She started down the ladder, thanking them profusely. Who knew how far that episode would have gone if Astrian hadn't come by?

She walked into her teacher's room, and Aeliean looked up at her, her eyes widening.

"Kiadora, did you not sleep? And your fingers!"

"No, I didn't sleep," she said flatly. "I've been up all night, thinking about this damn older woman. My friend caught me etching pictures of chains and shackles into my partially stone walls with my nails. It's a miracle I have fingernails left." Her voice was rising. The frustration and humiliation had returned, and she wanted to hit this damn woman who introduced her to these visions.

Aeliean only nodded. "The visions can be tough. We each react to them in our own ways. The ones who are truly clueless aren't changed worth a pile of dung. Growing is hard, stone has to be eroded before it can take on new forms. Now sit and tell me more."

Kiadora sat in the chair as Aeliean leaned against the sensory deprivation vat. Kiadora wanted to hold it all back, to not let this woman have the satisfaction of knowing she was even effected by these exercises, but before she knew it, she was off, unable to hold in the frustration.

"There has to be something I can do about the guilt. It's always the guilt of doing that to someone. My fingers look like this because I felt, at some level in my state of madness, that I needed to expunge all of this, to take the pain for that woman from another life."

She knew it was true, the memories came back slowly through the fog of madness, the thoughts of rage, the feeling that if she could just bleed it out, she could shed her own blood for that woman and everything would just be alright. Blood for blood.

"I figured if I could get the images into something else they could get out of my head also. The chains, the shackles, the blood…" Kiadora could feel the corners of her mouth begin to quiver. She wouldn't cry, damn it all. She ended by just shaking her head.

Aeliean had listened quietly, still rocking like a wave. The silence hung between them as Kiadora slowed her breathing and beat back the tears.

"The only thing I can tell you," Aeliean said at last, "is that what happened is in the past." Kiadora scowled at the obvious, empty placation. "It's not much, I know, but you're also usually shown these things for a reason, trust me. There is something to be learned and you will know it in time. You have to at least trust me on that."

Kiadora looked the woman hard in the eye, and Aeliean calmly returned her gaze. Aeliean's eyes were such an open shade of blue and her expression so earnest, Kiadora felt her own gaze fall to the ground. Aeliean was right. It was in the past, and she should move forward. Uranda had killed people in this life and had moved forward. And Broean hadn't been faking an addiction just for fun; she was meant to progress. It was up to her now.

"What's the plan for today?" Kiadora asked. Aeliean stepped away from the crate, and Kiadora's heart froze in mid-beat.

"There's a lid. Why is there a lid?" It had been propped on the crate behind Aeliean, casting a menacing shadow into the crate. "I'm going to be locked in."

"It's only water," said Aeliean smoothly and quickly. She had been expecting this. There was something rehearsed about how fast she offered the few words. "Come over here and take a look." Kiadora got up slowly from the chair and walked over to the tub.

It was the same dark basin filled with water, of course, as the one she used for that strange herbal bath and her past sensory deprivation exercises. But now there was a lid.

"You will float, only float, same as last time. Once the senses are eliminated, the mind can access the spirit realms far easier. This will cut further noise and stray energy from Eatheria. This is a necessary progression. You probably know what to do first."

"You lied, you said no lids," Kiadora said.

"Upon reflection, the Elders fear there may have been stray energy. This may ease the angst."

Kiadora scowled again and dropped her dress to the floor, fumbling with the thin fabric through bulky bandages. She stepped in and slid into the lukewarm water. Remembering her instructions, she started to float, keeping her bandaged hands above the water. Aeliean slid the lid over her head with a resounding thud. Kiadora floated there, listening to the rocking of the water echoing back to her. Then all was still.

It wasn't too bad, Kiadora thought. There was plenty of space between her and the lid. She could tell that before it came down, and she was left in the pitch black. Aeliean was right, it was far more quiet in here. Her breathing didn't feel restricted. It was just plain peaceful, actually. She let her mind settle and her breathing expanded. Still, she didn't want the same images. Her hands were damaged enough.

It wasn't long before the lack of noise or feeling started to make her feel slightly disoriented. She hadn't realized how incomplete the silence was last time. She had still heard the creek trickle in the distance and Aeliean creak her chair, despite the cotton. Somehow, she felt like she was floating. Then the colors came.

She saw red, then a penetrating white, one that was all around her and might as well have been in her. It was like she was passing through the light at the end of a tunnel. And somehow she was back on the street with the playhouse, with striking detail. She saw a sign advertising a fish market that never sat out at night and several of the bars that didn't serve lunch were now closed.

The street also looked a lot less idle during the day. The people who traversed the sidewalks did so with a swift purpose, clearly needing to be somewhere in a matter of seconds. One such man caught her eye immediately.

He had a large, brown overcoat on and a hat pulled down over his head, the kind of hat made out of the same material that Wellian had found to make their own hats out of, although this one looked more expertly fashioned. It had a stiff brim, not the flopping piece of material that barely passed as a sun hat that Kiadora had. His face was completely obscured.

Kiadora internally debated if she should get close to the man, wondering if anyone could see her. It was probably a hallucination anyway, but a feeling Kiadora couldn't fully identify told her to stay discrete. She looked down at her body, only to see nothing there. Strange, she always had an outline of a body in these things.

Still following the same gut instinct, Kiadora hid herself, or her line of vision, behind a restaurant poster for lunch menus balanced on an easel. The tall man headed past her, and she thought she saw a slender bulk under the overcoat. A sharp, metal edge just barely stuck out next to a chunk of deep brown hair. That was all she could make out of the man before he passed down the sidewalk.

And then she was back, floating in nothingness. And floating and falling. Kiadora felt her whole body convulse, as if tensing for the impact, sending waves of splashing echoes back in her direction. The feeling was gone, and Kiadora was squinting at the light as Aeliean pulled back the lid of the crate. Kiadora sat up.

The water now felt cold on her skin, and Kiadora was glad for the towel passed her way to dry off with. She hastily threw on her dress as she stood up and climbed out of the crate.

"Any visions?" Aeliean asked. Kiadora shook her head, without really knowing why. She had the feeling she just saw something that wasn't meant to be shared with anyone. Something secretive.

Kiadora told Aeliean about the red and white light, and Aeliean explained that it was a side effect of sensory deprivation. She went off for a while about something called a soul color or essence that could be viewed when the mind was allowed, but Kiadora only half listened. She nodded, pretending to be just fascinated, and then was excused for the day.

The thing that Kiadora could not get past the whole time was that she didn't feel like she did after she had come to after a normal "vision." Before when she had come out of it, it was like a dream. She only retained the main images, feelings and lingering madness.

Today she remembered that salmon was on sale at Nell's Fish

Market, and the lunch special of the day at Shyla's was elk battered in milk. And that tall man with the brown hair definitely had a weapon.

Tired of the plays, Kiadora sat at the The Royal Bizarre with some sweet drink called a honeysuckle something or other, Kiadora didn't remember the name the server had mumbled at her after she had requested something sweet. After taking each honeyed sip, she wished she could remember.

Maybe it was for the best, she thought, sitting back and looking at the silly, ignorant grins of the imitation monarchs on the wall. She remembered what Lisera had said about the tab chasers. Lisera had been kind to leave her those few copper pieces out of her meager wages. Still, it wasn't enough to enjoy too freely. After this, she realized, it would be back to bumming off of free shows up here and that would be her nights. As far as drinks and food, just the endless casseroles and watered-down berry juice that she got below. There had to be something she could do for money around here.

Kiadora took the last sip, letting the liquid sit in her mouth before she let the sweet concoction slide down into memory. She left her money on the table and headed out the door, pulling her mess of a hat over her face as she did so. As she walked back, holding her alcohol a little worse than she thought she would, she hit a man that made an odd clanking noise as she collided with him.

She muttered a quick, "excuse me," and looked back at the man, who continued hastily as if she had just passed through an invisible specter. She froze in place as she caught the dark brown hair. He was still tall as ever and this time she could barely catch the glint of several bayonet ends over his shoulder before he slid them back into place. Kiadora stood gaping in the middle of the sidewalk as the man passed around a corner, his face still hidden.

She headed back and went to bed, expecting to be roused from a vision at any moment. Kiadora realized the next morning, with no hangover to be spoken of, that it was neither dream nor hallucination nor vision.

Apparently, Aeliean had decided the sensory deprivation chamber was the best method after the "aura viewing" experience, as it now sat out at every lesson. Kiadora hated to admit it, but she was even getting used to climbing in the box. She never thought back to that terrible session under the Church, except for today, as she thought about how little it now fazed her. She tried to choke back a smile as she let her dress drop and sat once more in the lukewarm water.

Down came the lid and again came the red light, which went back into darkness. No white this time, Kiadora mused in some distant region of some unknown part of her.

In the corner of her vision, Kiadora saw a translucent light blue like water. All else remained dark except for the figure coming out from the side of her vision.

It's about time. The figure did not have a mouth to speak of, as all she could still make out was a watery oval, rippling around the edges. Still, she knew it spoke to her in an eerily deep voice.

"For what?" Kiadora asked. She did not speak the words out loud, rather they just seemed to be loud thoughts. Before she could wonder if it heard, it responded with,

For us to meet face-to-face. Didn't think you'd make it this far for a while there. Luckily, that Broean isn't a complete lump.

"What does Broean have to do with any of this?" Kiadora half said, half thought.

You think he would have faked the addiction all on his own?

"Wait, who are you?" The figure moved more into her line of vision and as it came fully around she saw that it had the outline of a small..otter? Or maybe a vole? Beaver? It had no distinctive facial or fur features by which to tell.

I'm in the outline of a groundhog, thank you.

"Sorry, I didn't realize I was thinking that out loud." It probably came off as more offensive than she wanted it to, considering she didn't know what this thing was.

I am your Ashilek. And there are no thoughts that are too quiet for me when it comes to your case.

"I don't understand." The groundhog still floated there, now its features taking on more substance. There were the two larger front teeth, the fur impossibly outlined in the water substance that the thing seemed to consist of. Two eyes were held in the substance, looking at her, and whiskers sprouted out.

Do you know what an Ashilek is? Kiadora thought back and remembered Narissa mentioning it to the Elders. But she did not know what the woman had been referring to. She did not think it would be a watery groundhog, at any rate. Kiadora shook her head. If there was even anything to shake, she did not know.

We take different forms, depending on when and where we are. I happen to be a

Water and Earth elemental right now, if you had not gathered that. I don't always look like this. It seemed impatient and resentful about the whole thing.

"Do you not like being a groundhog?" Kiadora asked.

Irrelevant. The point being, I am your spirit guide. I help you along your way, protect you if need be- so this is funny? Nothing got past this creature, even Kiadora's inner mirth.

"It's just, a watery groundhog is going to protect me."

Again, not my true form. The figure suddenly shifted into the rough outline of a man. *Does this please you more? I can turn into an outline of male genitals, if that would make you much more comfortable.* Kiadora didn't think she could blush where she was.

"No, you're fine." The being shifted back into the shape of a groundhog.

My point being, I am here to guide you, to help you in your spiritual journey. We've existed throughout time, across all cultures. On the surface, they think we are just mere action or will of their god. It is interesting that you are the only ones able to see us in these forms.

Kiadora just looked at the watery figure, not knowing what to think. What was she supposed to do with the creature? What would it protect her from?

I've already protected you from yourself twice. Once with Broean, and the other time I pulled you out of the flame, the form's deep voice echoed.

"That feeling of being drenched during the fire lessons when Sheir-kia did nothing, that was you?"

Yes. And you are to listen further. Can you do that? She could try.

Trying is not good enough. I will be around, keep your heart open. And with

432

that, she was back into nothing but darkness. And then she was back in the chamber with the old woman.

Kiadora stood at the table, refusing to pick up any instruments of torture this time. She looked down at the woman's terrified eyes. As she bent over to untie the woman, she noticed something. It really was her own hazel eyes that looked back at her, reflecting the slate gray of the walls, turning a slight, dull blue. The old woman also had the same small nose and slightly rounded jaw, but the rest was unrecognizable from the amount of wrinkles that adorned the woman's face. And the white hair also didn't help.

Kiadora pulled at the chains until they fell powerless to the ground. The woman stood up, strangely unscarred and unscratched from all that had been happening. The old woman smiled at her from across the table, and Kiadora was awake in the vat again with a twitch, the water echoing back at her at it splashed violently.

The lid opened, and Aeliean stared down at her, tilting her head at the grin that was on Kiadora's face.

"I did it," said Kiadora, as she took the towel again. "I released the old woman. And do you know what it means when you see your Ashi-lek in the form of Water?" Aeliean leaned against the crate and looked off toward the stream as Kiadora put on her dress.

"Did it have any other characteristics?"

"Yes, it was a watery groundhog." Aeliean nodded and looked back at Kiadora. "It didn't seem to like it."

"They are usually in imperfect forms at this stage. Seeing your true self is an advanced skill. At any rate, it felt you were spiritually ready to warrant such an appearance. I'm proud of you for that." Kiadora dropped the towel as Aeliean gave her a sudden embrace and she turned red. She didn't grow up with people showing much physical affection. She awkwardly patted Aeliean on the back and took her leave, feeling comforted that someone finally had pride in her.

CHAPTER 35

That night, she did not have any dreams of shackles or torture. Somewhere in there, however, she did see a salamander swallow a dragon. She also could have sworn she was walking on water across the pond on her family's estate, feeling strong despite the bitter cold.

And in an area past her peripheral vision, but a sector she could see nonetheless, waves rose and fell among the void, as if a head was nodding. The closer she looked, she realized the waves took the vague shape of a human head before falling forward in a nod, only to be reformed again. Then she floated in as free of a space as the deprivation chamber most of the night.

Odd word, she thought as she woke up, deprivation. It seemed to bestow as much as it deprived.

As she walked down to the dining hall, such as it was, she saw a table with large amounts of brightly colored cloth set out on it. It was usually set out right before major group rituals, and Kiadora remembered with a sinking feeling that the Great Union ceremony would take place soon.

She thought Regelend seemed a little withdrawn lately. She hadn't really seen him in weeks, except for the issue with her fingers. Even if Kiadora could think of something to try to do, she had to admit, something like that might be good for him. It was not like it was the worst thing they could make someone do, and he was too much of a prude. If she and Astrian had been asked, she might. For the good of the spiritual community, of course.

Kiadora shook her head. Why was she thinking about this? A couple of months ago she was right with Regelend on this.

Either way, she still found herself wandering over to the table to look through the various colors. Mostly this time of the year they had bright colors of green, yellow, purple and pink. But under a pile she saw a deep red sleeve sticking out with gold lace around the cuff. She pulled it out and found the fabric to have a stunning inlay of gold colored thread, weaving and spinning together in an intricate pattern like Aeliean was fond of wearing. She wondered if it was even supposed to be in here, but neither of the two women at the table made a move to stop her as she looked at it.

Was she supposed to pay for this? She looked around and saw other people just leaving with their choices, so she just walked away to go put it back into her quarters. It wasn't easy trying to find an area that wasn't covered in dirt, but she settled for folding it and putting it on her nightstand. Hopefully it wouldn't wrinkle too badly. On some level, she had already decided that she needed to look nice for the night of the ceremony.

After the morning meal, Kiadora made her way to Aeliean's room, only to be told that today would be their last day. These things came so fast down here now.

"That's it?" Kiadora felt stunned at her feeling of disappointment.

"Not necessarily," said Aeliean. "There is one more thing we are doing today. We're going to practice basic water scrying again. You can use this whenever you need it. You don't need a big, lumbering crate and lots of space. Because of what you have seen, this should be easier and yield more information than in the past." Aeliean motioned to the cushion that was by the creek once again.

Kiadora was already clearing her mind and slowing her breathing as Aeliean instructed her to, and the images came to the back of her mind as she stared at the water. They were distant at first, like watching a weak daydream. Then there was the flash of red mixed with white, and it was like she was seeing the images underneath the creek through the water, as vivid as if she was watching them unfold before her.

She saw the back of a head with long brown hair, the slight waves bouncing as the woman walked. The woman walked awkwardly and slowly, and as she turned a corner, Kiadora could see she was carrying a large crate. She could also see the side of the woman's face. It was Narissa.

She seemed to be walking along an underground corridor, which led up a ramp eventually. Now Narissa was on a dock and throwing the crate onto the deck of a ship.

"Ay, watch the deck. She's gotta hold against water, you know." The admonishment came from a lumbering sailor who was busy untying a sail farther up the deck.

"Not to mention the wares," said a tall man with dark brown hair who came walking up behind Narissa and boarded the ship. It could only be the man with the bayonets. He was gruff, the bottom half of his face unshaven. He still had that wide-brimmed hat pulled down low over his face.

"This junk is made to be durable," Narissa snapped as she came aboard as well. A second sailor, a boy, brought in the plank that bridged the ship to the dock. The larger sailor cranked up the anchor with the help of another man who looked to be about Kiadora's age.

The ship drifted out into what looked to be a wide river; Kiadora could see the coastline on both sides. She guessed it either had to be the Lanks or the Teilian river, the only two rivers in the country large enough to hold cargo ships. They started heading downstream and a large gust of wind picked up to speed along the process, picking up Narissa's wild, long hair that whipped around like snakes in the heat of attack. Kiadora could see that characteristic smirk on Narissa's face as her hair flew.

And then the stream was just water, bubbling and yielding nothing but the distorted images of the rocks below. When Aeliean said she could use this method whenever she needed to, Kiadora didn't think she had meant for this. It had been like watching the actions through a window. The details were crisp, and she knew that she had not just invented it. Knowing Aeliean, she had meant for Kiadora to view past lives. But this was happening now, and Kiadora was sure it wasn't something that was very copacetic if Narissa was involved.

Kiadora stumbled up from her cramped sitting position and thanked Aeliean for all of her help. She babbled out something about being glad she could know about her past lives and that she had at least seen the error in her ways as a torturer back. The two hugged as Kiadora headed up to her quarters, still uncertain of what to do about illegal weapons distribution.

It felt strange to be wearing color again, much less a well-kept garment that didn't make her itch. Kiadora ran her hand along the sleeve of the red and gold dress. She felt like a flower that had just bloomed its petals.

She was amazed that she had not done this sooner. It just had never crossed her mind to change from the riding clothes she had come down in, even though she saw the tables with the seasonally coordinated clothes every couple of months. Kiadora was just used to the gear and, she reluctantly admitted to herself, she didn't want to let go of what she wore on the surface. To assimilate the looks of this place would be to belong that much more, she realized. Not something she cared too much about until now.

Kiadora headed down to the Great Union ceremony. She figured she would give Regelend some support. She still hadn't seen him in the past couple of days and she was beginning to wonder if he would even come. Then she wondered if Astrian would come, too.

As she walked into one of the larger caverns, she could already hear someone playing on a lute, and she heard some drums going. Even on the surface, that sort of music was woefully out of style. Single players with acoustic guitars were the big deal at the moment, at least when she had left; most of them played fast cords and had strong voices. As the music grew louder, she could hear a spritely, lilting tune. Kiadora felt it somehow worked and could make a comeback. It was good for dancing, at any rate.

Kiadora walked into the cavern, which was already packed with a large crowd. People danced across the floor between tables set with food. Bright green and yellow paper lanterns glowed from the ceiling of the cavern and braided ribbons were somehow fastened to the craggy walls.

The first thing she did was scan the crowd for Astrian. The problem was, he really knew how to blend in, despite the hair. She looked for Regelend and Uranda, also nowhere to be seen. She picked up a small cup full of a red liquid. It tasted like some sort of a light berry wine. As she held the liquid in her mouth, trying to figure out what berry the concoction was made of (cherry?) a voice spoke behind her.

"I don't usually see you at these things. And that dress looks nice." Kiadora jumped, nearly spilling the wine on her red dress. She turned to see Astrian standing by the table. Did he come out of the rocks themselves? Still, she found herself fighting back a grin.

"Well, I've heard a lot about this one, with Regelend and all. I was going to try to give him some support, but I doubt he'll even show." She almost commented on how nice he looked, with a forest green, belted tunic. Did men care about those things though? She settled for just looking down for a napkin to wipe off the wine from her hand, which Astrian was already holding out to her.

"The participants are usually in a side chamber preparing," said Astrian as Kiadora thanked him for the napkin. Kiadora just nodded, suddenly very aware of how close Astrian was standing. They were off to the side so it wasn't even like she could attribute it to the crowd or the noise. She could have leaned a finger's width to the side and bumped his chest.

She made a job of wiping off her hand and glanced up when she was finished. He was looking between her dress and her face. He suddenly snapped his eyes away as she looked up. Kiadora kept hanging on to the napkin, not wanting to leave to go put it in a bin. Then she remembered the last time they spoke.

"I wanted to thank you for the other day. Sorry I was such a mess, I've been a lot better. See? No wounds," she said, holding up her hands. The herbal salve Uranda had given her had already reduced the cuts to light marks. Astrian's own hands twitched. He looked up from her hands directly into her eyes, the dark orbs flashing in the light from the lanterns above.

"We all get our moments here; it's not easy, what we do. I'm just glad I could help." He was now holding her hands. They were softer than she figured they would be, given his background. Then his lips were on hers, and they were in each other's arms.

After a few moments, Kiadora pulled away, laughing.

"They're just going to have us do the ceremony if we don't stop," she said.

"That's alright," Astrian said with a small smile. Kiadora actually found herself giggling.

"Later," she said with a wink. "I should find Regelend."

Astrian blinked suddenly. He looked startled and embarrassed.

"Of course, I was being…"

"A man. Come on, let's find the poor wretch." Astrian indicated the left side of the chamber. As they muscled their way through the crowd they found a side cavern. It stood oddly unguarded.

"You'd think they'd demand more privacy for this," Kiadora muttered as they walked in. They had just gone through the entrance of the cavern when a figure collided roughly with them. It was Regelend, looking panicked.

"Come on," he muttered. "They think I'm going to the bathroom." Kiadora and Astrian turned to follow Regelend as he nearly ran out of the hall.

"Well, where are you really going?" Kiadora asked.

"Anywhere but here. I'm done with this, I can't do it. Uranda will understand."

"I thought you had to," Kiadora said.

"I'm pissing on an entire damn spiritual belief, the one I'm supposed to practice. No, when I said I'm done, I'm done. I just can't live like this. I tried, I did." He spoke in a frantic tone, and Kiadora was shocked to hear him say damn, strong language coming from Regelend. As they ran around the classrooms, Kiadora realized Regelend was bolting for the waterfall exit.

"Regelend, just think about this," she pleaded. "Where will you go?" They were already running through the caverns on the way to the underground lake, Regelend shining a torch he drew off the wall further back.

"I don't know." Kiadora and Astrian just followed him up behind the waterfall and out the opening, Kiadora knowing they were both just intent to see if he would really leave.

"Regelend," Kiadora grabbed his arm and spun him around. She was actually choking back tears. He was the first to show her kindness when she was in the strangest place she had ever been. "Are you serious about this?"

Regelend only nodded. "I'll find my way."

Kiadora took a deep breath.

"Wait, you don't have to go out there abandoned. I know this doctor, he's sympathetic to what we are. But I'm terrible with directions, and I want to make sure you get there." 'And that he'll take you in,' Kiadora thought.

"They're going to want to know where you went," Astrian said to Regelend. "I'll tell them you bolted out of our sight. Kiadora, you were just at the ritual briefly to meet me, if anyone asks."

"It's not like I'm ever at those things," Kiadora added. "But do you think they'll buy it? I don't want you to get in trouble."

"Probably, he's the golden boy with the Elders," Regelend said, nodding towards Astrian. "You can't be such a scholar down here and not be, being close to becoming a Water Master and all."

"Then why did you pick him for the Children?" Kiadora asked.

"Because he's curious about everything," Regelend said. Kiadora squinted at Regelend, not believing the vague answer for a moment.

"And you two needed to meet," said Regelend with a smirk. "So, where's this doctor?"

"He's a couple towns over from my home. We can make it in an hour, but we have to take it brisk." Regelend sighed.

"Part of me feels terrible. They're going to need another couple for this."

"As if you didn't know we'd do it," Kiadora said immediately. Astrian smiled.

"I'll volunteer us in a couple of days, once this has died down," he said.

"Besides, we have to practice before that," said Kiadora with a smirk. "I'll see you later tonight." And Kiadora headed down the path with Regelend at her heels.

The walk was a little longer than Kiadora had remembered, but they got there in a little over an hour with the quick pace. All the lights were out in the doctor's small house. Kiadora felt momentarily shy, but then banged on the door anyway. She hadn't thought until now what she would do if the man happened to be out of town. But to her relief he groggily swung open the door.

"Kiadora, I thought you were away for your studies."

"I have a bit of an issue. My friend here is in trouble for what he is. He's like me. We just escaped. I know it's a huge risk to you, and I'll understand if you say no, but he really needs somewhere to be." Kiadora had been practicing the line all the way into town.

"Don't worry about it for a second. I'm tired of this sort of thing happening to people, and I would be happy to have some help around here. Who would I be to say no?" Kiadora beamed. She had been banking on this.

"He's running from the North, so I doubt anyone would know him down here."

"Still, I'll make sure he doesn't just go wandering out. We're not taking any chances. You go to the store, you hide your face," said the doctor to Regelend. "Say you're sensitive to the sun."

Regelend nodded, still trying to get his breath back from the near run across the countryside.

"Thank you, this really means a lot to me." Regelend said. "I'll sleep on the floor, I don't care. I won't take up much room at all."

"No, I'll get a bed set up," said the doctor, and without another word, Regelend was ushered in.

"I really have to get back, they'll start missing me. Thank you again." Dr. Iland nodded and shut the door.

Kiadora ran back, nursing the hopes that Regelend would be alright and that Astrian would still be awake.

CHAPTER 36

They had formed a circle, hands together, some heads tossed back, some bodies shaking. All their focus was directed toward Kiadora and Astrian. And something more, but Kiadora couldn't tell what.

It was strange. Kiadora thought she would be blushing more than she was. She certainly didn't expect to be slowly peeling away Astrian's clothes and him, hers. A couple of months ago, she wouldn't even be caught dead in the crowd. Her head started to swim as she pressed her hands on Astrian's sleek, pale skin. Kiadora's own dress fell away in a haze of red. She also figured, in some remote part of her mind, that she'd feel more cold in the dank cavern. But she was about to break into a sweat.

There was a smooth, green cloth on the ground, which Kiadora was thankful for as they nearly fell to the ground. And then it was like the large crowd wasn't even there. It was just her, Astrian and a collective feeling of life and warmth that wasn't entirely from the two of them.

"You'll need this. You have hard work ahead of you, and I can't have you with child. Mix it with water and drink once a month." Kiadora clutched a silk bag and opened it to find a green powder that smelled faintly like dried grass. "But don't open your mouth about it. The Elders would have my head. They think such a child would be sacred." Kiadora put the bag in her pocket and duly noted to drink the stuff.

She knew there were children around, though they did a good job of not letting them run freely through the compound. There was a play area, and many kids had chores around the place like dishwashing. Lessons started at age seven. But trying to manage parenthood in such a dank place was not part of the plan.

These instructions had been the first thing the woman said to her, making it the strangest introduction Kiadora had to a teacher thus far. Or anyone, for that matter. She didn't even know the woman's name.

The messenger had come abruptly in the morning, knowing to find her at Astrian's place. She wished they could have given her at least a day with him.

"You can probably gather that you'll be working with Earth right now." Kiadora could. The woman's room was a positive forest with potted plants everywhere, and herbs in various states of drying hung from where the woman couldn't fit the potted plants. Tall bookshelves housed leatherbound tomes with plant types printed on the spines.

"Come," said the woman, and Kiadora followed her down the corridor.

"I'm sorry, what was your name?" said Kiadora, nearly jogging to keep up with the woman's brisk stride.

"Tillana." Kiadora nodded, waiting for more, but she was out of luck. They rounded a bend, and Kiadora was stopped by a more impressive forest. Lines of plants grew under lamps, which were held by heavy ropes that came down from the high cavern ceiling. A piping system ran among the rows and sprayed water at intervals. All of this was set on a bed of soil that must have been a trick to import down.

Kiadora walked over to the lamps and looked up to see a soft glow from a flame existing above a plate of glass. But the light was far too strong to be coming from a candle.

"Fortified elementals," said Tillana briskly from behind. "There are workers adding their energies at all hours to get the needed amount of light. One of the few ingenious things those hotheads came up with." Despite the affront, Kiadora looked over at the row of men and women to the side, heads bowed and some muttering. And Kiadora had thought what she had done was impressive. How much could she learn to do?

Before Kiadora could spend too much time wondering, Tillana was shoving a spade roughly into her hands.

"You're done with that for now. This mulch needs turning, now get moving. And don't damage the roots." And with that, Tillana took her leave.

Kiadora didn't know what was stopping her from throwing down the stupid garden tool and bugging the people at the edge of the garden to find out what elemental fortification was all about. She then heard a sharp whistle and saw a man standing among the rows, pointing at where to start. Kiadora still didn't know what was forcing her to go over there, until he waved a pointed stick.

And so it went on for a couple of weeks. Kiadora practically limped up to Astrian's place after doing everything from turning mulch to harvesting to sprinkling new seeds. She was constantly stooping in the dirt, even that one day when she sang to one of the struggling plants. The man with the stick had complimented her on her voice, but it didn't make up for the days of loud commands shouted over several planted rows when she was barely done with her first task. Although she was almost pleased when the song plants started to bear fruit, she somehow doubted she had anything to do with it.

"Later you'll learn some neat little conjurations," Astrian said after a long rant session of Kiadora's. Kiadora propped herself on her elbow and looked Astrian in the eyes.

"Conjurations? Like the stuff the Shiekita of old were supposed to do? Can I summon a hurricane?" Astrian chuckled.

"No, things that strong are out of our realm. We're not gods. But you can use the energy signatures of the plants to grant you spiritual and situational benefits, like luck, health, prosperity, vitality, success. That sort of thing."

"Does it work?" Kiadora asked after a pause.

"I don't know. It could be argued that you create your own luck with your own ambitions." Kiadora laughed and hit him with one of the hard pillows.

"Thanks for cheering me up," she said, laughing, as he grinned and started to pin her down. No matter how tired she was, at least she could get her energy up for other things.

It had been a good couple of weeks since she had been back to her quarters. Despite always feeling so cramped, it now looked lonely to the point of feigning spaciousness.

She walked over to the small table nonetheless and searched in her drawer. The past couple of weeks of pure gardening had been too little. She needed something that was a little more exciting than a rake and some soil. And Astrian's company couldn't be relyed on all of the time.

Kiadora flicked on the lighter from Lisera. She let the spark catch and take on a life of its own before transferring the flame's residence to the candle. She below out the match and inhaled the smoke, savoring even that. It was nice to not smell wet soil and drying herbs, though she heard her peers swear by that heady scent.

And she had far from forgotten the visions from the surface. It would be great to know what Narissa and the man were up to, even if it was none of her concern. It would be something that wasn't a hoe, at any rate.

Kiadora sat before the candle and just watched, letting her mind go clear. But rather than falling into that world of iridescent particles, the flash of red followed by a bright white shone before her.

Then the tall man with the brown hair stood before a dark, lonely field. He turned towards her, his hat still obscuring most of his face. He motioned his head over to a wooded area at the edge of the field. Was that...? Kiadora looked around to see the cave they usually emerged from. So it was, the first wooded patch on the way to town. So close?

"I'll be waiting," the man said. And then it was just the flickering candle once more. Kiadora hovered on her bed for a moment, doubting if she should go. It could be an illusion or maybe a way to discover who was leaving the compound. What did she even know about this man? But she wanted to know more about him. She jumped up and headed for the waterfall exit.

Emerging from the cavern, she headed past the field the man had stood in front of. Right as she was coming around the bend past the wooded area, a figure leapt out and grabbed her wrist. She let out a small cry as she was forced to lurch to the side, nearly falling into the dirt. Kiadora regained balance, however, and saw the back of a thick head of dark hair pulling her deeper into the forest. They stopped on a small patch of grass between five trees draped with moss.

"Moss, protective stuff to begin with," the man muttered. He then shook Kiadora's hand roughly, wobbling her whole frame. "Cyrus. You've been watching us for a while." Kiadora frowned.

"Sorry, it was bad. I didn't mean to see anything I shouldn't. I won't say anything." It was starting to occur to her how stupid it was to follow this man into the woods. She clearly knew things she shouldn't, and it would be easy to knock her off here and now. Her ascension-by-razor diplomatic survival skills were fading.

But she still didn't sense any danger from this man, even if she couldn't tell what she was sensing with.

"No, that's just it, we need help," he said. Now seeing this man in person, he had an earnest quality to him, even if his face was obscured. His tone was like a neighbor asking her to help clean up debris after a bad storm, if she had the time.

"I'm sorry, I haven't been able to discern what it is you do."

"We work for freedom," said the man, as if it was the most simple task to be doing. "We know how much you hate it down there. That's what we all need, fundamentally. To see the sunrise, feel the cool night air, tromp through the woods. Meditate under the sun, the original and largest flame. Or see a play, perhaps," he said pointedly. How did they know? "Pity we should be denied such simple and fundamental things, don't you think?"

Kiadora nodded. Clearly this man had the upper hand, he knew where she went, but how, she didn't know. Besides, he did have a point that there was no arguing against. But how did he know, and what could she trust about him?

"They expect us to practice our craft, but we cannot enjoy its full splendor. Pity," he went on. "How are we to know true success locked away like this? We are supposed to stand for freedom and knowledge, but we stay locked away in our rat holes. No, it isn't right."

Rat holes. Narissa told him about her.

He was now a few inches from her face, and she could smell a bitter liquor on his breath. Still, she couldn't deny his words. "We should be free to make our choices and to reach our potential, is this not so, Kiadora?"

"Yes," she muttered, thinking about how great it was to see the sun for the first time in months. And that she hadn't even had the choice in so long. Now when she did, she had to hide it.

"You could help those things come about, go down as one of the makers of fate."

Kiadora looked out at the moonlight dappling down through the woods, the sliver of light playing over the trees that now looked young and vibrant, even in the night. A bed of daisies slept with petals closed in a nearby clearing. Despite the plants being shut for the night, they still looked healthier than what grew in the caverns. The lamp system was indeed ingenious, but it was still a pale imitation of the true light plants needed from up here. She yearned to see the flowers open and not have to sneak off to do it, afraid of being caught both by the Elders and the authorities up here. Rooting through flowers for no reason was the first sign of a Shiekita.

And Cyrus' words: *Makers of fate.*

"What do you need me to do?" she said. The man beamed under than wide brim, happy to have someone to clear the debris.

"I'll be in touch. I think you know how. Keep scrying." Kiadora nodded as Cyrus turned around and started to withdraw into the woods.

"Wait!" Kiadora said. "How do the Elders not see us? People down there, they…sense things." Cyrus did not turn and spoke to the trees.

"You let in the beings you trust or desire. It's your mind, after all." Then he was gone.

"So what have you felt?"

Kiadora had been directed to come to Tillana's room today by a messenger, and already she wished she was in the garden, if she could believe it.

"Felt?"

"Yes, in the garden. Around the plant life and soil. You know, the largest conduit of Eatheria?" Tillana spoke from behind a plant she was poking at with a spade.

"Um, dirt?" Tillana let out a sigh.

"If you're not going to say anything intelligent, at least make

453

yourself useful," she nudged a larger pot on the floor with her foot. "Hold this next to the fern."

Kiadora walked over and held up the pot, wishing to smash it on Tillana's head. Tillana gingerly lifted the plant out of its current pot and set it in the one Kiadora held.

"No matter, most of my students don't feel it strongly at first. I suppose you can't all be adept as I am after so long." 'So terribly sorry,' Kiadora thought. Tillana poured new soil onto the plant and directed Kiadora to another table.

She brought up a small plant with dark green leaves and deep purple flowers on it.

"Lavender, one of the most common herbs and the easiest to work with. Calms a person. Cup your hand around the base of the plant, between your thumb and forefinger."

Kiadora felt her ears go red. So the woman thought Kiadora needed an easy assignment, did she? But Kiadora didn't want to argue. She just wanted to get out of the room, so she did what she was told.

"Let your mind go blank, steady your breathing."

Kiadora did so, and the old sensation of tingling returned immediately. Feeling nostalgic, she wondered if she would collapse, but the feeling stopped right as her mind went racing. Kiadora switched her rapid breath to a slow rhythm. Her mind sank into that dark, but comforting, place where it was just her mind floating, suspended in a dark pool.

The warmth spread up her arm and through her chest, up through her head, down her legs and to her feet. She had never let it go this far, she had always panicked and stopped, or later, passed out. It was like being wrapped in a soft, wool blanket by the fire.

Small pinpricks erupted here and there, just under her skin. She expected it to be like the flame, she would suddenly just fall into another world with shifting particles and neon colors, but something different happened. In the back of her mind, she saw a few small specks of deep green light in the plant, flowing into her arm and swirling in various tracts and paths through her body. She looked down and saw no such thing, but in her mind she could picture it. It was like having double vision.

Just as Tillana said, Kiadora felt calm, more calm than in her entire life. It was like nothing had ever bothered her, and she could never be bothered again.

She started to feel her consciousness fade. She must have been entering that world between consciousness and sleep, because she didn't quite close her eyes, but she felt like she was about to nod off.

Then Kiadora felt her hand being lifted roughly. She could vaguely feel the leaves scratch her hand through the haze. She could feel her energy returning quickly. It was just like waking up from a short nap.

"Shake out your arms and jump a couple of times," Tillana ordered shortly. Confused, Kiadora snapped her arms out and jumped on the spot where she stood. She could feel something shaking out of her, but would never be able to quite define what.

"That grounds you back. And *that* is what you should be feeling," said Tillana, her back to Kiadora, as she moved to put the lavender plant away. "Go back to the gardens tomorrow, and as you work, feel that. Let Eatheria flow through you and get to know the energy signatures of the plants."

Tillana picked up the large fern and headed for the door, indicating with her head for Kiadora to get the door for her. Kiadora opened the door and let the other woman through, before slamming it shut.

Kiadora headed up the opposite direction, feeling cheated. She had just been offered one of the most therapeutic experiences of her life, and her teacher didn't even look at her afterwards. At least she had some errands to run tonight.

Kiadora stood in an alley, knocking on a back door. A sharp pain sprung into Kiadora's knuckle as she knocked. She figured it must be a splinter. While rubbing her hand on the back of her cloak, the door swung open violently.

"Letter for…" And that was all Kiadora could get out before a hand from the dark grabbed the letter out of her hand and slammed the door shut again.

"Nice manners," Kiadora muttered as she walked back out onto the main street. It was the same street as her usual haunts, but by the end of the day lately she was so tired from the gardens she didn't feel like doing much. And tonight she was supposed to report back to Cyrus. She had some questions for him anyway.

Tonight's errand had been oddly normal. A couple nights ago she delivered a bulky piece of metal to a woman missing her hair on the right side of her head. They had met at the back of a bar in the woman's own private room she had reserved. "Less eyes," was the only thing the woman had said when Kiadora asked why they had met back here and what the piece was. It had resembled a hunting rifle but had a barrel attachment added onto it.

The time before that was a paper bag filled with what felt like tightly compacted powder, which she gave to a man in a back alley in a neighboring farming village. Her only instruction, in that mossy grove with Cyrus, was to under no circumstances get it wet. Apparently, she didn't even want to know what would happen if she did.

She walked up the same country lane she always took back and found Cyrus behind a tree to the right. She could only tell it was him by his height. The rest of him was hidden by a large overcoat and that wide hat.

"He got it, then?" Kiadora nodded, veering off the path and stepping over the ditch to stand directly in front of him.

"What is this all about?" Kiadora asked bluntly in a whisper. "I had a door slammed in my face without a word, met a woman missing half her hair and I still *do* want to know would happen if that powder got wet, you know. I can tell I'm sticking my neck out here, and I want to know what I'm doing."

"Just know you are about to bring about great change," Cyrus said. Kiadora continued to stare him down.

"It is not wise to spread information around too much. I hardly know what it is these things are for. If one person gets caught or opens their mouth where they shouldn't, it's bad for the whole operation. You'll just have to trust that we are working for the good of our kind." And with a sharp turn, Cyrus headed toward the road and followed it back to town.

Kiadora walked back to the cave opening, lit the torch she kept there with Lisera's device and went back down to her quarters. She pulled back the curtain roughly and threw her hat down on her nightstand, the indignation of not being trusted rising all the way. "Seedy bastard," she muttered as she poured water into her basin, spilling a good amount all over her table.

"Who is a seedy bastard?" Kiadora jumped to find Astrian in her bed with his shirt off. They usually surprised each other like that, but she had been so preoccupied.

Kiadora regarded him for a moment. She knew no one should know, and she didn't want to get Astrian in on this. She was already fully aware that this held a lot of danger. But still the words came out before she could stop them. Kiadora always felt like she could tell him anything. Maybe Cyrus was right to not trust her. She sat down on the bed next to Astrian.

"What type of a powder is dangerous when it's combined with water?" Astrian cocked his head to the side, then looked off to the wall.

"I've read about some in passing that reacts to water as a bomb. Others just aggravate the skin. Some corrode the skin right off. Why?" Kiadora let out a sigh, knowing full well that she was running right off of a cliff but unable to stop.

"I met a man. I can't tell you his name. It's nothing like that," she added quickly.

"It wasn't a concern."

"Oh…thanks. Anyway, he wants there to be change, something new, something that's not…this," she said, waving her hand all around.

"Yes, *this*." Astrian nodded in complete understanding.

"I saw him while I was scrying, and he told me to come to meet him up top. That was after I saw what they were doing. Transporting things, guns in many cases. I wanted to know more. I also know this wasn't just some meditation vision. It felt like a fact of life, not something akin to a dream." Astrian looked at her with an expression that could have been admiration, if it wasn't tinged with concern.

"That's an impressive ability," he said quietly.

"Thanks. But I met him, and he said something great. That we could be makers of fate, that we could change all of this for the better. So I figured it was worth a shot if it would help. Since then I've been meeting people in dark alleys, delivering letters and that powder. The other night was a gun with a barrel on it. I asked him what this is all about. I feel like I deserve to know. He just said that I have to trust him and that he hardly knows anything himself. Apparently, they don't want the information to spread too far, in case someone talks." Kiadora clenched her covers. "Like I am right now." Astrian was silent for a moment.

"At any rate, we now both know what they're up to."

"Something violent," Kiadora whispered.

"They're a terrorist group, Kiadora. You don't want to get sucked into that." Kiadora turned her head away from him.

"But at least they're trying to do something about this. What, are we supposed to live like this forever?"

"It's worked so far. Better than killing."

"Come on, Astrian, you hate it as much as I do down here. You mutter in your sleep, you know. Always about the mines." Kiadora left the rest unsaid. There were nights when she had to remind him that he was not down there still.

"And I don't know for sure if the plan is violent," Kiadora plowed on. "They could maybe have guns as a protective measure against the soldiers that round us up. They're not going against peaceful foes themselves." Astrian still looked at her, a deep scowl on his face.

"Watch yourself," was all he said at last. She regretted talking to him at all about it. What was she thinking? What else would it have done but worry him?

"I will," she said, and she leaned in to kiss him, but he just wrapped his arms around her and they got under the covers to sleep.

CHAPTER 37

'Another day and that much closer to destroying my back,' Kiadora thought to herself as she threw dirt out of a hole and into a pile to her left. Kiadora was transplanting some tea leaf saplings. She resented that she was already thinking about the aches in her back. It wasn't like she was an old woman yet. She needed something else to think about.

Kiadora remembered Tillana telling her that she should be feeling some sort of energy while she was doing this. Maybe it would make the time go faster.

She let her mind go calm and blank. Though it was hard with all the physical work she was doing, she let her breathing go steady as well.

In the back of her mind, she could see the green particles. She turned her head in several different directions and could see them flowing by the millions through every plant, all with different colors, a cornucopia of differing energies. Again, she wondered if she would faint. But she didn't.

She looked down and cupped her hand around one of the tea leaf saplings she just planted back. Kiadora felt the familiar tingling, then the warmth. In her mind's eye she could see bright yellow particles go up into her arm, saw them travel across her body.

Kiadora almost expected to lose consciousness time, but did not. She actually felt her heart race just a little. It was like every ounce of her energy was returning and she felt like she could no longer just sit there. She had to move or it felt like her muscles would combust.

Kiadora bent over to get the next sapling, threw it in the hole she had made and covered it, happy to be doing something with her hands. She was positively ecstatic that she had the excuse to use her legs and jump over to the next hole, which she started to dig with vigor, throwing the dirt aside with flare.

All the while, Kiadora could see the particles flowing in an exchange with her body and several of the plants, some stray particles dancing on the surface of the leaves. The particles flowed into her body and out in a concentrated pattern directly at her heart, like she was now an extension of the plants.

She moved down the line quickly, getting her work done at twice the normal pace, until all of the saplings had a home in the ground. Kiadora stood up and could see in the distant, yet close, place in her mind the streams crossing between her and the plants. She now shared particle flows with the plants closest to her. Somewhere she had traded streams from other plants farther down the line with the ones closest to her without even feeling it.

Kiadora stood tapping her foot. She still had the need to do more. Kiadora waved to the supervisor of the day, who just nodded and waved her out. Looking down at the plant, she wondered how she could let herself go from their hold on her. Tillana had done the work last time. What had Tillana done, again, grabbed her hand?

Kiadora jumped back from the row of saplings and saw the connection cut instantly. But something was odd. She still felt like she could run across half of the country.

Without knowing what she was doing, she took off jogging out of the gardens and into the corridor. She ran down a path, taking another one she had never been down. She ran past several rooms she had never seen and then reached a stone wall.

Kiadora remembered not to go down just any corridor. The network of passages down here was immense, and no one even knew what was down some of them. A person could get lost forever, if they wanted to. Perhaps fall into another icy, underground lake.

She ran back the other way, sticking to the paths she knew. On her way through the compound, she ran past Aeliean, who only laughed and waved. A few other dwellers grinned at her and some said hello, like they knew her. She didn't know from where, but then she remembered some of them must have seen her at the Great Union ceremony. She felt herself go a little red.

It hadn't seemed like much of a big deal at the time. It had felt like just her and Astrian, alone with the intensity and slight awkwardness of their third time. But she kept running through the embarrassment, no matter how many people grinned and waved. Most just seemed to be grinning at the fact that they knew exactly what was going on.

She had seen a few people doing strange things herself. One man back on her second day walked with a tick, flinching to the left.

Although she didn't know if that was because of his studies with herbs or maybe he was just born that way. Another skipped through the corridors a couple months later, waving his arms in expansive circles. She hoped it didn't get as embarrassing for her.

Before she knew it, the main lights were dimming down. She returned to her quarters, breathing hard, but finally feeling like she had expended all the energy she needed to. Crawling into her bed, she was relieved Astrian wasn't there. She flopped onto her bed, had a passing thought of how mad he must be to not be around and was out.

The next day she was to work with lavender, the most common herb in the garden. She felt her heart stop at the feeling of not being able to stay conscious, like in Tillana's room. She knew there would be no excuse for not spreading mulch around these plants. It was the man with the stick who was watching her today. Kiand, she finally learned to call him after a couple weeks of work.

"These need new soil," he had barked, waving his stick at the rows of lavender plants. "Leave an inch untouched, and you'll never want to be back down here again." Then he threw a burlap sack of soil at her feet from where it was perched on his shoulder like an insipid parrot and continued down the row.

She bent down to untie the bag of mulch, gazing at the row of plants. And they happened to be in bloom, their striking amethyst was in sharp contrast to the green stems. Still, she could see bright purple particles running along the interior of the flowers, a few flying off the petals like usual. She didn't even need to touch it, just think about it and focus, she realized. As her concentration wavered, she could see just the particles around the edges of the leaves and petals.

The rest of the day, she worked in a calm daze. She expected to fall asleep but instead just felt at peace with the world. Probably the first time, a voice said at the back of her head through the calm. It was like her whole mind was immersed in a warm bath and nothing could bother her again.

At the end of the day, she walked back to her quarters still feeling like she was in that warm place that no one could touch. In her haze, she vaguely understood that she was smiling. She swung up the ladder, far more gracefully than the usual tired heave. She threw herself onto her bed, barely touching the curtain as she swept through.

She felt like she was floating, like in the sensory deprivation tub. Kiadora didn't know how long this went on, but was rudely jarred as the scene shifted and she was trapped in a narrow passage underground. She briefly thought that maybe she was following someone's view as they passed through the corridors of the compound, but she looked around and realized that the walls were made of jagged, chiseled rock and the width and height of the corridor were far too small.

There was a rumbling from overhead, and she heard a swear next to her. She turned to see a redheaded boy of about eight years of age in a dark blue jumpsuit. He had a pick hanging off his waist and strapped to his head was a small oil lamp.

"It's collapsing, not again!" he wailed. The boy didn't seem to notice her as he started running toward the exit. Kiadora couldn't feel her own legs move, but she followed him nonetheless.

Large chunks of dirt started to fall and large rocks came down right in front of the boy, grinding him to a halt. Still more dirt fell on him as he put his arms up to protect his head. Another rock about half his size fell right next to him before he could move a step and rolled down a small incline already created by the dirt. He let out a yell as the dirt pinned him to the large bolder.

Kiadora rushed forward in that eerie, hovering way. She realized she could pass right through the rock. Now in front of him, she held out her arms and looked down to see they were a transparent blue color, far more substantial than normal. Her arms passed right though him. The boy looked up at her, and his eyes went wide.

Then Kiadora was back in her darkened quarters. The lamps were dimmed overhead. It had to be the middle of the night. Marveling at the strange dream, she sat up and rubbed her eyes.

She knew that boy had to be Astrian. Maybe she missed him more that she was willing to admit. It had only been several days that they hadn't been talking.

As if on cue, the curtain swung back, and Astrian stood there in a woolen shirt and loose pants.

"How did you do that?"

"Do what?"

"The tunnel caving in, I know you were there."

"That wasn't just my dream? How did you know I was there and not just part of your dream?"

"You didn't see it, did you? Your nexus cord." Kiadora frowned at him in confusion.

"My what?" Astrian stepped in and let the curtain fall, becoming nothing but a shadow against the dim light.

"When your spirit travels out of your body it is held to your physical form by a cord. You had that cord," he said in a low tone. Kiadora grinned.

"Hm, so I saw your dream. You couldn't have been dreaming something more fantastic?"

"It happens nearly every night," he muttered. "Sometimes family members, sometimes me. There's usually no one there trying to save my life, though," he finished in a soft tone. Kiadora felt some of that love she still had well in her chest, despite their recent argument. She wanted to put an arm around him but wasn't sure if they even were together like that anymore.

"I'm sorry I butted in. It's the ultimate privacy invasion, really. It just happened after I went to sleep. I was working with lavender today. I don't know what it was with that plant."

"It's a strong herb commonly used to aid dreamwork."

Kiadora nodded as the silence just hung there. She wanted to apologize for her involvement with what Astrian thought of as a terrorist group, but she knew that it would only be a small cover-up for a larger problem, like wrapping up an arm in a cloth bandage when there was already gangrene. This was why she wanted freedom; for herself, but also for people like Astrian who saw underground tunnels crushing them in their sleep. Especially for Astrian.

And if she could do such amazing things with these herbs, maybe it was possible.

"I'm going back to sleep," Kiadora said. "Feel free to stay if you wish."

Kiadora reclined, and Astrian stood up. He hovered for a moment, evidently torn between walking back out of the curtain and staying. Kiadora watched him, not yet pulling up the covers, hoping he would stay. It would just be Astrian and his nightmares, otherwise.

As if picking up on what she was thinking, he joined her in bed. Maybe she wouldn't go back to sleep after all.

The next evening, after a strange day working with small pine bushes (she had spent most of the day craving immortality, which was just starting to wear off), Kiadora sat in the library paging though herbal manuals full of identification methods and uses for the plants, both fantastic and just medical.

She hadn't realized there were so many different varieties of plants. She had grown up around the same three basic types of trees and the grounds were kept well weeded. Most of the plants in the book were varieties that came from across the borders and from all reaches of the continent. A few came from a couple of other continents.

She didn't know exactly what she was looking for, just something to help her advance the cause above. Kiadora had considered dream invasion but didn't know what good a woman in dreams with a bizarre string attached could make people do. Society had long surpassed the view that dreams carried any world-shattering meaning, just latent fears and desires of the mind. And those were the people that even paid attention to their dreams.

She already had cinnamon on the mind. It was a powerful amplifier in general. But she couldn't seem to find anything that worked in her favor towards…what exactly? She realized she didn't even have a plan for what she wanted to achieve, yet she was already looking for tools.

Kiadora sighed to let off the mounting frustration. She didn't even know how to plan what she wanted to do. What use would she be to these people? She was supposed to make a difference? Kiadora had never so much as organized a sewing circle, let alone done anything terribly ruthless or history changing.

That was it. Some herb to help her be more aggressive and assertive. With renewed purpose, she went speeding through the book, scanning for anything with aggression properties.

And then she got to the poisons.

The passages under the plant names listed the common medicinal uses, or lack thereof: death. But the other properties where just what she needed: force, aggression, cunning, domination. The only question remained, where to find wolfsbane? Would they even have something so vile down here?

The next day found Kiadora in the gardens again, working with still more tea leaves. They used a lot of those down here. Just what she needed, to be more jittery.

She knew the garden caverns went on for possibly blocks, almost as large as a normally functioning farm on the surface, maybe larger. But there was still hard work to be done. She couldn't just go running through the farms, stealing herbs.

Kiadora worked through the day, trying to think of a way to be granted access after this was done. After a full day, she had come up with a plan so simple she still doubted she could be of any use on the surface. But it was the best she had.

She walked up to the head herbskeeper for the day and asked if she could walk through the gardens, see how it was arranged to work better and get a feel for the plant energies. The lanky woman looked up from a chart briefly and nodded. That was all it took?

She spent the better half of what felt like an hour wandering about the place, from cavern to cavern, up and down rows of greenery. Things were even labeled. How much easier could they have made this?

And there it was: wolfsbane. The blue flowers and spiky leaves sat innocently enough. No one was even around to watch her take it. She wondered again what such a plant would be doing down here and decided she didn't even want to think about it.

Kiadora lowered her hand down to it, and she felt an immediate rush. Her heart beat faster and she felt angry about something, though she didn't know what. In the back of her mind, she could see the dark red particles. They were faster and more discordant. She looked furtively back as she picked some and put it into a handkerchief she brought along, then pocketed it.

She could feel her face flush and had to steady her breathing. She wanted to go out and start a fight with anyone and for any reason, no matter the size, rank or skill of the man or woman. Kiadora realized with mounting anger that she did not know the first thing about controlling the actual pull of these plants once they had her. She went to her standard means of control and access to these powers, calming her breathing and letting her mind go blank.

This stopped her heart from beating so fast, but that undefined sense of rage still lingered dangerously at the corners of her mind. Then she remembered Tillana telling her to jump and shake her limbs, which she did, but she still felt the same. She immediately decided that the cinnamon would have to wait until later. Putting her mind still again, she carefully walked back to her quarters.

She pulled out the wolfsbane, opened the handkerchief and set it down on her table. The particles still flowed straight into her heart. Keeping her mind still, she took a step back, wrenching herself to the side. The flow stopped, and she began to feel an instant calm edge back into her mind.

Though she still felt tense. It had nothing to with the herb that sat silently on her nightstand, looking like a common medicinal herb found in bathroom cabinets on the surface.

She intended to let it sit out to dry, then use it. It would be less prone to rot, tear and disintegration that way. Kiadora put her hand under the table, trying to move the whole nightstand away from her head as quickly as she could. She moved the small table to the other side of the room where the herb could sit to dry. She quickly grabbed her pitcher, water and bowl, setting them on the ground, then placed the towel on her bed.

'Alright, now the cinnamon,' Kiadora thought as she swung out of the doorway and down the ladder. She was happy to be out of there.

Kiadora sat on her bed later, looking at the table still placed against the far wall, as far as it could be placed in such a small room. The herbs were finally dry after a couple of days. She had concerns about them being in such a dank root cellar of an area, but leaving her curtain open to the light and placing the table near the front of her quarters to get light had done the trick.

She could see the particles swirling around in the herbs, not flying off the surface of the plants. The cinnamon had a discordant flow, with no steady streams to speak of, though the red particles were brighter than the wolfsbane.

Kiadora let out of breath of apprehension and walked over to the table. With the way she had felt the other day, there was little telling what she would do with such amplifiers. But she had a purpose for them. Thinking of what she had to do, she picked them both up and felt the flow of particles enter deep within her. Even wrapping the cloth around them did nothing to stint the connection.

She put the little sachet in a front pocket and just felt the flow. It was more intense than the other day, which she attributed to the cinnamon, and it was harder to hold back the rising tide of anger. She had to pick a fight, rise up...harm something.

She quickly threw the folded cloth onto the table. The connection faded instantly. Now wasn't the time. It was the morning before a long day in the fields. But these herbs did what she needed them to do.

Later she would contact Cyrus. She needed to do more. He didn't have a say in the matter. On her way down the ladder, Kiadora wondered if that was the residue of the herb talking or herself. It was hard to tell with these things.

The candle leapt into flame at the touch of the match in Kiadora's shaking hand. It wasn't out of nerves. Kiadora was fidgeting after wearing the sachet for a couple of hours, wanting to see what the herbs would do. She had spent the time in bed, angry at the world. First it was Astrian for being such a jackass and not supporting her in this. She had sat up to go punch him but somehow had reeled herself back. That wasn't what she needed the herbs for.

Then the rage widened to old thoughts of her sisters and how she should go punch them right now. But she was supposed to be at a monastery far away, learning Hermetic pacifism, no less. After that, it had widened into a seething hatred for all who kept her down here. That was what she had been waiting for.

Kiadora sat up and looked into the candle, watching the flame whip violently back and forth, matching her own violent emotions. Despite the rising tide of anger, she calmed her breathing and focused her mind on Cyrus.

Instantly there he was, sitting in the dining room of an inn Kiadora did not recognize. She could only see some tables full of men shoveling stew into their mouths behind him, dressed in heavy traveling cloaks. To his right was the edge of a bar with waitresses walking around with large trays of food. It looked too normal of a scene for Kiadora's taste, considering what she was going to talk about and how she was contacting him. But she persisted.

"I'm doing more," she whispered, in a near growl. Cyrus' hat was pulled down as usual, but by the hint of a smile, she could tell he heard her and knew of her presence.

Do you even know what it is you want to do? He didn't move his lips, but she knew the words instantly.

"Anything," she said with a venomous urgency. "I'm sick of being cooped up here. I feel like I'm doing nothing, just these piddly errands. I want to really stick it to them." She could feel her blood boil as she uttered the words, like it would break from her veins and spill out of her body.

Literally? came Cyrus' silent voice.

"Yes, if need be," she was almost shocked on some level by the harsh, gruff quality of her tone. She had never spoken that way. Kiadora paused and spoke the sentiment that had been running through her for a few days, ever since the wolfsbane.

"I want to see blood run." Cyrus gave a curt nod.

You've said the correct words. We have to wait for volunteers for this sort of business. Then we know they are committed and can do what has to be done.

"Do you get a lot of volunteers?" Kiadora asked quietly, her voice returning to normal. Cyrus had acquiesced, he was no longer the enemy in this conversation.

More than you would think. His tone was even, as if discussing the harvest for that year. *Be at the normal spot, about the time the lights dim. Instructions will come.*

And then it was just Kiadora and her racing heartbeat. She didn't know if it was still the anger or excitement. Whatever the reason, it certainly wasn't apprehension.

Kiadora jumped as her curtain flew open. Before she knew it, she was on her feet with her fist back behind her head, about to strike. Astrian stood before her with his hands up, palms facing her to be as non-threatening as possible.

"Why so angry? I know we haven't been on the best terms, but I thought I would just stop by to see what was going on. I can't do that?" His eyes went instantly to the letter Kiadora had thrown down on the bed before she leapt up. She shifted to stand between him and the correspondence sitting out. She knew she should have written it in the dead of night, but Astrian hadn't been by in so long.

"Sorry, just jumpy lately." She had the herbs in her pocket, and the more she used them, the more she felt ready to fly at anyone.

"What is that letter I can't see? Love notes to someone else so soon?" She could tell he had meant the jab to be lighthearted by the smirk he wore, but it actually came out in a worried tone. She sighed.

"No, it's just...stuff for the movement. You can't say anything, but I've been doing more finally." Astrian instantly frowned.

"I had a feeling it would come to that. You remember what I said about it though?"

"Yeah, I know, but I have to do something." Kiadora sighed.

They were already reliving the argument they had a couple of weeks back, and he wasn't even in her door longer than a minute. Kiadora had hoped they could talk again, but not about this.

"It's probably strictly classified information, but who's it for, what's it about?"

"You're right, it is classified. Why do you care? You don't believe in the cause anyway." Kiadora could feel her voice rising slightly and reeled it back. She didn't need just anyone hearing about it. She shouldn't even be talking to Astrian about it. Some operative she was.

Astrian made a lunge past her and grabbed the letter. He was usually so calm and stoic, she hadn't been expecting the move. Before she could make a countermove, he had the letter held away from her. She jumped at him, but he grabbed her around the shoulders and held her back with a strong arm. Any way she moved, she felt like her collarbone was about to break. He scanned the letter with efficiency.

"Kiadora, this isn't you. 'Respect our demands or pay the price'? 'We will strike with a swift blade'? Kiadora, you can't do any of this. You cried once because I killed a mouse down here."

"It was fuzzy and cute. These are the bastards that kill our kind. Did you even read the top? It's for one of the officers of the guard who is in charge of beheading those possessed by Shiekita in the North. If we were in the wrong place at the wrong time, that would have happened to us. If they stop what they are doing, no harm will come to them."

Astrian looked at her calmly and slowly handed back the letter as he let go of her shoulders.

"Turn back, Kiadora," he said softly. "You'd sink to their level?"

"If it will free us." They looked at each other for a moment, both faces half cast in shadow. Astrian moved towards the door.

"Wait. If you talk, I'll know," Kiadora hissed. Before it was too late, she hoped.

"Don't worry about that," he said in a low tone. "Opening my mouth won't do any good. I have a feeling this goes pretty high up." And he was around the corner and gone. At least Kiadora had Astrian's complacency.

Kiadora wiped sweat off her brow. It had to be close to the time to leave the gardens. As she thought it, she felt a sharp poke in her side.

It was Tillana, holding one of those sharp tormentor sticks, as Kiadora called them. Tillana was in the fields on certain days and always demanded the heaviest workload to be done in the fastest amount of time. Kiadora figured she was probably here to make her stay late.

"You're being passed on," said Tillana curtly. Kiadora felt a grin spread over her face.

"Really?" She had never felt happier to be out of a session set. Although she estimated that it was her shortest time yet. The hard manual labor and the monotonous routine made it feel twice as long.

"We've watched your progress with energy flow interaction. It seems you've been manipulating pattern flows and mixing energy with different plants during your work, almost like second nature."

Kiadora nodded, waiting to hear more about where to report next. It was true that she didn't even need to try anymore. The particles flowed where she wanted them to almost the instant she wished. She let them flow as her whim took her throughout the day. It was something to do other that just move the soil.

It had clicked after she had started using the wolfsbane and cinnamon. Her need had been so strong that the connection seemed to establish itself almost instantly and the plant did her bidding. No, worked with her. It wasn't long before she realized she could work with any plant. The need was felt, the connection established and the particles moved where they needed to. It was like guiding a well-trained horse to take her to the nearest town. A slight twitch of the reins was all that was needed.

"So everyone else can see what I'm doing?" She worried for a minute that they would see her carrying out her orders.

"With this much plant energy and this close, yes." Kiadora held in a breath that she desperately wanted to let out.

"So what's next?"

"Air," Tillana huffed. "You'd be best doing something useful in the fields, but I don't have a say over such things." And Tillana turned suddenly and stomped down the row.

CHAPTER 38

Kiadora rammed the edge of the blade deeper into the man's thigh. He let out a yell as he struggled to get away, but the yell did not go too far past the gag she had shoved into his mouth. Kiadora had his arms bound and his other leg pinned with her knee. Blood was welling up around the bayonet and running to the left, touching her own knee. She smirked behind the cloth that was wrapped around her face, obscuring everything but her eyes. Blood ran, just as she had wanted.

"We told you not to put the woman to death, still you did. This is your punishment."

"Ou woe eh?" the man managed through the handkerchief gag.

"Very astute of you," Kiadora replied, not knowing or caring what he had said. She twisted the blade, feeling it scrape against bone. She yanked it out as she was still twisting, trying to make it as painful as she knew how.

"Let that be a lesson to you," Kiadora said. "In the future, we will not be so forgiving."

And Kiadora walked away, letting the man lie there in pain. She made sure to have him in an alley behind an inn. Someone would find him when they brought out the trash at the end of the night. It made her more likely to be caught herself, but she was willing to take the risk. She didn't want the man to die.

Kiadora left the bayonet next to a dumpster and took a left into a darker alleyway. She didn't need someone to see the dark, shrouded figure with blood on its brown travel dress. Kiadora would need a new dress and would have to dispose of the old one as soon as she was able. She cursed herself for not wearing the red one. The blood would be less noticeable. But this was the ratty one she wore from home; all the better for it to be consecrated to her new purpose.

She wove down the back alleys. Some she remembered from her many nights out, and others she memorized off of a map Cyrus had passed on to her to make a more stealthy escape. His instructions had been very precise, from what way to leave, to what to say to the man, to how to take down a man twice her size. She had never realized just how much of a weak point the back of the knees, the stomach and the nose were.

As Cyrus explained the sharp jab to the back of the knees with the butt of the gun, the debilitating blow to the nose and gut, and pinning the man down and tying his mouth and hands, Kiadora had doubted her resolve. She didn't know if she could be that strong and skilled against a trained soldier. But, as Cyrus had told her, they had a repulsive habit of going out drinking to celebrate the destruction of a Shiekita. Normally they would be turned over to the Church this far south, but this one has been reputed to turn cows dry. Incurable.

Thanks to the alcohol, it had been a simple matter of calling the man down the alley in a half seductive tone after he was done relieving himself in the gutter. The alcohol practically did the rest.

Carrying the wolfsbane had made it easier also. For the first time, she could let out the rage she had been holding back for weeks on this one man. It had felt great to hear him cry out when she sent the butt of the gun flying. Now she was just tired, as if she had expelled all the aggression she needed to for right now.

It had felt too great, she realized upon reflection. That man was now wailing in agony because of her, regardless of what he had done. She had the nagging feeling of futility towards what she just did. Kiadora thought she would feel more accomplished after the act. But what she did didn't bring back that woman who had been beheaded or halt her death. It was too reflexive.

She was now on the deserted country road leading back to the compound. A hand lunged out of a nearby bush and dragged her into the foliage. She let out a cry as she lunged to the side and felt her face get scratched by branches. Cyrus stood there holding her by the shoulders.

"Is it done?"

"Yes," Kiadora said irritably, brushing leaves off of her. "And do you have to greet me that way?"

"It's best to remain obscure. Did you say what I told you?"

"Yes, I told him that next time we wouldn't be so forgiving."

"Good...good," he muttered. "You'll get more instructions soon. Oh, and here. You'll need to change now. We can't have you carrying blood-soaked evidence into the compound." He handed her another plain, brown dress. Kiadora gave him a pointed stare, and he turned away as she changed. Then he took the bloody dress and started to move off into the trees.

Kiadora grabbed his shoulder before he moved off farther into the woods.

"I didn't save that woman. She's still dead." That old agitation was starting to return; she wanted an argument. It was one of those times she couldn't tell if the herb had anything to do with it at all.

"More may be saved in the future. That's the best we can hope for at this point," he said in that rough tone of his. And he was gone into the trees.

Kiadora woke up in the crumpled, red dress she had been proud of a couple months before. The one from Cyrus had been too coarse to sleep in comfortably. It was the cheapest grade, as if it was stolen out of someone's servant quarters. 'Knowing these people, it probably was,' Kiadora thought.

She got up, splashed her face and tried to straighten out her dress as much as she could. Kiadora walked out of her room, nearly colliding with the messenger who was just swinging off the ladder.

"You must come before breakfast each morning," the man said awkwardly as an introduction, looking down at the ground. He looked like he was bracing himself against an explosive argument. He probably was used to them, after such a ridiculous demand.

"It is to make you more pure and focused," he explained. Kiadora grimaced.

"And what if I don't want to?"

"They won't feed you, even if you try to get food. You're on the list." Kiadora scowled and just motioned the man down the ladder. She remembered the fits people had in the dining room when they had been denied breakfast. It had been something about purity and focus then, too. She had been worried it would happen to her, especially considering how terribly she and Narissa had gotten along.

But those fits never went anywhere, even if a few of those people had to be carried out. They all seemed to get used to it, none returned. So she let the spindly kid lead the way to her next tedious lesson.

It was another winding trip down several rocky corridors that ended outside yet another heavy, oak door. The boy instructed her to wait, and she was left with the gnawing hunger in her stomach and the vague wonder at how they got so much heavy wood down here. Much less afforded it.

She waited, sitting, for what felt like an hour before the door swung open. Kiadora jumped up to find herself standing face-to-face with a woman who had plain brown hair that was tied back tightly. Kiadora realized she would have used the word wrestled instead of tied, as the woman didn't seem to be too interested in making sure it was combed. It had that tangled and frayed look that meant her hair was neglected, rather than just curly.

The woman also wore a rather dull, gray traveling dress, similar to what Kiadora wore until just recently. It actually looked like the one Cyrus had just given her: coarse, tight and unrelenting in every way. The dress looked as if it was the first one the woman had picked up in a hurry.

The woman stepped to the side, holding an arm out to motion

Kiadora in. She had a tight, small smile on, as if the action wasn't a habit for her.

As expected, the room was as plain and dull as the woman. A wooden desk sat with two wooden chairs facing each other across the desk. Next to the chair, closest to Kiadora, was a writing board propped on its side. It was the type they used in schools in slightly poorer areas, which were held on the lap and written on with chalk. It was far cheaper than actual desks.

The walls had a couple of charts with arrows curving between cramped writing that Kiadora couldn't quite make out. A few displayed circles with small hash marks in them. A few plain, wooden cabinets completed the ensemble.

The woman walked over to Kiadora and put out a hand in a businesslike manner.

"Delandea," she said, shaking Kiadora's hand firmly. And then she turned to sit lightly down behind the desk. Kiadora assumed she should follow and took a seat, feeling like she was sitting before a teacher's desk after she had been called in for throwing rocks at someone who was teasing her.

"As you've probably gathered, you've entered your Air lessons. And at a remarkable pace, considering the circumstances. Congratulations on that."

"Uh, thanks…" Kiadora hadn't expected any compliments out of this woman.

"You are entering an extremely varied discipline. So as Air covers and encases nearly everything in the natural world and can work on many levels itself, so will your studies. There will be reading, writing and practicing hands-on exercises, so to speak. You will test your mind, your spirit and tax your emotions."

Kiadora remained silent. She dared not let herself actually feel excited. It sounded intense, and after her work in the gardens the word "varied" sounded like a trumpet from paradise. But she had a way of getting let down.

"Do you know of the spirits, the soul?" Delandea asked abruptly.

"I've heard of them. Mostly about how corrupt they can become if not praying enough, though…" Kiadora trailed off as she examined this woman's deep azure eyes. They had an intense, penetrating quality. She could tell they missed little, and something about the woman's gaze told of a deep intelligence. This woman knew things, and she knew that she knew things. Their bright quality nearly offset the rest of her plain appearance.

"Like most who come here, you have a lot to learn." Her tone was not condescending. It was merely a fact.

"Many things can be done with the soul and other departed souls," she continued, looking unblinkingly into Kiadora's eyes. "You can warp the soul, grow the soul, shrink the soul. The soul can transcend body, time and space. You can conjoin souls, destroy souls, and most importantly, learn from souls. They're the ultimate putty of the cosmos, but it had to be *done right* or a lot of damage can occur. The last thing we're here to do at this stage is to break down what the soul has worked hard to build up." "Damage?"

"We don't need to focus on that right now. If you do things right, you have little to worry about."

Delandea stood up from her desk and walked to a cabinet where she started pulling down scrolls from seemingly random places. She came back with a stack of about five scrolls and put them down on the table. She scribbled on a blank piece of parchment and handed the piece to Kiadora. It was a list of chapters from each scroll.

"I'll know if you don't read. Keep in mind, I can send you back to the gardens any day," said Delandea in a clam tone.

Kiadora felt her mood plummet. She assumed she was past the days of endless, mandatory study out of books. There had been nothing more tedious than reading ream after ream of text about things that transpired hundreds of years ago.

She felt further dread as she looked at the titles Delandea had jotted down: *Great Religions of the East, God in the Desert, Theological Views Through Time, When God Came to Man, Faith Without a Higher Power.* The last one just confused her. The rest would undoubtedly bore her.

What was more confusing was where these would have been from and who had written them and when. Things like this didn't just pop up in libraries on the surface. She only saw a few books from the surface in the libraries down here, not that she looked much. Anything on religion above was just endless talk and analysis of the Holy Text.

"These have been compiled by our advanced academic workers, the Surinas of Air," said Delandea, apparently reading Kiadora's look of confusion. "Some are recorded after travels, others are replications of texts found abroad. They're not always 100 percent reliable, so keep that in mind, but they get the gist of what they are talking about. And really, what is that reliable?"

Delandea let the question hang in the air as she retreated back to the cupboards. Kiadora expected still more scrolls, but instead Delandea brought forth a little mandolin. She walked back to Kiadora, cradling it gently.

"Have you ever had any experience playing music?" Kiadora shook her head. She had been instructed to sing in school a couple of times, but her voice always came out soft and shy. No one mentioned any striking musical ability, and Kiadora liked it that way. She didn't need people looking at her as she went through the religious motions.

Delandea handed the instrument to Kiadora, who held it the way she had seen performers hold guitars in the past, resting it on her leg, draping her right arm over it and holding the long part with her left hand.

"You're a natural already," Delandea said humorlessly. "Do you know why music is tied in with the element of Air?"

Kiadora frowned as she thought, no answers coming to her.

"Music is the expression of the soul, the ethereal, the untouchable. Just as Air is our driving force, but ethereal and untouchable," said Delandea. "Also, music is carried by Air. Many cultures think that their music can be taken up to a deity through Air. It is a common medium to the gods, and that is why it is the dominant element on the surface."

"Is that why we always sang so much in services?"

"Most likely. Now, calm your mind and steady your breathing. Play whatever you feel."

Kiadora hesitated, staring at the statuesque woman who stood before her. It seemed so unstructured for this woman.

"I...I don't know how to even play this thing, I don't even know what to do."

"You will."

Kiadora looked into those azure eyes, as clear and expansive as the sky itself. Kiadora closed her eyes and slowed her breathing. She let her mind float in that area of nothing, which seemed to resemble a dreamless sleep.

Opening her eyes and keeping that state, moving as a sleepwalker would, she let her fingers strum at the cords, instantly getting a feel for where the highest and lowest pitched strings were. She pressed down on the fingerboard with her index finger and pulled her other hand across the strings of the instrument, experiencing each note resonating. Somehow, the state she forced on herself made the sounds that much sweeter. It was like they were resonating at her core, each note warping her soul like Delandea said they could.

Slowly, a low and steady tune emerged, a melancholic lilt that steadily built speed and vigor. It was a simple and quick tune, like one that might be heard at the docks when bored sailors with limited musical training came to town and played tunes on accordians, but the tune kept those low notes and slight minor key.

Kiadora realized she could go for hours when Delandea finally placed a hand on her shoulder and squeezed slightly, bringing Kiadora out of it. She felt like she was just reaching her stride.

"That is what we call a Heart's Song or a Soul Song," Delandea said. "It is a person in their most connected state, their purest meditational form just playing what their soul dictates. They tend to be crude at first, matching skill level, but the basic notes and key are already there."

Kiadora nodded, running her hand over the strings at the base of the board. She wanted to keep playing more than anything.

"Eventually you will take the instrument with you. There are some caverns that are good for practicing without disturbing others. But right now we shall build skill here."

Kiadora's heart sunk, realizing that she had to leave the mandolin here. It already felt like an extension of her. Kiadora almost whined like a distressed puppy as Delandea came around the desk, took it from Kiadora and put it back in the cabinet.

Delandea came back toward Kiadora, scooped up the scrolls off her desk and dumped them into Kiadora's arms. She slipped the reading list between two of Kiadora's fingers.

Kiadora walked out the door and heard Delandea say, "till tomorrow," as the woman closed the door.

It was the first time, Kiadora realized, that she was actually in the library with any purpose, and she felt like she was noticing it for the first time, as a result. The library was far better lit than her quarters, and she figured she had less chance of falling asleep if she wasn't on her bed.

She glanced at Astrian, who was sitting in the middle of the room to the left of a crowd of people laughing at a book they had found. They both nodded curtly to each other as Kiadora found a desk among the bookshelves so as not to get distracted by the chatter. She remembered the libraries on the surface being a lot more calm and quiet. On the other hand, this library didn't have the same stuffy, moldering feel as the ones above. On the surface, the air always felt heavy with years of people reading the same thing through the ages. Everyone looked so bored.

This library was light, lively and full of people just looking for oddball tidbits of knowledge just for the fun of it, then sharing it with anyone who was around. It was one of the reasons she came in here when she was bored so often, she realized, even if she tended to stay away from large groups. She just loved the atmosphere.

As she got into her reading, she realized that the passages she had been assigned definitely fell into the category of oddball as well. Her reading consisted of several classifications of strange faiths she had never heard of: a nomadic tribe that thought mucus was a sacred blessing agent (they were extinct now), a desert tribe to the West that felt their god lived under the sand somewhere, some forest dwellers who prayed while hanging from top tree branches, a remote tribe to the Northwest that spent half the growing season harvesting corn at several intervals in the season to sacrifice to their slew of 20 gods.

By the end of her reading, which took about five hours by her estimation (the lights were starting to dim), her head was swimming with all the information she had just processed.

She read about countries far West that she barely even knew were there, much less anything about their religious customs. Somehow, Kiadora realized, she had gone her whole life just assuming everyone worshiped the same god in the same way as her people did. How could she have been so stupid? Apparently, there were as many ways to worship gods as there were people. Most of them insane, but still!

She actually looked forward to talking about this in class tomorrow.

CHAPTER 39

Kiadora barged through Delandea's door the following morning with her arms full of the scrolls she had been given. She dumped them onto Delandea's desk. The woman looked up with hardly a blink at being interrupted in whatever she was writing.

"I had no idea!" Kiadora blurted out. "There are so many ways to see gods, and here I spent most of my life thinking there was just the one way on the surface! Most of them are stupid, but just that fact that they are out there..."

Delandea shook her head and held up her hand to stop Kiadora from speaking.

"That's a common mistake made by new students to this area of study. You assume they are stupid, nonsensical, vague and weird. I did once, too. You will see that they are not so different in their own way. That is the point of comparative study. What similarities did you see?"

Kiadora sat down in front of the desk, miffed that she was not going to spend a whole day laughing at inferior ways.

"I don't know, they all seemed so different. Some have many, many gods, some have one like the Church, some have no gods…and their customs seem like they were just pulled out of someone's imagination."

"They were. But there's an undercurrent there I beg you to see. Think for a minute."

Kiadora stared dully at the ground, going over small tidbits of facts she had picked up from reading last night. There was the fact that the second harvest for the tribe to the Northeast was called the weepening, which Kiadora just thought sounded funny. The blessing agent, also known as mucus, was always dabbed right between the breasts of women, which was just awkward. And speaking of awkward, another culture didn't wear clothes during worship at all.

"They're just so different," Kiadora said. "I thought this was to just open my eyes."

"It's to start to," Delandea agreed. "But there's more. You have the same reading assignment tonight. I want you to come back with a list of similarities that you find."

Kiadora nodded, knowing that it would go as horribly as it was right now.

Then Delandea stood up and went right to the cupboard. Kiadora perked up when Delandea brought out the mandolin. She also brought out a booklet with the same hash marks on the cover as some of the wall charts.

"You remember yesterday?"

"Yes, the Soul Song. Do I get to do more of that?"

"Not quite yet. Now we will work on skill."

And the rest of the day was just that. Kiadora sat in the hard, wooden chair, steadily feeling a pain in her lower back growing while she held the mandolin and tried her best to memorize where she was to put her hand and how fast she was to play the notes in accordance with the appearance of the hash marks.

A taller mark meant she had to play the note longer and a line half that short meant she had to play it for half the time. After a while, the hash marks started to blur together for Kiadora, and she was forced to squint at the slight size differences of the marks.

The marks also sat inside circles, and depending on where the marks were in the circles, that was where she was to put her hands on the strings. Some patterns required her to stretch her fingers into seemingly impossible positions, and the tips of her fingers soon began to ache. This wasn't the spiritually deep and fun experience of yesterday by a long shot.

Delandea stood there, assuring Kiadora that it would eventually lead to a more rich Soul Song experience, but first one must put forth the necessary effort. She tapped Kiadora's fingers when they weren't stretched enough or her hand was on the wrong part of the fingerboard.

At the end of the day, Kiadora meandered out of the room, turning at a tap on the shoulder just outside the door. Delandea dumped the scrolls into her hands, the tips of Kiadora's fingers aching at the very touch of the scroll cases. Delandea gave her a quick reminder about the list, and Kiadora was alone in the corridor.

At dinner, Kiadora sat with the scrolls at her feet, wincing at the use of her knife. Delandea had said calluses would form, and then it wouldn't hurt as long as she kept her practicing up. Using a pen to write would be pure agony. She vaguely wondered why they had chosen such a painful instrument for her.

At the end of the night, Kiadora threw down her pen in disgust. In her bad mood, she had forgotten that she was right-handed and did the work with the fingerboard with her left hand, so she didn't want to scream in pain at the thought of writing a word.

Still, she remained hung up on the similarities of the several faiths. The more she read, the more she was bogged down by all the little details of what everyone practiced. There was no way sacrificing one of the village huts to be burned each year was anything like digging a hole to find God. These practices didn't even make any sense, let alone have any similarities.

Well, it had one. It was all stupid, and a waste of time and resources. But Delandea had said that was a mistake made by the new students.

Kiadora tapped her pen on the bit of parchment she was supposed to have filled by now. She had to write something; at least look like she had tried.

'They all…' Kiadora thought. 'They all…they all…they all *what?* Believe in something, even if it's stupid.'

"They all have faith in something and have practices to honor it," Kiadora wrote. She figured it would look like she had tried if she wrote at least four things.

"They all have ritualized practices," Kiadora continued.

"They all have to please what they believe in."

"They all do things to honor what they think of as god."

Kiadora looked over her list, knowing full well it was just restating the same couple of points, essentially. Maybe Delandea wouldn't notice.

"You're close," Delandea said, holding the list delicately between thin fingers.

Kiadora looked sharply at her teacher from where she had been staring at a chart on the wall.

"You have the word faith in here. The rest are just restatements of the same surface observations, and I think you know that." Kiadora smirked sheepishly.

"But you are close to getting at the heart of this, and you would have gotten there if you had not been so eager to finish. They all have faith, even if what they do looks silly sometimes. They have hunches about what cannot be seen directly, and they hold that very dearly in here," Delandea said. She tapped her chest over where her heart was. "That is why they do what they do. Expression of that hunch just comes to different cultures in different ways because it comes to different people in different ways."

"But doesn't that mean it's just the imagination, the way I would view a verbal story differently from someone else or see the true meaning of a play?"

Delandea let out a small smile.

"Yes, imagination and imagery play a large part in it. It is hard to explain at this stage, but you will get there and understand. This is a foundation course to expose you to the idea of faith experienced in different ways. It's not a lesson people come down here having experienced in our country."

"Does that mean I don't have to do that much reading after this?"

"Oh no, this is the stage where you learn all you can about the world and different practices." And with that, Delandea reached down behind her desk and brought up a large bundle of scrolls, about two-thirds larger than last night's bundle. It was so large that this one was bound with a leather strap and a thin cloth for easier carrying.

"You'll need all of these read by the end of your two days off." Kiadora nearly let her mouth drop open.

As if it was a warm piece of bakery, Delandea pushed the stack of scrolls toward Kiadora with a friendly smile.

"Let's get started on your music lessons, shall we?"

CHAPTER 40

Kiadora sent another shovel of dirt flying, the dirt hitting a tree in the dense forest. Now in addition to her fingers aching from her music lessons, her shoulders and arms felt like they were on fire. It had taken the better part of three nights, but digging a hole that was 9 feet deep was not easy. She had been able to see the flow of Eatheria particles around any major rocks and dug around them, but she still wanted to fall over. And the worst of the job was not even completed.

She hauled a large, tightly sealed crate out from behind a bush. She had been told that it would be here on the third night, so she had better have been done by tonight. Cyrus had told her that if she wanted to be really ambitious, she could put sharpened spikes at the bottom of the pit. He had said that with the utmost seriousness, and Kiadora had just stared. She doubted she could do what she needed to with the meat.

The plan was almost pathetically simple. Every night one of the town guards went traipsing through this area on his way to visit a sweetheart. Kiadora had to admit, the level of knowledge that these people had of the area was astonishing. It was Kiadora's job to pretend she had sprained her ankle and call him over. The pit was nearly invisible in the dark, especially after she threw a mesh tarp on the thing. She was just in the process of covering it with some early fall leaves when she heard a man come crashing through the bushes. Kiadora ran around the pit and dropped to the ground.

"Hello, is someone there?" she called.

The man emerged from a bush and stopped to look around for the source of the voice.

"Down here," Kiadora called again.

The man looked down, scratching at his side under his unbuttoned, dark blue guard's coat.

"Oh, God above, are you alright?" the man asked in a high tenor.

"No, I sprained my ankle. I was on my way to the playhouse, and I thought this would be faster." Kiadora let out a forced laugh, which she realized sounded more nervous than she wanted it to. She was also talking very fast. She hated lying.

"Anyway, I tripped on a tree root. You don't suppose you could help me into town?"

"Why sure, miss." The way he jumped forward and that high tenor made Kiadora think of a puppy eager to please. She turned red with shame as she realized what was about to happen.

Just as predicted, the man tread over the tarp, which promptly gave way. The man disappeared from sight. Kiadora jumped up and looked down at the man, or at the boy she realized, as he stared up at her in shock.

"What in the Otherworld, lady?" he yelled up at her with a whiny quality to his voice now. Kiadora retreated from the edge of the pit, resisting the urge to give the man a long stick to climb out with and explain that it was all a practical joke. She shuddered at the thought that if she had followed Cyrus' advice, the man would be impaled and dying a slow death already.

Kiadora went to the crate and started to work her fingers under a wax seal put in place to prevent any scent from escaping. She would throw the meat down on the man and expect the wolves to come.

"Let me out of here!" the boy yelled from behind. "This isn't funny, girl."

Kiadora stared down at the crate for a second, feeling like she was about to cry. As if the motion had been decided for her, she grabbed the crate and ran farther into the woods. She found a grove, undid the rest of the seal with a fast movement of her hand and dumped about two dozen steaks onto the ground. Her own mouth watered as she realized that she hadn't had a steak in over a year, at least.

'What a waste,' she thought. But she had to make it look like she dumped the meat, and animals would clear it out. Someone would find the man, they had to. This was a popular shortcut to the neighboring farms from the town, they said. His girl would go looking for him, at least, Kiadora reasoned.

Kiadora went running back and threw the crate down the hole. The man was still yelling, but she let her own hard breathing drown out what he was saying. She headed towards the path and went sprinting back to the cavern.

'Oh, damn.' Standing next to a hedge along the trail was Cyrus, with both hands in his pockets, waiting for her. He had on his dark, long coat and wide-brimmed hat like normal and looked like the shadow of a tree at first glance.

She halted beside him, still catching her breath. She grinned sheepishly.

"It's done."

"No, it isn't. Empty your pockets," he demanded in a harsh tone.

Kiadora dipped her hands into her pockets and came out with nothing. Cyrus lunged his arm forward and poked a hard surface in her pocket around her thigh.

"You didn't leave the note."

"Oh," Kiadora let out a little laugh. "So I didn't." It was a cryptic line that she was supposed to leave that read, "So as you trap us, so we trap you." It was to be pinned to a tree.

"That man isn't even dead," said Cyrus. It wasn't a suggestion, but stated as a fact. Kiadora just looked off to the hedge behind Cyrus.

Cyrus' hand shot out at her with lightning speed and he grabbed her chin in one hand. For a moment, Kiadora though he was going to bring a knife around to her throat.

"Listen, if you cannot perform the tasks as requested, we will not hesitate to dispose of you. That being said, we need you in this. You will get one more chance to complete a task as assigned. If that cannot be completed, let's just say the compound won't necessarily miss you."

He grabbed the note out of her pocket, let go of her chin roughly and withdrew into the hedge. Kiadora stood for a moment rubbing her chin, hoping it wouldn't bruise. A part of her almost wanted to call the man's bluff. Her sudden disappearance would look too suspicious. On the other hand, she didn't know how high this thing went up. It was possible she could die in the name of the cause and not a thing would be done about it.

As she shoved her hands into her pockets and walked back to the cavern entrance, she realized she forgot to bring the wolfsbane. 'Hm, no wonder.' Still, she thought with a pang of loneliness, if Astrian knew she was doubting these events as much as to forget the herb, he would be pleased. But she had no choice for her next job. If they ordered the entire slaughter of a village, she was in a place where she had to comply. No wonder Astrian had told her to turn back. She cursed herself for her foolishness as she entered the cavern to descend further.

Still reeling from the night before and Cyrus' threat, Kiadora knocked on the door to Delandea's room. She was instructed to come in and was greeted by a sofa placed close to the door. At least it would be a rest for her sore arms and shoulders.

Kiadora walked over to the desk and handed Delandea a small slip of parchment that she had scribbled a short paragraph on. It was to compare specific prayers from somewhere in the swamp lands, and Kiadora had knocked off the stupid thing in ten minutes.

"Please lie down," said Delandea without even looking at the parchment she placed on the desk after Kiadora handed it over. Kiadora gratefully rested her sore back on the sofa. It wasn't exactly plush, and the sofa was covered in a coarse material, but it beat the wooden chair. Kiadora stared up at the craggy ceiling, one of the many constant reminders that these were still just caves despite the lights, ornate doors and furniture. Delandea floated into view, her expression looking more harsh at a lower angle. Kiadora wondered briefly if she as in trouble, if somehow someone had heard about her recent deeds.

"Are you familiar with astral projection?" Delandea asked instead.

"Can't say that I am," Kiadora said as she let out a breath.

"It's the practice of detaching the soul from the body."

"Like in dying?" Kiadora nearly shrieked, sitting up. Delandea put a hand on Kiadora's shoulder and gently guided her down.

"No, not in the same sense. You are still connected to your body via your nexus point here," said Delandea, pointing at Kiadora's chest. Kiadora squirmed, being glad she wasn't a member of the mucus culture. "It's like there is a string holding your soul to your heart. Some people see it, and some people don't. I need you to go into a meditative state. I will be able to tell when you do, and at that point, you will follow my voice, and visualize what I say."

Kiadora nodded a little nervously and slowed her breathing, but then remembered the nexus cord she saw when dream hopping. Kiadora now worked to keep her mind clear. She now knew how instinctively, as she had a way of feeling like she was floating in a void almost instantly. It was the essence of peace.

From far off, Delandea's voice came.

"Focus on the darkness in front of you. Just see it, view it as if you were looking at any object."

Under normal circumstances, Kiadora knew she would just give Delandea a confused look, but in this state, it made sense. It was like she was becoming aware of the darkness on a whole new level, staring into the abyss that she usually took for granted. It seemed that instead of staring at the back of her eyelids, she was in a large, dark expanse that elongated the more she focused on it. Though it was a feeling, rather than a visual cue, as everything was dark.

"Hold that awareness," came Delandea's voice. And Kiadora floated in that expanded emptiness. Against her control, she could feel herself fly upward.

And then the colors started. She could see a deep brown, a lighter brown and shades of deep and vibrant green.

Unbidden, the alien sensations came next. She could feel a sort of… sturdiness in her middle. A coolness was near the bottom of her body, and at her top, she didn't feel her head, but hundreds of small, wispy segments brushed together in a single wave.

Kiadora felt the top of her sway, the middle of her steady as a rock and the bottom of her was cool, damp and seemed to be taking something in that she would never be able to give a word to. It was like…drinking. Out of many different feet.

Vaguely, Kiadora wondered if she should panic. But something about it just felt right, whole…natural. So she stayed wherever this world was and just enjoyed the sun warm those many wisps that made up her head. Then a realization hit: 'I'm in a tree.' And yet, for some reason, that didn't seem so weird at the moment. It seemed like that was just where she should be.

So she stayed, feeling the sun shift its position throughout the day, warming other leaves, she now knew. She could still see those same earthly colors. Her middle, her trunk, had small rodents running up and down it, but that was alright. What else was she there for, besides the small amount of gas she could feel flow out her leaves. What was it she provided? Oxygen, she had learned in school. Through it all, her roots drank and drank, taking in the nutrients and moisture from the soil, until she was satisfied for a while.

The sun started to set, and she could feel her leaves grow colder but not the same kind of cold that made her shiver. Just a sort of coolness that was more of a nonthreatening statement of fact. She wondered if trees slept at night and then thought of her own bed. She remembered Delandea must still be sitting by her. It must have been a full day that she was up here.

So how to get back? She remembered her own body on that hard sofa for a full day without food. With that thought, she could feel herself withdraw out of the leaves, down through the bark, out of the roots and travel through a dark brown substance that she knew was soil. She passed through gray rock as if it was nothing and was sitting up on the sofa with a start.

Delandea looked up from a book.

"Oh, good. You're back," she said in an even tone.

"I was a tree!" Kiadora said, pushing her hair back from where it had flown in her face. "For a whole day, and it wasn't even boring. It just felt right."

"I'm glad you cut it short. Some people leave for a month, and we have to feed their bodies with liquified food."

"Some people don't come back?"

"Poor young Hyan took up residence in a badger and can't figure out how to get back, despite the lessons."

"You have to teach a badger?"

"A badger with a human soul," Delandea corrected. "Smaller animals are easy to take over. He's accommodating. He comes down to us." Kiadora just stared as Delandea looked at her with the utmost serious expression. Then Delandea looked down and brought up a pail with a handkerchief over it.

"You'll want to eat. It's the ultimate way to ground your soul." Kiadora grabbed that pail with a muttered, "thank you," and she started devouring the bread that sat at the top. Under it was dried meat and some cheese that she couldn't wait for.

As she ate, she reflected on the experience.

"So was I really the tree?" she asked through a mouthful of cheese.

"Oh yes," said Delandea. "Everything is made of energy, of Eatheria, and the soul is the purest form. You combined your essence with that of the tree's." Kiadora nodded, not knowing what to say.

"And that expanding dark abyss I saw before I left?"

"We don't have a uniform explanation for that," said Delandea. "Many theories exist: some think it is a sort of holding ground that the soul goes to in preparation for higher workings, others think it is the view of a sort of metaphysical casing the soul is housed in that must be stretched to exit and still I've heard it said that we are viewing reality as it truly is: an abyss of total peace, free from the ego. Entire religions chase after that last one."

"There are a lot of theories for everything, isn't there?" Kiadora said as she swallowed the last zesty sliver of spiced jerky. Delandea handed her a glass bottle of water that came with the meal.

"We work in the realm of mysteries, Kiadora. If there was a unified understanding of everything, we wouldn't have our paths to find and follow. And then what would be the point?"

"It'd be easier," said Kiadora after downing the whole bottle of water in one go.

"But without evolution. Growth and learning abide in the heart of challenge. You can leave the pail here, the kitchen isn't open right now." Kiadora stood up and walked toward the door, feeling oddly invigorated. As she went out into the corridor, she was met with the dim lighting of after hours.

"Besides," Delandea called out through the door. "If there was really one answer to everything, all of us would have kept to the surface." She closed the door, and Kiadora stood there considering.

"Good point," she said to the darkness.

It was different this time. After the stretching darkness, she was flying up and up until she was sailing through the stars. Small points of light raced past her until they were nothing but lines. How long this went on, Kiadora could not tell.

And then she could feel herself hanging in a black void. It came quite out of nowhere. The stars disappeared and then she felt like she was going upward. Then she just hung there. She looked down for the first time and she saw it: her own body hung, naked, silvery and malleable like liquid metal. She could sense a cord that was going down and out of sight, the line back to her own body.

It had been weeks of sitting in that tree before she finally felt brave enough to venture into the sky. She didn't make the effort, it just sort of happened when she felt ready. Then there were the stars. Then after weeks there was peace.

She sat, or rather just existed there for some time. Just out of range in her field of vision she saw something move. It was a blue, fluid shape, lacking any sort of distinct form. She rotated her field of vision; how she did it she wasn't so sure since she felt like she was just floating among nothing. The blue form flitted to the side with her field of vision adjustment, hanging in the peripheral.

And Kiadora could feel herself being pulled back and back, until she was sitting up on the sofa next to Delandea.

"I saw someone…something, in that dark abyss," Kiadora said. Delandea just made a thin smile.

"What did it look like?"

"I couldn't see it directly. It looked blue, and then I was on my way back. I think I talked to him in the Water sessions. He was a little rude."

"The Ashileks can be blunt. They have a message to impart, and they forget human emotions sometimes. You're very lucky. Not everyone gets one. They tend to find those with the most to learn, the largest hardships to work through and the most latent curiosity. You'll most certainly be in for some interesting lessons. Now here's your reading," said Delandea, dumping a pile of scrolls into Kiadora's lap. "I want an essay listing the cultures' worship times and the reasons behind them."

CHAPTER 41

Kiadora walked into Delandea's room balancing the scrolls and clutching a paper of her own hasty cursive in one hand. Like usual, it had taken the better part of the evening, reading excerpts out of the scrolls Delandea had designated and writing a comparison of different worship times.

They met at all times conceivable, these far away cultures that Kiadora had previously not known existed. Some met during certain moon phases, others certain days of the week like Kiadora was used to and others gathered when the sun was at a certain point in the sky or on solstices and equinoxes. Still others gathered when the tides came in or when the hour struck noon every day. More gathered at sunset, and one culture gathered for worship when the town leader started her menstrual cycle.

The reasons spanned the boundaries of logic. All felt there was something distantly divine about these times, be it because they worshiped a sun god or felt a woman's time was a source of metaphysical power and therefore sacred.

The more complex civilizations met at times of convenience, like between conventional work breaks. Some breaks coincided with an intricate story. A region far to the South took off every two weeks for three days because they felt that was when their deity commanded it to a town leader, who heard it in a dream. Kiadora wondered if she could command two day work weeks if she told enough people that God spoke to her. Nevertheless, she had dutifully listed all the times and reasons per Delandea's written instructions, a paragraph for each type of gathering ("natural events," "day of the week," "time of day" and, for lack of a better category, "human reasons"). But still she had struggled. Many didn't mention why these practices were held when they were.

Kiadora dropped the scrolls on Delandea's desk and handed her the parchment.

"Here, a list of everything anyone needed to know about worship times. Except for some, I couldn't find reasons. I looked forever for some of them," she added hurriedly. She didn't want to have to do the whole thing over again. Plus, it had annoyed her. She wanted to know why a group of old men over in the Galadan Islands met at a stony outcropping every solar eclipse.

Delandea scanned the document.

"Good, some reasons simply aren't listed. Any conclusions?" Kiadora let out a long breath and stared at the rocky ceiling, thinking.

"Well, for one thing, it doesn't seem to matter what time people meet. It's all equally important to each of them." Delandea nodded her approval.

"Right. Did you know that we still have people down here who try to regularly engage in prayer weekly, like above?" Kiadora thought of the Children. It had been about weekly.

"I've heard."

"The Holy Text dictates it, of course. It was the number of days it took their god to banish the Earth Shiekita from the forests to make the world habitable for man. Not many people even remember that anymore."

"*I* didn't know that," Kiadora admitted.

"But you see, even those who don't even believe in the Earth Shiekita still hold this practice. Many of us feel that the notion of Shiekita is a bastardization of Eatheria. But still people pray weekly, even if it is not to what they saw as god previously. They pray to spirits, they pray to Eatheria itself or some just stay in that night to hone their meditation skills." Delandea threw up her hand and had started pacing. Kiadora felt startled. The woman was usually so composed.

"Come to think of it, there is a weekly period where the crowds about seem a little more sparse," said Kiadora conversationally, trying to break the tension in the other woman. Delandea stopped pacing and turned to face Kiadora. She took a breath and seemed to compose herself. Kiadora stared back, not knowing what to say.

"Sorry, such blind ignorance is too much sometimes. The point is, people do these things without even remembering why. The Elders will usually know, but these people don't. Sometimes these people will become the Elders and still never know. I had the pleasure to speak to the older men in the Galadan Islands."

"They didn't tell you why they meet just then?"

"No! I asked them several times in different ways why the solar eclipse, why not the lunar eclipse or the last day of the week or someone's birthday? They looked at each other, and then one said, 'because it's always been this way.' Imagine, a whole religious rite conducted at a certain time, and no one knows why!"

"Can't be a very good rite then," Kiadora said.

"Ah, but that's just it. It's beautiful. It's poetic, rife with intricate dances, and everyone walks away feeling recharged. And that's why you hit the nail on the head earlier. Sometimes, there are no reasons for beliefs and practices. The details don't really matter. It's felt on some primal level unique to the people. It's as if they're turtles, returning to the same breeding grounds by instinct. It gets frustrating to the higher reasoning capabilities, not having all the answers and not knowing why you have the answers you do. Sometimes, like the weekly prayers, it's habit, pure and simple. Or there could be a deeper power to the weekly cycle that we're not fully aware of. But sometimes, you have a whole group of people who meet at a naturally significant event because it just feels right. You're at a point, Kiadora, where you'll start to know things without knowing how the answers come to you. It's not strange, or unusual, call it intuition."

"Things? What sort of things?" Kiadora worried about the delusions people got down here. She thought back to when she could have sworn it was a good idea to walk into a fire.

"Things you'll know are the right answer without a doubt when they hit you. You'll learn to see the reality from the delusion." Delandea stared pointedly at her, and Kiadora could tell they both shared a mental image of Aeliean. "Not everyone can, but you'll get there. You already found your Ashilek, after all." Kiadora stared at the floor.

"What if he's a delusion?"

"They'll tell you things you can verify independently. Is there any such way to do so?"

"Yeah, I have to talk to a man. Do you know where I can find Broean?"

"He takes pride in stocking the Eternal Fires. You can go there now. The music lessons can wait." Kiadora nodded, said thanks, and was out the door.

On her way through the corridors, Kiadora rubbed her thumb against the tips of her fingers. Delandea had been right, the calluses had formed. It was also easier to read the music now; she didn't have to stop to remember what a marking meant. Some shorter songs she even had memorized. But there were still the more complex cords and faster songs to master, which still left her hands and arms aching afterwards. She wandered down the hall and made it to the Eternal Fires faster than she had hoped.

She had been back often to meditate since she went on with the other lessons. She always left feeling recharged, like she could tackle anything. She came close to once a week, she realized.

The familiar warmth of the flames hit her face as she entered, shadows dancing on the walls. In many ways, they rivaled any play on the surface. Broean sat at the edge next to a large stack of wood, watching the flames intensely. He quickly heaved a large log into the right side of the flame.

"Broean!" Kiadora called as she walked up. "How's it been?" He looked around and grinned as he saw Kiadora.

"Hey, kid, thought you'd be back."

"You know what I'm going to ask?"

"You have to verify your Ashilek somehow."

"So you saw him?"

"Clear as day. He's a spirited fellow. You should like him in time."

"In time? He was sort of rude."

"They all take some getting used to. Eatheria has a way of handing you exactly what you need. That's not always easy. So he told me to use the drug trick. " Broean lifted a large metal rod and poked the fire with. "Said you needed a smack to the brain, and that should do it."

"But how did you know it was him? I mean, I dream stuff all the time, it doesn't mean it's a spirit."

"It's a strange feeling, but you know when you dream and are spoken to. The dreams are more…real…hard to explain, anyway."

"No, I get it," said Kiadora, remembering seeing Cyrus for the first time. She watched Broean select a smaller log and fling it into the middle of the fire, trying to forget those moments.

"What did he look like?" she finally asked. "I mean, when I saw him, he was a blue groundhog. Do they always look like that…like…"

"A solid, liquid and gas all at once?" Broean offered.

"Yeah."

"They take a true shape later. You'll find his shape. Their shape tends to mirror your personality."

"So it will look like me?" Broean let out a husky laugh.

"Not quite. You'll see." Kiadora stared for a moment.

"Well, I actually left a lesson to come find you, better get back."

"Who you got?"

"Delandea." Broean nodded.

"Hard, but good."

The darkness spanned once more. She didn't know how long she was there, but as she half expected it would, the blue, shimmering being reappeared.

Follow me, it said in its ageless, curt voice. Kiadora saw it dance to the right and felt herself move in that direction. It wasn't that she was being pulled, but more like she wanted to go in that direction and her line of vision made it so. She saw the blue form dance off in the distance, too far the see any sort of a shape. Kiadora knew she was moving forward, though there were no visual cues to reveal the fact.

Farther away, in a cylinder around the Ashilek, she could see a blue-green so radiant it was like coming out at the end of a tunnel. The new color expanded until Kiadora was immersed completely.

"Where am I?"

Just feel it.

Kiadora let a wave of sensations overtake her. First there was the certain feeling of...vastness. Kiadora knew she didn't take up the usual human height and weight of a woman. That same feeling of presence and control spanned outward into obscure distances.

Everything was blue, everything felt fluid. In the outer edges of her presence she could feel a sense of rolling: back and forth, back and forth.

But for as wide as she was, she was also deep. She could feel the warmth at the top of her and coolness at the bottom. Innumerable

515

objects moved within her, but it was fine. It felt like they belonged there, much like the small animals in that tree. The sea life was a fluttering sensation across her vast presence.

More than that were the emotions. She felt calm, more calm that she had ever felt in her life. If there was an epitome of peace, she was now peace itself. And there was a level of benevolence that she never knew: all things came from her and all things depended on her, so why be angry? They were all hers. She let herself float in the peace, loving everything in a way she thought she never could. Kiadora could have stayed like that forever.

After a while she heard, *Remember this, damn you!*

Then the blue was fading and her presence was shrinking. She was back in the dark pool of complete nothingness. But the calm and munificence remained.

Then Kiadora was sitting up, feeling a little more jolted. Slowly, she felt some of the mental pressure return: the readings, the musical cords giving her trouble and Cyrus.

'Damn it.'

Remember this, damn you, the spirit had said. But the slight dampness of the remote caves came back. The dampness was a sensation Kiadora had come to associate with isolation, unlike the fluid inclusion of what she was beginning to realize must have been the ocean.

"Have you ever been to the ocean?" Kiadora asked Delandea, who was sitting and reading a scroll by the sofa. Delandea regarded her for a moment.

"A few times," she said. "I was a street child, so I went where I wanted."

"I've never been there," Kiadora said. Her parents where always tied up in some political business Kiadora never followed too closely. "I wanted to, but trips were always just to close shopping centers." Delandea nodded. Kiadora could tell by the other woman's intense glare that she wanted Kiadora to get to the point.

"I've never been to the ocean, but I...was the ocean. That must seem crazy." Delandea stared with a shocked expression.

"So soon?"

"I guess. So this is normal?"

"Not many people can integrate with an elemental body as big as that. I sat in a rock for months. That was your spiritual energy, the flow of Eatheria that makes up you, integrating with the energy of the ocean. You took on one of the single largest elemental bodies this planet possesses, Kiadora. After that, it's Air and Earth itself."

"Oh." Kiadora looked at her hands and fiddled with her fingers, feeling like she should have something more profound to say. "It was nice. Peaceful. I never felt...love on such a grand scale." She felt like a sissy for even saying it. Soft emotions were never a popular topic of conversation on the surface, and they were downright weaknesses in the higher courts. But still, she had to remember that feeling, for some reason.

"Make sure you carry that with you," said Delandea, as if reading Kiadora's mind. "That will be all for today." Delandea moved off to the desk with her scroll and sat down to review it further.

Kiadora left the room quickly before Delandea could remember to pass along an assignment. She walked along the normal corridors, barely looking at where she was going. What a random thing to feel, she decided. The ocean. Was it possible for the ocean to even have feelings, or was that her?

She was almost at her ladder when a man with stubble and a limp bumped her on the shoulder.

"Cyrus, tonight at lights down," the man muttered and continued on his way as if he had said nothing. He, of course, meant the usual place next to the path. Kiadora sighed and swung herself up on the ladder. It was so close to being a good day.

As she reclined, she realized something. They needed a physical messenger to contact her. There would be no random access to her mind, now. Not from them.

CHAPTER 42

Later that evening, just as the lights shut off, Kiadora bent down and grabbed the dried wolfsbane she kept in a cheesecloth pouch besides the head of her mattress. Such pouches were up for common pickings in a supply closet outside of the gardens. The thin cloth allowed for better energy transfer, she had heard in passing. Kiadora felt the soft texture of the cloth, knowing that most herbs were used to aid in meditation, sleep or even lovemaking. Never something like this. She knew it would be bad tonight. After the last few gaffes, they would expect her to prove herself. And she was acting by way of threat.

The compound won't necessarily miss you, Cyrus had said.

The astral projection sensations of earlier this afternoon still played around the edges of her consciousness, their dance once a strong jig now fading into a subdued waltz. It had felt wonderful, being that connected.

The compound won't necessarily miss you.

Kiadora closed her hand around the herbs, feeling their jolting energy travel up her hand like a light electric shock. In her mind's eye, she could see the dark particles make their jagged pattern up her arm and into her heart. She immediately felt her heart rate quicken, and the plant's Eatheria spread to the rest of her body almost simultaneously.

Kiadora looked around at the cramped surroundings: the damp walls of sod, the lumpy mattress, the craggy floor. No, she deserved better. There was just too much to be mad about to stay down here. She put the wolfsbane in her pocket, feeling the energy from the thing pulse through her. She immediately leaped out onto the ladder, was on the ground before she knew it and was jogging toward the exit of the compound quickly and quietly. She made her way through the narrow path past the underground waterfall probably a little too fast for safety and was out in the cool night. The nip of autumn was starting to settle in at this time of night. It wouldn't be long before the leaves fell and then where would Cyrus hide?

As she came up the path, he was behind the leafy hedge where he always was. He thrust his hand out, but Kiadora stepped to the side and made her way into the woods, the moss drooping around them. He let his arm go down and seemed to regard her for a moment from under that hat. He stood as still as the hedge that surrounded him, and Kiadora had trouble figuring out what he was assessing.

"You seem to have come ready," he said in that gruff voice that yielded neither emotion nor compliment. Kiadora nodded, trying to hold an earnest gaze with a man who never showed his face. For how close they were, she still could only see the stubble on his chin.

"You'll need all that resolve. Are you aware of the baker's house in this town? I believe they have the family name of Willowmoat." Kiadora stared off into the leafy hedge, trying to picture the home. It was strange, she thought as she continued to stare into the hedge. For all the fear of Earthly energies, families still had names from the natural surroundings of their indigenous ancestors. As a result, hardly anyone ever used their family name anymore. Sometimes, Kiadora flat-out forgot hers: Oakforest, Oakbriar? Oakwood, that was it.

Finally, in a flash, it came to her.

"You mean the log house across from the well?"

"That's it. You get to torch the place." Cyrus threw a small match-box at her like he was a jovial parent throwing a child candy. Kiadora caught it as he rummaged around under his cloak and handed her an unlit torch.

"Remember what I said last time. Make a good job of it, and you'll go far in this." Then the man was gone into the brush. Kiadora stood looking at the matchbox and torch. Better get this over with, she decided. Kiadora set off down the path as quickly as possible, staring at the swiftly moving path as she sped towards town, making sure to keep her hat pulled over her face.

Once in town, she was at the little cottage before she knew it. It stood off to the edge of the town. Kiadora had passed it several times on the way to the theater. She only knew it belonged to the local baker because she remembered the smell of fresh pastries. There were sometimes dozens and dozens of cakes and muffins sitting out to cool. Why did it have to be this place?

Now the little cottage sat dark and quiet. Kiadora moved past the well in the middle of the courtyard and around to the back of the house, marveling at how there was once a time when she would look at a little two-room home such as this and wonder how anyone ever grew up in such a small place. Now compared to her quarters, the place seemed like a venerable palace.

All she felt was the intense desire to get his over with. She felt jittery, like she had too much coffee. She struck the match on the wood that made up the exterior of the cottage and lit the torch. She didn't know how you went about lighting a house on fire, exactly. She watched the torch ignite and hold the wild flame. Was there a best way to do it? For lack of any better ideas, she quickly threw the torch on the ground so it was resting on the bottommost log of the cabin's undulating wall.

Kiadora jumped back as the flame took to the wooden wall imm-ediately. It climbed up and out at an alarming rate. She retreated back to the field that the house sat on the edge of. Kiadora resisted the urge to run screaming from the home, assuming they'd put it out. Surely, they'd have to notice something like that. And it couldn't be her fault if they caught it in time. Then again, the house was dark, so maybe they weren't home. Kiadora knew it was a desperate hope, being this late at night.

The flames were now roaring in all directions. They had encased the roof and flames were coming out of the windows. Kiadora stood transfixed, vaguely wondering if she could still help them. In addition to the dark, jagged particles of the wolfsbane, her mind's eye could see the hyperactive red, yellow and orange particles of the flame. It was like the Eternal Fires, but more immense and now terrifying. She could feel the energy of the flame as it leapt out towards her. There was the heat, as well as a tingling sensation. She withdrew farther, not wanting that sinister force touching her. Kiadora had heard in passing about the duality of these elemental energies, dark and light. Now she understood.

The flames grew, and she could feel the heat once more. She turned to run, hoping more than ever that they weren't home after all. It was dark, she couldn't have known; surely Cyrus wouldn't hold her responsible if all she did was burn a house down. It would send the threat. Still, she could feel herself shaking as she ran.

And then, from behind her, the small scream of a child: a piercing, high pitched wail of unmitigated pain. Kiadora rammed her fingers in her ears and kept running, crashing through the brush.

When she felt she was out of hearing range, she brought her hands down and kept running until she was at a path. She looked back and the only thing in the distance that she could see of her deed was a rising plume of black smoke that she could hardly make out in the night. Kiadora glanced along the path, realizing she was lost. She usually never came this way and certainly never took a path out this far into the wheat fields. She didn't want to go back to the town, so she just continued meandering along the path.

After a time, she could see a figure coming through the field to her left, walking hunched and low. Her already pounding heart jumped into overdrive as she wondered if it was possible to run into thieves this far out. But as the figure drew closer, she saw the wide-brimmed hat and musty cloak. She stopped and waited for this specter's inevitable arrival.

"Good job," Cyrus grunted as he approached. "Won't be a single survivor." Kiadora could feel all the blood drain from her face and limbs. She wavered where she stood, about to collapse. Cyrus thrust out a leathery hand and grabbed her shoulder to keep her steady.

"I heard a scream, a girl," Kiadora said faintly, staring at the ground. She refused to even look at the man.

"The smoke is usually enough to knock them out when they are asleep and then they burn quietly. The girl must have been a light sleeper." He said it so casually. And then Kiadora had to voice what had been floating around the back of her mind since she received the torch.

"They say we do this, we burn houses. That's why we can't walk among the others." Kiadora lunged her hand out to the front of Cyrus' cloak, grabbing the stiff material as she still swayed where she stood. "I did that tonight. I lived up to their worst expectation!" Before she knew it, she was shouting.

"That's the point," Cyrus said calmly. "Don't you see? They create their own monsters. There will be a note during the coming investigation. I'll leave it. It will say, 'Not demons, were it not for you.' I'm quite proud of this one, really." Kiadora could feel herself swaying less now. She still shook, but not out of rage.

"How can we claim we deserve equality when we destroy, just as they say?" Kiadora shook the man's cloak, and his hat fell back just enough. She jumped back as she saw two gaping, empty eye sockets.

"You're blind," she said.

"I can see Eatheria within. That is all I need to move within this world. They tell of how damaged you were when you came, of what they did to you. You got off easy." He now spoke in a low tone, pulling the brim of his hat down once again. Kiadora just shook her head, her mouth agape.

"Why?" she breathed.

"I didn't understand it, not at all. Eatheria, I mean. There was an accident. I still don't really understand how I did it. I loved the wind, felt free when I could be above everyone, on some high cliff. I always longed to fly. It didn't take long to realize there were the particles, the energy flow. I could sense them, connect with them. Call the winds, as it were. It didn't take long for people to notice the controlled ebb and flow of the breeze around me. I tried to explain it, to tell them how harmless it was. I was careless.

"The threats started, and I knew they'd come. When they did, I ran and felt cornered. I blew half the town away, destroyed it, knocked it down. I panicked. It was in front of most of the town. They say my eyes glowed silver when it happened. I don't know. That could have just been an exaggeration. Either way, there is a lot of superstition floating around about us. In my old town they believe the power lies within the eyes. So they removed the problem.

"They do their best down there, but there are understandable gaps, especially in those early days when the Elders first established the compound. The world is large. They got word of the event afterward, found me in a government child facility when it was too late. My family didn't want me at that point."

"I'm so sorry," Kiadora said, almost in a whisper.

"The real bitch about it is that if someone had just been around to teach me, to help me understand, I wouldn't have been so destructive in the first place. If people just understood…

"But that's why we do this and why we need your help. People don't listen to reason or committees or careful explanations. They pay attention to the actions, to the violence. The dramatic is their pathological obsession.

"You'll be shaken for a few days or weeks, but it will fade. I just hope you can remember that what those damn Elders do is talk and talk alone. You really proved yourself tonight, kid. The next plan is going to be your main event. We'll send a messenger. Head back the other way on the trail, take the first right fork. That'll get you home."

Then Cyrus was moving away back off into the field. Kiadora watched him glide deftly in his world of pure energy and space.

Kiadora staggered into her cramped room and fell onto her lumpy mattress. She took the wolfsbane out of her pocket and threw it behind her mattress. Immediately, she felt a little more calm, but not enough.

The low light from outside filtered through the colorful curtain, casting blues and yellows, greens and reds. All the same, as it always was. For some reason, Kiadora expected it all to be different, for the world to come crashing down, for up to be down and down to be up, inside to be outside, for all of it to just somehow shift fundamentally. But it was all the same, like she had done nothing, been nowhere. Like it all didn't matter.

She threw herself down on her mattress, staring up at the dark, root-filled ceiling. Like thousands of veins, she thought for the first time. Like the veins of her heart, stretching out into the darkness, doing nothing but holding decomposing animal waste and debris up.

Kiadora closed her eyes and saw it: the flames. She heard the small girl scream.

Kiadora remembered the last time she was floating through the darkness, going to where she felt love, connection, peace.

Remember this, damn it, the Ashilek had said.

She was trying, but it felt more distant than ever now. Nevertheless, she tried to let her mind go still. If she could just get back there. The scream went on, the flames flashed through her mind. Kiadora willed it away, willed herself to that dark place where there was no guilt, no fear and no terrible deeds.

Slowly the darkness came. Kiadora watched it, watched the darkness like it was a show. Focused on it, felt it, was it. Then the form returned. It was a flickering red shape. It had a form this time: that of a large lizard. A very large lizard, with a long neck and large head. She had seen it before, in a picture book from childhood. Someone was always throwing a spear at it, as if that would pierce the thick hide. Somehow, it always did. The thing always breathed fire. A dragon, like from the play.

"Do you taunt me?" Kiadora asked without intending to.

There is something you must see. Come.

The darkness was stretching again, in that invisible but very real way. But the darkness never let up. The movement stopped abruptly, and now there was just pain. It was a level of pain Kiadora did not know existed. It was like every nerve had been battered, damaged.

Then the images came: the surrounding flame in a haze of gray smoke, stretching from the wall to the entire bed. The fire was absolutely everywhere. Kiadora was small now, like when she was about five years old. Moving backwards yielded an even larger, scorching pain in her back. Then there was the scream Kiadora knew so well. A move to the side was met with the floor, but the pain spread. The scream kept going.

It happened fast now. Vision went as she felt herself thrashing and rolling on the floor, and the pain spread to her face. Then there was just the pain. Only the pain.

Then the pain fused with a growing weakness. Steadily the weakness began to surpass the pain...

Kiadora passed into the first type of darkness: the area of no pain and little consciousness. If Kiadora felt like she had a real body here, it would have been shaking. The dragon returned, Kiadora now realized. Its scaly face turned towards her, a gaze of pure fire that danced among red eyes.

"You ass! Why show me? What am I supposed to do about it now?" Kiadora would be hurling as well, if she had a body.

You miss the ocean, don't you?

"Yeah, that's where I was trying to go."

Escape won't cure this. You'll just drive the memory deeper until it eats away like a smoldering ember. You'll have erased all the progress you made so far.

"You tried to stop it. You wanted me to remember that connection."

What Cyrus has failed to remember is that what you do to others, you do to yourself. I won't allow you to forget that.

"But what am I supposed to do?" Kiadora asked again. It came out as more of a wail than Kiadora intended it to. "They're going to expect me to keep hurting people."

You'll know.

Then Kiadora was getting up from her bed. There would be no sleep tonight.

CHAPTER 43

Kiadora stumbled down the ladder, drowsy as ever. It had been just as long of a night as she figured it would be, only more so. The longer the night dragged on, the more resolved she became in knowing what she had to do.

This couldn't go on. She couldn't keep hurting people like this. Astrian was right all along. She had to turn them in. Somehow.

Kiadora rounded a bend and was at her teacher's door again. It felt like it took all of her strength to open the door. She didn't know where that full body ache had come from. It wasn't like she had to dig a grave this time, or at least not a literal one. As she entered, Delandea looked up, and her brow furrowed immediately.

"Have you been ill?"

Kiadora shook her head as she sat down on the stiff, wooden chair that was in place of the sofa. The mandolin sat out next to it. She didn't know how she would bring herself to play anything today.

"No, just some bad dreams," she picked up the mandolin, giving herself a mental shake as she did so. At least it was something else to focus on.

"So, what scales will I be practicing today?"

Delandea looked at her for a moment, clearly debating pushing it. She held Kiadora's gaze for a little longer.

"It's dreams of the Church. It happens sometimes. I'm fine." Kiadora held Delandea's gaze, willing herself to sound sincere. She had never had to lie so convincingly in her life. Finally, Delandea broke her gaze.

"You're actually finished for now. You've also learned nearly every cord you need to know. There will always be more for the future, trust me." Kiadora nodded.

It must have been months. There were days where there would be nothing but the endless drill of every note that must have been known to man. Then the writing. Kiadora felt like she must have recorded every religious origin, practice and experience ever conceived in the history of man. The earliest recorded beliefs came from the cave drawings where entire cultures decided they came from something else. Some fell from the sky, others sprang up from the mud and one decided they came from horse manure. But it was always initiated by something. Someone or something wanted them there. And it was for a highly individualized purpose. One culture had to grow wheat or demons would attack. Others decided they were simply there to enjoy the earth. But it was *always* some higher purpose. Kiadora still figured it was rationalization, a purpose to keep going.

What she didn't expect to happen was to have it all blend into one collective practice in her head, with theirs included. What started as silly rituals from distant lands began to take shape: it all melded into one continuous circle of intuition, then devotion, then symbolic action and finally rolling into intuitive experience. It all seemed to happen the same: someone felt there had to be more and dearly wanted to be closer to that sense. So they saw mud as sacred or they danced under the full moon or built a house of worship. Then groups started to show up and everyone felt something that the text didn't quite capture. They must have, Kiadora reasoned, because they kept doing it. Certain rituals spanned hundreds of years. And because of her time with the Eternal Fires, that tingle she felt when she was in the woods as a child and, most recently, the sense of being one with the ocean, she knew how they felt. There was just...something more.

And Kiadora could feel it as she held that mandolin on her lap. That...something. She cursed herself for not being able to explain it better to herself. She could describe anything: plants, feelings, thoughts, love...but this defied all of that. It simply was.

"You know what to do," Delandea said softly. Kiadora looked up sharply. That phrase again. Everyone figured she was so smart, but if she was, those people...

Kiadora took a breath and stilled her mind. There was nothing she could do about that now. She let her mind settle into that place of complete peace and began playing.

Quickly it emerged. The song contained the basic sounds and slow lilt of the original tune, but now it was more complex. She had set up a definite minor key, and all the right notes combined to make a sweet, sad tune. She had heard something similar at a funeral once, but that had been more simplistic. At one point, she had somehow set up a round with herself, playing multiple notes in quick succession an octave apart from each other. The song echoed cries of sorrow against itself, keeping low and long. The last note ended on a trill, and she realized she had tears in her eyes.

Delandea sat looking at Kiadora, her eyes red and barely holding back tears.

"That was my Soul Song, wasn't it?" Kiadora said.

Delandea nodded.

"What have you all been through?" she asked softly, bluntly.

"Oh, you know…" Kiadora's voice wavered, and she looked off to a chart on the wall: a circle with the hash marks she now knew so well. She could now play it. It was a series of cords in the G major key.

"It sounded like a funeral march," Delandea pressed. Kiadora only nodded back.

"I've had some death to mourn," Kiadora said. Still, as she said it, she realized that she was breathing easier. Her chest didn't feel so tight, and her head felt a little clearer. It was like she had bled some of the sorrow out through her instrument.

"I see," Delandea said. Silence hung in the air, and Kiadora began to fidget.

"The Soul Song can be taxing and at times traumatic," said Delandea. "It shows you at your rawest. You may leave early today." Kiadora nodded and was out the door without a word.

On her way down the corridor, more tears came. She turned her face toward the wall, hoping no one would see her. It wasn't uncommon to see people walking around in odd moods. She'd seen everything from tears to random, lone laughing. She just always figured she could be the composed one.

"Hey." Kiadora felt a hand on her shoulder and looked up. Great.

It was Astrian, the last person she wanted to see. He was staring into her eyes, as if trying to read her problem.

"It's nothing, just a thing from lessons," said Kiadora, as she wiped fiercely at her eyes. But new tears quickly replaced the old.

"No, there's more." How did he always know these things? Kiadora only remained staring at the wall. The last thing she was going to do what meet his gaze.

"They made you do something, something you'll never be able to take back, didn't they?" Astrian said in the lowest of tones. He was in close now, and she could smell the morning grits on his breath. For some reason she felt aroused. She mentally kicked herself for thinking of that when she had blood on her hands not even a day old. What right did she have? For that matter, what right did she have to enjoy anything ever again?

Astrian put an arm around her. She tried to shrug it off, but he kept a tight grip.

"I'm not leaving you alone like this. That fact that you care means you failed to become the monster they want you to be." Kiadora glanced over at the catch in his voice at the end of that last sentence. His eyes looked brighter, more slick than usual. She bit her lip as she realized he was about to cry. Men weren't supposed to do that.

"Come on, I have the afternoon off," Kiadora said, moving forward out of Astrian's arm and gesturing with her hand. "Are you busy?"

"My teacher sent me to the pools for reflection. I'll tell him I wasn't feeling well if he asks. Says I've been bottled, locked up lately, need to look inside at things." He put a finger up to his eye and wiped several times, trying to make it look like he was rubbing at a piece of dirt. They wound their way down the corridor and out past the cubicle rooms.

"I've worried you." Kiadora said after a lengthy silence. They were now standing at the foot the ladder, staring up. "You thought I'd work to be callous to it all."

"At any cost. You can't stop a person like that."

"You didn't think I could fight it?" Kiadora asked in a low tone, now hurt.

"A strong enough conviction can make a fool of anyone, Kiadora. It's just a matter of whether that conviction makes you the right type of fool. A lot's happened to you that can make anyone the wrong type. But not you." He was smiling now and staring at her with those watery eyes again.

"Come on," Kiadora said as she went up the ladder. Astrian followed, and they both sat close to each other on her bed facing the far wall.

"I'm going to have a lot ahead of me if I'm going to make this right again. But I can't back out now. There's been threats." She took Astrian's hand in hers and took a deep breath.

"A whole family, Astrian. I had to burn down the house, with them in it." Her voice was shaking, and the tears were coming back. She had to fight to keep her voice low. He suddenly lunged and had her in a hug. Now her whole body was shaking.

"The father was an active board member of the Church, s..some high-ranking chair. Made a few comments about us publicly, about…about how he thought there was a large group of us living in the area with the crimes and all. Everyone thought maybe we traveled, others figured it might have been criminally insane pranksters. I've been reading the papers up there." She pulled away and held Astrian at arm's length.

"They don't just go for those they see as guilty, Astrian. They go for the close loved ones as well."

"Kiadora, I'm an Eatheria user. I'm not one of the oppressors."

"If I left, they'd come after you," Kiadora whispered, undeterred. "My boss has been through worse than I have, he's unhinged. Everyone not working violently for freedom is an enemy. The hate radiates off the man if you look closely. Otherwise, I'd probably say to shit with it and walk, not give a damn what happens to me."

"You don't mean that. Redemption beats out a tragic death any day. We're not going through all of this to die without purpose."

Purpose. It came up again and again in her readings. Every culture forged one, no matter how trivial.

"You have the ability to do something grand here," Astrian pushed. "You know what to do."

"I have to trip them up in their own game, don't I?" Astrian said nothing, and they both just stared at the wool bed cover. "That sounds easy until I think about how to do it. Will anyone above even care about what I do?"

"Kiadora, those above live a life that consists of continual inundation with bad information. If neither of us developed this awareness for one reason or another, we'd be on the surface with jobs, feeling enlightened when we went to services and deeply suspicious of anyone with a shred of difference. No one's been around to tell them any better. They don't deserve the violence."

Cyrus' voice echoed in Kiadora's head: *If only someone understood…*

"They have to know about us." Kiadora said. "But not like this. Not with the burnings and the deaths. I have to stop those first. The town guard will want justice, and it's what they deserve. Once that happens, the real work will begin."

Astrian leaned over and kissed her warmly, lingering. Then he pulled away.

"I've spent too much time down here. We all have. I've been here 14 years, I was 10 when I came. I learned to read down here," he said, shaking his head. "You've never settled for that complacency. That spark will help you. It will help the *two* of us, more if we can find them." Kiadora let her arms find their way around Astrian's back.

"I love you," she said, before she even knew what was out. Astrian grinned.

"I love you, too," he said, and then they were lying on the bed while Astrian kissed every bit of her skin he could reach.

CHAPTER 44

It had taken several weeks and at least six hand cramps, but Kiadora finally threw down a thick scroll onto Delandea's desk with gusto.

"There, my final thesis. Now I can progress to…what is after this, anyway?"

"Not so fast, give me a chance to read this. Go practice your Soul Song." Kiadora grinned and turned around to a chair in the corner where she found the mandolin. As she picked it up, she realized that the instrument would probably actually play a light tune today.

She was surprisingly proud of her work. Her heart had sunk when Delandea handed her a scroll that was as thick as her own thigh and told her to fill it with a unified theme that she was able to pull from all of her readings from the past several months. Kiadora had panicked and whined that she didn't even know where to start or what to write about.

Delandea had told her to search her heart. Her mind would do the rest. Delandea then handed her every bit of writing Kiadora had compiled from her Air lessons to date.

Scowling all the way out the door, she headed for the library and sat staring at the stack papers before her. It had to at least be half the height of her chair. Kiadora didn't realize how much her work had amounted to.

She had sighed and picked up the first paper on the stack, her latest about origin stories. And it hit: the odd spark every culture shared. The fact that they were always there for a purpose and the creation stories reflected that in every instance.

Kiadora had spent a few weeks wondering about her own purpose. She seemed only capable of causing misery. 'This can't be all there is,' she thought to herself several times. Life was boredom, mixed with confusion and sprinkled with horror. If her life was a pastry, it would poison anyone who ate it. The only time she felt right was in a trance state, and she still wondered if any of that was even real at times.

But these cultures, even if they sounded stupid, they had it figured out at least. A jungle culture had decided that because they were dropped on the earth by birds, their entire purpose was to tend to the sacred blue parrot that was native to their area. They set out offerings for it and even had high holidays in its honor. Its annual mating period was an orgy of offerings and prayers to the god that the birds embodied. A town youth was chosen, one per year, to go out into the birds' nesting area and live among them with nothing but his or her bare flesh. And they always came back with more reverence for the birds than before!

When the people died they would meet this parrot god face-to-face (or face-to-beak) and somehow merge with its consciousness, where they would reincarnate as a parrot and watch over the following generations. Kiadora couldn't get her head around how merging with the Great Parrot would cause them to be reborn as a normal parrot, but it had a nice, circular continuity to it. And when your life revolved around parrots, it was less time burning down houses.

So she searched the library looking for every creation story she could find, from an entire civilization that was molded out of mud to first man being birthed from an iguana. Somehow, she could always find a way to relate it back to purpose: the mud people were now an industrious farming community and the iguana folks were quiet desert dwellers. She sat in the library, her back cramping on the stiff, wooden chairs, and recorded all of these stories and related each one to its respective civilization's current societal structure and activities. And they all had some stated greater purpose.

Kiadora's hand now hovered over the instrument. She looked up at Delandea, who was plowing through Kiadora's cramped handwriting. Delandea unfurled the scroll at a remarkable pace, but a hair faster would have told Kiadora that the woman was just scanning. Delandea tended to chew on her bottom lip as she read, not betraying any sense of greater mirth. It was a rapid and quick concentration that Kiadora realized she could never possess if she tried. Kiadora sat waiting, the other woman not even noticing that Kiadora was not playing.

Delandea finally looked up from the scroll and looked over at Kiadora.

"You're close," was all she said. Kiadora felt all the wind leave her as if a great vacuum had been attached to her lungs.

"Well, what did I get wrong?"

"They all have meaning, and yes, it is tied to their creation stories. You are right there, and quite smart to pick up on that." Kiadora felt her cheeks go red.

"However, something as resounding as purpose comes from a higher plane, Kiadora. You need to go back and look at these stories again, *carefully*. If you're stuck, just meditate. It will come. Take as much time as you need."

Kiadora stood up, just a step away from fully shaking. She put her instrument down, trying not to throw it into the wall. Delandea handed the scroll back with a hard look into Kiadora's eyes.

"When you understand, you'll be glad you looked deeper," said Delandea.

And then Kiadora was in the corridor with the heavy scroll she thought she'd never have to hold again.

Kiadora sat staring into the Eternal Fires. The flames leapt and danced as they always did.

Kiadora had spent what must have been a couple weeks just drifting around the compound. Every time she looked at her scroll leaning against the far wall in her sleeping quarters it seemed to taunt her, and she felt like she needed to go out.

The library just reminded her of work, so she always found her way to the underground lakes, where Astrian was doing high level Water elemental work of some sort. Usually she just sat next to him as he gazed in a trance. Once when there weren't many people, she had tried to wade in the lake out of boredom, but was immediately driven out by sharp cries from the three people who were there.

"You're getting your energy into it!" a man had yelled from across the lake, the echo magnifying his outrage. Astrian had to explain to her in a quiet tone that too much of a person's personal Eatheria could set the water off balance. It needed to be as pristine as possible for the high level of meditational work that was done with it. Kiadora had just stared.

"Look, you wouldn't drink water you had just dipped your foot into, would you?"

"No."

"Same thing." Kiadora looked back out across the lake.

Then she felt offended.

"Hey, my particles can't be toxic to your precious lake!" Astrian sighed, wrenched out of the beginnings of a trance.

"You should know how the different energies that make up Eatheria interact with each other. You've used the wolfsbane enough," he added in a quieter tone. "You don't go around never influencing anything, no matter how subtle." Kiadora smiled at him. He was so wise, even when peeved. That was a level of depth Kiadora hoped she could one day possess. Maybe it was time to start trying.

"I'm off to the fires." Astrian just bid her farewell with a small smile.

And now she was at the bonfire, hoping it would take her somewhere. She remembered her last truly intimate foray with the flames here and hoped there were enough people paying attention to pull her away, if it came to that. She had spent plenty of time here, but in the way anyone would spend hunched around the fireplace in winter. She worked with candles when she wanted to meditate. It seemed safer.

But it was now time to pull out all the stops; she didn't want to let her previous hard work go completely to waste.

Kiadora focused on the flames, letting her mind go as blank as always. Her breathing steadied, and soon it was only her and the frantic flames. The swirling particles leapt into view, the frenzy of reds, oranges and yellows a welcome and familiar sight.

As natural of an action as falling asleep, Kiadora could feel herself rise up and out of her own body and pitch into the flames. Kiadora wasn't concerned as she felt her essence intermingle with the flame itself. No one came forward to stop her and without quite knowing how she was aware of it, she knew she had separated from her physical body. It was more of a feeling of common sense than any statement of knowledge, like the common sense that one had to breathe to stay alive.

She could feel every tendril of her that leapt up toward the air, seeking the oxygen she desperately needed to stay burning. Kiadora could feel the greedy consumption of the logs, and every part of her twisted in every direction imaginable.

She couldn't exactly see the people around the room as their consciousnesses melded with hers, all was red, yellow and orange, but she could feel them like she felt the air or the logs. They held their own swirl of particles, crashing through bloodstreams, flowing in and out of the nose and mouth, and penetrating every bit of tissue.

Particles extended into the space around these people and to the ground under them, touching the people close to them. Some particles flowed heavily into the flames in a torrent of new energy, each with a composition as unique as the last. She could feel them combine with her in a steady stream of constant change. Some particles carried emotions of sorrow, mirth or rage. In whatever stance they hit, they immediately melded and were purified.

Again, Kiadora could feel herself rising up and out into a dark void. There a wolf form hovered directly in front of her. She could plainly make out the tides and currents that made up the blue, liquid form of the creature. He had his mouth open, pulled back in a canine grin with a flat tongue showing. It seemed like the smile that invented all mirth.

You've made it, but there's still more to see. Come.

Without protest, Kiadora followed the form through the void, moving in that unknown way that was purely felt. She hypnotically watched the wolf's tail move back and forth like the wave in the ocean and realized that she was now staring at actual waves as she crashed into the sea. She had always wanted to go to the sea, had heard stories of men who spent their lives riding the waves and skimming the waters in large crafts. In daily life, she could never imagine such a body of water so large that it spanned most of the planet.

Now, it felt like something she had always known. She could feel parts of her crashing on distant shores she didn't know and would probably never visit. Kiadora knew she had done this before, but now it was on another level. She didn't just feel the ebb and flow of the waves or the peace towards the life she harbored. Kiadora felt full compassion for that which she nourished. It was a level of love that she didn't know even existed, beyond what she felt the last time she was here. It wasn't the passionate love she had just for Astrian, the concern for a friend she felt for Regelend and it wasn't that theoretical love she was supposed to have for a father who cared more about politics than her.

It was like she was in love with everything that existed then, did exist and would exist. Everything was her concern, her charge, and letting it come to harm would be unthinkable.

As she experienced this, she realized her awareness was not just that of the ocean, but she was the stars, the moon and the cellular material of every being. There was no end to what she touched. She touched the beginning of time, the present and the end of time. Somehow, previously believed empty space was not even immune to her presence.

Through it all, she saw how the particles flowed. It was a stunning macrocosm of particles flowing in and out of every single thing in space, even the "empty" bits. But as she watched at this scale, Eatheria did not seem to be individual particles, but one surrounding energy that was felt more than seen. Space had no bounds. A small stirring of energy in the belly of a fish could, in just another moment, be contributing to the cosmic outpour of a flare from a distant star. Kiadora could feel all these patterns at once, though she didn't know how she could register such information simultaneously. And all the energy flowed directly through her at some point or other. It passed through all humans at some point and then was off to spend some time in the atmosphere of a distant planet.

And then Kiadora could feel the awareness shrinking, receding out of the stars, out of other humans, out of the oceans, and then she was back in the void. The wolf hovered in front of her, still grinning that primordial grin.

All Kiadora could do was stare.

So...?

"I had no idea..." Kiadora said. She paused and looked off into the void. Then: "Will I ever be able to control it? Like the wolfsbane and extinguishing flame?"

The wolf let off a grating chuckle.

A mortal? Surely not, not in the way you are thinking, at any rate. We'd be foolish to give anyone that kind of power.

Kiadora felt dejected.

But there are other ways, the wolf said. *You'll realize them. After this, you'll realize them.*

Then Kiadora could feel herself falling until she was staring at the bonfire once more. She looked up, but it felt like a different reality she was observing. She regarded the other people at the edge of the flame, the flame itself, the walls, the ground. All were connected. It was like the rusted out gears of her mind were breaking free of decay and falling into place for the first time.

She rose and left the fire, moving swiftly, almost gliding. As she came into the common area, she realized by the dimmed lights, with pleasure, that it was nighttime. There was something she needed to do that she had been putting off for too long.

Kiadora hoped that her hunch was right, that Cyrus would know she was there. She had been waiting for a good while and had arrived with the single thought of, 'Cyrus, get over here. Now.'

The man came crashing out of the brush behind her. Kiadora turned as he was righting his large hat as he did so.

"Did you hear?"

"I could sense your urgency," Cyrus replied.

"My family," Kiadora said, cutting right to the point. "They control the education system, you know." Cyrus nodded.

"We know."

"Get ahold of them, and you control the flow of information. You control minds." Cyrus grinned.

"Great minds think alike."

"I can go back," Kiadora said. She looked out in the direction that her family's estate was. She kept her breathing steady and willed her heart rate to slow down. "Start a fire, plant bombs, whatever you need."

"Bombs would be best. You'll receive further instructions."

Kiadora nodded and turned to leave, fearing she could keep her composure no longer.

"Kiadora," Cyrus called from behind her. Kiadora turned. "You seem different."

"It's all connected." Kiadora said. "The longer we stay out of it, the longer it doesn't mean a damn thing."

Cyrus smiled wider and gave Kiadora a firm pat on the shoulder. Then he turned into the brush and was gone. On the way back, Kiadora puzzled about how such a man could feel the web strongly enough to hear her call but could block out the misery.

Kiadora once again slammed the parchment onto Delandea's desk. Delandea picked it up wordlessly and began to read while Kiadora sat in the wooden chair in front of Delandea's desk and stared at the floor.

It seemed like hours, though Kiadora knew it could never be that long with the rate at which Delandea read.

Finally, Delandea put the scroll down, waves of Kiadora's perfectly groomed handwriting falling in torrents over Delandea's desk. Kiadora looked up slowly to find Delandea staring at her with a wide smile.

"Now, you have it," she said in a matter-of-fact tone. Kiadora had reworked the whole thesis, including the same information with a different interpretation. It wasn't the creation stories that gave purpose, it was the feeling of connection. The creation stories merely expressed that in metaphor. The farms were connected to the mud, and the desert people were connected to the scaly creatures around them. It was just an extremely narrow view.

Kiadora grinned back.

"So what now?"

"Well, first of all, this now belongs to you." Delandea reached under her desk and pulled up the mandolin, handing it to Kiadora. Kiadora took it gingerly, as if clutching it too hard would disintegrate it into the dust of dreams.

"You can play the Soul Song anytime you want. They can be quite enlightening at different times."

"They change?"

"It's hard, but yes, sometimes they will." Kiadora thought of playing it now, but sort of wanted the experience all to herself. It always felt like stripping nude in front of another woman, something she still hadn't gotten used to.

"Also, there is the matter of what element you will choose to work with on the closest level possible. You will reach the level of Master with this element and may eventually teach others."

"Wait, so you're moving me up a level?"

"Correct, you will, in essence, be graduated from the level of Sitrina to Surina, that of one working to master one element."

Kiadora slouched back in her chair. A few days ago, she would have yelled, "Fire!" But today, after becoming one with all four at once, she wasn't so sure she wanted to study just one.

"What if I don't fully know which one I want?" Kiadora cringed as she asked the question, fearing they would send her through all her past lessons again.

"Then there is a placing ceremony. You are... *positive* you do not know which one?" Delandea looked at her closely, her stare drilling into the back of Kiadora's mind. Kiadora had been vaguely aware that her story of nearly leaping into the Eternal Fires had spread far. People whispered and pointed at her in the library after the occurrence. Maybe she should just say Fire?

Wait, what was she thinking? How long was she going to stay around this place exactly? She had plans. But she wondered about the feasibility of just leaving one day. Lisera did it, but it didn't seem as easy as just stomping off. And there was Cyrus. Maybe if she could just see the damn Elders everyone spoke so much about...

"Who does the placing ceremony?" Kiadora asked, daring the hierarchy of life to actually cooperate for once.

"The Elders." Kiadora had to use every ounce of restraint to keep from laughing.

"I'll do it, the placing ceremony, I mean."

"I understand it is quite the ordeal. They've only had to do it for three other people as well. You are *sure* you need to do this?" Delandea asked again. It was time to be blunt.

"Look, I didn't write such a stunning thesis by books alone. There was this…this vision, or something. I was the moon, the stars, the ocean, I was everything…it was amazing! And now you are asking me to limit myself? I'll need some guidance if I'm about to follow one narrow road."

Delandea just stared at her with her eyes wide.

"The Transcendence? You have experienced the Transcendence? I've only read about it. It's rumored the Elders can do it, but no one knows for sure. I suspected based off this…" said Delandea as she waved vaguely at the scroll on her desk. "But I didn't think anyone so new…"

Kiadora stared at the woman, her brow furring. She didn't think this would bring so much attention to herself. She thought it was just a place most people got to eventually, like puberty, marriage or old age.

"I'll put you in for a placing ceremony with the Elders. They'll want to see you, at any rate. Do a lot of meditating, more than usual, you'll need to prepare yourself."

Kiadora stood before the Eternal Fires, just after the lights dimmed. There was only the fire tender there, who looked like he was about to fall asleep. She stood with the packet of wolfsbane in her hand, feeling the prickle and rising rage that had no internal source. Fire, the great purifier and purger, would take care of it.

She threw the wolfsbane and cinnamon into the flame, feeling the prickling and the rage soar away with it. The flame leapt where she threw the herbs, and in her mind's eye she could see a small wisp of blackness rise from where the packet had fallen before it was overtaken and extinguished by another tendril of flame.

CHAPTER 45

Kiadora regarded the back of Wyland, her red curls bouncing merrily and her rainbow of an ensemble swirling like the particles Kiadora had come to know so well. Kiadora wondered when the last time was that she interacted with this woman. Sure, Kiadora had seen her on a number of occasions, especially at those public rites. But the woman was also in a hyperactive state of overseeing costumes, drinks and the whereabouts of the rite participants then. Kiadora thought she could never have anything to say to this woman, and now that she was being abruptly led to the Elders, still no words formed in her mind, except the vague thought that she would have expected such a hectic woman to change somewhat. But Wyland looked as bouncy and overexcited as ever, the several metal necklaces jangling at her throat as she walked. Maybe you reached a point where you became what you were meant to be, Kiadora mused.

Kiadora's thoughts were interrupted by an abrupt stop in front of a craggy entrance, the same Narissa had dragged her to the last day of her introductory lessons. A man with a vacant stare sat there, and he looked up at the two of them with glassy, pale fish eyes.

No words were exchanged. The man nodded to Wyland, gave a slow, lingering look into Kiadora's eyes and retreated back into the cave.

As they waited, the gravity of the situation finally hit Kiadora. She was to go in front of the Elders, the mysterious council of people who were as feared for the myriad of legendary punishments as revered for their unearthly wisdom. Kiadora could feel her hands begin to get moist. She glanced at Wyland, who had a small, calm smile on her face. When Wyland had met Kiadora the first thing that morning, she had practically sang in a bright tone normally reserved for songbirds that Kiadora's placement was to be today. Now Kiadora felt sick.

Even if she wanted to place, she had no idea what these old nutters would make her do. She had heard in passing it was normally weeks of fasting and intense visionwork down by the lakes, but in some cases it would vary. No one quite knew what they were going to get. One man who was now a Master had to hang from hooks for a week. No one knew how these bizarre rituals were chosen, but the general consensus was that the Elders could somehow see into your soul and know what was needed for you specifically. Kiadora hugged her arms to herself, as if that would stop anyone's penetrating, otherworldly gaze.

The man with the glassy eyes drifted out of the cave once more and gave a curt nod. He stood back and held his arm out to indicate his permission to pass. Wyland gave a bow and went in. Kiadora rushed passed, not wanting to linger around the man with the dead eyes.

They walked down a long, narrow passage with walls that jutted out in odd places. Soon, Kiadora could hear a fire raging and they came out into a cavern.

Kiadora expected something with a little more fanfare. Some thrones, fancy rugs, maybe at least some pillows for them to sit on. Instead, she was met with a group of nine people, seated in a semicircle around a medium-sized bonfire, not quite as big as the Eternal Fires. It would be like something a person would light to cook food in the forest. She got the immediate idea that it was there for light and nothing else. There was no store of wood, she noticed, upon looking around. No, this was lit for her.

The nine sat cross-legged with backs straight and arms resting on their knees, all keeping a very ritualized stance. Most had gray hair, a few had deep wrinkles. The youngest seemed to be middle-aged, though it was hard to tell. The woman had wrinkles and hair as blond as in her youth. She recognized the steel-haired and eyed Elder of Studies, Eledina. All nine dressed in clothes that had long ago turned to rags.

They all stared at her with the sort of intense gaze that saw beyond what stood before them. Under their silent gaze, Kiadora's sweating hands seemed to renew and double their efforts to soak the fabric of her dress that she realized she was gripping. Did they want her to do something with the flame?

Kiadora took a deep breath. She could say this.

"I do not wish to place," Kiadora stated in a clear tone.

The Elders looked at her for a second longer and then turned their gaze toward each other. They regarded each other, and Kiadora could see small twitches of mouths and eyes narrow. She realized after a moment that they were communicating silently. What were they debating that they couldn't say in front of her?

"We understand you have experienced the Transcendence," croaked an old woman with shock white hair and black eyes in the middle of the group.

"That's right," said Wyland, speaking for Kiadora, her tone now clear and strong as well. "She has become as the trees, the air, the water and fire, she has seen all.

"However," and now Wyland turned her gaze towards Kiadora. "That does not mean you have an in-depth enough of a knowledge. There are certain paths to take to the highest levels, one of which is to know yourself and know your strengths. They say you have a knack for Fire. You will show the Elders."

"But why limit myself?" Kiadora said, almost in a yell. "My God, it's all connected, it's a web, you must all know that. You've been doing this long enough."

"And a web has individual sections, small pockets. Those parts make up the whole, we each have our place. You must place within an element," said Wyland.

"The way I see it, ma'am, we're all the string, and that's made of one piece," said Kiadora.

"But no one can truly see the whole web," said Eledina, her calm gone, the gray in her eyes a true steel now. "We've come close in here, but it's through the details we see the whole. You must decide on an element to become an expert in."

Kiadora regarded them all, her arms beginning to shake. So this was how it was going to be?

"Then I request to leave. There's more to be done than sit in a cave. I know I'm not the first to make such a request, you can't intimidate me into staying."

"And nor do we wish to," said the old woman in the middle. "We have no use for those unwilling to stay. However, if you so much as think of revealing our whereabouts, we'll know. And then you won't think we're so inactive."

"Very well. I'll head out immediately." Kiadora turned and walked out of the cavern, her back straight, feeling every pair of eyes on her. She mostly expected it to end that way. She knew full well they had no use for the unwilling, especially those who bucked the hierarchy.

After a second, she realized there were footsteps behind her. She turned to see Wyland following her, a sad expression marring her pale features.

"I'll need to have Lid open the way," she said in a quiet tone.

"Meet me by the furnace two hours after lights-out."

Kiadora parted ways with Wyland at the end of the cavern, nearly tripping over the guard. She muttered an apology and continued, not looking back at the man. It was still early, so she swung up to Astrian's quarters. He sat up the instant she parted his curtain.

"I need to say good-bye," said Kiadora. "I refused to place, they said I must, so I'm leaving." Kiadora looked at the root-covered wall, like veins encasing them all and giving life. On the other side of the council caverns, back where she admittedly did have some good times, it seemed childish. She briefly wondered if she should go back and take it all back.

She looked over at a rummaging sound Astrian was making and found him rooting through his one drawer. He was pulling out an old handkerchief, a comb and a flat, black stone she had seen him kick around and balance on parts of his body. A miner game, he had said.

"What are you doing with that?" Kiadora asked.

"Packing, of course."

"Wait, no, you're higher in the studies, you have more here! I didn't think you were serious. Not really."

"What I have here doesn't compare to you," he said in a whisper, as he tied up the comb and small stone in the handkerchief.

"You...you sure?" Kiadora said after a stunned silence.

"We'll manage," said Astrian.

"We'll have to wait until two hours after lights-out," Kiadora said. Astrian nodded. He then spent the rest of the day teaching Kiadora the stone game, stopping only to pick up some spare clothes from a supply closet. Right after the lights dimmed, they had one more tryst in Astrian's quarters for old time's sake, and then Kiadora went back to her own quarters to get her things.

Kiadora swung off the ladder and pulled her curtain back. She looked at the messy bed, the small dressing table and the pitcher of water. Her home for what must have been over a year, maybe two. It wasn't much to look at, and certainly not pleasant. The sheets on her bed had a permanent layer of dust. But it had been home; it was like a part of her soul rubbed off on this place. But Kiadora walked over to her bed and picked up the mandolin. Her soul could rub off anywhere, really. She put her mandolin under her arm and grabbed her hairbrush and towel, then set off down the ladder to where Astrian was waiting for her.

"We have to go out through Lid's. Wyland's waiting of us," said Kiadora. Then a thought terrorized her. "Will they let you go?" Astrian gave a half grin back at her.

"They're letting you go." Kiadora nodded, and they headed towards the furnace.

They found Wyland waiting outside the cavern that had waves of heat radiating from it. Somehow Wyland's curls had gone frizzier around her glum expression.

"You showed so much promise," Wyland said, tears now falling. She embraced Kiadora in a hug. Tall order from a woman who Kiadora had only talked to twice. Wyland pulled away and looked at Astrian.

"You too, I should have known." She hugged Astrian as Kiadora looked off to the side, resisting the urge to punch the other woman. Wyland let go and motioned them to walk into the door that led to the staircase to Lid's.

"He knows you're coming," Wyland called after them. "If the children show potential, consider sending them down here." Kiadora felt several muscles contract around her heart and let out something like a hiccup. Astrian chuckled and urged Kiadora up the staircase.

They emerged in the freezer, which was still as cold as ever. They walked out to find Lid standing in the kitchen alone, jovial and smiley as ever. He gave them a welcoming pat on the arms as they walked through. After he shut the door, he rotated around to them like a large spinning top.

"Funny, Lisera said you'd be up this way again...and who's this?"

"Uh, that's Astrian," said Kiadora, knocked out of a haze of confusion. Lisera really did know her better than she thought. Astrian gave a small smile and shook the large man's hand firmly, his hand disappearing well past the wrist.

"Now, I can put you two up for tonight, but you'll have to find a place to go after that. I'd never keep this place open if I gave out rooms for free for too long."

"Free? No, we can pay..." said Kiadora, her voice trailing off as she realized that no, she couldn't. She owed too many people for their kindness: Lisera's drinks, the free plays, now a free roof over her head. Her family had names for people who couldn't pay, mainly "prisoner."

"That's very generous of you," Astrian cut in. "But we can find..."

"Nonsense," Lid roared. "Up the stairs on your right, third door on your left. And I don't want to hear any more about it." Despite the stern paternal tone, he still had that wide grin of his.

Kiadora and Astrian glanced at each other and headed out the kitchen, up the stairs and to the third door on their left. Astrian pushed it open to reveal a humble chamber with a double bed, a small table and two chairs.

"It's like a palace compared to where we came from," Kiadora breathed after Astrian shut the door. "Look!" She knocked lightly on the wood paneled walls. "No sod!"

Astrian sat down on the bed and then jumped slightly as the mattress gave a little under him.

"The mattress isn't as hard as a rock, that's a nice change."

Kiadora put her mandolin and other items down on the table, then walked over next to Astrian and threw herself down on the bed, relishing in the bounce like when she was a small child.

"Not as bouncy as the ones I grew up with, but I'll take it!" said Kiadora. Astrian ran his hand over the soft covers.

"We slept on stone-hard cots inches off the dirt," Astrian said quietly. Kiadora sat up.

"I'm so sorry. I shouldn't rub it in." Kiadora felt herself blush, as if she was meeting him for the first time. Down underground they were all society's castaways. Now, back on the surface for good, she was painfully aware of how different the worlds they came from were. Still, she had no intention of going back home, so what did it matter?

"So, what do we do now?" Kiadora asked. "There's no way either of us is going back to where we came from." Then the truth sunk back in. She'd have to. "I should send Cyrus a message."

Astrian nodded, and Kiadora immediately closed her eyes. She remembered hearing in some lesson or other that it wasn't good to scry so close to another person, but with Astrian it just felt like another part of her was next to her. She steadied her breathing and let her mind go still. After a moment, she willed her awareness outward and focused her will on Cyrus. So natural, so easy now. It all just clicked.

And then she felt him. For the life of her she couldn't tell how she knew it was him. Something about the bitterness, the rough edges to the personality. If he were a shape, it would resemble something like those prickly burrs she picked up on her dress in the summers after a day in the field. It was so essential, it couldn't be faked.

I'm not at the compound anymore, you'll have to reach me in other ways, she said.

We know, came his voice. *We'll reach you this way. Scry nightly.*

And then she was alone. Always so brisk, that one.

"He knows," she said. They sat in silence for a moment.

"So, what do we do now?" she asked again.

"I've been thinking, we have an instrument. It was nice of them to not cast us off with no means of an income," Astrian said. Kiadora stared at him for a second before what he was implying sunk in.

"You mean you want me to play? In front of people?"

"Sure, you played in front of your teacher. How about you let me hear it, I haven't heard it for a while, and I'll bet your Soul Song is enchanting." Kiadora turned red.

"I can't play that for money! It'd be like stripping naked on the street."

"You can play it here." Kiadora looked at him, lips pressed, and then broke at that curious gaze of his. She went over to pick up the instrument and sat on the chair, hard and unyielding as the one Delandea had her sit on. She ran her fingers over the strings, checking the tune of it. She adjusted a few middle stings and then let out a long strum over all of them.

Immediately, there was a banging from the opposite side of the wall Kiadora sat next to.

"No music, keep it down! Some of us are here to sleep!"

Kiadora and Astrian started laughing.

"Paper-thin walls, good to know," said Astrian, with a glint in his dark eyes. "Anyway, you are good. Good enough for people to pay us on the street."

"And what'll you do, watch the money? It would be boring to follow me around like that. I mean, I know we have bigger plans, but we need to eat."

"I can sing." He stared at her earnestly, a mere statement of fact. Something in his steady gaze told her he was good and knew he was good, but it wasn't a boast.

"You can show me tomorrow, I wouldn't want our friend to knock the wall down."

CHAPTER 46

Kiadora glanced down as another coin was thrown into their hat. She continued to strum on her mandolin, the low tones complementing Astrian's gruff baritone. Given the state of his voice, she would never have pegged him as a singer in all of eternity. But somehow the gruff tones lent passion to the old folk songs he knew. It hadn't been hard for Kiadora to harmonize her instrument to the tunes. Astrian had found an old hat in a dumpster behind a clothing store, and that was their cash register.

It was amazing, really. People just threw money at them like it was no object. They quickly learned that the well-to-do areas were the most willing to spare a coin, after all, there was plenty where that came from, and there always had been. It was a meager wage at the end of the day. The earnings barely covered food and modest lodging, but there was a freedom to it that acted as an added benefit no amount of coins could make up for.

At the end of the day, stretched out next to Astrian in lodgings that still felt like a palace compared to a sod hole, she wanted to go on doing this forever. Though by morning, after the nightmares of torture, spiritual teachers making ridiculous demands and odd dreams about her old quarters caving in, she remembered that this was just a way-stop on the path to greater planning.

And sure enough, just as Kiadora was starting to get acclimated to the life of a roaming minstrel, the message came while scrying in a lamp one night. There were no words to it, she just knew of a certain door, not too far away, behind a certain store she had passed a dozen times.

Kiadora turned to Astrian.

"It's time," she said. He looked at her for a moment and nodded. She began to get up and put on a gray traveling dress as coarse as her old one she had left the compound in. As the rough fabric fell over her body in a depressingly familiar way, she looked longingly at her performing dress, a spirited diamond pattern in red and green.

Astrian started to get up behind her from where he was lying on the bed.

"What are you doing?" Kiadora snapped. Astrian gave a pointed stare.

"Don't be stupid, I'm not just staying here."

"They probably know you're not on their side!"

"They'll just have to change their mind when I show up to help. Tell them I had a change of heart, that's why I left."

They stood for a moment staring at each other like they were trying to melt metal by gaze alone.

"Fine, but you better not get injured or die, I'll hate you forever for it." And they both strode out the door.

They went down the same streets they traversed every day to find a decent spot for playing, rounded into an alley next to an old bar and found the door Kiadora already knew all about. Whitewashed, large crack on the left side. This was it. Kiadora and Astrian glanced at each other as Kiadora took the handle and swung the door inward. Not locked at least, Kiadora thought. Astrian turned and fumbled at the wall. A lamp cast a paltry, wavering light on a room that resembled a small shed on the inside.

The only item in the room was a single crate. She walked up to it and peered in. Small items in black sacks sat in a heap inside. Astrian walked up and picked one up, weighing it in his hand.

"Explosives, not unlike what we used in the mines to cut into some of the deeper reserves." Kiadora reached down and picked up several straps that hung out of the crate like sleeping snakes.

"Oh, they don't mean for me to…"

"That's exactly it," said Astrian in a grim tone. "I imagine they don't want these going around in a suitcase."

Kiadora bent down again. Pulling on the straps dislodged a diagram. It detailed how to place a fuse through several bags to form a line, like some macabre string of party lights. And a note below:

Place these within the family quarters tomorrow morning. We will get the rest.
-C

Kiadora grinned. So they would be there.

Kiadora nodded to the guards who stood at the entrance of her family's home. They nodded back, obviously figuring there was no threat in Lord Belac's daughter. Kiadora remembered that the others said they would be around, and she realized just how little the guards deserved their monthly wages. Kiadora had long ago realized that they were there for show, anyway, a reminder to others of her father's resources and importance.

As she reached the door, Astrian following silently behind her, she looked down to check the state of her cloak. She had fastened it securely and the bulk easily concealed the small, stringed bags of gunpowder strapped to her chest. Kiadora had no intention of setting them off, but if she was pulled aside by Cyrus, she would be forced to prove her intent. Given the temperature of the day, the cloak seemed like overkill, but Kiadora could just say she was feeling a bit cold and under the weather if anyone asked.

Astrian had blatantly refused to strap anything to himself and wore his usual brown tunic. He just said he would explain that he would help place the "little death pouches." He had said those words with a grimace.

Kiadora took a deep breath before she pushed the heavy front door open. The expansive entry hall with its ornate staircase stood still and empty. Of course, she would not be greeted happily. Everyone was always so preoccupied around here. Astrian hovered outside the door, and Kiadora had to gesture him inside. His eyes went slightly wide as he took in the polished marble stairs and gold-plated busts of old lords of the house.

"It's not as impressive as it looks," Kiadora muttered. "It's all shine and no substance."

"I don't think I've ever been in a room so large."

"It's not the type of household that's easy to get attached to." For the first time in her life, Kiadora actively felt ashamed of her family's expansive home. "They'll be up in their quarters. They rarely leave those areas."

"Where did they think you were, anyway?"

"The Hermetical Order," said Kiadora, feeling an instant jolt. How was she supposed to behave? Hermetical? Then again, her family probably didn't know a thing about the society of divine contemplatives other than that they were prestigious and kept Kiadora out of their hair.

Kiadora practiced the slow, steady breathing she learned to keep her heart from pounding. She had no reason to worry, the police were on their way now to investigate an anonymous tip Kiadora had written with her left hand to disguise her handwriting.

It had just been so long since she'd seen these people; she hoped seeing them would not make her revert back to her old habits of watching the floor too much and letting her eyes well up with tears of frustration. That wasn't the person she wanted Astrian to see.

She reached the family quarters door, dark wood carved with a lavish scroll design. She knocked briefly before she opened the door. Kiadora's mother looked up from some elaborate needlework she was doing and let out a small gasp.

"Kiadora, it's you." The small wisp of a woman stood up and walked slowly to Kiadora, as if Kiadora was an animal that would become startled by sudden movement. "How was the Order? Are you better?"

Kiadora hadn't expected her to be so blunt this quickly.

"Lots," Kiadora said truthfully. "No fainting." Kiadora followed her mother's gaze, which was trained curiously on the doorway. Kiadora looked back to find Astrian hovering just outside the doorway again, like a servant who needed permission to move from room to room. Kiadora realized that's probably what he felt like in a place such as this.

"Come on, Astrian, you're allowed to walk through the doors." He stepped inside and slowly walked up to stand beside Kiadora's shoulder.

"This is Astrian, I met him at the Order. He's from a large holding in Currenteen. He's..a friend," Kiadora lied. Astrian looked her hard in the eye, and Kiadora willed herself to keep her face straight. She always had a habit of grinning when she lied. But the real problem was that through Astrian's hard stare, she could sense his offence at the fact that custom demanded he be of higher standing just to be in this room. No wonder he kept to the doorways.

Kiadora shifted her gaze to her mother and found the woman smiling. Kiadora remembered her disapproval to Tahn, the only friend she had managed to make in these parts.

"A friend, you say?" her mother said incredulously.

"Yes."

Just then her father walked through the door, wiping ink off his hands with a handkerchief. He immediately let out a rare grin.

"Kiadora! Back during a break? It seems the Order has helped greatly, you're holding yourself taller. And who's this?"

"Kiadora says he's a friend," said Kiadora's mother in an overly chipper tone that suggested she knew otherwise.

"Kiadora!" Ashila's shrill enthusiasm rang through the chamber, and Kiadora found herself thrown into a hug. "It's been too long, I though you would have returned by now. Oh, and you've brought company!" Ashila shifted over to give Astrian a small curtsey. "Are you from the Order as well? I'll bet you have eyes for this one," said Ashila with a giggle, tilting her head toward Kiadora.

"He's a friend!" Kiadora yelled. The last thing she showed up for was her family to start planning a wedding for her.

"Finally have a voice on you now, do you?" Dehlia asked from a doorway in her usual sardonic tone. Kiadora felt the familiar constriction in her chest but looked Dehlia in the eye now.

"Dehlia. It's been a while," Kiadora said in a curt tone to suggest that a while longer wouldn't be such a bad thing.

Then the world was upended. A massive boom echoed through the house, simultaneously throwing them all to the ground as the walls gave way in all directions. Kiadora saw a flash of red hair as Astrian threw himself onto her.

As soon as it began, it seemed to be over. Rubble lay here and there, but while much of the walls had collapsed, stronger load-bearing areas had seemed to keep most of their structure. Kiadora got up and looked over Astrian, who seemed to be in once piece. Her father was standing up, brushing dust off his tunic, and then Kiadora looked down to see her mother.

The woman lay on her side moaning, her lower back covered in blood. Kiadora saw a trail of wood leading up to the woman, some hunks of furniture blown from the next room. Kiadora's mother was standing just too close to it all.

Kiadora reached for her mother. Lady Melanone looked up, her face the very picture of agony. The woman's thin hands reached out and grabbed Kiadora's hands. With a jolt, Kiadora realized this was the first time since she was very young that her mother had touched her. Kiadora held her mother's hazel gaze, the same as her own. Her mother looked at her with the distant look of someone at the gates of death. She took a moment to focus and then looked stunned. It was as if she was seeing her daughter for the first time.

"You've become something strong," her mother wheezed. "Do great things, things greater than I've done."

Her mother's eyes closed and her breathing stilled.

Kiadora felt the tears start to fall.

"I already have plans," Kiadora whispered, hoping on some level her mother could still hear her. Kiadora looked up and realized that Astrian was kneeling over Ashila, trying to stunt blood flow with a torn part of his tunic on the side of her sister's head. Half her head seemed to be nothing but blood.

Kiadora's father was over by the doorway where Dehlia had been standing, a piece of drywall now in the way. He was trying to call around the rubble to see if Dehlia would still answer. Kiadora heard muffled words and her father pressed one ear against the rubble.

"She says she dived out of the way of a falling panel just in time," Kiadora's father said.

Despite everything that had gone on between her and her sister, Kiadora felt a flood of relief. But Ashila wasn't so lucky. Kiadora looked around for a way out and found the door jammed in an awkward angle. To the side of that was a small strip where she could see the hallway. Kiadora threw off a comment about finding help and headed toward it, hoping she could slip through. She just fit, grazing her back. As she emerged into the hallway, she found the corridors to be in better repair, and the closer she moved toward the middle of the house, the less damage there was. At one point, everything looked normal, save a chandelier in the hall that had come crashing down.

At the top of the main staircase, she met some police officers, no doubt the men who had come to investigate the tip. She noticed they had cut their own new doorway in the rubble.

With them were two men in dark suits and a bag of medical equipment. Kiadora felt a tinge of admiration for the men who had thought enough ahead to bring medical personnel with them. Kiadora told the men there were survivors, one badly injured. It felt like she was speaking in a dreamy haze, and she led the two doctors and a police officer with a large saw back up to the ruined family quarters.

The men couldn't fit through the small opening, so she watched as they cut the the gap she went through with the large saw. Every moment they took was agony. She called to Astrian, who said her sister was still alive. Finally, a large chunk of wood paneling gave way and the men were in. Kiadora followed and watched as the men cleaned the blood off the side of her sister's head. She had hoped the blood made it look worse than it was, but that was only partly true. Small debris had torn away much of the skin on the left side of her sister's head. Her hair was a matted mess and was being promptly cut away, the hair Ashila went through great lengths to style. Her ear was badly cut up, much of the skin hardly looked like skin. The men worked quickly to remove small bits of wood and other debris Kiadora couldn't identify. The debris had come about half an inch from taking out Ashila's eye.

Kiadora shuttered as she realized how much worse this could have been for them all, how much worse she would have made it. They were lucky the plans apparently didn't account for time wasted with a family reunion. She looked down and realized she still had explosives on her and a police officer a few steps away. The medical team assured Kiadora it was all surface, that Ashila would be fine, save some sca-rring. Kiadora excused herself and moved through that same haze, trying to find a place to throw off the cloak and explosives. Down the hallway, she tore them off and threw them over a broken wall into a room that was once a random study.

Astrian walked up behind her at one point and started telling her about how a second explosion could ignite the whole thing. Kiadora stood, trying to consider this, but her mind didn't seem to want to move beyond simply ridding herself of the explosives. Astrian also started on about how she shouldn't wander around a structurally unsound building on her own, but it washed over her. With every moment she started slipping out a little bit more. Every time she remembered her sister's torn up head or that chunk of wood sticking out her mother's back, she started to drift away a little bit further.

Then she felt it at the edge of her mind, the sharp point of someone else's consciousness. She didn't know how she knew what it was, she just knew. And that person was the in danger. Everything about the person's mind cried out with desperation.

Kiadora took off down the hallway, moving too fast for Astrian to keep up. She lept over fallen beams, dodged blown-in walls and leapt down stone stairs. There on the lower level, near the back of the house and stuck in a back storage room, was Narissa. Kiadora peered in the small opening. The home was all stone down here, but Kiadora was now certain that the blast had come from outside, on the lower levels. This part of the house had been nearly pulverized. It was only by extreme luck that Narissa was merely trapped in a small stone prison, a bomb half rigged behind her.

Kiadora regarded the woman, still holding Narissa's consciousness in her mind. And just in an instant Kiadora was in, knowing in that intuitve way. Like the knowledge that she was breathing even when she wasn't focusing on it or that her heart was beating when she was asleep. It had to be fact or she couldn't experience life so clearly.

Now it was just Narissa's life coming all at once, each detail vivid.

There was the deep, intense love of a clear sky on a sunny day and the simple pleasure of a deep, clear breath taken. Memories of cornfields that seemed endless drifted past. The short perspective of a child barely glanced over the new, early summer stalks. And there were the suspicious looks from other farmhands as she gazed and took long, lingering breaths. Those looks become accusations later.

And then there was the fear, the crushing feel of the walls. The knowledge that the ceiling was too low, just *too* low, the air too stiff, the people too close. Always too close. And the anger at *them* for forcing it on her.

There was the guilt, the shame. In a scene, Kiadora could see Narissa pleading with the Elders. Eledina's steel gaze bore into the core of Narissa's mind as she demanded the students receive better. The sexual bits should be done by compatible teachers, not just anybody. Males should teach females and vice versa, or same sex, if it came to that for some. Eledina explained in a cool tone that new students came so trained to be disgusted by their own bodies that they needed to be broken. Only calculated, isolated sensation could do that. They weren't setting out to create a generation of students who were in love with their teachers.

Yet it had happened. The experience had awakened feelings in a girl who didn't know how to handle them. One of Narissa's. They found the girl dead by one of the underground lakes with the smell of poisonous herbs on her breath. Friends said they noticed her raving earlier that day about demons making her like it too much, making her crave things she shouldn't from another woman. They'd figured she'd get over it. And Narissa hadn't noticed, hadn't been able to talk to the girl, tell her it was alright. So now there was the guilt constantly roiling under the surface.

The intellect was astonishing. Long terms Kiadora never knew were even words came to mind with complete definitions, historical context and cultural relevance. And it was for any and every branch of learning. There was so much Narissa was able and compelled to soak in, she was made an introductory, general knowledge teacher. The thirst was more than a compulsion, it was purpose itself. Knowing just for knowing.

And now there were the surface dwellers, those Narissa was in charge of watching: priests still espousing a hatred for those damn Shiekita, doctors with hokey and expensive cures, humanitarians who offered bread before dragging people to the Church, the pitying, yet smug, looks of the workers in the houses for the possessed. With each person, hope of freedom died more and more until the despondency turned into a growing rage and all the images of war and violence that went with the rage, both symbolic and real. But the rage had been tempered by doubt as the movement became more extreme, hence the half finished bomb.

And Kiadora was back in her own head, staring into the clear blue eyes of the woman. The cold distance was gone, replaced by the frightened gaze of a child.

Kiadora reached in through the rubble and grabbed the woman's hand.

"I'm going to work on this, I don't care what it takes," Kiadora said.

Kiadora let go, and Narissa reached for Kiadora's shoulder, squeezing it tightly with one hand. From the teary eyes and the look of understanding, Kiadora could tell the other woman was in her head, also.

Kiadora could hear people moving above their heads now and began to shout that there was someone stuck down here. Narissa made to hide the bomb behind a slab. Three burly police officers came around the corner by the stairway and quickly started to move what must have been 70-pound slabs of rubble.

Astrian came in tow, throwing his arms around Kiadora, babbling about structural instability again and not knowing where she went. Narissa was offered a hand from one of the officers, but leapt out of the new opening by herself without assistance. Kiadora offered a quick, mumbled excuse about this being a new serving woman. Once the officers' backs were turned, Narissa nodded a quick thanks.

CHAPTER 47

"There's a tribe to the east of here, in the desert, that meets weekly to comb the sand for water. They believe that divinity is in the life source they can find. It's a type of ritual, a worship service for them. All across the world people meet like this, like we do for the weekly services, but they do not necessarily sing, they do not necessarily meet in a building, they do not silently pray. Divinity takes all forms."

Kiadora took a breath as she watched the crowd, all faces held with rapt attention. It had been easy, all she had to do was stand on an empty pear crate and start talking to people about her worldly travels, start telling tales. She had never seen these places, of course, but she figured it would lend her credence. She couldn't very well reveal the actual source of her knowledge.

Astrian had said in his parts they had traveling storytellers, people who would stand on the street corners and tell tales; it passed as a free form of amusement for the poor and the weary folks of the area. As long as the tales didn't go beyond the light and fanciful, the act was fully encouraged for keeping morale up among the mine workers and their families. It had become a sport to see who could come up with the wildest of tales among the locals. A person on a raised platform just needed to start talking, and a crowd drew as if the ground was sloped to the person and the crowd was a river.

It hadn't worked at first, until Astrian pretended to stand around and listen, then people came. Astrian stood in the crowd asking questions and Kiadora responded, until....

"People in the desert? Why should I care about them, then? It's not like they follow the true God," cried a faceless man from the back. Astrian, standing in the front row to the left of Kiadora, glanced back with a panicked look. Kiadora searched for the man, but could not find him. Not again.

"That's pretty interesting, though, the things people come up with," Astrian commented loudly.

"More than just interesting, they see the point. Divinity can be found all around us." Kiadora took out a candle and match from her pocket. She lit the candle as people watched curiously. She could read the confusion in their eyes. 'So was this a street performance, then?' they seemed to think.

"The flame can destroy, but also provides heat. Watch how it grows." Kiadora held up the candle, seeing the flow of Eatheria. She willed the strings of particles to expand and the flame grew from the size of a grape to the size of a grapefruit.

The crowd gasped, and people began talking excitedly. She could hear cries of, "do you think she really did that?"

"So as I am connected to the flame, so we are all connected. We sense the divinity in us all. That is why as we gather in services, others

577

comb the sand. God is all around us."

"Horsecock!" shouted the man from the back. "I know what you are, you're just one of those Shiekita!" And then the faces turned, like they always did. The curiously melted into fear and then, in the next instant, to hate. Kiadora looked down at Astrian, and they both nodded. Time to leave. There were now angry shouts from the crowd as Kiadora stepped back into the alley they stood in front of and Astrian slipped around the corner. A few people continued down the alley after them. Kiadora saw a rock fly over her head and clang into some trash cans. They reached the end of the alley, Astrian making great time despite his limp, and took a sharp left and ducked under a loose fence. They were out of sight and walking into some corn stalks.

"I don't think this will do," Kiadora said, once they were far enough away. "Eventually they'll start putting up posters for me. The country will be plastered with want ads for my head."

Her eyes felt scratchy, like they sometimes got in springtime around certain weeds. It was the salt of her barely held back tears again.

She had imagined this being much easier. Kiadora had felt people would be open to new ways, an alternative to the tyranny of the Church. Maybe all the time underground had made her lose touch. She had envisioned curious faces of those who had never seen a benevolent alternative, only the propaganda and the houses for the possessed. Each time she had felt she was making progress, there was always at least one person to act as the trigger switch for the group's collective indoctrination.

They went crashing through the corn, becoming steadily breathless as they dodged potholes and tried to crush as few crops as possible.

Just as Kiadora was wondering how large the damn field was and where they would go next, they saw a blond head move through the corn, barely discernible amongst the green and gold of the late summer crop. Kiadora grabbed Astrian's sleeve to stop him and she pointed. Both held their breath and started to stoop down.

"It's no good, I see you there," came the man's voice. The man's familiar voice. Could it be?

The stalks parted, and there was Wellian with a large grin on his face.

"Wellian, how did you…" Astrian started.

"I heard you were in the area; I was looking for you every day. I was in the crowd and knew things would go bad, so I headed toward where I knew you would be coming out. It was your only exit."

Kiadora stood speechless. Such acuity seemed out of place in a man who otherwise thought a bird would take him to paradise. When she finally found her voice, Kiadora asked, "Why were you looking for us?"

"Figured you'd need a place to stay. Come on." And he turned and led them through the field. They passed over a dirt path and just as Kiadora thought he'd turn, he went headlong into more corn, stamping down everything he passed.

The field of corn finally ended after a while, and they found themselves in a mostly barren field with only a few small trees. They headed across that and over a small hill. Just below the hill, out of sight, was a broken-down barn. Despite her gratitude, her heart fell. She was hoping they'd have a real house. A few holes at the top of the place made it look like it'd be drafty at night.

She hated to admit it, but her return home recently had only reminded her of what she would always be used to on some level. Not that she'd ever go back home, once they rebuilt. She didn't even know if she'd revisit.

She didn't worry about those bent on revenge. Much. They had arrested all the people in charge of the blast, save Narissa, whose employment as a servant was vouched for by Lisera. She knew there were ways to wiggle out of the sentences, but the evidence had been pretty rock solid. As for those convicted escaping, it was always a possibility, but Narissa had said the authorities had apprehended them all. The blast and panic had sent most fleeing- right into waiting officers. Narissa divulged where the others were by "accidently" walking into them with several officers.

That, and there was the way Dehlia looked at her now. The general derision had melted into outright hate and accusation. Kiadora could tell Dehlia knew Kiadora's sudden reappearance and an attack on the home very well might not have been coincidence. Where her father's and sister's eyes has softened, Dehlia's cold stare had followed her all the way out the door. Kiadora had then realized that nothing she could do would make her alright in Dehlia's mind.

She'd always be a freak.

And now here she was at a broken barn with the bird people.

Wellian led them into a side door, and they found the interior converted from a simple stable to makeshift living quarters with old, overstuffed furniture, a table drug up from somewhere and even a rug to cover a good portion of the dirt floor. At a small table Torren and Aela sat playing a game of checkers. They looked up at the sound of the door and made small gasps.

"Kiadora!" Aela shrieked in a squeal more fitting of an eleven-year-old girl. "He said he'd find you! And Astrian, the faithful adherent!"

Kiadora looked back at Astrian, alarmed. Astrian raised his eyebrows, frowned and shrugged to show his own confusion.

"Have a seat," said Torren, gesturing to two chairs next to him. "It's not a short way out here."

Kiadora and Astrian both walked over to the chairs and sat down slowly, Astrian limping worse than ever, as if they might startle someone. Aela and Wellian regarded them with eager expressions; only Torren looked truly relaxed.

"We heard what you two are trying to do," said Wellian conversationally. "That can't be easy."

"No, we're running into...trouble," Astrian said, every ounce of his frustration showing on his normally placid face. "I knew there would be resistance, but they're even more rigid down here than from where I grew up. I didn't expect so much violence."

"For some reason, I thought this would be downright easy," Kiadora said. "Show some people we're not the stuff of nightmares, let word spread. I mean, people should like a friendly demon, right?" Torren chuckled.

"If it were that easy, the compound wouldn't exist. No would have had to create it as refuge."

"But you can do it, you can make others see the way," said Aela.

She moved to put her hand on Kiadora' forearm, but then pulled away as if remembering who she was talking to. "You're chosen."

"Whoa, wait. What?" Kiadora jumped up from the table.

"You experienced the Transcendence before anyone else at your skill level. Reena is still there, she was just made a Matrina of Air. She hears these things. You were chosen from above to bring a new era of peace." Kiadora laughed nervously, out of simply having no idea what else to do.

"So no pressure, right?" She looked wildly at Astrian for help, who sat staring at Aela as if she had green skin. Then he trained his dark eyes on Kiadora and looked back to Torren.

"Listen," said Astrian. "It's been a long walk. I hate to impose, but we haven't had anything to eat all day." The minstrel money had been tight with them having to keep a low profile from all the violence.

"Of course," said Wellian, who jumped over to a brown sack in the corner. "I'm afraid all we have right now is corn."

Astrian and Kiadora lay next to each other in blankets on the floor. Kiadora looked up at the stars through one of the holes at the top of the wall. Due to the overhangs, Wellian had sworn they rarely got water in. Astrian had fallen asleep immediately. The man could sleep anywhere. But Kiadora lay awake, wondering at what Aela had said.

What did it even mean to be chosen? She didn't feel that way. No great voice had spoken to her out of the sky, no holy hand of righteous judgment had pointed to her. She had experienced the Transcendence, and that had been great, had helped set her on this path. But it seemed that it was something others could do if they tried to or wanted it badly enough.

And, what she really hated to admit, that sensation was starting to fade. There were days she forgot what the Transcendence felt like.

The days of crowd jeers and hiding and little food. Those were the days she found it difficult to love them all, to even care. But still, at her core, she remembered what it had felt like, to be combined with them. She still saw the web. It flowed through her, it's gossamer strings spreading from her heart. Still, she felt like she should have some great radiance erupting from her every moment of the day. All the great prophets in the Holy Text seemed to have it. The foreign tribe leaders she read about down below seemed to exude it.

Looking at Astrian, who was turned away and taking slow, steady breaths, she got up and headed up to the hay loft. She needed to be alone, maybe to meditate. The length between each of her meditation sessions was getting far too long, like her meals. She had read about people who starved themselves to achieve better meditation, but with her it seemed to go in reverse.

She tiptoed across the floor between inert bodies. They all slept on blankets on the floor at night. Curiously, no one had taken up residence on the couch, lumpy as it was. Maybe the dirt had just become too familiar to everyone.

She grimaced as she put her first foot on the ladder up to the hayloft, expecting a loud groan of the old metal to wake everyone. Luckily, she was able to ascend relatively noiselessly, reminded of her old quarters with each rung she passed. She hoisted herself up onto the loft and was met with several paintings stacked against the wall. Apparently someone was quite the artist. One pile had price tags on it, evidently the rejects of some art fair. An easel and a set of paints stood in another corner.

Kiadora walked over to regard the paintings; it had been a while since she had been able to admire true art. And then she stepped back with a gasp.

She stood looking at her own face, turned toward the sky. It was an artist's rendition, of course. Everything was better than in real life. Her complexion, which usually had some sort of awkward redness from sunburn, heat or even shyness, looked too milky perfect. Her figure was too full, her breasts larger than normal. It wasn't the figure of a woman half starved and always on the move. Her nose was a little too small and round, not quite as angular as normal. Her hair had some golden blond colors worked into it, rather than the cool, light brown of normal. But there were her hazel eyes, the overall likeness to her features unmistakable. She wore a blue, flowing dress. Somehow, light emitted from behind her head, casting a radiant arch.

"Like it?" said a whispered voice. Kiadora jumped and turned to find Torren standing there, a mild smile on his face.

"Did you do this?"

"No, this was all Aela, she has the artist's touch. I couldn't paint a straight line."

"She really was serious about this chosen thing." Kiadora glanced back at the painting, getting more sickened by how wholesome it was with each passing moment. She looked back at Torren.

"We all are." Torren held her gaze with an earnest stare, the moonlight through the small window doing nothing to lessen its intensity.

"Well, what happened to your bird? You were waiting for him. It was your prophesy they were following."

"I know, I redid the matrix. Came up with a whole new set of dates, and those failed as well. We didn't even get a mortal bird the second time or the third. Left the compound at last, just so we could focus on it. Then I realized it wasn't about the answers the matrix came up with. Aela and Wellian kept on about it though. Until they found you. Then the Ollox wasn't a bird anymore and paradise wasn't so far away." Kiadora shook her head.

"I don't understand…"

"Don't you? Doing what you do, you should." Torren had moved to the side and was fiddling with the edge of a cloth covering another canvas. "It's all the same, it doesn't matter. You know that." Torren threw the cloth off of the second canvas and there was a painting of the Ollox. It soared among the clouds. The sun was behind its head, casting the same radiant glow as the halo in Kiadora's painting. Torren stood regarding it.

"People like Wellian and Aela, they need this, Kiadora. And I suppose I do, too. I'm still here. I've been thinking of working on another matrix, about you this time. Haven't decided what to ask it before I start though. For the others, of course," Torren added hastily.

Torren crossed his arms in thought, and his sleeve fell down to reveal the mangled, mottled skin underneath.

"The matrix distracts you, doesn't it? From that," Kiadora said, indicating his arm.

"That's a very simple answer, Kiadora." Torren gazed out the window now.

"I can't save you," Kiadora said, coming over and placing a hand on his shoulder. She expected him to withdraw like Aela did. Apparently she wasn't quite an untouchable demigod yet, not to Torren. "And you don't expect me to. It doesn't matter if it's a bird, or a woman, or a sky god."

"Now you get it, kid," said Torren. "All they need is something, and you're on the track to making it you. Make sure it's something that we can all grow with this time."

CHAPTER 48

Kiadora sat in the backstage of the playhouse, the very one she and Astrian had gone to their first night out. That last night in the barn, Kiadora had spent the small hours of the morning racking her brains on where they could go and what they could do.

It had been so obvious she had smacked herself on the head. A playhouse that already offered controversial plays with beefed-up security just sat waiting for her to cash in on a connection she had to Lisera. She had requested to see the owner, who had asked her to demonstrate her abilities. Then she had offered to give a stage show in the agreement that she was allowed to make the performance deeper once word spread. The man's eyes had practically shone gold from all the thoughts of the stuff floating around within. And the rest of the house believed in what she was doing.

Now was the night before her fifth show, and word had traveled fast. The place was packed to see the woman with the illusions. Still, she wondered how many people would only see illusions.

She sat tracing the scar on her chest. It had become a nervous habit since these new, larger crowds. There was something grounding in the simplicity of the act. It reminded her of her time in the gardens below and helped her understand why Lisera had become a house-keeper. Kiadora vowed to find a place to start a garden, somehow. Something to ground out the stage fright. Astrian played with his stone to calm himself near showtime.

Astrian came up behind her and placed an arm around her shoulder. Since he was no longer required for crowd control, he could showcase small amounts of Water control instead. He had joked that it wasn't so different. They both wore matching black performing suits with vests; they had resisted gaudy sequins as if they were allergic.

"I wonder why that's all we can do." Kiadora said.

"Hm?" Astrian asked.

"You know, I can only control the size of the flame, and I can put it out, but I can't generate it, can't grow it too big. You can only control the bowl of water you have."

The crowd went wild for his antics of using the water to make it rain and dancing his little water figure across the stage.

"Because," said Astrian in a matter-of-fact tone, "if we could do more consciously there'd actually be Shiekita." Kiadora stared at her-self in the mirror, her face heavy with stage makeup, imagining being able to generate a massive ball of fire at will. There was a time in her life when she would have sent it straight for the Church while there were people inside.

"Huh," she said.

"There are visitors for you," called a stagehand. Kiadora nodded and in walked Regelend, followed by Uranda.

"You guys!" Kiadora yelled as she ran over to hug them. Regelend and Astrian exchanged a nod as Kiadora fell back. She noticed for the first time Uranda was holding a small bundle, which moved.

"Is that..."

"Our son," Regelend beamed, "thought you'd like to see him." Kiadora went over to look into the small bundle and a tiny, smushed face looked up at her. Uranda even had a small, tight smile. What passed as a smile for her, anyway.

"Doesn't quite look like either of you yet, but congratulations!"

"He's very handsome," Astrian put in for the two of them.

"How are things at the doctor's office?" Kiadora asked.

"Well, we also wanted to tell you about that," Regelend said. "After spending considerable time with us, Iland's – sorry, Dr. Iland – decided to stop finding a cure. Granted, he said it was because he saw we could 'function normally and even produce healthy offspring,' to use his words, but that's huge news for the compound."

"That's great!" Kiadora nearly shrieked. "I'll send a note to Narissa." Regelend raised an eyebrow.

"Narissa's the first one you want to go to?"

"Yeah, a lot has happened since you left," Kiadora said.

"Kiadora decided to get involved with a terrorist group," Astrian said with a pointed stare at Kiadora. Regelend and Uranda just stared. Kiadora burned with shame. She knew a part of Astrian would never get over that, even if his love was true.

"I learned from that... boy did I learn. Anyway, I helped save Narissa's life and was able to read her thoughts for a while. There's a lot to her, Regelend.

"Anyway, we're all going to have to get together for tea. And do me a favor, can you take this to Lisera with this note? She's at my old home." She handed some money and a note to Regelend.

"Sure, what's this for?"

"For a drink a long time ago. And a thank you note. My father doesn't pay her what she's worth. I can't get out much, security won't let me," she said with a scowl. Regelend nodded and tucked the two items away.

"So what are people saying about this thing?" asked Astrian.

"Needless to say, you're the talk of the area. Most people like the show, think it's all a neat illusion. We've come to see what you're doing for ourselves, we've heard so much about it." Kiadora's heart fell.

"Is that it?"

"Some people say it's the work of the Shiekita. Tahn's the loudest," then Regelend went red, realizing just what had slipped out. Kiadora gave a wooden smile.

"It's alright, Regelend, I don't mind hearing it. Maybe someday he'll understand. Funny, and I used to look to him for understanding." Kiadora glanced over to see Astrian peering at her with a curious gaze that was just a little too intense.

"An old friend, that was all." She squeezed his arm in reassurance. Then a lantern above the door went on.

"We have to go on now, but see us after the show," Kiadora said, ushering the three out. Kiadora and Astrian went up a winding staircase and went to the edge of the stage.

Kiadora took a breath. Just illusions to people, huh?

"Let me do the introduction," Kiadora said to Astrian as the curtain went up. Astrian glanced at her and then nodded. They walked onto the stage, and it was indeed a packed house. She could only make out the shapes of heads, but as her eyes adjusted, faces in the first few rows gained features.

"What you are about to see tonight isn't an illusion," Kiadora called out to the audience, her voice carrying because of the amazing acoustics of the theater. "It's from a greater connection, a greater web of energy called Eatheria. We all are bound by it, connected by it. Every evil act sends ripples across it, every good act does as well. It would make sense to make your acts good, then, yeah?"

Kiadora's face burned with embarrassment; she had never been very good with the performing arts, and now was no exception. But then again, that wasn't what this was about. And Aela made her realize one thing: the artists would come and make this all pretty. However she phrased it, she'd eventually have a halo and be speaking in lyrical verse.

"As part of my own awareness of the web, I can do this." She picked up a candle from a small table, lit it with a match and held it up for all to see. Then she once again expanded the flame, faster and larger than any trick candle had the capability to do.

The audience lost it with wild applause and cheering. She could hear snippets of admiration for the excellent, advanced stage props she had and her heart sunk again.

Then Kiadora looked down in the first row at a child who was looking at her with a rapt gaze. The girl held a toy, but she was far too old to have such a toy with her, especially out in public. The girl's steady gaze, flooded with intelligence, told Kiadora that she wasn't simple. The girl held up her toy. It was a large, stuffed spider sitting on a cloth web. The girl plucked one end, shaking the whole structure, and gave a benevolent smile. Kiadora smiled back.

It was a start.

Get a free short story featuring Narissa and Astrian!

Visit livelylit.com

Subscribe to the newsletter to receive a free downloadable PDF of the story.

Also at livelylit.com:

-Find out about giveaways, contests and sales on books

-Updates on future books

-Author blog featuring news, musings and tips on writing, plus more!

ABOUT THE AUTHOR

Michelle Lovrine lives in Wisconsin with her husband and three corgis. She looks at pictures of large libraries the way some people read erotica, and her favorite way to die is to be crushed by a massive pile of books.

www.ingramcontent.com/pod-product-compliance
Lightning Source LLC
Chambersburg PA
CBHW050119030726
47505CB00007B/1938